i

The Sapphire Bell

Louise Furley

The Sapphire Bell

ISBN: 979-8-9859963-8-8 (Paperback)
ISBN: 979- 8-9859963-7-1 (eBook)

Cover art by: *Pixel Mischief Design*
Photo: *Courtesy of Shutterstock*

ALSO BY LOUISE FURLEY

The Sapphire Bell

Prologue

Hiding out at my Aunt Edna's in Vero Beach has given me time to recover my sanity, but regretfully, I had to fold up the rose-colored glasses I used to view the world with and put them away.

Raised by parents whose marriage was still intact, I considered myself lucky to have been the most important person in their lives. They hadn't spoiled me with money and material things, just nurtured me with comfort and such a feeling of security, I always knew there was a safety net under me.

A happy-go-lucky kind of guy, I graduated from college without overly straining myself, quickly landing a great job with a computer company. Cushioned by family and a close-knit circle of friends I had known for years, I had never really experienced strife or tragedy...or bone-chilling fear.

Then, almost as if the wind had changed direction, something blew so slowly into our insulated and woefully innocent world, we were unaware of the cunning malevolence until it had entwined itself into our lives.

A burgeoning dawn woke me one winter's day. Fingers of light crept into the room pestering my heavy lids. I opened my eyes to blazing streams of fire burning across the dark sky with such brilliance, the kaleidoscopic radiance surpassed all other mornings that had preceded it.

It was the beginning, it was the day the fresh bloom of love captured me. Suddenly, my black and white world soared with rainbows of color and wondrous joy.

1

I tried hard to protect my newfound precious bounty. My life before this unparalleled day had been like a glass of colorless liquid, pure and clear, maybe even a little dull, what you see is what you get.

But, add just a drop of any foreign, unknown substance and the liquid becomes blurry, unfathomable, changed. I had been living in an Eden, a lovely uncontaminated world filtered by family and friends, an ordinary life.

Then, like a plague eviscerating my very soul, an intangible and inexplicable foul abomination insinuated itself into my life, staining my unblemished paradise to a hideous blood red.

My soul tainted with the blood listed heavy, full of devastation, would it ever lighten and turn upright again?

Chapter One

Anyone would kill to live in the town I happened to be born and raised in with its sunny days and seductive nights. Shady Bay is a suburb of Indigo Isles, a city quietly pulsating deep in the heart of south Florida.

Many of the roads run along the spider branches of Hidden River. Sleepy cypress and water oak trees droop over the river and shore, shading the creatures of the water and the boaters floating lazily along with the current.

The city gets its name from the deep indigo hue of the river. Local residents know where the best fishing is, and every kid has visited the secret ponds where they can feed the ducks and watch the turtles bask on the banks.

Shady Bay is small, most everyone knows everybody's business, or at least someone knows someone who knows you.

I was on my way to the kitchen to see if my wife Julia was fixing my favorite lunch of honey-smoked ham and sharp cheddar cheese slapped on a crusty loaf of Italian bread.

I planned to wash down each delicious bite with a frosty Heineken and had just entered the kitchen when the phone on the wall rang, startled me. My immediate thought was, *who would be calling this early on a Saturday morning*?

On the other end of the shrilly ringing phone was the irate and ancient voice of Mrs. Anderson, our widowed next door neighbor.

Her cracked weathered voice shrieked through the airwaves, "Rusty Dixon!"

I held the phone away from my ear while acknowledging it was in fact I who had answered the phone. The creaking voice continued, albeit a little less strenuously.

"Rusty, that exhibitionist wife of yours was out on the lawn again at dawn this morning, picking up the newspaper attired in only her underwear! You must speak with her and tell her this has got to stop!"

The voice continued, quivering with self-righteousness and age, "This is a decent, law-abiding neighborhood and blah, blah, blah...."

I waited until the voice ran out of steam and began to taper off. To mollify Mrs. Anderson, I agreed it is totally unacceptable behavior.

My wife Julia has been a tad absentminded lately, yet she is a kind hearted person. Also, Julia is pregnant so I feel we should allow for some aberrant behavior. I pacified my neighbor as best I could.

I told her I would speak to Julia and try to get her to stop and think before she leaves the house and make sure she's fully dressed. Actually, my wife has a very cute figure, but generally she hides it with layers and layers of oversized clothes, usually my clothes.

As I hung up the phone, the topic of conversation bustled into the room. Julia's normally perky face looked distracted. A contemplative cast replaced the twinkle in her pretty eyes, and her red hair was in disarray from its normally neat, shoulder length bob.

"Everything okay, honey?" I asked her.

She didn't answer right away. She moved to the refrigerator and started taking out ingredients to make lunch. Now I was positive something was wrong because she was making tuna fish and I hate tuna fish!

"Julia, what's wrong?" The question came out more forcefully than I intended.

She put down the can of tuna and looked up at me. Her green eyes, blurred with unshed tears looked like twin spring leaves caught in a churning stream. My stomach clenched in alarm. I grabbed her arms to steady myself more than her.

"C'mon, sweetie, you can tell me anything. Is the baby all right?" I knew my voice was squeaking, I couldn't help it- Julia is only a few months pregnant, but due to her petite frame and oversized clothing, you couldn't yet tell she was with child.

She turned her head away, and then looked back at me. Her lower lip trembled and one tiny tear slipped down the reddening apple of her cheek.

"Rusty... I think someone is spying on me and I'm so scared!" She flung herself into my arms. Burying her face against my chest she began sobbing.

Pulling back from her, I echoed, "Someone is spying on you?"

She leaned into me, nodding her head up and down against my chest leaving damp smears on my shirt.

Struggling to keep my voice gentle, I demanded she answer me. "Tell me what's going on, baby." My hands gripped her arms so tightly I thought she'd complain, but she just sniffed and wiped at her eyes with the back of her hands.

I stared at the top of her bowed head waiting for her to answer.

She stood back sniffling, still rubbing her eyes. After taking a deep breath, she said, "Okay, well, the other day, um, Wednesday I think, I was vacuuming the den and...well, you know how I hate to get my clothes dirty, so usually I clean wearing just my undies. I was wearing that pink lacy set you bought me from Victoria's Secret. You remember, it has those tiny straps and the peek-a-boo-"

"Julia!" I interjected. I was becoming exasperated and this was not the time to get distracted by visions of my curvy wife in sexy garments. "What happened?" I asked again.

Tossing her head, her red hair swung over her shoulder, she continued, "Oh, I was bending over and trying to clean under your favorite old stuffed chair, when I thought I heard a sound outside the window. You weren't here, you were down at the park with the dogs I think. So I glanced at the window while I was still leaning over and my hair was in my eyes, and I thought I saw someone... I mean, a face looking in the window.

"But when I pushed my hair out of the way and blinked and looked again, the face was gone. I dropped the vacuum and went over to the window and peered out. I looked around but I didn't see anyone.

"I figured it must have just been the meterman or something passing by. So I went back to cleaning." She shrugged, unconsciously pushing her hair off her face like she must have that Wednesday.

"So, then...yesterday, it was really early, hmmm..." she pressed her lips together with a finger on her chin, eyes looking upward, her red brow crinkled then she looked up at me.

"Yeah, it was around five a.m. I came down early because I couldn't sleep. So I slipped on an apron, you know because I was naked and I didn't want to get splattered with hot grease. I started to cook you some fried eggs and bacon for breakfast.

"I was just setting that heavy iron skillet on the burner, when something at the kitchen window caught my eye. I jerked my head towards the window but it was empty. I decided it was all in my mind.

"The dogs were upstairs sleeping with you in our room, and if there were any strangers or robbers around, the dogs would have run downstairs barking all over the place. You know how they are when someone unknown passes by. It's so hard to calm them down," she ended with a sigh.

Yes, I thought, that's true. Our dogs, Muffy and Boris, were generally pretty active burglar alarms.

Julia brought Muffy home first around two months ago. She came in one day, sopping wet, hugging a dirty lump of shivering fur. My wife's beautiful auburn hair was darkened by the rain and plastered to her head.

Her jeans and t-shirt dripped big blobs of brown water on the kitchen floor. I didn't know who looked more bedraggled, my wife or the pitiful, shaking, soaked mass of smelly fuzz she was holding in her arms.

Julia said she'd found the poor thing in a torrential rainstorm, cowering under a park bench. When she picked up the black cocker spaniel, it had whimpered and slathered her face with wet sandpaper kisses. That was it. The dog was ours forever.

Muffy had no tags and we put up some found dog notices around town, but she belonged to us from that night on.

Then, a week later, I came home from a long, head splitting day at work. As I pulled the Bronco into the driveway of our split-level house, my eyes were abruptly drawn to a white and tan, shorthaired mongrel that was tied to a palm tree in my front yard.

The mutt was standing calmly, tongue hanging, observing my wary approach. When I exited the Bronco, the dog started growling, and then barking ferociously as I moved closer.

Instantly, I ceased all movement as the animal lunged at me ignoring the rope that was slashing at its throat with every leap it made.

"Julia! Julia!" I yelled for my wife four or five times before she came springing out of the house.

"Doncha just love him!" she exclaimed as she ran over to the canine. Immediately. The dog stopped yelping and slobbered all over her face with his globule tongue.

Apparently, again as Julia was walking through the park, she watched as a hot dog vender chased off a dirty scrawny whelp. The sorry looking critter, according to Julia, looked hungry and frightened.

So of course she must bring him home as well. This cur, like Muffy, also had no tags, and after no response to the notices we posted, Boris too became a member of our family.

I viewed the dogs as protection for my wife and our soon to be infant addition. But, she treats them like they're her children, pampering them terribly and spoiling them outrageously.

Anyway, unless they know you, and even sometimes then, the pups, as we call them, go into bark and growl mode before we can even hear a footstep on the porch.

So I tell Julia I think her pregnancy is causing her to be a little extra nervous and easily spooked. "Listen honey," I began gently rubbing her shoulders, "sometimes when a woman's hormones start changing, all sorts of erratic behav-"

"I am not imagining things Rusty!" she cried. "I was just outside checking for the mail when I noticed something glinting in the grass on the ground underneath the kitchen window.

"I went over and I saw a candy wrapper lying there and next to it was a footprint...and- and...it wasn't yours Rusty, because it was too big! So see, I am not wacky and hormonal, someone is really peeking in our windows!"

She sobbed, "And I'm so scared!" and hurled her tiny body into my arms.

"Okay, okay," I murmured, stroking her back. "We'll call the police and report this. Maybe they can have an officer stop by or maybe drive by a little more frequently."

"All right." Sniffing, she wiped her nose with a paper towel.

I went to telephone our local authorities and she left to go upstairs to wash her face and put some clothes on.

Chapter Two

It wasn't long before I heard the doorbell ring. I answered the door to two of our county's finest.

The female police officer's stiff nod of greeting was one quick snap of her head, down-up. Barely moving her thin lips and without any inflection in her voice whatsoever, she introduced herself.

"Hello. I am Officer Bridgette Newman and this is Detective Mark Patterson. You called to report an incident?" She sounded computer generated.

One hand clutched a clipboard tightly to her chest, the other she extended as rigid as a stick to me. On the tall side and somewhere in her twenties, her figure was trim and angular but a hint of muscles lurked under the blue uniform.

Exuding a serious, no fooling around attitude, her smile was for politeness only- it was gone in a blink. I'd hate to say it was more of a grimace than an actual smile, but…at least she tried.

Short brown hair curled neatly behind small, earring-less ears, pale grey eyes regarded me with suspicion. I guess to her everyone was probably up to something.

Stepping forward, I pushed my wire-rimmed glasses back up my nose and shook her hand.

"Yes," I said, "thank you for responding to our call." In turn, I shook hands with the detective.

He was tall as well. We met eyeball to eyeball, but he was around forty years old with crinkles around his eyes and just a smattering of grey at his temples. The rest of his chestnut brown hair clipped neat and short looked pretty thick.

I couldn't stop my hand from rising to my head, automatically trying to plump up my own fine locks.

Officer Newman was dressed in our county's police uniform, but the detective was wearing a suit. I call it a suit but I suspect he bought it at Sears.

"Mr. Dixon, I've come along with Officer Newman to hear your report because we've had a few of the same type of complaints in and around this neighborhood for the past few months. We believe the suspect is one and the same in all of the incidents reported. Do you perhaps have a description of the offender?"

The detective's smile wasn't much warmer than Newman's, his lips looked like they wanted to wrinkle into a purse, but he settled for letting his lower lip stick out a little. I put my arm around Julia's shoulders and pulled her forward.

"Officers," I said, "this is my wife, Julia Dixon. It is she who has been the 'observee' of this thug each time. I've never been present nor have I noticed anything out of the ordinary lately."

Smiling shyly at the detective, Julia peered up at him through golden eyelashes. "It's a pleasure to meet you, Detective Peterson."

"Ahem..." The detective coughed, slightly embarrassed. He tugged at his tie. "That's uh... Patterson," he corrected her, nodding slightly.

"Oh!" Julia put her hand to her mouth and giggled engagingly. "I'm so sorry, but I'm terribly unnerved by all this." She has the sweetest smile and she directed it straight at Patterson. She didn't even glance in Newman's direction.

"That's no problem, Mrs. Dixon, people get my name wrong all the time," he reassured her, giving her a much more generous smile than he had offered to me.

He was obviously smitten with my petite pixie. Her emerald eyes and rosebud lips buy guys over right away, they had worked with me!

Julia and I had met at a local hangout called the Turquoise Cove Bar and Grill. It's a cheery place with a relaxed atmosphere.

The dimly lit dining room is comfortable and pleasant with worn blue booths and a cluster of tables covered with yellow and blue plaid tablecloths.

Candles oozing down wine bottles, and daisies popping out of blue glass vases centered on each table add to the cozy ambiance.

The oblong-shaped bar on the other side of the dining room has plenty of room for friends to gather and gab. In the back room there is a pool table where I've lost many a rowdy game of billiards while gustily swilling foamy dark ale and sharing jokes with my pals.

Julia had been sitting on a cushioned bar stool, slowly sipping a lime-green margarita. She looked dynamite in a silvery, sequined and beaded, intoxicatingly short dress.

The top part of the dress exposed her creamy shoulders, and the whole outfit, fitting sleekly to her body, shimmered and twinkled every time she moved.

Burnished titian hair was held back elegantly with a silver comb, and shiny earrings blinked through loose wisps of hair every time she bent her head to the straw. She reminded me of festive tinsel reflecting all the light in the room.

She was supposed to meet a date, but he had stood her up. I don't usually speak to strangers, especially when I'm hanging with a group of friends. But, she kept glancing shyly through her eyelashes in my direction looking so pretty and forlorn.

Julia looks vulnerable, as she's barely over five feet tall and hardly 98 pounds. She has this way of gazing up at you like you're the most important and handsomest man in the entire world.

We dated and married within six months. We had to hurry the wedding along once we found out about Dixon Junior. My parents were not too thrilled about the expediency of the ceremony. However, notwithstanding the unexpected bundle of joy, I am head over heels in love with my redheaded gal.

Ahhhh... I put aside my reminiscing. I have yet to meet Julia's family, much to my folks' chagrin. We were going out to Boise at Christmas, but at the last minute her mom called and said her dad had pneumonia, and that we'd best wait and plan on another time.

I've never even spoken with them. Her mom calls several times a week, their phone bill must be astronomical! And the few times I've answered the phone I've only chatted briefly with her brother Cliff.

He's always a bit cool and abrupt, not a cheery or warm sort of chap. I assume he's probably not too happy that his little sister married a man her family has never met and knows nothing about.

Julia doesn't talk a lot about her childhood. I don't think it was a tremendously happy time. On the contrary, it sounded quite unremarkable and lonely the little she does tell me.

Chapter Three

Detective Patterson asked Julia if she could describe the face she saw at the window.

She had little to tell because she hadn't actually seen anything. She closed her eyes tightly to try to remember everything.

The detective waited patiently for her to relay the events that had occurred.

"Well," she hesitated, "it was so briefly there, and I was practically upside down with my hair obstructing my view. I just saw a face." She stopped, her eyes darted back and forth, flashing yellow specks as she tried to recall details.

She looked towards the window, her eyes narrowed, as if she were struggling to recall what the stranger had looked like.

"I think the person was white, you know- Caucasian, but I'm not even sure if it was male or female. I keep thinking it was male, but I guess in these situations one would tend to believe it's usually men that peek in windows."

She shrugged her shoulders and turned her palms up. "I really saw more of blank figure than an actual face. It disappeared so quickly I thought I had imagined it."

Shaking her head slightly, she said, "I'm sorry, I wish I could tell you more."

The detective and Officer Newman were both writing as Julia was speaking.

"Hey!" I exclaimed. "We may have physical evidence of the intruder!"

I watch a plenty of re-runs of those police TV shows like CSI and COPS so I felt secure in my knowledge of police buzzwords. Beckoning to the officers to follow me, I led them outside and around to the front of the house.

Mumbling something about watch out for dog poop, I stopped and pointed to the ground under the window. We had left the candy wrapper where we had found it, nestled amongst the lavender impatiens and next to at least a size 13-foot print.

"See," I said as I gestured excitedly at the evidence, "someone was actually standing here secretly watching my wife!" Then I started getting angry.

Flailing my arms about, my voice escalated in volume. "We want protection!" I demanded. "We want the perpetrator caught and sentenced to the fullest extent of the law! The electric chair is too good for this hoodlum!" I ended with my arm aiming rigidly up and my index finger stabbing at the sky.

The two officers ignored me as they knelt in unison to the ground in front of the object half hidden in the garden.

"Let's get a photographer out here to get a picture and a measurement of the print," Detective Patterson said to Officer Newman.

"Yes, sir!" Newman snapped. She didn't salute or click her heels together, but she might as well have.

"And bag this wrapper and run it over to the fingerprint guys. Maybe they can pick up a print and we can possibly match it to a known felon, that would make things easy," he said as he poked at the colorless cellophane with his pen.

"See if they can determine what kind of candy it was and maybe the manufacturer. I really doubt it'll do us any good, but every little bit can help."

Officer Newman nodded affirmatively as she wrote notes on her clipboard.

Julia and I stood awkwardly holding each other as we watched them.

Newman went over to a black squad car that was parked behind my Bronco.

Detective Patterson turned to us and brushed off imagined dirt and wrinkles from his trousers. The smile he directed toward us was patronizing as he buttoned his suit jacket and straightened his paisley tie.

"Please, Mr. and Mrs. Dixon, I really don't believe you have anything to be concerned about. These voyeur types are generally innocuous. I suggest you keep your curtains drawn for a few days and periodically look outside and note anything peculiar or any strangers hanging about."

He glanced over to where Officer Newman was putting one of those yellow tapes that state 'police-do-not-cross' around the scene of the crime. The radio that was strapped to her shoulder squawked in bursts of metallic chatter.

We stood idly as we watched her open a plastic baggie, and using tweezers, she gingerly picked up the clear candy wrapper and popped it into the bag. Zipping the bag closed, she folded it neatly then shoved it into her shirt pocket.

"That's all we can do for now, Mr. Dixon," Patterson said. "The photo and print crew should be here shortly. You don't have to bother with them. They'll just photograph and measure the print and probably make a cast of it. Please stay away from the area until they say it's clear."

He started walking to his car and I strolled along beside him, my hands in my jean's pockets. I had calmed down, but the guy's condescending attitude bugged me.

"Well," I started, "are you going to put surveillance on our house? Will the police check on us? Should we buy a gun?" Once the officers left, I knew anxiety and fear would start needling Julia and me. I was already getting edgy- I could hear my voice rising to a squeak again.

"Mr. Dixon," there he went again with that patronizing air, "honestly, I don't think you have anything to worry about. You have an attractive wife, which normally might keep the suspect coming back. But, since we've made somewhat of a scene here with the police tape and car, and once the crew gets here and takes pictures...well, I think that should pretty much run off any suspicious types lurking in the bushes.

"Voyeurs tend to reside in the area they're peeping in. He's sure to have spotted all this activity and go search for new stomping ground. However," he continued as I opened my mouth to protest, "we will request extra police monitoring in the neighborhood. We will probably use unmarked cars, as we don't want to scare off this guy if we haven't already. We want to capture him. With this type of offense, we need to catch him in the act."

He opened the door to his nondescript white Dodge. As he climbed in, I peered inside.

It wasn't apparent it was an official police car until you got close enough to see the blue dome light perched on the dashboard, the police radio and other official equipment.

I turned and walked back to where Julia who had trailed behind us, was waiting at the end of the driveway.

Officer Newman had already driven off, and Detective Patterson was pulling out onto the street. He drove away, heading towards the main highway.

Julia and I strolled slowly up the driveway to the house. A flock of green parrots flew noisily overhead, clattering like a group of old ladies at a tea party.

We could hear the repeated bouncing of a ball. Jimmy Stedman was dribbling a basketball up and down the sidewalk in front of his house a few doors down.

The sky was pure blue with very few puffs of clouds to cool the hot day. We live in an old, but lovely neighborhood. Quaint, rustic homes mingle with new flamboyant abodes. Every house is uniquely different.

Our small beige house with hunter green shutters is sequestered almost exactly in the middle of the neighborhood. We have a medium sized yard, and an eye-catching awning of vibrantly lilac bougainvillea drapes lushly over our front doorway.

The grass beneath the vine is dotted with delicate petals. Loosened by the wind, they fall silently like purple snowflakes.

Three royal palm trees stand in a triangle in the front yard, and wrapped around the house is red hibiscus that the zebra-striped swallowtail butterflies and hummingbirds love to frolic around.

At the foot of our driveway is a mailbox in the shape of a pig. That was Julia's idea. Sometimes I don't get her sense of humor. She says she likes the 'homespun country' look. Hence the pig, and a bunch of cow and rooster designed items scattered around the kitchen.

As soon as we got inside, the coolness of the house chilled us a bit after being outdoors in the hot sun.

A small shiver ruffled Julia's body. She rubbed her arms with her hands and walked across the living room she had decorated with overstuffed, floral-spattered furniture. She stopped in the doorway looking like a little schoolgirl in her yellow sleeveless blouse and matching shorts.

"I'm going to go finish preparing lunch. Remember, we're going over to Mike and Sandy's tonight for dinner, of course Steven and Heather will be there too." She disappeared into the kitchen.

Oh good. After lunch I have time for a nap and maybe I can catch some baseball scores on the tube.

We get together with our friends every few weeks or so at one of the three couples' homes. The host couple supplies the food and the guest couples provide beer and wine.

Sometimes in the summer, the girls make fancy drinks like frozen banana daiquiris and tart sea breezes. Everyone gets a little intoxicated by the end of the evening, but since we all live in pretty close proximity, it's no big deal.

Mike and Sandy Casey's grandmother lives with them, and she usually watches their adorable tow-headed, two year old, Bonnie.

I decided to go into the kitchen and supervise Julia's preparation of my lunch.

Chapter Four

We pulled up in front of the Casey's two-story Tudor around 7:00 and parked behind Steven and Heather Hazelhursts' yellow Saab. I was glad tonight we were eating at Mike and Sandy's.

I like Heather, now don't get me wrong, but she can be a snob and cooks like one too. For hors d'oeuvres, she smears goose liver all over dry tasteless crackers.

And for dinner, she serves the scrawniest looking chickens. Lying half slimy and half charred on a bed of curly purple lettuce, they look like the smelly pigeons I see strutting along the ledge of my office building.

Heather tries to turn plain green beans into something exotic by calling them haricot verde or varicose veins or some kind of fancy name. Worse, the rock hard, boiled red potatoes look unappetizing swimming in a greasy pool of oil and garlic-sprinkled with coarse pepper, they look like little bald men left out in the sun too long.

Now, on the other hand, Sandy Casey can make a lasagna that is so aromatic and tastes so authentic, you feel like you're sitting outside on a sunny cobblestone street in Venice, relaxing under a striped umbrella with a glass of red wine cradled in your hand.

I can close my eyes and imagine gondolas leisurely drifting past, my foot tapping rhythmically to the romantic crooning of the mustachioed gondolier.

Sandy puts so much into her mouth-watering pasta, you don't know with every forkful if you're going to get a chunk of spicy hot sausage or a bite of tangy meatball. My mouth was already salivating like Pavlov's dog.

"C'mon, sweetie, let's hurry inside!" I grabbed Julia's elbow and rushed her up the pebbled walk to the front door.

The beautiful cedar door with the cut glass window was standing invitingly open.

Hauling a case of Red Dog beer, I pulled open the screen door and yelled, "Hey! Where is everyone?"

Julia followed behind me, lugging a six-pack of kiwi-strawberry Snapple, her drink of choice since the pregnancy.

"Hey man, where've you been? I'm ready to get some ribs barbecuing on the grill!" Mike Casey burst into the living room.

Grabbing the cold beer out of my hands, he pecked Julia on the cheek, snatching her pack of Snapple as well. Heading out of the room with both packs of drinks under one huge arm, he urged us to follow him.

"Everyone's outside on the patio since it's such a warm evening," Mike said, pointing towards the back of the house.

Mike is a big, beefy effusive man that does everything in a large and loud way.

When we reached the kitchen, he yanked two beers off the pack and tossed one to me. Retrieving a glass from the cupboard over the sink, he dropped in some ice cubes then sloshed a Snapple into it and handed the drink to Julia then placed the rest of the beverages into the fridge.

"Hey guy," I said, "what's new? Are those cans of paint I noticed stashed alongside the garage?"

"Yeah," Mike replied, pulling the tab on the can, flipping open his beer. "The ball and chain has been after me to get on with some house fixing upping. You know how it is, it never ends..." sighing heavily, he took a huge gulp of beer.

He turned towards the door and said, "I've gotta get those ribs going, c'mon outside." He motioned to us to follow him.

We left the kitchen and continued through the family room. The sliding glass doors were open to let in the balmy night air.

Through the screen door, I could see Mike's wife Sandy with Heather and Steven Hazelhurst in the dwindling sunlight, casually sprawled around the patio table with their drinks in front of them, munching on potato chips.

Mike shoved open the screen door and sprang out onto the patio.

"Hey!" he boomed. "They're here, I can start cooking those luscious ribs!" He went over to the already smoking grill that was further in the back of the yard.

Popping open the lid, he poured lighter fluid on the charcoal until it was saturated, then he tossed a match in and stood back as the flames instantly flashed, leaping spasmodically skyward.

When the flames died a bit, Mike picked up a platter full of succulent ribs. He stabbed each one with a long barbecue fork and plopped them on the grill. The meat sizzled the second the fat hit the hot metal.

The aroma of spices and caramelizing fat, mixed with a hint of smoky charcoal, drifted alluringly across the lawn and over to the patio. I stood for a second, sniffing the air like a dog.

I felt Julia tugging my hand so I turned towards the patio. "Hi guys," I greeted as we moved up to the group sitting around the table.

After setting my beer on the table, I pulled out a chair for Julia then plunked myself down on a padded cast iron seat. A circle of greetings rang out, Steve and I high-fived.

After we got settled, Steve shoved his chair back and stood up.

"I'm getting another beer, can I get anyone a refill?" Steve asked politely.

We all shook our heads. No one wanted anything so he went into the house to get his sole libation.

Steve is a cool guy but he's a little on the nerdy side. Actually, I guess the three of us men are all a smidge geeky. That must be why we're such good friends.

Steve and I went to college together. I studied computer science, and Steve majored in economics, but we shared some of the same electives.

Steve met Heather in college also. I think Heather majored in husband hunting. I never saw her study, but I did see her schoolbooks. I think she bought the books so guys could carry them around for her.

Heather spends a lot of time and money on her appearance. Her hair is so blonde it's almost white like platinum. She keeps it cut short and kind of spiky. Her hair is always so salon fresh, you can see the hairspray glistening from ten feet away! The spikes look so sharp I'd be afraid to touch them.

Rarely have I seen Heather dressed in the same outfit twice. Even when we're all picnicking at the beach, she wears full-face makeup, naturally she doesn't go in the water. Her acrylic nails are painted blood red, and she's always wearing expensive new togs.

Way too skinny for my tastes, Heather is so thin, I would fear she has anorexia if every time I saw her she wasn't eating something or sucking on one of those water spritzers. Her career apparently is shopping and going to the spa.

I'm pretty sure she thought Steve was going to zoom up the financial ladder and give her the rich luxurious life she always believed she deserved but wasn't born into. Heather is a hothouse rose living in a daisy greenhouse!

Steve does okay in his research and development position at the Ft. Lauderdale Fiduciary Bank. But, he's too nice and has too much integrity to make really big money. So, Heather builds a facade, and plays the role of a wealthy socialite with a middle class income.

Heather and Sandy have known each other since middle school when Heather's family moved into town from Saginaw, Michigan.

Growing up on the same street, Sandy and I have known each other since we were in diapers.

Sandy met Mike when he came to her parent's house to fix their septic tank. The pipes in the ground had been spewing noxious brown water for hours, flooding the entire back yard. The whole neighborhood had a lingering odious smell for days.

Mike has worked with his dad since he was 17 in his uncle's plumbing company called 'Pipedreams'. The slogan on their work van says 'when you get that sinking feeling - call us!'

Years ago, while Mike and his father were sweating away in the hole they had dug in her backyard, teenage Sandy dressed in Daisy Duke shorts and a cropped t-shirt that exposed her midriff, flitted back and forth bringing the digging duo pitchers of icy lemonade and freshly baked chocolate chip cookies.

Mike worked out with weights then, he had a well-muscled torso with a taut, washboard stomach. He'd pull off his saturated shirt, and apparently his rock-ribbed, buffed chest would send young virginal Sandy into breathless palpitations.

Once Sandy's parents became aware of her worshipful lust for the grimy plumber, and Mike's mutual passionate interest, they tried to limit contact between the two would-be lovers.

But, Sandy's infatuation for Mike was obvious to anyone who observed the two together. No one could keep them apart. When they weren't joined at the lips, Sandy would talk nonstop about Mike's virtues, opinions and plans for their future.

I'm sure Mike still loves Sandy, and they are very comfortable together. However, I think Mike has a roving eye.

I don't know if he's ever acted upon his desires, yet I've been out bowling with him, and sometimes afterwards we stop and have a few drinks at various local pubs.

And, well, Mike is quite the diabolist flirt. The few occasions we've been out late at night, I've left him lounging on a bar stool drunkenly leering down the open blouse of whatever ingenuous young damsel is sitting next to him.

Now though, after several years of reposeful marriage and lack of his once regular body building exercise, Mike's burly body is still big, but he's beginning to look more like an Irish Fred Flintstone than the burnished Sly Stallone he once resembled. His black hair is still thick and glossy, but there are specks of grey lurking there.

Mike's wife Sandy has always been like a sister to me. She's soft, round and friendly and speaks with total candor. If she doesn't like your new plaid shirt, she'll come right out and tell you the colors make her want to puke.

After a few years of wedded bliss, Sandy is probably aware of Mike's wandering attentions. Sandy was born to be a wife and mother, and she mothers Mike along with little Bonnie. As long as Mike doesn't seriously rock the boat, I think she will overlook his occasional outside interests.

Julia was regaling the girls with the events of our peeper's activities. She described the times she thought she was unknowingly being observed, and our subsequent report to the police.

"Oh my God!" Sandy exclaimed, obviously mortified. "You're kidding! Are you serious? How creepy!" she sputtered, gawking with wide-eyed horror and disbelief, first at Julia, then at me, and back to Julia.

"Your flesh must be crawling!" Heather said to Julia, her nose crinkled in distaste. Yet, she leaned forward in intense interest, her eyes taking on a sensuous, half-lidded appearance.

"What's he look like? Were you naked?" Heather trembled unconsciously, her mouth was slightly open, her small pointy tongue slid all around the outside of her lips.

Oh my gosh, I thought, this is turning Heather on. She's envisioning someone secretly watching her! So there is some fire inside that cold, pale body of hers.

Julia's head swiveled back and forth between the two women as she recounted all the gory details of the past few days.

Now that I think about it, all in all it didn't seem to be that big a deal. But boy, the looks on the three ladies' faces were enough to write one of those lusty, busty romance novels!

"What's going on?" Steve strolled out of the house with a wine glass of Chianti pinched between two fingers. "Are you talking about a new movie?" he asked, re-seating himself at the table.

Heather dragged her attention away from Julia, and recapped what we had been discussing.

When Heather had excitedly completed her version of our story, Steve's concern was noticeable as he questioned, "Did you call the authorities and report this?" He looked from Julia to me.

"I mean, I've heard these guys can go from peeping to raping and killing people!"

Steve looked anxiously around the group. Almost as thin as his stick-figured wife, Heather, he has short, crew-cut blonde hair, and super thick glasses.

Heather attempted to make him wear contacts some years back, but he has some type of visual impairment that makes contacts impossible. Between the hair, the eyeglasses and the penny loafers, you expect to see a pocket protector too. Steve's a great guy, yet he is the epitome of the word nerd.

At that point, Mike left the grill and lumbered up to the table.

"What're we talking about?" he bellowed. Crashing onto a chair, he slammed the empty crushed can of Red Dog on the glass table.

"Mike!" Sandy scolded. "We can hear you, we're all sitting only 12 inches apart, and please watch the table, you'll fracture the glass."

She turned to Julia and said sympathetically, "You poor darling, you must feel so violated!" She patted Julia soothingly on the shoulder.

Heather licked her lips again and inquired eagerly, "Do you think he's likely to come over to our neighborhood?" A bony hand fluttered at her flat, yet heaving bosom.

"Oh Steven!" Heather cried, suddenly clutching his sleeved arm. "You have to protect me, what if he broke into our house and raped me?!" She actually sounded more hopeful than fearful.

"Okay, calm down Heath, I'm here, no one is go- going to hurt you," Steve stammered. Puffing out his concave chest, he gulped the sweet burgundy wine to support his manly bravado.

When we finished telling the story for the third time, Mike threw his large head back and guffawed.

"Oh puhleeze," he snorted and stood up with his hands on his hips, shaking his massive head. He chuckled, looking around the table at us.

"Some poor slob that ain't getting any at home, sneaks around the neighborhood looking in windows to get his jollies. You really have to feel sorry for the twerp. That kind of guy has got to be harmless."

One side of his mouth pulling back into a half smile, shaking his head back and forth again, he strode back in the direction of the steaming grill.

"Mike's right," I said taking a swig of beer. "We're getting way too melodramatic about this prowler. I'm sure the cops will catch him soon and throw him into the pen where he belongs."

"I think we should all be a little more careful when we're alone," Sandy said. Plucking a potato chip out of the bowl, she snapped it in half then tossed one half into her mouth.

She stood up and ate the other half, wiping her hand on her jeans. "But for now, I think we should eat and have some fun, and change the subject to something more pleasant and less perturbing. Okay?" She looked around the table, we all nodded in agreement.

Satisfied, Sandy grabbed a couple more potato chips and headed towards the house.

"I'll help with the food," Julia offered. She got up quickly and went inside the house with Sandy.

"Ohhhh," Heather moaned. "I guess I should help too, but the goings on in the neighborhood are so titillating, my heart is beating so fast...with...um, fear, I'm afraid I might faint!" She fanned her face with a napkin, sliding her glance around at each of us.

We three men just looked blandly at her then started a conversation amongst ourselves.

With a beleaguered sigh, Heather reluctantly left the table and also disappeared into the house.

After a minute or two, Mike went back to supervise the ribs.

Steve and I talked shop while consuming chips and quaffing beer.

The sun was almost completely gone now leaving just a trace of pink in the darkening horizon. It was still warm and since we were way in the back behind the house it was pretty quiet.

We could hear the infrequent car pass by out front. Somewhere a dog sporadically barked, and from the rear of the yard Mike was singing off key, but loudly to his smoldering ribs.

The girls returned to the patio, arms laden with tableware, creamy potato salad, corn on the cob, baked beans, biscuits, tossed salad and brownies for desert.

"Wow!" I exclaimed leaping up to help the girls set the food on the table. "There's enough food here for ten third world countries!"

Mike came running up with a huge serving plate stacked high with the most incredibly wonderful smelling, gooey ribs.

Steve had gone back into the house and returned carrying a red tray that was filled with glasses of wine, cans of beer and a couple of Snapples.

He reached in and out with the drinks, dodging arms and heads as everyone was trying to put something on the table. We were chatting and laughing, spilling food and splashing drinks as we all finally sat down and began passing food around the table.

Soon, our plates were piled sky high with the delicious food.

Chapter Five

We had a merry time gorging ourselves on all the delectable victuals, and catching up on each other's lives.

When our orgy of eating ended, there was barely a morsel remaining. Sitting back groaning we patted our evermore protruding bellies.

Gas lanterns hanging interspersed about the patio flickered little spots of orange haloes all around us. I hardly remember noticing Sandy quietly lighting the glass lanterns.

We sat in camaraderie silence for a few moments. A multitude of satisfying sighs traveled around the table.

Heather cut into the peacefulness, trilling in her high-pitched girlie voice, "Did I tell you guys that I'm going to open a boutique?" She glanced expectantly around at the group, false eyelashes standing like exclamation points encircled small pellets of hazel.

"Really?" Julia said. She was folding her checkered cloth napkin neatly and pushing it through a wooden napkin ring that was carved in swirling lines.

Sandy likes to mix formality with the laid back. Sometimes we're eating burgers on china plates and drinking Kool-Aid out of champagne glasses.

"Tell us all about it, Heather." Julia smiled, encouraging her.

"Well," Heather said eagerly, "I don't have all the concrete plans yet, and Steven is going to have to work a lot of overtime to come up with the money to bankroll this project, but he's all for it, right honey?" She grinned at Steve, who looked pretty weary, yet nevertheless nodded weakly at her.

"Anyway, it's going to be a small store at first, but with top named designers, and only the most exclusive merchandise. I'm thinking of renting one of those fancy shops that are strung along ultra-fashionable Las Olas Boulevard.

"Only the most elegant, hauteur collection of outfits will be displayed in my windows. I intend to attract the extravagant, wealthy people who aren't even planning to buy anything but are only window-shopping.

"I want them to be so taken by the splendor of my ensembles that they are swept into my store by their unbridled desire to possess one of my finely made frocks!" Heather took a breath, her painted face shone with ecstasy.

Her enthusiasm increasing, she continued, "I even have the outside of the shop designed and a theme depicted." Beaming, she looked around at each of us to see if we were at rapt attention.

Everyone was listening to her except Mike. Mike was looking at her, but you could tell his eyes were glazed over and he was really thinking about something else.

Steve was nodding and agreeing with everything she was saying, but he looked pretty tense.

Sandy humored Heather by asking polite questions about who would be some of the designers, and where on Las Olas she would like to be located.

I glanced at Julia. She was watching Heather, almost studying her, while sucking on the straw that poked out of her glass of Snapple.

I tried to stifle a yawn. Boy did Heather bore me with her 'I want' attitude. And where in the heck did she think poor, overworked Steve was going to get this ton of money for heaven's sake. The poor guy is already up to his neck with charge cards and loans.

Plus, he already works late into the evenings and all day on Saturdays. What does she want anyway, for Steve to get another job midnights and Sundays flipping burgers at the Branded Bull?

Jiminy Cricket, I thought, what a self-centered woman Heather is. Why doesn't the lazy sloth get a job herself?

Steve should really stop being a doormat and make that girl start pulling her own skinny weight. She sure helps me realize what a gem I have in my wonderful wife.

I smiled lovingly at Julia, brushing her foot with my sneakered toe. She turned towards me, our eyes locked in a private embrace.

"So," Heather droned on. "I've spoken with Dimitri, the architect that works in Steven's building and he's quite excited about my idea. He's already drawn out some plans. He says the exterior of the building will be that polished black marble with the gold veining."

Unconsciously, she ran one hand up and down her arm, caressing her skin. She licked her lips again then reached up and tweaked at some of the blonde spikes sticking out of her head like razor points.

"The smooth, ebony marble will make a dazzling foil for the bronze statue of Freya, the mysterious and ancient Nordic goddess of love and beauty I want displayed at the store's entrance."

"Well," Sandy said, "that sounds very exciting and so enterprising. I can't wait to see the completed project. Although," she smiled kindly at Heather, "I don't think I'm the kind of customer you're looking for. I probably couldn't afford a pair of stockings from your opulent shop."

"That's *boutique*," Heather sniffed nobly.

"Whatever," Mike muttered.

"Anyway, that's okay, Sandy," Heather stated magnanimously. "Since you're such a good friend, I can probably give you a small discount on any minor item in the shop, I mean boutique. Of course I can't discount any of the really good stuff you know, after all I will be there to make money. There won't be anything cheap or tawdry in my shop."

Totally oblivious to her own bragging, Heather sipped her wine while managing to keep her pencil-thin nose high in the air.

"Well thanks buddy, that's very generous of you," Sandy replied sincerely. "Well," she said pushing her chair back, "I guess it's time to clean up this mess."

Sandy got up and with Julia helping, started packing up the remains of our repast. They carried plates and bowls back up to the house. Belatedly, I remembered the Casey's grandmother.

"How's Grandma Amy?" I asked Mike.

Mike erupted with a tremendous belch.

"Eeew how gross!" Heather wrinkled her nose in disgust. She hurried away from the table, jiggling a tray piled with dirty dishes.

Mike snorted as he watched Heather tripping across the lawn in her spiked sandals and skin-tight, short-shorts that deliberately exposed the bottom portion of her skinny butt. Her derriere looked like two small halves of white grapefruit rock and rolling to an uneven beat.

She caught up with Sandy and Julia. We could hear them discussing the boutique. Heather's high-pitched voice carried all the way back to the patio.

"Oh, Grandma is doing pretty well," Mike replied, yawning. "Her arthritis bothers her some during the summer storms, and she gets up and around more slowly these days. But for an old lady she's incredibly active. She chased Bonnie around all day today, then bathed her and read her a short bedtime story.

"The poor woman, she was so bushed by time Bonnie fell asleep we practically put her to bed with the tyke. She's a real blessing to us though, a real blessing." Mike sounded quite reverent not hiding his awe and respect for the elderly grandmother.

He made some more revolting and foul reverberations then said, "Hey look, I got us some stogies." Mike pulled three smooth Coronas out of his shirt pocket and handed one each to Steve and me.

"Oh man," Steve grinned as Mike ran a cigar under his nose. "We haven't enjoyed one of these since your sister Yvonne's wedding in April."

"I thought you quit smoking," I mumbled to Mike as I lit the end of my cigar and began puffing.

Mike draped one arm around the empty chair next to him, and crossed one heavy leg over the opposite knee. He squinted at me then tipped his head over the back of his chair, blowing out slow, spiraling smoke rings.

His eyes followed the rings as they floated up, dissipating into the black night.

"Yeah, sorta," He grunted through the side of his mouth as he continued to puff. "I quit smoking cigarettes, Sandy wouldn't get off my back because of Bonnie. I went through the gamut of gum and patches and stuff but I finally quit."

His expression melted into pure bliss as he sucked on his cigar. "But I just can't give up the occasional Cuban."

"They're so relaxing and macho," Steve piped in, happily toking on his tobacco.

Between puffs and periodic discourse, we nibbled on nut-filled brownies. We could hear the clatter of dishes and girlish laughter wafting down from the kitchen where the women were tidying up.

"So how's the plumbing business going Mike?" I asked, lounging back in my chair.

"Oh," Mike leaned forward, cigar still in hand, his huge forearms rested on the table and his back hunched. "We were making money hand over fist, but gee, lately we're having a hard time drumming up business.

"Uncle Bruce put some ads in the newspaper but business has been really slow. And you know it's a stinking dirty job. Sometimes I think I'll never be really clean again. Sandy is always complaining about the permanent black gunk under my nails. She knew what I did for a living when she married me."

Angrily, Mike put a can of beer to his mouth and chugged the whole brew in about four seconds. Then he crushed the empty can with one hand. We were all getting pretty blitzed at this point. We had not stopped drinking since we arrived.

"I know what you're saying," Steve slurred. "I'm just exhausted all the time. You know how it is...I work 14 hours a day so we can afford all the things Heather thinks we should have. Then, she gets all whiny and pouty when I can't...uh...you know...come to full attention for her when we...uh...." suddenly red-faced, Steve looked everywhere but at us.

His eyes dropped to the table. "It's not like she wants it very often man, but when she does boy, I'd better be freaking Superman and be able to last forever and perform tricks! Any other time she's perusing her manicure over my shoulders."

"We understand," Mike commiserated with Steve, clapping him on the back.

I nodded my agreement. Although in all modesty, I must say that I have never had a problem in that area. However, knowing Heather, she can be a demanding and critical person. It can't be too easy being intimate with her.

Mike winked at me. "It happens to all of us dude, at one time or another. The booze can get me once in a while, but if the chick is hot enough-" Mike stopped abruptly, stuffed his cigar back in his mouth and stared at the table.

At that moment, Sandy and Heather came out of the house dressed in bathing suits.

Sandy was carrying a pitcher of a clear liquid, Heather had four cocktail glasses entwined in her fingers.

Oh gag me, I thought, Heather was wearing a friggin' thong! There were sharp bones sticking out everywhere. I couldn't see one curve on her body. *Ack*, I turned my head away fast before I saw more of her exposed white skin.

Sandy was at least wearing a navy blue one piece with a little skirt attached. Sandy always has been a touch pudgy, which was cute and sexy when she was a teenager, but now she was really packing on the pounds.

She and Mike were beginning to look like preview for the Big Butt Family Show. Sandy had pulled her straight brown hair back into a ponytail, which unfortunately only accentuated her round face and plump cheeks. I had to look around Sandy to find my tiny wife.

Ahhhh, there she was.

Julia was still wearing the white lace sundress with the pink flowers on it. She had white sandals on her wee feet, and a small white bow in her long hair that was curling softly from the evening's humidity.

I smiled at her. She was carrying her purse, I had a feeling it was time for us to go.

"Lookit!" Heather squealed. "We made a whole pitcher of martinis!" She carefully set the glasses on the table, giggling when one of them tottered back and forth in danger of falling off the table.

Tucked under her arm was a jar of large green olives. She twisted the lid off, stuck her fingers in the jar and pulled out a shiny green olive with the red pimento still in it. Heather looked at the olive she held between her thumb and two fingers and then she looked over at Mike.

Mike was still sitting at the table. His shoulders hunched and his arms were crossed, resting on the table. His head was bowed, but his eyes were turned up, he was watching Heather.

Without taking her eyes off Mike, Heather put the olive she held to her lips and licked it. Then she put part of it in her mouth, pulled it out slowly, then she did it again, but this time she bit off an end.

She chewed for a second, then lowered her jaw so her mouth hung open like a Venus Flytrap. Dropping the rest of the olive in, she chewed loudly, swallowed, then licked each finger, still staring at Mike.

I was the only one watching them. Mike looked over at me and smirked.

Sandy was pouring the contents of the pitcher into the four glasses. Her movements drew Mike's attention.

"Why in the hell are we drinking martinis?" he grumbled, scowling at the martini pitcher. "What's wrong with my beer?"

"Oh Mike, you big baby, we wanted to try something potent and different." Heather laughed at him. She sauntered over to the table where Sandy was pouring the martinis. Reaching into the jar with her fingers again, she pulled out a couple of fat olives.

She dropped the olives into a full glass and handed it to Mike. Mike sat back in his chair and grunted, but he took the glass from Heather.

"Yeah honey," Sandy added. She had finished emptying the container of martini mix. "Don't you feel like doing something different, maybe something really wicked and totally way out sometimes?" She sipped her martini and sighed, a contented smile spread across her chubby face.

"Okay guys, let's get crazy and do something wild!" Steve had been so into his cigar he hadn't seen the exchange between his wife and Mike. He reached for a glass.

Holding the martini up to the group in a salute, he yelled, "Cheers!" Then he heartily slurped down the fiery cocktail.

I was impressed. He didn't choke or turn red, just held out his empty glass for more.

Julia was pointedly staring at me.

Placing the butt of my cheroot into an ashtray, I slid my chair back, and stood up stretching and yawning.

"Well guys, it's been great amusement and sumptuous chow, but we gotta boogie, Julia has to get her rest."

Mike and Steve also stood up, clapping me on the back and each kissing Julia on the cheek. I put my arm around Julia as we left the group.

"You all be good and don't do anything I wouldn't do!" I called out.

Walking with Julia towards the house I half-turned and looked back.

Heather was leaning over Mike, holding an olive to his lips. His sullen expression had cleared.

Steve and Sandy were standing by the Jacuzzi talking.

In the back of my intoxicated mind, I thought there was something wrong with this picture, but they waved at us as we exited and the thought slid right out of my head.

We hopped into the Bronco and headed home. Julia drove since I was too busy singing raunchy ballads I learned in college at the top of my lungs.

Chapter Six

The summer weeks passed quickly. The weekends seem to go by so fast sometimes it feels like I never leave the office.

Today began like most others. I spent a few minutes in the morning shooting the bull with my boss, Artie Stillwagon.

He was sitting at his desk going through receipts and tapping some of the numbers onto an adding machine. Guy still lives in the dark ages.

I was standing slouched against a bookcase gazing out a window. The sky was bright and cloudless, the sun blinding. When I looked away from the window, there were spots in front of my eyes like the ones caused by the flash of a camera.

Blinking to clear my vision, I cupped my hand over my brow to block the glare and looked back out onto the street to watch the people passing by.

Most of the residents in the town were at their various jobs, but there was still a steady stream of traffic. Groups of mostly women, many in pairs, bustled past the store.

Carpathian Computers is a great name for a computer company. Artie wanted to name his shop after something strong, enduring and mighty, so he titled it after the mountain range in Europe.

While working in the repairs department, periodically a salesman will ask me to come out and explain a particularly technical operation of a computer to a confused customer. We offer classes on Tuesday evenings on how to become computer friendly with one's new and expensive purchase.

Of course, there's always going to be problems with computers, new and old, so I have good job security and make a pretty good dime. I come home Friday nights and give my paycheck to Julia. She balances the checkbook, pays the bills and gives me a weekly allowance.

She puts away a chunk of my earnings into a savings account for our awaited Baby Dixon. By the time the babe is born, we should have a good bit of money in the bank to pay for all those infant needs. I think all that's better handled by the woman. They know what they and the newborn need more than a sad sack guy like me.

I was a single child, lived in a dorm in college, then I moved back home to be nurtured by my mom until I married Julia. I'm not exactly the exciting, dangerous type. I like to have fun, but I stay on the safe side. Just give me an easy chair, a beer and a TV remote and I'm a happy guy.

I work on computers all day at the store, so that's the last thing I want to see when I get home. I count myself extremely lucky that I found and courted a super girl like Julia so easily.

My grandfolks have a good deal of money and I may or may not see any of it when they die. My parents and I have always lived frugally. I'm not exactly cheap, but one needs to look out for the future, not to splurge and live extravagantly. Save for the rainy day, that's my motto.

A few months ago as soon as we found out Julia was pregnant, we had immediately decided to get married.

Since we needed to move the wedding along quickly, we took a long weekend to Las Vegas and tied the knot there amongst the glamour and excitement of the city that never sleeps.

Avoiding the tacky, Elvis type wedding service trappings, and hasty non-romantic drive-thrus, we searched until we found a small, charming yet traditional white chapel with a gingerbread exterior.

The minister and his wife were kind and soft-spoken. The inside of the chapel was austere but they had softened it with mellow golds and subtle cream colors. Bouquets of multicolored spring flowers were bursts of cheerful colors throughout the tiny room.

While the minister's cordial wife played the organ with hushed gentleness, candles flickered and glowed on a small alter creating an ethereal atmosphere. I've heard Julia describe her dress several times since the wedding.

Apparently it was 'the perfect' dress. Of course I thought she was radiant in the ice blue, floor length gown, with bits of miniature violets and baby's breath threaded in her French braided hair.

She took my breath away when she entered the room her eyes were so big and solemn. Calla lilies and white roses were cradled in her arms and she had the most beautifully serene smile, what a shining picture of happiness and joy.

Next to the patient minister, wearing a rented black tux and ruffled shirt, I stood nervously waiting for her. The minister's wife had pinned a white rose to my lapel and I had remembered to tuck a pressed white handkerchief into my breast pocket before leaving the hotel room.

My new, black dress shoes were polished to a high gleam. The final touch was the gold pocket watch my dad had given me last birthday. I decided I looked quite debonair.

The ceremony was over so soon, it was hard to believe we were bound together under the eyes of God forever and ever, till death do us part. Wow! How scary.

But, one look into my new wife's adoring eyes as she folded into my arms for our first kiss as man and wife, my soul delighted with love so powerful, I felt physical pain in my heart.

Hearing the minister sigh and his matronly wife twitter, I reluctantly pulled away from my beloved bride, cherishing the look of amore emanating from her expressive eyes.

We drank fruity champagne in fluted, gold-rimmed crystal glasses to celebrate. Chatting and laughing with the pastoral couple, we signed the declaration and legal paperwork of our marriage.

Thanking the pleasant people for their sincere service and warm blessings for our newly joined life, we prepared to leave, excited to share our news with our closest friends.

When we pushed the heavy oak door open, silver bells chimed joyously overhead as we exited the chapel and entered the world as now one integrated whole person, instead of the two separate people we were when we entered.

"Hey Rusty!"

Interrupting my musings, Bob Noble, one of our best salesmen and the office supervisor was standing in the doorway.

"Can I borrow you for a minute? I know it's almost lunchtime but I have a lady out here that just bought that new Mega 1,000 charger and she's having trouble getting it to work." Bob smiled half-pleading with me.

I glanced at Artie, he was intensely studying his adding machine tape and making notes.

"Sure," I said. "Let's see how quickly we can get this problem fixed." I slapped Bob on the shoulder and we left Art's office and went into the showroom.

It took a lot longer than I thought to adjust the new equipment and explain how it operates to the customer. It was past 4:00 already, and I never did eat lunch.

I was just going out the door to the Calico Catfish down the road for a blackened dolphin sandwich and a basket of Cajun steak fries, when Jill, Artie's secretary called out to me.

"Rusty, you have a phone call, says his name is Steven." With her hair swept up into a prim bun, eyeglasses and skirts that ballooned past her knees, Jill looked older than she really was.

Her demure appearance did not successfully hide the mischievous sparkle in her eyes.

She reminds me of a commercial where after using some type of perfume or something, she suddenly pulls the pins from her hair, whips off her glasses and tosses them over her shoulder.

Shaking her now loose, luxurious hair, she yanks off her full skirt to reveal a skimpy, sexy outfit underneath then she breaks out into song and dance showing how using this new perfume has somehow made her more beautiful.

Now with men lined up around the block waiting for her, her life becomes more exciting!

Fortunately, Jill couldn't read my mind or she'd be a bit flabbergasted, but she'd probably laugh at my silly characterization of her. She held my phone that I'd left on her desk out to me, dangling it lazily from two fingers.

Smiling my thanks, I took the phone from her. I was pretty curious, Steve has never called me at work before. I haven't heard from him or Mike since that last get-together at Mike's at least six weeks ago.

For privacy, I went into the studio area where I work. Pulling a stool over to a worktable, I sat down, and clicked the cell to answer the call.

"Hey man, what's up?" I said jauntily into the phone. Pulling out some drawers, I searched for perhaps a forgotten candy bar or even a piece of gum to stem my hunger pains.

"Hi Rusty," Steve sounded odd, hesitant. "Um, how's Julia?"

Darn, there was only junk in the drawers, small parts, tools, pieces of wire, paper clips, bolts, screws, nothing edible. I shoved some stuff around, but the drawers were bereft of food.

"As beautiful as ever," I responded. "You sound funny Steve, what's going on?"

"Have you spoken with Mike or Sandy lately?" he asked.

"Naw, I haven't seen or heard from the four of you in five or six weeks, not since the barbecue." I stopped talking, he sounded like he had something on his mind but was stalling.

I figured he'd eventually spit out why he was calling. Hugging the phone with my chin and shoulder, my right leg swung while I continued my search for food. There was silence for a minute.

"Gee Rusty, I have to tell you something, I've got to unburden myself," his heavy sounded distressed. "I just don't know how to begin... I was such an idiot...we were all big stupid idiots..."

Now Steve spouted an angry, "Oh man...."

"C'mon Steve, give, what the heck is going on?" I could hear his ragged breathing through the phone.

"Oh man," Steve repeated, "that last Saturday night we six were together at Mike's...you and Julia left early...boy were you smart to leave when you did."

Silence again. Then, "You just don't know, but, our lives traipsed down the hot path to hell right after you guys left. We were drinking really heavily that night, even more than usual. Parts of the night are a blur, I can't even remember everything.

"I sure remember though, the toilet hugging, and the excruciating headache the next morning. In fact, the throbbing headache didn't go away for a long time and I couldn't eat for two days after without heaving-"

Interrupting his appetizing dialogue, I said, "Listen Steve, I know what hangovers are like, get to the point if you have one."

He cleared his throat and said, "Okay, okay. Anyway, somehow as the night progressed, my wife seemed like she was all over Mike. Normally they can barely tolerate each other, but Saturday, whew...there was some heavy physical stuff going on."

"That's unusual. Wait, what do you mean by physical-"

"Then Heather started feeding Mike olives like she was Cleopatra and they were grapes. She'd put an olive to his mouth and wait until her fingers were totally enveloped by his lips before slowly pulling her hand away and reaching for the next one. With each olive, Heather leaned in closer and closer to Mike."

Steve took a deep breath. I vaguely remembered seeing Heather behaving oddly as Julia and I were leaving the party.

Steve continued, "So anyway, uh, Sandy and I were lingering over by the hot tub, sipping our drinks and making small talk, mostly about Bonnie and the cute things she does and the new words she's learning.

"We were talking to each other but our eyes kept drifting over to Mike and Heather. Why one of us did nothing to nip things in the bud right away I don't know, I just don't know...I sure wish we had now...I wish I could go back and do things over." Steve's voice grew real quiet, real sad.

I didn't make a comment, I had no idea what to say.

"So...the night seemed weird...like in and out. Like one minute I was totally lucid and the next I was enclosed in myself, not seeing or hearing anything except the roar in my head I guess from the alcohol." He stopped talking again.

I switched the phone to my other ear, my swinging leg stopped moving and I stopped rummaging for food.

"Keep going," I encouraged Steve, although I was beginning to feel some trepidation, the story sounded like trouble to me.

Actually, I wasn't sure I should or wanted to hear any more. "Maybe," I cut in as he started to say something, "maybe you shouldn't tell me anymore, Steve."

"But I need to talk to somebody man, I've gotta confess, and you're my best friend. Who else am I going to tell?" Steve whined.

"Okay, okay, go ahead and tell me if you feel I can help," I said, holding my breath.

"Anyway," Steve continued, "the next thing I know, Heather climbs up and sits on Mike's lap facing him with her legs straddling his waist. Then they...uh...start sucking face and groping each other like they were alone instead of in public in front of their spouses.

"I mean, they were kissing for real, mouths open, tongue and all, not like the little pecks we usually give the girls. Heather was only wearing a minuscule bikini. I guess I should have stopped them, gee, after all we are married, but I felt so detached from the scene, like I was watching a movie under water or something. I felt weird like I said."

"What did Sandy do?" I asked.

"Sandy just kept staring at them like she was watching two strangers. We had stopped all pretense of talking by then. She just kept drinking her martini and staring at them. I guess we were so drunk by then we couldn't react.

"Neither of us seemed to be able to make any purposeful actions. Maybe we were afraid to try and stop them."

Um," heck, I had no idea what to say.

His voice filled with dejection, Steve went on, "We just stood there, gaping at the two of them kissing and fondling each other. Mike's hands are roaming all over Heather's body, and she wasn't being shy with her hands either," Steve said wryly.

"Yeah," I murmured, "shy would not be the word I'd use to describe Heather."

"Anyway, so then Mike untied the back of Heather's bikini top, not that there was much there to begin with, and he lets the top drop on the ground. Before he could touch her, she hopped off his lap and took his hand pulling him to stand up." Steve sucked in a ragged breath.

"Then, totally uncaring that she was topless, she tugged on his hand, dragging him over to where Sandy and I were standing by the tub. With a goofy look plastered on his face, Mike tottered so drunkenly after Heather, I thought for sure with every step he took that he was going to fall, tripping over his big feet.

"When they got near the hot tub, Heather pushed her bikini bottoms down to the ground then shamelessly kicked it away. Totally bare-assed naked, she set her cocktail glass on the edge of the Jacuzzi then stepped down into the steaming tub.

"Once she was in the water, she pushed off from the wall, floating backwards, her arms were wide open, inviting. Cackling like a hen in heat, she called to us to join her."

"Hens don't go into heat, Steve," I interrupted.

"Whatever. Anyway," Steve went on, "already tearing off his clothes, Mike quickly joined Heather in the tub. Heather taunted Sandy and me, yelling to us to let loose and enjoy ourselves, to join them in the water. She splashed water at us, mocking us, calling us prudes and chickens.

"Mike settled next to Heather in the bubbly water, and ignoring us as if we weren't standing there, he reached for my wife and pulled her to him. Their hair was soaked and their faces were shiny and red, steam swirled around them- kind of like it was cocooning them inside their own personal cloud. They locked lips again."

Rusty pictured Steve shaking his head, his eyes glazed over recalling the night.

"I don't know what else they were doing because the water went up to their necks and the bubbles fully covered them. I looked at Sandy and she shrugged. Tipping her glass up, she drank the last bit of her martini and set the empty glass next to Heather's on the rim of the pool.

"Then she stood straight up, and with one fluid movement, she peeled off her suit, dropping it on the ground, next to the pool railing. She stood for a moment, silently looking at me.

Then, she sighed really, really heavy, like with... resignation...and she joined the others."

"And then?" I prompted.

"Mike grabbed at Heather, but she would squeal and move just out of his reach, teasing him to chase her. Sandy just huddled against the side of the tub, trying to look nonchalant.

"I felt absurd standing there clothed while they waved to me, jeering and goading me to come in. I guess I'd had enough alcohol to dull the walls of my modesty and my senses." He paused.

Shame making his voice shake, "And, well...I stripped off my jeans and shirt and got into the tub too," Steve's sigh was so woeful his last words were barely audible.

"Holy cow Steve..." I was surprised at them. But people get carried away when they're drinking and all normal censoring is diminished.

"That's not the most moral or puritanical thing you could have done, but I don't think it's that abominable, it's not the end of the world." I yanked at the door of a cabinet attached to the wall next to the phone. It snapped open.

Yes! There was half a tube of Certs sitting on the shelf. Thank heaven for someone's bad breath! I ripped a candy out of the package and threw it into my mouth then folded and pocketed the rest. It was stale, but beggars can't be choosers.

"That's not all of it, Rusty," Steve said. "That was only the beginning."

"The beginning of what?" I questioned.

"It was the beginning of the end," Steve choked dramatically.

Jeepers, the guy really sounded distraught. I took my glasses off and pinched between my eyes. "Tell me the rest, Steve." I sighed.

He made an indiscernible sound then said, "The rest of the night is quite vague..."

Guilt stammered his words, "I...I...remember Mike suddenly standing up in the middle of the Jacuzzi with a swoosh, he was holding Heather like a doll in his arms. She was clinging to his neck, giggling and kicking up her heels.

"Her head was hanging back, and she was shaking it back and forth, laughing and laughing, she didn't freakin' stop laughing." Steve sounded angry again.

"Then Mike stumbled up the tub steps carrying Heather, showers of water drops sprayed all around them and onto us. He turned towards us, smirking. Sandy and I were gaping wide-eyed at them.

"He said to us, 'We're going into the house and do the nasty. You're welcome to join us.' Then, he turned as if he'd already forgotten about us, and with *my wife* still in his arms, he brazenly marched up to the house, leaving a trail of wet splotches behind."

Steve was quiet again for a minute. I waited anxiously, I feared he hadn't finished.

He hadn't. "Sandy and I were like stone statues. We didn't move a muscle for a few moments, our mouths hung open, we didn't even blink. Then, slowly we turned to each other.

"Looking through my glasses foggy with steam, I remember Sandy's face was flushed from the heat of the pool. Little beads of sweat ran in rivulets over her temples. She looked hazy and ghostly through the steam from the heat of the tub.

"Everything was heavy and slow moving, like rowing through a swamp in a humid Louisiana night. We stood up simultaneously, our nakedness forgotten. Without saying a word,

I held my hand out to her and she placed her hand in mine. Both of us were trembling as we moved towards the house.

"I recall I couldn't feel my legs, and there was a rushing sound in my head. I couldn't think or feel. I seemed like a zombie, a walking empty shell. Soundlessly, as if in a trance we entered the house."

I didn't dare interrupt Steve's story, he was certainly holding my interest.

His voice empty and stoic, he went on, "Surprisingly, there was a stillness to the home. I guess we expected to hear Heather's lascivious laughter and other torrid sex noises. After all, Mike is a loud man in all other aspects, why should his love-making be any different?" Steve sounded indifferent, but I could hear muted sniffing, then he grew silent.

I let a minute or so go by then I grew impatient. "So, then what?" I prodded.

Boy, he sure had my undivided attention now. I was absolutely aghast at their behavior. It was like listening to porn, but these were close friends I knew, or thought I knew. Wife swapping? I was bewildered and dumbfounded.

I could hear his deep draw of breath before he said, "Well... I'm ashamed to say...but...uh, Sandy and I cautiously tiptoed into the guest room. We didn't know where the others were and the last thing we wanted was to walk in on them. They must have been ensconced in the master bedroom.

"The guest room was as empty as it was dark. We didn't turn on a light, we just fell onto the bed in an awkward embrace, like two pieces of puzzle that didn't fit. We fumbled at each other, bumping noses as we clumsily kissed." A mortified groan uttered out.

"We were so uncomfortable and self-conscious...it was agonizing...but too late to turn back. We never said a word to each other." The sound of self-contempt corroding his voice was unfamiliar to me.

"Listen," he sounded tired. "I don't need to go into the explicit details, I hardly remember them anyway, thankfully. But needless to say, we did 'it'. I don't know how I was able to function after the gallons of alcohol I consumed, but I did. Most of the actual, uh...act...uh...is kind of murky, thank God. I just recall lying there on my back afterwards, staring at the ceiling.

"I could hear Sandy breathing next to me. I peeked over at her without moving my head. She was lying on her back too, her eyes seemed fixed on the ceiling fan. I could see her eyes following the paddles listlessly, endlessly circling the base of the fan. We weren't touching, just lying there wordless, not sharing our fear, shame, embarrassment, regret. It was awful."

His sigh pushed statically through the phone. "She got up first. There was a towel hanging over a chair. She picked it up and wrapped it around her nude body. Without a word she left.

"I lay there for a few more minutes until I started feeling cold and clammy. Then, I got up, dressed and without looking or waiting for Heather, I jumped into the Saab and blindly aimed the car for home." Rusty pictured him shaking his head and blinking in bewilderment.

"The drive home is a total fog to me. I don't remember it at all. I just recall struggling with the door lock, stumbling up the stairs and collapsing on the bed. My body and brain were mush. I must have fallen asleep immediately."

He hesitated, I waited.

Clearing his throat, Steve said, "The next day when I woke up, Heather was beside me, sound asleep, snoring like an old fat man. I never heard her come home or get into bed. I rolled over...my stomach lurched, my head beat and my body throbbed." He choked out a bitter laugh.

"Waves of nausea and dizziness hit me. Scrambling out of bed, I slammed my hand over my mouth and ran down the hall to the bathroom and puked my guts up."

"Thanks for sharing the gruesome aftermath, Steve," I muttered, my lip curling.

Standing up, I tucked my loosened shirt back into my trousers, the phone still held against my ear with my shoulder. I was pretty shocked. The Caseys and the Hazelhursts have been

47

my friends for years. Steve's description of their behavior sent shock waves through my brain. I was speechless.

"Hello Rusty, are you still there?" Steve's haggard, whiny voice jarred through the phone.

"Yeah, yeah Steve, I'm here." I started pacing. I walked a few steps in front of the steel door I had closed for privacy.

There was limited cell reception in the room. After only four steps on the yellowing floor, the bars on my phone shrunk to 1. I turned and paced four steps in the other direction. I brushed my hand raggedly through my oat-colored hair, disheveling it even more than its regular messiness.

I took a long deep breath, not sure how to respond. I said, "Well, that's quite a little tempest of sin you guys created, Steve. I have to confess I can't believe what you've told me. I mean it's so bizarre, man. So not like you guys, our group."

He didn't say anything so I asked, "What's going to happen next? What're you guys gonna do now?"

Pulling the Certs from my shirt pocket, I unfolded the cover and unraveled the silver lining to reveal the next candy. Prying the fusty green and white speckled mint from the package, I flung it towards my mouth. It bounced off my chin and flew onto the floor.

When it hit the floor, the mint rolled across the floor to the far corner of the tiled room. I cursed under my breath.

While waiting for him to respond, I tried to picture myself in his position- ick- I shook my head to dispel the picture. There's no way I'd cheat on my babe, and there's no way Julia would ever cheat on me. This was new territory for me, I didn't know how to help my friend.

I stared at the mint across the floor. Holding the phone with my right hand, trying to stay in the cell reception area, I squatted down and reached out my left hand stretching as far as I could, my middle finger was only inches from the candy.

I could almost touch it when I heard Steve's plaintive wail. There were only three green candies left and I hated to waste one.

Oh well, I took out the crumpled pack and ate another mint.

Steve was sniveling into the phone.

"I don't know what we're going to do!" he cried. "So far Heather and I are acting like nothing untoward ever happened. We behave like we didn't violate a couple of major commandments, we are sure gonna fry in hell. Neither of us has mentioned that night or Mike and Sandy. I..."

He gulped loudly. "I guess we'll just go on as we always have, after all, we equally sinned. I'm not sure how to act around Mike and Sandy. I'm not sure how to act around Heather for that matter. I have no idea if she even knows about Sandy and me. Even though it's all her fault, she'd still kill me if I told her."

Sucking on the mint, I said, "I don't know what to tell you, Steve. You guys have made a huge mistake and I don't know how you're going to get over it. Your one night of debauching madness probably ruined the friendship between all of us. I'm not going to preach at you or anything, but gosh Steve," I sighed.

"I don't see how you can look Sandy in the eye, or be pals with the guy who just slept with your wife practically right in front of you. And your marriage vows...bro..."

"I know," Steve whimpered. "I guess I'll have to wait and see how everyone else acts and take my cues from them. But, I don't even know how I feel. My wife slept with one of my best friends, as did I.

"I feel so dirty and degraded, and right now, I'm so disgusted with both Heather and myself, I don't know how I feel about her right now either. The love is not there, I don't know if it'll come back, and I sure don't like her much right now either. But, who am I to judge? I'm equally guilty. It's all so grotesque and confusing." His anguish came right through the phone wires.

There was silence again except for Steve's bouts of melancholy sighing and gnashing of teeth.

"Anyway," he finally shuddered, "thanks for listening buddy, it helped to get if off my chest and relieve some of the pain and shame I'm feeling."

"That's okay, pal, anytime you need to talk..." I consoled him. "You can call me and we can hit the Turquoise Cove and soak up some cold ones and hash through your life. You know, maybe you can talk to the minister at your church, you know, confess and stuff, that might help."

I didn't know what else to say, I've never been in the position of Father Confessor before. I'm not beyond the occasional little white lie, but adultery is outside of my realm, it's just not right.

"I'm really ashamed, Rusty, I don't know about telling a preacher...he'll judge me and...what if he tells someone? I don't know..." he broke off.

I said quickly, "Steve, priests don't judge and they don't gossip, that's their job, that's what they do. They're supposed to listen, maybe give a little advice, dole out a little punishment like some Hail Marys or something...then you feel better and you go home forgiven. The guilt is supposed to just wash away."

I don't know if that's what I'd do, but it sounded like something good to tell him.

His voice faint, Steve sighed, "Okay, maybe I'll try it, what do I have to lose, really...anyway... I have to get going, my lunch hour is way past, and, and ...you know... Well thanks for listening buddy...I'll, uh, let you go, okay? Talk to you later, bye."

The phone clicked dead.

I clicked my phone off and set it on the counter next to the tattered, wispy willow patterned wallpaper. Boy, I thought looking around, this place can sure use some new decorating. It's kind of dreary and dull.

Faded linoleum floor, grey walls, metal cabinets, wooden work tables laden with computers and parts, tools someone is going to be in trouble for leaving out.

I plunked down on the stool, my shoulders rounded, I rested my arms on my knees. Lowering my head into my hands, I groaned out loud. What a decadent bunch of fools, I thought to myself.

One selfish dissipating night and six lives are changed forever. I can't imagine those two couples will be able to be friends again. And where does that leave Julia and me? Can we keep both couples as friends? Do we want to be friends with any of them?

I shook my head back and forth, my palms covering my eyes. "Crap!" I spat out. I decided I'd better call Julia and tell her about our friends' deviant behavior.

Looking down at my watch, I saw it was nearly 5:00. I stood up and reached for the phone again. Wow, the earpiece was still hot from being pressed against my ear for so long. I dialed our home number.

After three rings, Julia's light breathy voice answered, "Hello, Rusty."

"Hi Baby," I sighed with the weight of my friends' sins on my shoulders.

"You won't believe what's happened..." I filled her in on all the gory details. When I finished, she agreed that our friendships were probably over or will be greatly strained.

I told Julia I was going to have to work late and not to wait up for me. She needed her undisturbed rest for her health and for the bambino's.

Sometimes when I work really late I bunk down in the den downstairs so I don't wake her. I'm not the most graceful guy in the world, and there's a rare table or footstool that I haven't managed to kick or trip over.

I get the munchies too, so I usually creep into the kitchen and get a beer and some mixed nuts and watch a late- late show. Then I crash on the cracked brown leather couch in front of the tube.

Sometimes when I wake up in the morning there's a worn, but still fluffy quilt tucked around me. That meant Julia rose early to walk the dogs and she covered me on her way out. What a darling she is, always thinking of my comfort. I made an audible sigh, missing my kewpie doll of a wife.

I stuffed my phone in my pocket after we said our good-byes. Eating the last of the Certs, I crumpled the pack and tossed it into the little wicker wastebasket under the counter as I left the workroom and strolled back into the showroom.

There were around four or five customers milling about looking at merchandise. Bob the salesman was talking to a young couple that was learning about one of our newest computers, the 'Quixote Factor'.

The couple was earnestly staring at Bob, but it was obvious the deal was very complex, and they were struggling to follow what he was saying. Bob adjusted his red and black silk Armani tie, and straightened his silver stemmed glasses as he patiently described the merits of the computer.

Browsing in the book corner was an older, balding man wearing a charcoal grey sweatsuit that needed washing and had seen better days. His grey athletic socks were stuffed into grubby white Nikes. One of his laces was untied and dragging, and one of his pant leg was shoved sloppily into the top of a worn out elastic sock.

That sort of guy always surprised me. He looks like a grubby derelict from the railroad tracks, but he buys the most expensive top of the line computers made. You certainly can't tell a book by its cover!

Up at the front counter, Lisa Marie, one of our cashiers was checking out a young male customer at the register. The youngster was buying a video game.

Lisa Marie is a sweet, quiet, unassuming girl. She's always pleasant and everyone likes her. Anything you ask for, Lisa Marie will amicably get it for you. We need ten more like her in the shop.

"Hey Lisa Marie-" I slapped my hand on the countertop. She turned and cheerfully smiled at me, revealing a mouth full of perfectly pristine teeth.

Handing the young guy his change and receipt, she held the bag containing his new purchase out to him. As the boy grabbed his purchase, Lisa Marie turned back to me, her blonde hair swished in front of her pretty face.

All grins, the kid mumbled a shy thanks, ducked his head and ran out the door clutching the bag.

"I'm gonna zip down to the Calico Catfish and get some dinner. I'll be back in around an hour. It looks like a late night tonight. The Deluxe 3000 Malcolm Ostrander dropped off needs to be fully dismantled, updated and cleaned and put back together by 9:00 tomorrow morning. Mr. Ostrander said he has a big assignment he has to get completed before his business trip to Rome next week."

I barely covered my mouth as an enormous yawn overcame me then grinned sheepishly at Lisa Marie.

Her eyes, the color of a misty blue spring in Ireland, softened as she nodded in agreement. Dual dimples creased her cheeks and rubescent lips curved into a warm smile. Young Lisa Marie is such a strikingly beautiful girl, boy if I weren't happily married I'd-

"Oh Rusty, you poor guy. You're so overworked and you hardly ever get to see your pretty wife during the week." She smiled at me sympathetically.

"Oh well," I forced a groan, "the life of the wicked you know!" Laughing, I waved to her as I exited the store.

Her lilting 'Bye!' squeezed out as the door clanked closed behind me.

I couldn't wait to get to the restaurant, if nothing happened to stop me I should get there in less than ten minutes.

Chapter Seven

Hitting the sidewalk, I walked south towards Orangetree Lane. The Calico Catfish was only a few blocks down the road from there.

The sun was swinging over to the west lengthening the shadows. Dense, threatening clouds loomed out west, it was raining somewhere over the everglades. Although miles away, I could see a black cloud with a cascading storm flowing beneath it.

The sun streamed down in feathery white strokes through a hole in the center of the cloud, like a gigantic strobe light from heaven. I could almost hear God commanding from above, "Dance my little lambs, dance!"

I've always felt that some superior being was pulling my strings and directing my life, especially when things didn't go the way I wanted them to. Of course, I've been saved by plenty of miracles as well, so who knows what's really going on?

Strolling past closing antique shops, I could still hear the occasional tinkle of a bell as someone entered or exited a store. The traffic was getting heavier as it inched towards six o'clock, an hour already past the five o'clock escape time.

Even though it was in the dead of summer, hot and humid as heck, the roads were still packed. They weren't as overflowing with snowbirds from other states like in the mild winter, but the place never really slows down.

The city gives the appearance of lethargy in the long broiling summer months, but the people just slip from their air-conditioned cars, to their air-conditioned jobs to their air-conditioned homes, waiting for that first welcomed cold front to seep down from the north and make the land comfortably habitable again.

But thank goodness there's some of the summer left before the northerners cram into our concrete paradise, clogging our space.

The whirling of mechanical thunder, the sound of metal slicing rapidly through air, drowned out the other noises of the street. I put my hand to my brow to shade my eyes and looked up.

High in the sky, was a helicopter, its propeller blades cutting through the air with a chopping rhythm. The aircraft hovered loudly for a moment; then it swooped down, made a quivering loop then quickly flew off out of sight. It was a news-copter checking out the traffic during the rush hour.

Thankful that I wasn't in a car, I rounded the last block and turned onto Fallen Palm Ave. Loping up the stone walk leading to the Calico Catfish establishment, I enjoyed the vision it portrayed.

The restaurant is surrounded by an expanse of verdant grass and several tubular palm trees curving towards the sun, their fronds listing gracefully in the light breeze.

In the center of the lawn is a majestically gnarled, Sweet Bay Magnolia tree with each lofty branch uniquely twisted and sporting lustrous, pearl white blossoms.

Now, folks tell me constantly that there are no magnolias this far south. They insist it must be something else that resembles the tree. So of course I have to drag them out here to prove this one exists. It's worth it though, because then we get to have a great dinner here at my favorite seafood restaurant!

Making my way up the walk, butterflies suddenly swarmed out of the surrounding bushes like a handful of tossed, colorful fluttering confetti.

The restaurant's wide, blue wood planked verandah was covered with patrons lounging on swinging benches and rattan chairs with glass tables. Ceiling fans strummed gently overhead.

People chatted sipping piña coladas and tropical rum drinks. Everyone looked relaxed and content. That's why I like the Calico. It has old southern charm and hospitality.

The owners are genteel natives. They create an impression of a Caribbean island, languid and serene, immersing customers in tropical colors and island friendliness. The overlarge wicker chairs have rounded, fanned hi-backs to provide a bit of coziness and privacy.

I visited briefly with Holly the cheerful hostess as she brought me into the bar area for quicker service.

Sitting on a tall bamboo stool, I rested my elbows on the smoked glass table and ordered a Heineken and lunch from my waitress, Pamela.

Eager to please and peppy as always, Pamela had a beer to me in minutes. I sipped my beer and grazed on some peanuts piled in a wooden bowl while I waited for my sandwich.

My eyes wandered around the restaurant. I could hear a quiet murmuring about the place, an occasional burst of happy laughter bounced off the paneled walls.

The customers were peacefully enjoying their drinks, food and company. The hum of the cookery unconsciously relaxed me.

I took a deep breath and a big swig of beer, firmly pushing my friends and their smutty behavior to the back of my mind.

What's going on in this world? I wondered. First a degenerate is peeping at my wife, and now my closest friends have collectively lost their minds. To hell in a hand bucket - that's where we're headed for.

Carroty-colored curly hair bouncing gaily off her shoulders, Pamela whisked my blackened dolphin sandwich and a basket of piping hot, Cajun seasoned steak fries right to me.

"Ow!" I yelped, dropping the sizzling fry I had picked up, it burnt my finger it was so hot! I plunked my thumb and forefinger into my ice water, submerging the lemon that was floating in it.

Pamela burst out laughing. I glared at her. She quickly hid china blue eyes behind lashes the shade of melted orange sherbet. She peeped at me with a grin.

I sniffed indignantly, trying to hide my injured pride.

Her impudent lashes laced freckled cheeks as peels of riotous laughter rang out of her mouth.

"It's not that funny Pamela Darning," I chided ruefully, glowering at her. Pulling my fingers out of the water glass, I dried them on my linen napkin.

Pamela held her order book up in front of her face to hide her mirth, but I could see her shoulders shaking and her head bobbing as she tried to contain her amusement.

As the server removed her giggling body from my injured presence, I delved hungrily into my sandwich. I was so ravenous I never looked up once until there wasn't a crumb left.

With food still stuffed in my cheeks like a chipmunk, I licked my fingers and considered dessert. Everyone knows stressed spelled backwards is desserts, granted I wasn't exactly under a big load of stress at this moment, but there's something to be said for preventative medicine.

Feeling pretty stuffed, I decided to just go with a small scoop of vanilla ice cream, with maybe just a spoonful of hot fudge and a sprinkling of nuts over a dollop of whip cream. I needed the ice cream like I needed five thumbs. I'm a tall beanpole, but I do have a burgeoning paunch.

I suppose I should drink less beer and exercise a little more than just moving from the couch to the fridge and back. I do think about exercising occasionally, but I can usually put it off until I forget about it again for a while.

After practically licking the empty bowl, I paid my bill, added a hefty tip, then trudged back to the shop.

It was well past seven when I pushed open the glass door and entered the store.

There was one customer in the showroom and he was at the register. Lisa Marie was handing cash to him. She glanced up at me, smiled a welcome then turned her attention back to the customer.

Other than those two, the room was empty. During the dinner hour we get very few customers so the other employees must be taking turns at supper breaks. I went into the breakroom.

Aaron, one of the cashiers, was chewing on a ham sandwich, his eyeballs glued to the paperback in his hand. A brown paper bag sat squashed on the table in front of him, and a Coke was sweating a wet circle on the laminated wood tabletop.

"Hya," I called out as I went to the small refrigerator and took out a cherry soda. "What'cha reading?" I asked.

Aaron looked up briefly and then quickly lowered his eyes to his book. "Murder mystery," he mumbled through a mouthful of bread. He obviously didn't want to be bothered.

I said, "Don't get any ideas, ha ha..."

He ignored me.

Leaving the kitchen, I wandered down a narrow hall, painted an exciting plain battle-ship grey. I passed several doors before reaching the workshop. The room was vacant. The other service people had already gone home. I've been putting in a lot of overtime lately.

Popping open my cherry soda, I tossed the metal tab into an bowl on the counter and took some healthy swigs before sitting down and getting started on Malcolm Ostrander's computer.

With that peeper terrorizing our neighborhood, I really should get home as soon as possible. Maybe I should call Julia and make sure she locked all the doors and windows and keeps the dogs close to her until I get home.

I couldn't help but suppress a grin, it was kinda cool having someone besides myself to worry about, I must be growing up. I hopped off the stool to go get the phone.

Frowning, I stuffed the phone in my pocket and walked slowly back to my stool. Julia hadn't answered and I'd let it ring a thousand times. And the answering machine wasn't on.

I shrugged and shook my head. She was probably just in the bath or something and couldn't hear the phone. I figured I'd try again in a while. I pushed up my sleeves and reached for my Phillips.

Chapter Eight

Ahhhh...done. Emitting a tired yawn, I stretched back in my chair.

Finally finished with the computer, I taped a yellow stickie with the customer's name to the monitor, so if I wasn't there in the morning when he came in, someone would know it was Mr. Ostrander's computer.

My mouth opened as wide as a cavern, another immense yawn escaped. *Whew, how late is it anyway?* I looked at my watch. Eleven thirty, darn, time to go home.

I put away the few tools I had used, flicked the light switch off and moved into the hall, pulling the door closed behind me. Everyone had gone home.

Turning off the hall lights as I passed through, then into the kitchen and out the back door of the store. I pushed the heavy security door closed, making sure I heard the lock click before I turned away.

It was still warm and muggy out. But the night was enchanting as only a south Florida night can be. I stopped next to my Bronco. Pulling keys out of my pocket, I gazed up.

Luminous crystal stars were sparkling from the cushion of a velvety, onyx sky. There was only a whisper of a breeze, and even that was tepid, not refreshing.

Sweat trickled down my face, yet that didn't spoil the sublime twilight. The lovely evening urged me on to rush home to the beauteous night's only rival, my gorgeous wife! I climbed into the Bronco and sped home.

I parked the Bronco in the driveway behind Julia's compact, dark blue Toyota. The lights in the house were off, but Julia had left the porch light on for me. What a sweetie. I stuck my key in the door and opened it soundlessly.

I assumed Julia was in bed asleep since all the lights were extinguished. Oh well, I figured I'd just crash on the sofa in the den so as not to awaken her. I didn't need to go into the kitchen. I was still kind of full from dinner and I was feeling tremendously sleepy. I just went straight into the den.

Not even turning on the TV, I plumped a small, crocheted pillow encircled with fringe. Cramming the pillow under my head, I laid my weary body gently and slowly onto the couch, falling asleep the second my head hit the pillow.

I awoke suddenly, disoriented. Did I hear a noise?

I squinted at the clock on the VCR, I'd removed my glasses when I had first sacked out. The red numbers were a little blurry. Maybe it was just the normal wiggly digital. It was 12:30. I'd only been asleep for 30 minutes or so.

Click I definitely heard that.

Bolting upright, my head snapped towards the entrance to the den. The door was slightly ajar. It was dark except for minimal moonlight that subtly outlined objects in the room.

I heard another sound. A footstep? I got up and crept quietly to the door.

With one finger, I inched the door open wider, then slowly poked my head out and looked around. I didn't see anything.

Wait! The first door down the hall was the nursery and the door was open about a half an inch, I could see a light on inside the room.

What the heck? Was it Julia? But she never gets up in the middle of the night, and she sleeps like a rock.

The den opens into a hall on one side of the room, and into the family room on the other side. A hallway leads out of the den.

Down the hall is first the nursery, then a huge linen closet, the laundry room and last is a door to the garage. Opposite the hall, on the other side of the family room is the kitchen with its café doors.

60

Just inside the foyer to the left of the living room are the stairs to the second floor. We call the house a split-level because there's only eight stairs going up to the three bedrooms and two bathrooms upstairs.

"*Julia*" I whispered loudly. Silence.

"*Juliaaa*!" I hissed a little more intensely. I could see no other lights on in the house.

I was pretty sure Julia was sound asleep up in our bedroom or she would have had many lamps illuminating her path. She has such a phobic fear of stepping on a bug with her bare feet that she always makes sure her way is well lit.

Whoosh

I heard the sliding glass door in the family room suddenly shoved open. Immediately, I pressed myself flat against the wall and held my breath.

I counted to five then peered around the corner of the door. Adjusting my eyes to the darkness, I watched a dark shadow of a figure stepping stealthily from inside my family room and out through the open glass door to the back yard.

I blinked.

Did I imagine that? Am I dreaming? Suddenly, I remembered the neighborhood peeper. I was sure I'd seen something, an image of a tall, stocky person wearing pointy-toed boots played back in my mind.

Without any further pondering, I grabbed my glasses and ran out of the den to the glass doors then pushed my head out.

The intruder was slipping along the back of our home, his boots barely making a sound shuffling through the dewy grass.

Stepping through the door, the heat of the night hit me in the face like a furnace. I crept along the leafy yellow hibiscus bush that wrapped around the back of the house.

Holding my breath, I clamped a hand across my mouth lest I screamed with fear and tiptoed to the edge of the house.

Keeping my back plastered against the wall, I twisted my head around the edge of the building. Slinking around the corner, I trampled the caladiums and hid behind a scraggly bush.

Pushing the leaves aside, I ignored the thorny branches scraping my hands while trying to peek through the screen of the wide foliage.

I almost didn't see the man blending into the darkness as he moved swiftly through the neighborhood. Darting from our house to Mrs. Anderson's next door, I jumped behind dominoes of coconut palms lining the street, one after the other.

Luckily it was dark, or the stranger would have been able to see my slightly rounded belly and gangly arms and legs sticking out from behind the poles of trees.

Seeing the guy turn a corner, I sped up my pursuit. Breaking into an irregular jog, I tried to stay close to the shadows of houses, scooting through the open spaces and using trees, shrubs and vehicles for cover.

I followed the man down several streets then out along the highway. When we hit the main street, I moved more openly and bravely.

The man walked briskly and with such confidence, I was pretty sure he didn't know I was following him. Still moving furtively, I closed the distance between us.

There were very few vehicles on the road. Every couple of minutes or so, a car would whiz past producing the only sound in the steamy still night. There wasn't even a trace of a breeze, the air heavy with humidity.

My hair was already dripping with sweat and my shirt was soaked. I wiped my forehead with a sleeve so the perspiration wouldn't drip onto my glasses and distort my vision.

We moved rapidly along the main road, passing shops and businesses. The buildings were all closed, but some had security lights on outside.

I tried to stay concealed in the shadows the lights cast, barely missing tiny lizards with slippered feet that skittered across the cement under my fast descending hi-tops. I could hear the grass rustling as the bigger iguanas scampered through to get out of my way.

The bright amber moon was almost full. A few misty clouds swam in front of it causing the stars to twinkle. The streetlights were so far apart I was secure that I couldn't be seen.

Thank goodness earlier when I had fallen asleep with my clothes on, I had forgotten to remove my sneakers. I'd have pretty sorry feet by now, and if I hadn't grabbed my glasses I wouldn't be able to see three feet in front of me. I probably would have wandered out onto the highway and been creamed by a young mother in a speeding minivan.

*Whoa...uh oh...*the guy slowed way down...

Abruptly, I back-peddled and zipped behind a telephone pole.

Turning suddenly, the man disappeared behind a closed gas station.

I jogged to the station on my toes quietly avoiding the fallen palm fronds that littered the parking lot. Soundlessly, and very, very slowly, I looked around the back.

Starting from the gas station, a narrow alley ran only a short distance before it assimilated into the night's blackness. I took a deep breath then stepped into the alley.

It was darker in the alley because the cool silver moonlight was blocked by tall apartment buildings. In the dimness, I could scarcely make out trashcans lining one wall of a building and used junk and garbage piled haphazardly against the other side.

Inching snail-like into the alley, I looked around warily for the intruder, he might be lurking in a doorway ready to pounce on me. It was so dark it was difficult to identify objects strewn about the alley.

Treading as carefully and as quietly as a Native American stalking a deer, I stepped over trash trying to avoid stomping on crinkly leaves.

Eek! I jumped back, barely stifling a shriek as a warty brown toad hopped out and bounded off, vanishing down the alley. *Damn toad*. My heart was beating right out of my chest!

Breathing slowly and deeply to calm my shaking nerves, I stopped and looked around.

Silence. Empty. *Where'd the guy go*?

Nuts, it looks like he got away. I moved quickly through the alley. As I got close to what seemed to be the end, I thought I heard a creak, like doorknob turning, or door opening.

Moving more cautiously down the dark passage, I thought I had reached the end but saw there was another branch to the alley. Something was looming in the craggy corridor, noiselessly camouflaged against the brick walls.

Oh my gosh! There he was!

About 20 feet down the second alley, he stood motionless, cornered like a trapped rat. It was pitch black, except for a single light bulb shining through a broken dome directly behind him.

The bulb's blinding light outlined the silhouette of a person. I could only make out his size. Big. I couldn't even tell if he was looking at me or at something behind me.

"You!" I called out, pointing a trembling finger at him. "You've been spying on my wife! I'm making a citizen's arrest! Please come along peacefully!" I instructed the stranger.

"And what the heck were you doing in my house tonight? How- ugh!"

Severe pain, crushing blackness.

Chapter Nine

"Rusty? Rusty?" Down a long, dark tunnel, way in the back of my throbbing, foggy, tortured brain, I could hear my wife's distressed voice calling me.

"Uhhhh..." I tried to move, piercing pain screamed from the back of my head. Moaning, I struggled to open my leaden eyes-but it was blinding light, burning, stinging agony!

"Rusty?" A cool hand pressed lightly on my forehead then lovingly smoothed my hair back off my brow.

Wincing, I again attempted to open my eyes albeit very, very slowly this time. I squinted at floating blurs that finally settled into recognizable forms.

Julia was gazing down at me, concern altering her comely features. She was sitting on the edge of the bed I was lying on.

Staring at me also and dwarfing my tiny wife, judging by the white coat and stethoscope hanging out of his pocket, appeared to be a physician.

"What happened?" Groaning, I struggled to sit up. The doctor stepped forward and pressed my shoulders firmly back onto the bed.

"Mr. Dixon," the doctor frowned. Sounding terribly serious, he said, "I am Dr. Jules Rothschild. It seems that you were clobbered on the back of the head with a heavy object. The police found you alone and recumbent on the dirt ground in an alley."

I blinked painfully from him to Julia and back.

"A woman in an apartment said she was awakened by a disturbance coming from below her window. She looked out and saw you lying there. She thought you were just a drunk passed out from over intoxication, but she called the police anyway, lucky for you."

As bad as I felt at that moment, I don't know how lucky I really was to be alive.

"We don't know what occurred, I guess you have a lot of explaining to do…" He looked pointedly in Julia's direction.

She was nibbling on the nails of a couple of fingers, her big green eyes peered anxiously over her knuckles at me.

The doctor swung his glance back at me. There was no judgment at my behavior in his voice or demeanor.

"Since you have regained consciousness, you're probably going to recover nicely, but you will have a nasty headache for a few days. We've filled you with all sorts of medication, so you'll probably be out like a light pretty soon."

He nodded, his smile indulgent. "I'll leave you to your lovely wife, but only for a few minutes, you need your healing rest." The doctor, on the far side of middle age and balding, patted my shoulder kindly then discreetly left.

"Oh Rusty, I was so worried! What on earth were you doing in a dark alley in town in the middle of the night?" Close to my ear, Julia's voice was loud and high pitched revealing her anxiety. She clutched my hand, her eyes stretched wide with confusion.

"Uh...well..." I was a little embarrassed at my audacity, and just beginning to realize my foolhardiness in pursuing an unknown criminal in the middle of the night into a dark alley. Gee, I was kind of an idiot.

Feeling pretty sheepish, I tried to explain to Julia what led me to my appallingly stupid actions. My story sounded boneheaded to my own ears.

"That was so dangerous Rusty! That thug could have killed you. Promise me you'll never do anything that crazy again. Promise me Rusty!" Julia cried, fiercely hugging my neck.

Even with my face smushed against her breasts, the throbbing in my head increased with a vengeance. Feeling too weak to argue, I promised Julia I'd be more prudent in the future if the same menacing situation arose, and call the police to do the chasing.

Appeased, she smiled. "Okay, honey." She leaned over and kissed me tenderly on the top of my head.

Nervously pushing her auburn hair behind her ears, she sat back and frowned at me. "I didn't even know you were gone, you know. The phone rang around 5 this morning, it was the hospital calling. Fortunately you had your wallet on you.

"I would have been frantic if I had woken up and you weren't there- with no note or anything. I hope you've learned a lesson, I don't need a heart attack at my young age you know." Relieved that I was okay, she ruffled my hair, smiling to take the sting out of her words.

I yawned. She stood up.

Tugging at the thin blanket and crisply sterile sheet, Julia pulled them up, motherly tucking them neatly under my chin.

"I'd better get going and let you get some rest. The dogs need letting out then I'm going to the supermarket to pick up a couple of things. I'll stop by later after lunch, maybe I'll sneak you in some of those chocolate devils-food cookies you like, okay?"

She looked around, apparently forgetting where she'd left her purse when they'd first let her in to see me. Spotting it over in a chair, she turned back to me. She bent down and kissed me lightly on the lips.

I could feel her hair tickling my face as my eyes drifted closed. She smoothed the blanket again, obviously reluctant to leave me.

I peeked up at her through slits of heavy lids, she tucked her loosened t-shirt back into her jeans and tiptoed to the chair.

I nodded agreeably to her suggestion of cookies – "*Ow*" Boy, did that smart.

Julia picked up her purse, pausing at the door.

Through my drug-induced vision, she looked like a fuzzy little red-haired angel. She pressed two fingertips to her lips and blew me a kiss, gracefully wiggling her fingers at me as she gently closed the door.

I sniffed. Her fragrance lingered. It was piquant, citrusy, intangible. The more I tried to smell the scent, breathe it in, the more elusive it was.

Yawn...the sedative they had given me must be taking effect...I let my aching eyes close and drifted into dreamless slumberland.

What seemed like only seconds later, a shuffling noise disturbed my sleep. Gingerly, to avoid pain, I opened one eyeball.

I was looking straight into the steady gaze of Detective Patterson. The other eye flew open.

"Mr. Dixon, I'm happy to see you're no more the worse for wear after your adventure the other night." He was attired in the same suit but different tie he was wearing the day he took the report at my house about the peeper.

"Detective Patterson, what brings you here?" Cringing, I squeezed my eyes together as I pushed to a sitting position. *Yowzer, was I ever sore* I must have crashed hard on the ground after being slugged. My elbows hurt and my hands were scraped raw.

Next to my bed was a nightstand with a reading lamp, a pitcher of water and a glass. The room was tiny but private. Thank goodness I have great insurance.

Over in a corner of the room, I saw one of my small suitcases. Julia must have brought me a change of clothes.

Patterson was sitting in the only chair in the room. He leaned forward, poured a glass of water from the pitcher and handed it to me.

"I'm curious Mr. Dixon..." The detective settled back in the chair, crossing his legs. "First, you call us out to your home to report a voyeur. Now I find you in the hospital with some crazy story about having pursued an intruder from your house. And don't tell me it was a robbery because the police found your wallet in your pocket."

He uncrossed his legs and leaned forward again. His brows arched quizzically over sober brown eyes. "What exactly is going on?"

I could feel my own brows drawing together as I echoed him. "Going on? What do you mean 'what's going on'? What are you talking about?" Annoyance and pain roughened my normally boyish voice. I gulped at my water, half of it dribbled down my chin.

"I'm not accusing you of anything, Mr. Dixon," he said politely. "I'm just inquiring if there's anything you want to tell me." He relaxed back into the chair and re-crossed his legs.

His expression placid, he calmly raised one eyebrow, his movements and tone of voice mild- making me look like the bad guy by being upset.

His insinuating questions and arrogant manner made me just plain angry. I thumped the glass down hard on the table next to me and leaned my upper torso towards the detective.

"Listen Patterson," I ground out, glaring at him through narrowed eyes. "I'm a regular, hardworking, no trouble kind of guy. I don't know what you're implying, but there's some creep following my wife around. He breaks and enters into my house to do whatever ungodly acts he's intent on committing." My fists clenched in impotent fury.

"I try to protect my helpless wife and my home and nearly get killed doing it. And you come in here like some kind of bullying cop with a Dirty Harry attitude, implying all sorts of-"

"Mr. Dixon, please calm down." Patterson waved at me with one hand. His other hand loosely clasped the arm of the chair.

"I said I wasn't accusing you of anything. We're only noting that here's a man whom we've never heard from before, and suddenly he's come to the attention of the police twice in a short period of time." His arms rested along the arms of the chair, he drummed his fingers on the ends and stared intently at me.

Struggling to sit up straighter, I twisted around and pulled at my pillows, fiercely stacking them against the headboard.

Punching them in place, I carefully leaned back into the hard, hospital-issued pillows.

Grimacing in pain, my teeth gritted and my eyes clamped shut. Sighing painfully, I put a hand to my head, rubbing it testily. I squinted at Patterson. He was just sitting there benignly watching me.

"Detective, I realize you're just doing your job, but interrogating me like I was some kind of con fresh out of the pen intent on committing some sort of murder and mayhem, well, you're fishing in the wrong creek. I," pointing emphatically at my chest, wincing at my jerky movements. "I am the one being harassed and persecuted."

Fuming, I crossed my arms in front of my chest and sat staring blankly at the wall in front of the bed. Before he could say anything, I swung my head back in Patterson's direction.

"Which reminds me, have you found the peeper yet?" I looked at Patterson, now my eyebrows innocently rose in question.

"Uh...ahem...we...uh...that...is...well..." Patterson shifted uncomfortably in his chair. He tugged his shirtsleeves down over his knuckles. Then he yanked the ends of his jacket over the sleeves, twisting the cuffs around, he examined the buttons.

He avoided looking me in the eye. His dark brown eyes shifted all around the room, looking everywhere but at me.

"Um, we uh...are still getting reports of voyeur activity near but outside of your neighborhood. We don't have any solid leads yet, but we are working on it. Peeping is hardly a big concern for the police. Murders and robberies take much more precedence, you know." He sniffed importantly.

His gaze came back to me, but he looked no higher than my chin. He cleared his throat then looked at his watch.

"Well," he said standing up. "I've taken up enough of your time. The doctor said you will be good as new after a few days of rest." He nodded then turned towards the door.

"If you think of anything important regarding your assailant, or if you decide you have something you need to tell me," he held up a hand as I opened my mouth. "You have my number. If I can't be reached, leave a message with Officer Newman or the Officer of the Day. I hope you feel better soon." He smiled at me, only one side of his mouth turning up.

He exited, the door closed behind him in automatic, slow spurts.

Uhhhh...I relaxed, sinking heavily into the pillows. Hoping for undisturbed rest, I let my aching eyes drift closed again.

Chapter Ten

Sitting in a chair, dressed in a t-shirt and jeans, I crossed my sneakered feet at the ankles and propped them up on the bed.

I was watching the Road Runner stop suddenly, then abruptly step to the side as the Coyote zoomed past him. The Coyote halted, suspended in mid-air for several seconds before he realized what happened.

Plummeting like a rock, he smashed on the hard ground at the foot of the cliff. The squashed Coyote, tongue drooping out of a crushed face, looked up to see the head of the Road Runner peering down at him from the top of the mountain.

With zero expression, the bird went 'beep! beep!' and sped off, leaving a cloud of dust in his wake.

The door opened, Julia entered the room looking radiant and gorgeous as ever. Her captivating smile brightened her gamin face as her very presence lit up the sparse room.

I realize we're newlyweds still in the honeymoon phase, but I hope I always will feel this way about my wife.

Dancing lightly across the floor to where I was seated, she wrapped her slender arms around my neck and hugged me, then kissed the top of my head.

"Hi my poor, injured darling." She looked into my eyes, her lips pursed, the worried look from yesterday crossed her face. She kissed me briefly, softly on the tip of my nose.

"How's my brave warrior feeling?" Tenderly, she patted my head, smoothing back and disentangling my untidy coif.

I grabbed both her hands and pulled her onto my lap, eagerly peppering her pretty face with happy, baby kisses. She captured my face in her hands and pressed her full lips to mine. Our mouths parted as we sank into a deepening, passionate kiss which turned frenzied-

"Hello there!" A hearty, annoyingly jovial voice barked, interrupting us. We jolted apart and gaped guiltily at the intruder with the bad timing.

Dr. Rothschild was standing there, grinning affably at us.

"I see we're feeling much more in the pink!" He looked directly at Julia and winked.

Red-faced, Julia sprang off my lap. She immediately straightened her short yellow dress, re-hooking the gold belt that had loosened during our heated foray.

Still a bit shaky, I stood up. Pretty sure from Julia's amorous ministrations I looked like a newborn duckling, I quickly combed my mussed hair back with my fingers. After a quick wipe on my jeans I held my hand out to the doctor and he shook it.

"I believe you are free to leave, Mr. Dixon." His smile was natural from years of practice and seemingly sincere. One blue eye winked kindly at me.

"I've signed your discharge papers, you can complete them at the front desk. I don't foresee any problems, you seem to be healing well." He grinned at Julia.

Still blushing, she turned her head. Twisting a lock of hair between two fingers, cheeks bright pink she pretended to be interested in what was going on outside the window.

"Please call any time if you feel any additional pain or discomfort. Take three or four Ibuprofen every six hours for the next few days, that's all you should need." We shook hands again.

He straightened the ever present stethoscope hanging around his neck and opened the door.

"Thanks Doc, I'll be sure to holler if I have any difficulties." I said.

"Again, feel free to call the hospital if the pain doesn't substantially decrease by the end of the week, or if you experience blurriness or excessive dizziness. Mrs. Dixon." He nodded at Julia.

She smiled at him, her cheeks still a bright pink. She turned to face him, her hands laced behind her back, she twisted slightly side-to-side looking up at him with her shy green eyes, the yellow dress fluttered around her knees. "Thank you Doctor, I'll take good care of him."

"I'm sure!" Doctor Rothschild chuckled as he left.

Julia turned to me, grasping my hand. "C'mon hero, let's go home and get you into bed."

I leered at her as I rose. "Exactly what I was thinking!" I patted her on her firm tush.

"Rusty! Cut that out! Someone else might come in. Let's go." She scooted out of my reach, running to stand by the door.

We were supposed to wait for a wheelchair, but I picked up my suitcase and holding hands, we left the hospital room to go sign the discharge papers and head home.

By the time we arrived at the house, I couldn't keep my eyes open. The drive had just exhausted me. Apparently I wasn't as recovered as I thought.

Julia lugged my suitcase into the house, and I wearily trudged up the stairs.

"You hop into bed, honey, and I'll fix you some herbal tea and buttered toast," Julia cheerfully called from the bottom of the stairs.

My head and body were aching by time I climbed between the stiff coolness of the clean sheets. I don't remember if I ever had the tea and toast, I just careened into a deep sleep.

I was being chased by something unseen down a dark, gloomy alley. There was not a sliver of light in the cloudy black sky. Suddenly–

Yellow eyes flickered menacingly in the night - ugly bats with razor-sharp teeth flew threateningly overhead. Leathery wings flapped all around my head. Then they attacked!

Terrifying screeching raging through the night they started diving at me, narrowly missing my head as they swooped back and forth.

"Aaaaiiiiii!" Screaming in hysteria, I waved my hands over my head to ward off the maniacal bats and ran blindly down the crooked alley.

Sticky cobwebs on the walls grabbed at me, trying to keep me there. Bricks in the buildings gouged my arms as I stumbled, bumping and scraping them while I hurtled down the alley looking for an escape!

My heart was hammering, my eyes wide open- my hand clutched my throat, the air was heavy and clammy and eerie-

Running, I tripped over trash and splashed clumsily through puddles. The only sound in the night was my rapid loud breathing and my pounding footsteps.

Glancing over my shoulder, I tried to run faster, but the sidewalk turned to goo, it clung to my ankles and sucked at my feet. I couldn't lift my legs anymore, I was sinking, being drawn down as if pulled and sucked by quicksand.

The husky intruder was in front of me. The huge, black shadow of him moved closer and closer...*I tried to shout for help, I couldn't—*

"Rusty baby," a honeyed voice whispered in my ear.

I could feel a soft breast pressing against my arm. "Wake up sweetie, you're having a bad dream. Here's some Chamomile tea and crackers, they'll soothe and calm you."

Julia helped me to sit up. I shook my head and took some gulping, deep breaths, dragging myself away from the nightmare.

My wife held a tray containing a china teacup, a matching sugar bowl and creamer, and a plate lined with Saltine crackers and small wedges of cheese. She sat on the edge of the bed, crossing one slim knee over the other. Wearing red shorts and a sleeveless white blouse, she looked so crisp and clean.

Julia spooned some of the sugar into the steaming tea, added a dollop of cream and stirred it gently. Tapping the spoon on the rim of the cup, she set the spoon on the saucer and handed the tea to me. I sipped the herbal tea with the subtle orange taste. Julia placed a lump of cheese on a cracker and handed it to me with a paper napkin.

After taking a big bite, talking through a mouthful of food, I said, "I am so blessed with you my sweet, little nurse. I don't know what I'd do without you." My eyes swam with salty tears.

"Now Rusty, you're supposed to be resting," she scolded gently. "Drink up and sit back, I'll read to you until you finish and fall back to sleep."

She got up and pushed a rocking chair over to the bed. Picking up a book by Agatha Christie, she began to read about that tenacious busy body, Miss Marple. Julia's melodious voice carried me once again off to a more peaceful sandland.

Awakening slowly, my head was fuzzy with sleep. It was nighttime. The curtains were still open at the bedroom window. Through the glass, I could see the gilded moon a soft glow in the inky heavens.

I reached over on the bed next to me and felt for Julia. My hand patted an empty space. Rolling over, I squinted in the darkness to see if she was anywhere in the room. Although it was pitch black, I could see I was alone in the room.

My head cocked slightly as I heard the familiar squeak of the front door opening. I listened as it closed and latched. The room lightened slightly as the living room light clicked on.

Suddenly, I heard heavy breathing and pattering feet running into the room. "Oomph!" I expelled breath in one burst as two drooling, hot-breathed, furry bodies trampled excitedly all over the bed and me.

"Okay pups, okay!" Rubbing their ears and bellies, I blithely ordered the dogs off the bed. When they hit the floor, they ran in circles, yapping and chasing each other. Then they ran off, I could hear the clatter of their paws clippity clapping down the stairs.

I sat up, swinging my legs over the side of the bed. "Julia?" I called out. "Julia!" I called more loudly, urgently.

"I'm here, Rusty," she murmured from the bottom of the staircase.

I heard her light step on the stairs. Even as slight as Julia is, every other stair groaned as she tread on it. I saw her outline in the doorway.

"How are you feeling, sweet pea?" Her musical voice warmed me even from the doorway ten feet away.

"Did you go out? Where have you been?" I asked sounding like a sulky child.

"Oh," She shrugged vaguely. "I took the pups for a walk down at the beach."

"This late? Do you think that's safe?" I tried to sound more like a mature adult. "Especially honey, with what's been going on lately?"

I glanced at the digital clock on the nightstand. Its red light displayed the time, 12:02 a.m. Wow, I'd slept for almost 12 hours straight! I still felt woozy. Boy, those must be powerful pills the doc had given me for my headache.

"Oh Rusty," Julia said tiredly. "I had the dogs with me, I was perfectly safe." She sounded weary, strained.

I suggested, "Why don't you climb into bed sweetie, I'll rub your back." My voice softened as I patted the bed.

"That sounds wonderful. Let me take a quick shower and change my clothes." She turned and was gone from the doorway. It must have been terribly humid out, I thought, her hair looked damp.

I opened the drawer in the nightstand and took out a scented candle in a crystal bowl and a pack of matches we keep there for special occasions. I struck the match against the jacket and it sprang to life. Holding the flame to the wick of the candle, it sparked and immediately the fragrance of vanilla filled the air.

Then I fluffed the pillows and folded down Julia's side of the bed. Snuggling under the sheets warmed by my body, I closed my eyes with a longing sigh and waited patiently for my alluring wife.

I smelled her tantalizing perfume before I heard her enter the room. Lying down with my head propped up on my hand, I watched her.

She was an entrancing vision in the flickering incandescent light. Wearing only a scanty, rose colored negligee with scarlet trim, she slid onto the sheets. So waifish, the bed only moved imperceptibly under her.

Slipping her tanned legs, graceful as a ballerina's under the covers, she settled in with her back was to me, pressing her supple derriere against my side. Her fiery hair feathered like fine mink on the white pillow.

I reached over and tenderly stroked her creamy shoulders. Slowly pushing a ribboned strap off her shoulder, I replaced it with a sweet kiss. Ever so lovingly, I kissed her neck while running one finger lightly along her arm.

The bed trembled with her sultry shiver. My hands skimmed over the shiny sheerness of her chemise, fingering the lace that encased her exposed, rounded cleavage. The material was silky in my palms.

I rubbed it gently over her smooth skin. A moonbeam shone vaporous through the window. The quicksilver light reflected a warm glow off Julia's skin and shiny sheath.

Squeezing her upper arms, my ardor-heavy breath nuzzled Julia's slightly damp neck. Clutching her thick wavy strands of hair between my fingers, I rubbed my face with the lustrous tresses.

When I tugged on the locks almost violently, Julia moaned. She squirmed and arched her back, pressing her body harder against mine. Desire heated my being, filling me with excruciating pleasure. My legs tingled with hot electricity.

Fervently drawing her closer, my arms enveloped her, crushing her against my chest. She twisted to face me, her lithe body pressed urgently against my highly aroused frame.

Her eyes, seductive stormy emeralds in a tumultuous sea melded with my impassioned, blue-green orbs. She moved her face enticingly, slowly towards me. Her dewy lips parted, she brought them tremulously to mine. Our mouths joined.

Greedily I covered my wanton wench's sylph body with my own...

Chapter Eleven

℘rrrrrrring!!

I slammed my pillow over my head, covering my ears. What in the heck is that incessant, blaring noise that's rupturing my eardrums?

"The alarm Rusty! The alarm!" Julia's muffled voice cried.

Damn! The stinkin' alarm clock. The person who invented them should be shot, then whipped, then their head cut off then-

"Rusty!" That shriek, louder than the alarm, galvanized me into action. I reached out a long wiry arm and smacked the button on the clock that was causing all the racket.

Then, with ill temper, I batted the offending box off the night table, hurtling it across the room. I sniffed, satisfied when I heard it crash against the far wall, hit the ground and finally lay silent.

"Feel better?" a mocking voice next to me teased.

I rolled my head on my pillow and turned back to look at Julia.

She looked like a sleepy moppet. Her mussed hair, a jar of gingery sand in the early morning light, covered half her face. I could barely see her half opened eyes peering through the curly locks like a timid coquette.

I pressed my nose into the downy pillow, inhaling the pleasant detergent odor that was still present. Yawning and stretching my sparsely hairy arms over my head, I reached up as far as I could, my legs rigid in the opposite direction.

"Uuhhh..." I groaned then yelped out another bodacious body wrenching yawn. Shaking my still groggy head, I sat up and swung my skinny legs over the side of the bed. Rubbing my eyes, I yawned some more and scratched my head.

Pushing off the bed I stood up. My headache was mostly gone. No more excuses to stay home from work. Oh well. I looked back at the bed.

Julia had virtually disappeared. A few burnished locks curled across the pillow, but the rest of her was deeply buried under the jazzy afghan, crocheted in a myriad of vivid colors that my aunt Leta had made us for a wedding gift. We set the air conditioning really low at night, so it was pretty chilly in the ruffled bedroom. I hated to leave the toasty bed.

After a steamy shower, shaving and quietly dressing in a starched, white long-sleeved shirt and black Dockers, I tiptoed down the stairs carrying my socks and black tasseled loafers. I needed some instant energy in a mug to get my engine running.

When I yanked the chain of the glass chandelier hanging over the kitchen table, a soft light came on.

Filtered strands of light from the kitchen window and door were already picking out pieces and parts of the dim kitchen, painting them with yellow splotches.

Humming the tune, 'nothin' but blue skies, do I see...' I took out the can of ground coffee beans and a filter from the cupboard over the sink. Hmmmm, I pondered, since I rarely do this, I had to guess how many spoonfuls of coffee for however many cupful of water.

I don't bother to read the instructions on the can, that's too much trouble. They never seem to be right anyway. I think they give measurements for those tiny, fancy teacups. Nowadays we all have our own humongous mugs with our favorite sayings on them.

My mug is in the shape of a baseball, and a bat is its handle. I play softball with some of the guys at work, so one of the fellows gave me the mug last year for a grab bag gift at an office Christmas party. I get a kick out of the saying on the side of the mug. It says, 'touch my mug and I'll slugger you!'

I looked down at the filter full of coffee. It looked pretty full. I took some out. Appears too little now. I put some back in. Hmmmm, I added some more for good luck. After placing the filter into the coffee holder, I slammed it into the machine.

Filling the empty coffee pot with cold water, I poured it through the top. There, nothing to it. I don't know why the girls in the office are always whining about having to make the coffee.

Strolling to the front door, I opened it and looked out. It's gonna be a scorcher. *Phew*, already 80 something the thermometer says and it's only 6:00 a.m.

I was practically drinking in the air there was so much water in it from the humidity. Even the palm trees looked droopy from the weight of the heat.

Great! There's the paper right on the front porch! The paperboy missed the grass and flowers and the puddles, and landed it where it belonged for once.

Reaching down, I scooped up the Bay Chronicle. Re-latching the front door, I padded barefoot back into the cheerful kitchen that was increasingly brightening from the rising sun.

The cherry red kitchen counters and the cupboards stained a light oak bring out the sparkling white appliances. The backsplash designed in ceramic tiles painted with red cherries and green leaves is our latest addition.

The glass chandelier was pouring rainbows onto the natural oak table and all around the room where the sun was spreading it.

Hearing the final gurgling of the coffee machine, I poured a steaming mugful. A candy pink box of Dunkin' Donuts was on the counter. Julia must have picked it up last night.

I opened the lid and hungrily looked inside. I decided on the custard-filled with the chocolate icing. Reaching in for the delectable doughnut with one hand, I took out from the cupboard a small, green enameled plate decorated in summer chintz with the other.

After dropping my doughnut onto the plate, I grabbed my mug of hot java and carried them to the table. Pulling out a matching oak chair, I sat down while reaching for the paper. I slurped a mouthful of black Joe before checking the headlines. Hmmm...the coffee's not bad.

Picking up a plump pastry, I opened my mouth wide to take a big bite, already tasting the resplendent richness in my salivating mind, when I heard a knock at the kitchen door.

Still holding the unbitten sweetness in my hand, I turned my head towards the door. The bottom half of the Dutch door was a thick, white pine. The top half was filigree glass that was partially covered by snow white, sheer swag curtains.

Through the curtains, I could see Sandy Casey's affable, plump face framed in the window. She smiled solemnly and waved at me.

Reluctantly, I set the doughnut back on the plate. With a brief, longing look back at it, I went to the door to let my friend in and find out what she was doing here at the crack of dawn.

Opening the door wide, I smiled questioningly at my normally amiable friend. She looked uncommonly subdued this morning.

"Hya Sandy, what brings you here so early on a workday?" Greeting her, I ushered her inside the kitchen. "Have a seat." I gestured towards a chair. "Would you like a cup of coffee?"

Sandy pulled out a chair, and sat down heavily on the red quilted cushion. "Yes Rusty, thanks, I could use a cup of coffee." An abstracted smile flashed across her face.

Her generally sunny disposition seemed suppressed and sad. She sat there, glumly, her hands folded in her lap atop jean shorts. She didn't move, just stared without blinking past me to the white wall in front of her.

I poured a now lukewarm brew into a Garfield shaped mug, and placed it in front of her. Retrieving a second plate from the cupboard, I set it next to the mug.

Sandy clasped the mug in her hands, but she didn't drink any coffee. After refilling my cup, I dragged my chair back out and plunked down with one arm stretched out flat on the table, and the other clutching my baseball mug.

I gently inquired, "So Sandy...what's up?"

Sandy turned somber brown eyes to me. Her tawny lashes were fringed with wetness.

"Oh Rusty," she cried, sounding horribly woeful. "It's Mike…" Her voice was so dejected I thought she was going to break down right in front of me.

"Sandy honey," I grasped one of her hands in alarm, "what is it?"

She took a deep, shuddering breath. Her slumped shoulders straightened a bit. "I know Steve told you about our degrading transgressions that last night we were all together…"

She looked away from me, pretending to study the small watercolors of various fruit Julia had hung on the walls lining the doorway of the kitchen to the hall.

Creeping redness tinged her neck and climbed to her face. She blushed with shame and embarrassment. Her eyes darted to me then she quickly looked away.

"Steve told me he told you all about it the other day when I unexpectedly ran into him at the grocery store," she continued dolefully, regret encumbering her words. "It was mortifying seeing him, for both of us. As much as we wish we could un-ring the bell, we can't undo what we've done, but we just don't know how to go on…"

She shifted her ample body in the chair. Her fingers toyed nervously with the top button of her black and green plaid, short-sleeved blouse. Crossing her sandaled feet, she picked up the mug and sipped some of the contents.

Obviously not really tasting the thick acrid brew, she pensively drank a little more before setting the mug down. She had declined my offer of a doughnut with a shake of her head. Now she was staring at them vacantly, not really seeing them.

She cleared her throat. "Anyway, Rusty, did you know that Steve moved out of his house this weekend?"

"What? You're kidding!" I cried incredulously, my mouth hanging open in surprise. I gawked incipiently at her, my disbelieving eyes jumped to her dejected ones.

"Yeah, he said it was so uncomfortable at home, too much to function. He and Heather weren't speaking and they were trying to avoid each other. Apparently..." she stopped and looked towards the door blinking, tears shone on her cheeks. Her dark eyes were awash with lugubrious tears.

"Oh Rusty," she cried, "ever since that horrible night, Heather and my Mike have been secretly seeing each other!"

"What?" I said, not sure. "You mean they're having an affair?" I was astounded!

"Yes, it's true. That's why Steve moved out. Heather was cranky and irritated because he wouldn't bankroll her boutique scheme and she blurted it out, to hurt him." The tears were streaming down her face, sliding off and splashing in miniature puddles on the table.

"Oh my gosh..." I didn't know what to say.

"Yeah, I guess Steve got the wind knocked out of him, and he left so he could focus and think, decide what to do. I think he was also afraid of what he might do to that scrawny cheating plastic witch he married." Sandy's face clouded with anger and her eyes spat venom.

"Things were so acrimonious between them, I believe he was scared he'd lose control and slap the conniving tramp." It was obvious by her furious expression she wished Steve *had* socked Heather once or twice.

"So," she said, dashing at the tears streaming down her face. "Steve packed a few things and left. He's staying with that hairdresser friend of theirs, you know, that pretty girl with the long, straight brown hair. She's been to our house a few times for parties. Lizzie, uh, Lizzie Pierce is her name. She works at the Clip and Flip in Sherwood City."

Sandy drank more coffee and eyed the doughnuts. She reached in and pulled out a white sugar-powdered, lemon filled. She set the doughnut on her plate but just sat and glared gloomily at it, not touching it.

"Do Steve and Lizzie have a thing going on too?" I asked. At this point I'll believe anything.

Sandy shook her head, still staring at the doughnut. Her arms were rigidly next to her body and she was sitting on her hands. "No, I don't think so... Lizzie's just a nice girl. I think she feels badly for Steve. And Steve had no place to go. Both of his parents as you know passed away a while back, and his only brother John, moved with his wife and daughters out to Denver when he got that terrific job offer from the government. Steve stayed here of course because of his job."

She drank some more coffee. I just didn't know what to say to her. My heart went out to this desperately unhappy friend I've known since grade school. First Steve, and now Sandy spilling their pain. Comforting words totally escaped my rattled brain.

"There's more, Rusty." Sandy sat back in the chair. Her eyes were pools of wet darkness, pain puckered her familiar features.

I waited.

Sandy gulped loudly. "The worst part Rusty, is...is...I ran home from the store and Mike was there...and I confronted him with what Steven had told me. And...and..." She hiccupped and the tears poured down her face.

"And he confirmed that he and Heather had been sneaking around and having clandestine meetings in a cheap hotel in Sherwood City. He admitted that, that Saturday night we barbecued was the first time they'd had sex together, but for the last year or so, Heather had been coming on to him.

"She'd brush up against him, lean over him, just barely touching him with her body. He said whenever they were alone she'd get real close, and 'accidentally' brush his, uh...you know."

Embarrassed again, she looked down at the table, her pudgy cheeks reddening more. The tears slowed, she sniffed loudly.

"He said she'd playfully slap his butt when no one was looking. He told me that it was inevitable that the affair would happen with all of that teasing. That Saturday night we all got so drunk, their inhibitions just melted away. They just didn't care what Steven and I thought.

"But that night was just a precursor, sort of a sexual appetizer to them. So they carried on the affair until Mike decided he was

86

pretty much done with her. Apparently they've been intimate enough times that he was satisfied and her nonstop yakking wasn't worth the sex.

"It must have been totally for curiosity, you know Mike usually goes for the big busted more voluptuous women...he's always said Heather is a mouthy, self-centered bony princess..." She took a couple of quick bites out of her doughnut.

Sandy raised her bleak eyes to mine again. Her entire being bared her misery. Then her shoulders slumped again, her head hung down. Grief shadowed her red-rimmed eyes. Her snub nose was red as well, and her lips were puffy and turned way down at the corners. Even her plain brown hair looked lank and dull, it hung limply around her sad face.

I got up and got the coffee pot, brought it to the table and heated up our cups then I went back to the counter and replaced the pot.

When I returned to the table, Sandy was wiping her eyes and brusquely blowing her nose into a paper napkin. What do you say at a time like this? I just looked at her wretchedly sad face and waited. Sandy dabbed at her wet eyes.

She was staring down at her coffee while absently pulling tiny shreds off her napkin, rolling them into little balls between her fingers then dropping them in a pile next to her plate.

After taking a quavering breath she said, "So...so Mike and I had a huge fight. Thank goodness Grandma Amy had taken Bonnie with her to her regular Wednesday Bible study class. Oh my poor little girl..." Sandy started weeping again.

"What are we going to do about the baby? What do we tell her?" she wailed.

"Listen Sandy," I said. "Mike has always been a great father, uh...a good husband, provider..." I didn't know where I was going with all that.

Sandy smiled through her tears. Her nose was crimson and shiny, and her eyes were swelling. Sandy was not a woman poets would write about, expelling starry eyes and ivory skin and all that. But she is a warm, loving person.

"Anyway," she snuffled. "I accused Mike of being a lying cheater, and he said I was a lazy, fat pig and..." she snatched another napkin from the holder on the table and held it to her face sobbing.

After a couple of deep breaths, she said, "And then, hic, he said he was leaving, that he was going to go to his boat, 'The Bonnie Lass' and stay there for a while. He grabbed some clothes, some food, his cigars and stamps, and of course he wouldn't forget his precious beer, and a bottle of Jim Beam."

She took what was left of her doughnut and shoved it into her mouth and chomped furiously. Swallowing, she reached for her coffee and drained the mug, clunking the empty cup on the table.

"I don't know how he'll survive on that tiny boat. It barely sleeps two, and the galley is so cramped." She sighed. "Oh well, I'm sure it'll only be temporary...I mean..." she broke off as more tears welled up.

"I just don't know what to do, Rusty. I keep saying I don't want the philandering adulterer back...but then I realize I love the big lug...sniff...and I miss him...and what about our daughter? I can't raise Bonnie without her papa!" she cried mournfully, wiping her eyes, her lashes were spiky from the tears.

I reached over and patted her hand. "Sandy, I am so sorry. You know I think the world of all of you guys. I don't pretend to understand what happened, but I know you're all suffering. I think you guys desperately regret that Saturday night." I sat back and smiled weakly at her.

"I believe if you all give each other some space and time to think, and maybe forgive, perhaps broken fences can be mended." I shifted in my chair.

Sandy was staring blankly again. She was looking in my direction, but I could tell her eyes weren't focused on me.

"I can't see any of you splitting up. You're made for each other." I shrugged, turning my palms up. "Heather has always had Steve by the nose, he's always been mad for her...and you and Mike," I pointed at her.

She looked at me.

"You and Mike are a team. I don't think Mike would know what to do with himself if you weren't there to take care of him."

Sandy nodded, dabbing at her wet eyes with a fresh napkin.

"And I can't see Mike living a bachelor's life. He can't burn water for heaven's sake! And Bonnie..." Sandy's face saddened further.

I continued, "Mike will always be a part of her life. There was no prouder man in this world the day you had that little lass." I smiled, remembering Mike, chest bursting with pride, passing out cigars and candy cigars to everyone in the waiting room at the hospital that night.

Sandy smiled faintly. "Yeah." She said, "He was her proud papa. He floated on air for weeks, grinning like a buffoon." Her eyes became dreamy as she recalled the event of her daughter's birth.

"Bonnie just had to blink funny, and if Mike thought she was about to cry, he was there in a heartbeat, cuddling and cooing to her, anything to stop her little tears. He did everything to get her to raise her sparkly baby eyes to his adoring ones." Her smile broadened.

She nodded emphatically, her chin jutting out. "You're right, Rusty. I'll forgive him and he'll be back. I just have to wait and let some time go by." She made a humming noise looking thoughtful, also a bit smug.

"I'll teach the son of a bitch," she snapped. "I'm gonna make him pay, and pay good before I let him come back!" A mischievous grin lightened her gloomy expression.

"I'll make him court me like he did in the beginning. He's going to have to work at it and earn the right to be in our home again. First, he's going to bring me flowers," she clicked off on one finger, counting, "then, dinner in a fancy restaurant," she clicked off a second finger, "and dancing," she clicked off a third.

"I'll play hard to get, Rusty," Sandy said, the misery clearing from her dark brown eyes. "But, eventually I'll let the big dope 'catch' me again!" She laughed cheerfully, her plain face glowing once again with happiness.

"Oh, Rusty," she exclaimed. "I am so glad I came over here! I knew you would be the tonic I needed to get through this!" She shoved her chair back and bounced over to me.

Leaning over, she gratefully hugged me. Standing up, her hands were clasped in front of her pudgy waist. Her body jiggled all over with joy and hope. My deflated friend was now her normal jolly self again!

"Sandy, you and I have been good friends since forever. Your pain is mine you know. I'm so happy I could help. I just know everything will be okay!" I grinned at her and took a huge chomp out of my heretofore untouched, doughnut.

Oowee wow! The richness of the cream filled my mouth. The chocolate icing clung rapturously to my tongue. Boy, my taste buds were singing a glorious song! I hastily gobbled the rest of the heavenly, sugary creations.

Sandy plopped down in her chair. Picking up another powdered doughnut, she made greedy fast work of it. We licked our fingers in genial comradeship.

"Well, Rusty," Sandy drank the last drop of her coffee and set the mug down. She tapped her napkin to her lips with ladylike etiquette. Crumpling the napkin, she dropped it on the plate, empty now except for a few teeny crumbs missed by her wet fingertips.

"The only other thing that's been on my mind and driving me nuts lately, is Grandma Amy."

"Grandma Amy?" What about her? Is her health failing?" My concern was evident in my raised brows.

"Oh no, quite the contrary." Sandy shook her head in consternation. "She's been slipping out of the house late in the evening for the past few months. When Bonnie's asleep and Mike and I are watching TV in the den, apparently she's been sneaking out the back kitchen door. She doesn't return until the early hours of the morning!"

Perturbed, she continued, "We noticed when Bonnie wanted a drink of water one night. I got it for her and I thought I'd check on Grandma and see if she wanted anything. I knocked softly on her bedroom door, which normally she doesn't close all the way, but that night it was shut. I called out to her but there was no response.

"I carefully opened the door in case she was asleep, I didn't want to wake her. She wasn't there! I checked all over the house. I looked in the kitchen, bathroom, everywhere, but she was gone! Her purse was missing too, as well as her car. I told Mike, but he said I should mind my own business. The next day," Sandy reached for a third doughnut; honey glazed, and took a bite out of it.

Talking with a chunk of doughnut pressed in one cheek, she continued, "In the morning, I asked her if she'd gone out last night. She looked at me like I was insane and said, 'Of course not. Where would I go?' I had no answer so I let it drop.

"Then, a few days later it happened again! For the past several weeks now, she disappears about three times a week. Mike told me to leave her alone that she obviously doesn't want us to know what she's doing. So...well, what do you think she's up to?" She pulled off a piece of the pastry and shoved it into her mouth, gazing quizzically at me.

"Gee Sandy, I have no idea. Where would an elderly woman go in the middle of the night? Bingo perhaps?" I shrugged my shoulders and glanced at my watch. "It's certainly a mystery, but right now I've got to get going to work." I stood up.

"Oh Rusty, I'm so sorry! How selfish of me!" Sandy jumped up and snatched her car keys off the table.

"No Sandy, it's okay." I patted her hand. "I always have time for you, my dear friend, always. You can count on my Jughead ears to be stuck straight out, waiting to listen to your woes, and of course your good stuff too, anytime!"

She hugged me tightly. "Thanks Rusty. I'm going to get started right away on my 'get Mike back' plans!" She walked to the door.

"See ya, Rusty!" she called out happily, eager to begin working on her husband handling agenda.

Seeing her head to her car, I sat down and pulled on my socks. After pushing my feet into shoes, I plucked my truck keys off the counter where Julia had dropped them after bringing me home from the hospital.

Passing the kitchen table, I grabbed up the newspaper, still folded from when I retrieved it off the porch and tucked it under my arm.

I quietly latched the door closed and sauntered to my Bronco. Ahhh, I sighed. Life is good. I was feeling smug and buoyant, reveling in my genius of getting my two friends back together. Feeling pleased with myself, I drove off to work.

Chapter Twelve

"Hey, hi!" I greeted fellow employees as I entered the store.

Bob Noble waved to me from a far corner. It looked like he was taking inventory of our oldest section of computer accessories.

Lisa Marie, a fetching picture as always at the front desk, was shining up the glass counter with spray cleaner and a paper towel. She called out a merry hello and kept rubbing.

I went directly to Art's office. He was sitting in his leather chair. His scruffy loafers were propped up on his desk. He was chatting in his professional tone into the phone. I could see other lights blinking crazily on the phone. It appeared Artie had a host of calls waiting. That's a good sign. Busy means business. Business means dollars!

Art motioned for me to sit. I pulled a heavy chair, fortunately on wheels, to the front of the desk and sank down into the comfy leather chair. I still had my newspaper, so I flipped through the front page. Artie rambled on, ending one call and clicking on to the next.

"Hello Stan! What's the good word? Selling anything in the new line?" Artie yelled heartily into the mouthpiece. Art talked at length to Stanley Woodfield, one of our wholesalers.

I finished a quick perusal of the front and local pages, and was thumbing through the sports section when Art finally set the phone down and greeted me.

"Hey Rusty my man, how're they hanging?" He smirked at me, shoving the phone to the side of his desk, out of his way. Art is a white-shirt and tie, professionally serious boss, but he can still surprise me sometimes with the rare crass remark.

"Uh, just fine Art. Everything's great," I replied, folding the paper and laying it on the desk.

"You still besotted with that hot little number you forced into marriage?" Art laughed, teasing me.

"Yeah, Artie, the little woman still has me bewitched. I fall in love with her more every day!" I crowed, a proud rooster.

"You are one lucky dude, Rusty. I'd give anything to be in your shoes, to have that babe home waiting for me!" Art said.

"Oh sure Art. You wouldn't know what to do if Connie ever left your butt!" I informed him. "You'd come sniveling around to all of our houses every night, begging for us to feed and comfort you!" I bantered back. Laughing.

Art pushed his chair back, the wheels rumbled over two feet of hardwood floor. He reached over to a cabinet next to his desk, and pulled out a thick, black book. Holding the book, he kicked the chair back to his desk.

"Let's go over some of these invoices, Rusty." Art opened the book. Still working old school ways, he handed a pad of paper to me. I took my Waterman pen out of my shirt pocket then flipped the pages of the pad over until I reached a blank page.

"Okay," Art said. Wearing his reading glasses, his nose buried in the book, his right hand was poised over the adding machine. "Let's begin with Darylrymple's South Beach store." Art started calling out computer models and matching numbers. I dutifully wrote notes.

We worked steadily, without interruption for around two hours until we heard a light knock at the door.

Jill, Art's secretary, entered the office with two steaming cups of coffee. Just what I needed, I thought as I stretched my cramped body. Removing my glasses, I rubbed my neck. I'd been sitting in the same position for some time, and relished the idea of a break and some refreshment.

Art barely glanced up. He briefly acknowledged Jill's presence then continued the analysis of the paperwork in front of him. Later he'd have Jill enter them in a proper Excel sheet. Funny for running a computer company he was so old fashioned the way he did things.

"In the nick of time, Lois Lane!" I kidded. Thanking Jill, I gladly accepted the black coffee, sweetened with one spoonful of sugar. Jill has known me long enough to know how I like my coffee.

"You're very welcome." Jill smiled at me while setting Art's coffee cup next to his left hand. Art mumbled his thanks without taking his eyes off the book. I winked at Jill as she discreetly left the room.

Art and I plodded through undisturbed with our work for a couple more hours. I could see lights on Art's phone intermittently lighting up, but there was no sound. Art must have turned off the ringer.

Most business people call him in the early morning, knowing he doesn't like to be interrupted in the late morning to early afternoon. Jill screens his calls and only contacts him on the intercom if there is something important to deal with.

Around 1:00, I could hear my stomach growling. I laid my pen down and looked at my boss. "Art," I said. When he didn't acknowledge me, "Art," I repeated louder.

He looked up at me, a little dazed from being pulled from the complexity of his work.

"Wha-?" He blinked.

"I'm hungry," I said, sounding like a kid in nursery school whining to his mommy.

"Oh!" Art looked surprised. "Well, I guess if you have to stop..." He emphasized the 'have to'. He looked back at his records book.

Gosh, now I really felt like a crybaby. But gee, a guy's gotta eat. I'm still a growing boy! Well, sort of. Only now I'm growing out instead of up. Feeling guilty, I stood up.

"I'll, uh...be back in um...an hour, um or so..." I said as I made my way to the door.

"Uh huh," Art harrumphed. "Take your time, I'll be here." He never looked up.

I made my get-away, closing the solid door behind me. Man, that guy is made of steel. He works ten-hour days, and I seldom see him eat or take a long break. That's certainly not me! I need rest and fuel to keep this Beetle Bailey boy happy!

I hurried back to the break room. We always order Chinese delivered on Tuesdays. Jill anticipated my desiring the Asian eats, so she had ordered my regular choice for me.

"Jill, I don't know if Artie appreciates you, but you are the queen in my parade!" I gushed, reaching hungrily for my egg drop soup.

Jill laughed and left the break room with my ten-dollar bill in her hand. The room was filled with employees.

Lisa Marie, Aaron and Cybil were chatting over chopsticks at one end of the table. At the opposite end, Maggie and Ted were reading their fortunes. They had impatiently cracked the cookies open, and were now giggling over their future romance and wealth. Jim Salva sat across from me, already digging into his chow mein.

I slurped down my soup and began chomping on fried rice and shrimp.

Jim was re-hashing the baseball game that played last night. The Padres trampled the Marlins. We had some small bets going around the shop. Most of us had lost. They won once, but the Marlins were doubtful to get to the Series again this year with new players. Oh well, hope springs eternal.

While Jim was describing a home run slammed in by Sanchez to me, I eavesdropped on the conversations going on around me.

Ted was extolling in great detail to Maggie, the date he went on last Saturday night. Apparently he liked the girl well enough, but she wasn't the one he planned on taking home to mother. It sounded like he wanted to just jump her bones and get on to the next conquest.

Maggie was shaking her finger at Ted, trying to instill some chivalry into his horny head. Good luck. It'll be a long time before some bird snaps up that worm. And I mean worm!   Ted is a cad. But he's a funny and likable chap, it's too bad he's such a rogue.

Occasionally, I responded to Jim's diatribe of the game that I had also watched. I turned my ear, half listening to the discourse at the other end of the table. Setting down a half-eaten crunchy shrimp, I took a swig of cola, then picked up a greasy egg roll, dipped it generously into some duck sauce, then stuffed a good portion of it into my mouth.

The other employees were reading sections of today's paper, relaying out loud stories and tidbits of information that had struck them with interest.

"Uh oh," Cybil said, "it looks like the President is up to his old shenanigans!" She read a scandalous article out loud reporting that the President and a woman, not his wife, were found in a compromising situation by a celebrity guest who was visiting the White House.

"Ooooh, here we go again, the dog!" Lisa Marie said, shaking her head.

"Yeah, what a creep!" Aaron agreed. "Hey," he exclaimed, laying the paper down on the table in front of him, his pepper steak forgotten. He pointed to an article. "There was a murder in Sherwood City last night."

"So, what's new, this is south Florida!" Cybil shrugged, hot mustard was smeared on her chin. She swiped at it with the back of her hand.

"Yeah, but check this out, listen-" He started to read the article. I turned my head back towards Jim who was now explaining to me what team he was positive was going to win the Series.

"Anyway," Aaron said, his voice raised in volume over the rest of us. "'A white male was found murdered in his bed last night at the Lost Lagoon hotel, located on Foxglove Street. In the dingy hotel room, police discovered the body of Thomas Clifton Allen.

"Mr. Allen had apparently been shot once in the chest and died instantly. A second bullet was found lodged in the mattress next to his head. The bullet they dug out was unusual, according to Ballistics.

"It had been hallow-pointed, which is not that abnormal, however, this bullet was gouged out by hand. On the floor, next to the bed, was the body of a woman.'"

We ignored him, continuing chatting about the game and the cheating president.

"Hey guys, listen to this!" Aaron called to get our attention. "'The white female, identified as Annibelle Grace Cranston, was found nude, lying on her back on the floor, near the bed. She had allegedly been shot in the head and chest while still on the bed, then, after she was dead, she had been dragged onto the floor.

"The police said the sheets were still partially on the bed, and the rest were scrunched under the body of the victim. The peculiar thing,'" Aaron read on, he was getting thoroughly engrossed in the story.

"'Was that the woman's head had been brutally bludgeoned after she was already dead. Her face was smashed and beaten beyond recognition.'" Aaron seemed to be relishing the gory facts he was reading.

"'Stranger still, police stated, at first unidentified, white dots, or large flakes of powder, thought at the time to be cocaine, were scattered all over the woman's face, chest and surrounding area on the floor, like a dusting of snow.

"Shards of broken glass were imbedded in what was left of the skin on her face. Police also picked out of the bloodied head, pieces of what appeared to be parts of ceramic figurines.

"'There was no evidence of a struggle or robbery. Ms. Cranston's purse was on a table with cash and an ID in it. The driver's license identified her under the name of Gracie Cranston.

"'When police ran her fingerprints, the full name of Annibelle Grace Cranston came up. The FCIC NCIC report revealed Ms. Cranston had been arrested in the past for petty crimes such as writing bad checks, prostitution, and shoplifting.

"'The male victim, also through fingerprints, was identified as Thomas Clifton Allen. Mr. Allen had a record as well. His priors included petit theft, check fraud, gambling and selling stolen property.'"

Sticking his nose deeper into the paper, Aaron said, "Listen to this, this is interesting. 'Other than the purse, there was no other evidence that the female resided there. The police surmise that she was either an infrequent girlfriend or a prostitute.'"

We gave up trying to yell over Aaron, so we half listened to him, nodding in his direction occasionally. I continued to gorge myself on shrimp and fried rice.

"'The police had detectives investigate the figurine and broken glass that was embedded in the female victim's battered face. They discovered that the item was from the famous sculpturer, *Ivan Hammondstone's Special Series Six Collection.*

"The collection is a group of six replicas of Hammondstone's snow globes titled, *The Belles of the Ball.* The doll pieces found stuck in the victim's face were the last, and the most recently produced in the series, called *The Sapphire Bell.*

"'The famous artist had designed a hand carved image of a beautiful woman, molded from fine, bisque china. The figure was attired in a satin, voluminous sapphire blue dress, with a flouncy white petticoat, and matching sapphire slippers.

"'Draping from her delicate neck was a silver ribbon displaying a sapphire bell that nestled in the hollow of her ivory throat. The collection has been sold through magazines.

"'Each snow globe is uniquely created, and only one a year is produced. Hammondstone owns the originals, and he claims they are not for sale. The reproductions, however, are quite popular, numbered, and sell out shortly after they are exhibited.

"'According to the police, the murder may have been motivated by unpaid gambling debts. A number of newspapers and bulletins referring to horseraces were found scattered about the dreary room.

"'The authorities are being so descriptive of the murder scene in hope that someone would come forward, maybe the pizza delivery guy or someone that new the couple. Police are contacting local known bookies to see if...' "

"All right already Aaron!" Jim cut in. "It's just a murder for Pete's sake. It's not like there's not a million of them in south Florida! The dead hoods were no one we know so WHO CARES!" Jim shoved a chopstick laden with white rice into his mouth and chewed loudly.

"Really Aaron, I agree," Cybil said. "I'm trying to eat and I don't need to picture a naked woman with her face brutally disfigured by someone in a rage, pounding and pounding a snow globe into her head until the glass breaks, and a man with his blood and guts hanging out lying next to her, a-"

"Oh thanks Cybil, I wasn't even listening. Thanks for the gory description. You guys are really gross, c'mon cut it out!" Ted snarled, sounding cross.

"Fine. I thought the figurine bashing was kinda cool, you know, beaten after death by a doll, just forget it." Aaron huffed and stuck his face in the paper, ignoring the rest of us.

We carried on a light conversation until the clock on the wall reminded us it was time to return to the coalmines.

I piled up the empty boxes that had contained my lunch and tossed them into the trashcan. After bidding a pleasant 'cheerio!' to the rest of the group that was also cleaning up, I strolled back to Art's office. The door was open and Art was talking with a man in a black suit.

"Hey Rusty," Art said to me, "this is Jack Francis from Euro Enterprises." We shook hands, I stepped back. "You can go on to work in the shop, Rusty. I'll be occupied for a while." Art smiled at me and turned his attention to Mr. Francis.

Dismissed, I left the office and headed to the repair shop. I was just as glad. I'd rather be working in the shop than reviewing endless dull numbers with Art.

I worked a relatively short day and went home early. Dinner was ready on the table when I got home. Meatloaf and mashed potatoes awaited me, as did Julia on tiptoes to buss my cheek.

"I missed you today, sweet pea," she whispered in my ear. "Wash your hands, dinner is ready."

I hurried off to the bathroom.

Chapter Thirteen

After we ate and cleaned up the dishes, we went for a leisurely walk around the neighborhood.

We strolled hand in hand along the sidewalk, nodding and waving hellos to our neighbors. The Stedmans were tidying up around their yard, they waved to us.

The sun had dropped way over to the western horizon. The shadows were long, stretching the darkness of the houses and trees.

Ellie Cook, pushing her six-month old twins in a double stroller, zipped past us on in-line skates.

Birds in trees were still chirping to their friends all perched in a neat row on electric wires. We stopped on Waterlily Bridge to watch the jumping fish in the canal. Mullets in mass schools, leapt abruptly, making frenzied splashes up and down the river as they moved along with the current, chasing an even smaller food chain.

Banshee, the Dewey's fox terrier ran up to the end of their fence, barking a furious warning to us. I was glad we had had left the pups home, playing in our back yard. The sky darkened as the sun melted in to the firmament.

We made our way with unhurried ease down the street back to our house.

When we arrived home, Julia went through the house to the back and let the dogs in. We all settled in the den to watch Frasier re-runs.

A week or so later, I came home early and Julia had prepared meatloaf for the third time that week.

"Hey Baby doll," I said to Julia, "what's up with the burger chow? Don't I give you enough dough for real food?"

Julia was setting the table. She placed the silverware on the tablecloth then returned to the kitchen, she came back out a minute later with the salt and pepper and a butter dish.

"I need to talk to you about that, Rusty." She set the condiments down and turned to me, her hands on her hips.

"I know we'll get things for the baby when we have a shower, but there's some special things I want to get ourselves. Like, there's a particular crib I think is best for the baby. It adjusts as the child grows, and is considered to be the safest for infants.

"And, I've found this really neat playpen that is incredibly versatile. They say it's perfect for the active kid!" Julia went back into the kitchen and returned with plates and glasses.

"The furniture is kind of expensive, Rusty, because it's very well made and designed to last. But, it's the best, and we'll be able to use it for our next child too!" Julia hugged my arm, her shining eyes gazed up at me, imploring me to understand and agree.

How could I ever say no to my pregnant wife pleading so prettily?

"Take all the money you need, honey. We want nothing but the best for our pending pabulum sucker. All the overtime I've been putting in lately should be mounding up the moulah. And besides, I can always eat peanut butter sandwiches for lunch." I wrapped my arms around Julia's slim shoulders and hugged her to me.

"But," I warned. "I'm still looking forward to dinner at the Seahorse Chalet on the beach this weekend. We'll just charge it. I think it's important that we celebrate the anniversary of the night we met!" I looked down at Julia, squeezing her shoulders.

"Oh Rusty, you are so romantic!" Julia cooed. Pressing herself against my chest, she looked up at me and said, "Sometimes I feel that you and I are living in a fairy tale. I dream that I am a beautiful princess and you are the dashing prince that has just rescued me from the jaws of the ugly, fire-breathing dragon!"

I grinned at her whimsy.

She went on, "You're carrying me off through a magical, green glen. We're sitting high up on your magnificent white stallion and you're holding me tightly against your chest.

"At the end of a meadow is our storybook castle. There," Julia sighed, "you and I and our children live happily ever after, with the seven dwarfs to mow the lawn, and the evil witch to be our housekeeper of course!" Julia joked, dispelling the spellbinding fantasy she had been spinning. She giggled and stood on her tiptoes to kiss me gently on the lips.

I laughed too, and made a secret promise to myself that my lovely lady would never want for anything. I hope she always looks at me with adoring eyes, like I'm her prince ready to rescue her for eternity!

But for now, I scooped my princess wife up into my arms and carried her away, up to the stars...or up the stairs to the bedroom!

By the end of the week, I decided I should give Steve a call and see what's up with the temporary bachelor.

"Hey big guy!" I yelled into the phone as Steve answered. "How's the bad boy bachelor making out?"

"Hi Rusty," Steve replied. "Things are looking up!" He sounded ten times better than the last time we talked.

"Oh yeah? What's happening?" I asked.

"Well, Heather and I have been talking some. She admitted she'd been feeling stifled lately, and because I've been working so much, she's been getting lonely. She said she only had the affair with Mike to stir me up and get my attention. I can understand that!"

Give me a break, I thought. The reason Steve is gone at work so much is because Heather pushes him to make more money for her! What a line of bull she's been feeding him! I only said, "Oh yeah?"

"Sure, Heather just wanted some romance back into her life. So, we've been going out to dinner and the movies a couple of times. No sex yet, we're sort of just dating again."

"Uh huh," I mumbled. Oh sure, that would be Heather. Dating and presents without the putting out. The grasping bitc-

"Yup!" Steve said cheerfully. "Things are going really great. Heather has been warmer and more pleasant. Like she's really making an effort to be nice to me!" Steve sounded happy.

Duh, I thought, since when is it an effort for a wife to be 'nice' to her husband? Steve still has his head in the sand. But, it's not up to me to give him a slice of 'real life' pie.

"That's nice," I said noncommittally. Heck, it's the exact thing Sandy's doing.

Mike probably told Heather what he has to do to get back into Sandy's good graces, and once Heather realized Mike wasn't going to be her meal ticket, she needed to get Steve to forgive her and take her back.

I couldn't picture Heather as a plumber's wife anyway. She was always making snide remarks to Sandy about the smell that sometimes clung to Mike and his grimy fingernails.

"And," Steve said eagerly, "Heather says if things keep going well, soon I can move back home!"

Apparently Steve forgot it was HE who had moved out, NOT that Heather had kicked him out! Steve's making it sound like the whole sorry incident was all his fault. What a bonehead!

I felt like poking him in the eye and saying *'wake up Steve! You're married to a gold-digging slut who's going to use you and abuse you until she bleeds you as dry as she is!'*

Now I was starting to wonder if Mike was her first extra marital romp. No wonder she seldom wanted sex with Steve, she's probably too tired from doing the yard guy, and the pool man, and every stock boy in town!

Well, I'm not the one to tell Steve what a sucker he is, the poor sap. He'll learn on his own. Or, maybe he'll continue looking through his rose-colored glasses, pretending all is fine with the world. Maybe he wants things that way.

I don't want to be the messenger that gets killed for delivering the bad news for Pete's sake! If he wants to stay in his dream world, let him.

"Gee Steve, that's super. I'm glad things are turning out the way you want," I congratulated him.

"You bet, man! I'm thrilled. We're going to our ten-year reunion at the Golden Gill on the beach on Saturday night. After that, Heather says she'll let me know if and when I can come home. You guys are going too aren't you?"

Damn, I had completely forgotten about our college reunion! Steve, Sandy and I had all graduated together. Sandy had taken Liberal Arts. She planned on going into the advertising field. But, she never seemed to get around to seeking full time employment.

Sometimes, before they had Bonnie when money was tight, Sandy worked part time at the local drug store. After Bonnie was born though, she and Mike decided to have a stay-at-home mom. In a way, that wasn't the best thing for Sandy.

I think her not having a job or career has made her stale and too dependent on Mike. If she were secure in herself and her ability to support herself and Bonnie, I'm sure she'd throw the bum out. But, oh well, we live the pages life writes us I guess.

"Sure Steve, Julia and I are going. I totally forgot all about it!" Now I remember Julia telling me she got a new dress for the event.

"Hey," I asked Steve, "what about Mike and Sandy? What's the deal? Have you heard if they're going?"

Steve made a snorting sound. "I'm not sure, and I really don't care. Mike's as good as dead in my book. I'll always care for Sandy, you know, but..." he cleared his throat, "that friendship is pretty much dirt under the bridge."

"That's water under the bridge," I corrected him.

"Whatever," Steve replied. "Anyway, I'm really looking forward to it. It'll be like when Heath and I first started dating in college. I'm hoping seeing familiar faces will bring back happy memories, that she'll run back into my arms and things will be the way they used to be." Steve trailed off wistfully, thinking of good times passed.

Actually, there never were good times with Heather. She was always directing Steve, ordering him about. 'Do this, do that, buy me this, take me there.' However, Steve always acquiesced, giving her whatever she wanted.

He even supported her when she dropped out of college and refused to get a job. Heather led Steve firmly around by the ring she had through his nose.

"Anyway," I said, "I wonder if Mike and Sandy do come, if they'll be there together. It's really Sandy's reunion, but I recall her saying she'd gotten two tickets for her and Mike, and Grandma Amy is all set to baby-sit." I told Steve about Grandma Amy's nocturnal travels.

"Hmmm, how interesting." Steve pondered a minute. "You know, I thought I saw her driving that old, four door sedan of hers a few days ago, with a man in the passenger seat. They were driving down Main Street in Sherwood City, and it was well past midnight.

"I beeped the horn and motioned to her, but she zoomed down a side street and out of sight. I just figured it wasn't her. Besides, what would an old lady be doing out that late at night?" It sounded like he was scratching his head.

"It couldn't have been Amy. And I didn't recognize the man. But, it was pretty dark and I couldn't see into the car that well."

"Who knows," I said with a shrug. "You think you know someone, and then 'poof' they're not who you thought they were!"

"No kidding, Rusty, I definitely know what you're saying. Well, I've got to get going." Steve sighed.

"I've got a few more hours of work I can do at home for the project I'm developing for the bank. This one is going to bring in some substantial financial gain for the R & D Department. I'm hoping all these extra hours will pay off. I need to upgrade my lifestyle. A huge bonus or commission would really set us up!" Steve sounded optimistic, hopeful again.

"Hey Steve, you stick with it. Build your career into something great, I know you can do it!" I tried to sound encouraging. "So...we'll be seeing you Saturday night. We'll be the ones in the finest duds!"

"Coo, bro. Okay, well then, catch you Saturday. Say hi to Julia for me, later man." He hung up.

Chapter Fourteen

"Bye Steve," I said to the already dead receiver.

I wandered around the house looking for Julia. I found her in the nursery. She was dusting and polishing the furniture and some of the special things she'd been collecting for the baby.

Already there were Winnie the Pooh pictures on the wall, and a lamp with Piglet cross-eyed, trying to look at a butterfly that was clinging to his nose.

A new white dresser was against the wall, presumably already stuffed with infant clothes. Julia's back was to the door; she seemed engrossed in her cleaning.

"Julia," I said to get her attention.

"Oh!" she cried. Startled, she lurched towards the door, her hand clutching her chest.

"I'm sorry baby! I didn't mean to scare you!" I made swift steps to reach her. She moved towards me, patting her chest. She took my hand, led me out of the nursery, and closed the door behind her.

"Rusty," she admonished me, "you know I don't want you to see the nursery until it's done. I want to surprise you." She frowned at me.

"I forgot honey. I'm sorry, but I looked for you and couldn't find you."

We walked into the kitchen. Julia opened the fridge and took out an orange soda. She pressed a glass to the icemaker. Miniature cubes released and clunked into the glass. I went to the refrigerator myself and took out a cream soda.

We carried our drinks to the table and sat down. Julia had placed a coffee cake and plates on the table earlier before she'd gone into the nursery.

She cut a thin slice of brown sugar and pecan topped cake and set it on a plate. Dropping a fork on the plate, she handed one to me.

"Thanks baby. Mmmmmm, I love coffee cake!" Not waiting for her to cut her own piece, I grabbed my fork and dug in.

"Just a small piece for now, Rusty. Dinner will be ready in about two hours. I didn't know you'd be home from work so early or I'd have prepared it sooner. I know how much you like to eat the minute you get home." Julia delivered a dainty piece of cake to her mouth.

Cutting a large forkful of cake, I shoveled in a mouthful of flaky sweetness.

"I just got done talking with Steve," I told Julia as I sliced another bite ready to sail onto my awaiting taste buds.

"He said he and Heather are dating again, just like Mike and Sandy. That's got to be the silliest think I've ever heard! Married folks dating, ridiculous!" I drank some cream soda, ice cubes bounced off my nose.

"I think it's very romantic." Julia sniffed. "Maybe this whole wife-swapping adultery thing will bring both couples closer together."

"You've got to be kidding, Julia, they're married for Pete's sake! You get married so you don't HAVE to date anymore!" I shook my head in disbelief.

Julia shook her finger at me. "Contempt prior to investigation, that's what my uncle Bill used to say."

"What? That sounds like 'don't knock it 'till you've tried it!'" I said, cake crumbs flurried out of my mouth. "Are you saying you think WE should try this swapping deal?" Incredulous, I shoved in more cake.

"Don't be silly, Rusty. I have no desire for any other man but you, you know that!" She grinned at me. "I just think it's wonderful that they're all trying to patch things up, trying to make their marriages work. What's up with you anyway? You're usually the most romantic guy in the world!"

Julia tipped her head back, drinking her soda. She licked orange foam off her petal pink lips

"I am happy for them, you know I am. In this case though, I think Sandy should kick Mike to the curb, and I think Steve should date some other women and get a perspective on what a normal, decent female is like. Heather was about his only girlfriend.

"He was always so shy and geeky, he never had the nerve to ask girls out. Heather only went out with him because she had an eye for the future and Steve looked like the one with the best prospects for earning the biggest bucks. Anyway, I hope he finds someone as terrific as I did!" I smiled tenderly at Julia, pressing my knee against hers.

"You say the sweetest things, Rusty." Julia stood up and leaned over in front of me. Her hands on her knees she smiled at me, her lips inches from mine.

I couldn't help it, my glance slid down to her shirt that draped low as she bent in front of me. I was oogling my own wife!

She stood up and put a lid on the coffee cake, knowing full well I couldn't be trusted not to take another slice of baked delight. She kissed me on the top of my mop and carried her empty plate to the sink.

Drinking the rest of her soda, Julia said, "I talked to Sandy earlier today. She sounded pretty happy. She said Mike took her to the Turquoise Cove Saturday night for dinner. On Sunday, she said he came by and she cooked a pot roast while he played with Bonnie and changed the oil in her car.

"Sandy said Mike brought her flowers. I guess it was only the bouquets you can buy from the guy who sells flowers by the side of the road, but still..." Julia picked up my plate and glass and took them to the sink. "It's the thought that counts."

"Yeah," I said facetiously. "Mike's a real thoughtful guy."

111

"Besides," Julia turned towards me, leaning her back against the sink. Her arms were crossed in front of her chest. "Sandy said Bonnie had been crying and crying for her daddy. Sandy was at her wit's end trying to occupy a two-year-old and attempting to explain why Daddy isn't there at night to tuck her in."

Her brow furrowing, Julia gazed idly out the window. "I think that even though Mike is a cheating bastard-"

My eyes whipped to her face, I've never heard her curse before. She looked so serious, like she was recalling a past experience, and a none too happy one either.

"Every child needs both parents and they should make every effort to fix their problems for the sake of the children, regardless if they can't stand the sight of each other!" Julia looked like she'd bitten a sour apple.

I shoved my chair back and went to her and gently touched her shoulder. "Are you okay honey?" I said softly in her ear.

Julia blinked twice, clearing away the vision she saw and looked at me.

"What?" She looked slightly dazed, and sad, as if she'd pulled back from some long ago, painful memory.

"Oh Rusty," she moved away, turning back to the sink. She placed the plates and glasses in the sink. Turning on the water, she filled the sink with bubbly suds.

"It's just that I firmly believe Mike and Sandy need to work things out and make a stable home for Bonnie. They chose to have her and she deserves nothing less. Besides, Grandma Amy is still disappearing during the week.

"Sandy is terribly puzzled, but Amy refuses to tell anyone where she goes. If Sandy asks her, Amy denies ever leaving the house. She makes up something like she was in the other bathroom or something goofy like that. She's obviously hiding something, but Mike told Sandy to leave her alone, let her have her little secrets, he said."

Nodding, I mumbled, "I agree."

"But Sandy is worried Amy might be getting Alzheimer's and could endanger herself or someone else venturing out at night and wandering around." Julia started washing the dishes with a scrub sponge.

"Which reminds me, Rusty. There's a spectacular baby stroller I found at the mall. You'll really like it when you see it." Rinsing the cutlery she dropped them in the drainer.

I got up to leave the kitchen. "I don't really know strollers from bassinets, Julia."

"But you'll love this carriage, Rusty. The problem is, it's much more expensive than the one we originally looked at. So...well, I need a little more money for this one." She continued rinsing the dishes.

"Wow," I said with a hearty exhale, "this babe is costing as much as the Empire State Building! But, like I said, only the best for our emerging embryo! Whatever you need honey, just take it out of our savings account, I'll sign the withdrawal slip."

I stood in the doorway, hands in my pockets. "I guess we'll be seeing the Caseys at the reunion on Saturday night. Maybe by then they'll have solved the mystery of Grandma Amy's midnight missions." I watched Julia as she neatly cleaned up.

"Hey, she could be just sneaking out, and taking dancing lessons! Wouldn't that be a hoot!?" Chuckling, I went back to the kitchen table and picked up the evening paper. Then I made my way to the den for some current event scanning, and maybe catch a snooze.

"Call me when dinner's ready!" I called out as I left the room.

I heard Julia's faint, "Uh huh" and splash of water as I moved down the hall.

We sat down a few hours later, and enjoyed a juicy roast beef and some apple pie for dessert. I planned to hit the sack early. I was pretty pooped from all the work I've been doing lately.

Julia was getting the leashes out of the closet. Although it was still light in the early evenings, I worry when Julia goes out by herself at night. She only had to call the dogs once, and they immediately came running into the room.

They get all excited, their tongues drooling, and tails wagging. They're practically beside themselves, wriggling in glee with any opportunity to go out. I kissed Julia, reminding her to be careful.

Pointing first at Muffy, then Boris, I instructed the pups that it was their duty to watch over and protect their mistress from any potential mischief-makers.

The three of them left the house in an ebullient flurry of fur and barking. Barely able to keep my eyes open, I trudged up the stairs to put my poor, weary body into bed. I couldn't wait to recline my exhausted rack of bones on the spongy mattress.

We spent the following evening quietly. Ordering pizza and soaking up a few beers, we watched the Thursday Night Movie.

The week passed by quickly.

They finally hired someone at the store, so I didn't have to work as much overtime. We looked forward, my sweet wife and I, to the exciting event of my reunion at the end of the week.

I was curious to see who would show up, especially if the carousing couples that used to be our best friends would be there. It'll sure be interesting to see how my other old school chums have changed.

I couldn't wait!

Chapter Fifteen

"Julia!" I yelled for my wife for the third time. "C'mon honey, we've gotta go! The tickets say 7:00 and it's already 7:15!"

"I'll be right there!" she called down.

I've heard that before. I looked at my watch for the hundredth time. Women! I swear, they don't start getting ready to go until the time they're supposed to be there!

I twitched my tie in impatience. Patting my pocket, I checked to make sure I had the tickets to the reunion. Opening my jacket, I reached in and pulled them out.

The front of the tickets blared: '**Come one, come all! Get together again! See who's old, see who's still young, divorced, rich, a different gender! Re-live your college days! Feel the thrill of the unknown you experienced years back before you entered the real world!**'

Inside it read: 'Join us from 7:00 p.m. to 8:30 p.m. for cocktails and hors d'oeuvres. A full course dinner will be served following the cocktail hour.

Meet old friends and make new ones on the air-conditioned, glass enclosed deck of the beautiful Golden Gill restaurant. Most of the seating area has breathtaking views overlooking the expanse of our magnificent ocean!

After flavored coffees and gourmet desserts, your dean, August Treymane, and your class president, Colleen Stewart, will

MC an evening of awards, special presentations and hilarious recollections of your college life.

Between events, enjoy dancing with your past and current lives, in the exquisite Candlelight Ballroom. The dance floor extends in a horseshoe over the water, out into the star-filled night. Guests will feel as if they're dancing magically suspended over the great wonder of the Atlantic!'

The invitation ended with, 'You don't want to miss the chance to leap for an evening back into the past. To live and love again, young at heart, one more time....'

I tucked the two tickets back inside my suit pocket. Straightening the black jacket and blue silk bow tie, I again looked at my watch. It was 7:20!

I ran my hand through my thickly moussed hair, and turned towards the stairs to call out in frustration to Julia to shake a leg.

"Oh my gosh!" My eyes and mouth widened in awe.

A stunning vision was poised at the top of the staircase. My gorgeous wife hesitated, then, like a mellifluous dream, resplendent in a rich, sapphire cloud, she floated gracefully down the stairs stopping within a meter from me.

"Julia!" I exclaimed, admiring her outfit. "You look extraordinarily beautiful!" My voice resounded painfully from the emotion that overwhelmed me as I drank her in.

The pure satin gown held up by air thin straps, clung to her sensual shoulders, skimmed her feminine figure then billowed into an elegant bell to the floor.

The gauze skirt whispered a million starbursts. It rustled musically as she took a step closer to me. The deep blue of the dress enhanced the vibrancy of her flaming hair. She had brushed the locks back into a smooth chignon, pinning it in place with two tiny, matching sapphire bows.

"You think I look all right, Rusty?" My wife looked over her shoulder at her reflection in the long hall mirror.

"I've never had a dress this glamorous before. Heather and Dimitri helped me choose the gown from her new boutique collection. I wasn't sure if it wasn't too much." She smiled imploringly up at me, her head tilted endearingly.

"But don't you look handsome and suave, honey, in your new Gucci suit! It was well worth the money we charged on the card!" Julia smiled at me as she combed my hair, neatening it with her fingers.

She stood up on her toes to lightly brush my lips with hers. Dainty, silver pumps peeped out from under the full skirt as she moved to get her purse and silver wrap.

"Honey, you are going to be the belle of the ball! The other women will pale majorally in comparison to your radiant beauty!"

I couldn't believe what a fox I'd married! Boy, those old friends, and enemies too, are going to be so jealous of me, ha!

Julia turned sharply, giving me an odd look. Then she bent her head down as she put her keys in her purse and said, "Do you have the tickets, honey?"

I nodded affirmatively, patting my pocket.

"What about your phone to take photos?" she inquired.

I swiveled on my heels and went in search of the moment catcher.

We drove in Julia's car since we were all decked out. My truck lacks that bit of grandeur that Julia's dress warranted.

We cruised along A1A, parallel with the ocean, until we arrived at the Golden Gill.

The place was jumping!

The parking area and steps to the entrance were flecked with people dressed in their finest attire. The ladies looked like strolling roses, all different colors and styles of dress.

The men sauntered with the women on their arms, dashing in the splendor of new clothes purchased especially for this evening. Limousines pulled up and people emerged like they were stars arriving at an awards gala.

We left the car with the valet and entered the marble foyer of the grand hotel. The area was perfumed with numerous floral displays. An enormous tropical flower arrangement was placed on a glass table in the center of the atrium. Lavish reds and blazing oranges splashed shouts of color, radiating from porcelain vases.

We followed the other excited guests down the carpeted corridor to the French doors that opened into the party room.

The Golden Gill was so named because the main ballroom was gilded in gold. I felt as if I was a setting in a priceless golden ring.

Crystal chandeliers sparkled from the vaulted ceiling. Paintings, encased in ornate gold frames, decorated the walls that were papered in the palest, softest hint of gold. Electric lamps glowed in aureoles along the walls. Garlands of gold tinsel draped from doorway to doorway.

The tables were set in parties of eight, the Gorham China and silver stemware polished to perfection showed off the tables in grandiloquent style.

The ballroom was extravagantly designed, just a shade from being gaudy. Glass bowls of gardenias were on tables permeating the air with their strong essence.

Against two walls, bars were conducting a brisk business. Nervous ex-schoolmates were lined up for some social courage in a bottle.

As I escorted my lovely wife into the festive atmosphere, I felt a spurt of exhilaration. I was secure in having Julia on my arm. She is a refined, yet gorgeous young lady contrasting with garishly made-up women who were struggling to appear sexy and still teenage!

Julia prevailed as a fresh, dewy buttercup surrounded by withered stringy vines. I was so proud to be able to show her off to my previous comrades of classes.

"Rusty," Julia exclaimed, gaping all around herself in the wonderment of a child at her first grown up party, "this is awesome, it's so incredible! I feel like I'm standing in a rhinestone studded Christmas box!"

I nodded in agreement, shivering with excitement as my eyes took in the glamour and frivolity all around us.

"Rusty dahling!" Someone shrieked in my ear while simultaneously dagger-like fingernails jabbed holes into my shoulder.

Glancing with concern over possible damage committed to my brand new, extremely expensive Gucci suit, I recognized the heavy New York accent, and tower-high, beehive hairdo.

"Mindy Morgenstern!" I greeted my old classmate, leaning in to receive her kiss that barely brushed my cheeks on either side.

"Why Rusty you big sweetie, you look fabulous! Who's this lovely lady you're clutching so tightly?" Mindy nodded towards Julia, flashing her a wide, toothy welcoming grin.

Mindy was the warmest, friendliest person I have ever met. She just loves everybody and will hug even the surliest person into a cheerful mood. On the downside though, Mindy Morgenstern can talk a person to death! She believes she's the expert on everything, knows everyone and has simply been just everywhere!

I introduced Mindy to Julia.

While shaking hands, they sized each other up. Apparently they each met with approval because Mindy immediately began chatting with Julia as if they'd known each other all their lives.

Shy as always, Julia attempted to answer Mindy's shotgun questions with a congenial smile.

"Who've you cornered this time honey?" An equally New York accented, yet softer voice cut in. Mindy turned to invite someone else into our group.

"Dahling, you remember Rusty Dixon from that horrible stats class I could nevah pass. Look how wonderfully he's filled out from that skinny stroke he used to be!" Mindy patted my ever-expanding belly that protruded slightly over my belt.

"He's gone and married this tiny beautiful girl!" Mindy pointed to Julia who was blushing and staring down at her silver pumps. Mindy pulled the man closer as she bussed his cheek.

I shook hands with Morey Goldfab, another old classmate.

"Rusty, I'm Mindy Goldfab now," Mindy explained. "Morey and I got married a few months after graduation. I chased him for four years and finally I wore him down and he gave in and made an honest woman out of me!"

Mindy hugged Morey's black, Givenchy-tuxed arm.

Morey smiled tolerantly down at his wife's overly made-up face. He obviously adored her, but was not showy about it. We chatted for several minutes, catching up on our lives.

Mindy told us she and Morey were now living in Boca Raton in an exclusive, mostly Jewish community. They have four children and apparently another on the way. The Goldfab family is active in their temple and immersed in a heavy social life.

If I know Mindy, their house is never empty. Mindy's parents always had friends and relatives in a steady stream, coming and going from their wealthy Palm Beach home. As outgoing and boisterous as Mindy is, I'm sure her house is just as busy.

Mindy gossiped nonstop, pointing out people she recognized.

There was Craig Simmons, she confided. Too bad about the embezzling charge he was facing...and over next to the bar with a cocktail in her hand was Marla Wesson, married four times already for heaven's sake!

"Can you imagine," Mindy whispered behind her false nails, "what a meshuga her latest husband must be, Marla took the other three guys for everything they had! Her brother is an attorney, so of course she's nevah on the losing end! There's rumors y'know, apparently the new husband really likes the booze...and poor Nancy Gail Smith-"

Mindy gestured to an overweight, pasty looking woman who was balancing on crutches while stuffing a peeled shrimp, dripping in red sauce into her capacious mouth. Her small piggy-eyes were darting all around the room. She watched the servers as they tried to scoot past her with their laden trays piled high with diverse hors d'oeuvres.

Mindy carried on in her nasally voice, "Always the schlemiel that girl! Look at her with that huge cast on her leg; just like she was in college, always falling down stairs and running into doors, she's got to be blind as a bat!"

We all watched Nancy awkwardly hobbling while chowing.

"She schleps her five kids to all sorts of classes, ballet, karate, anything so they'll not turn out as clumsy and accident prone as she is. The sorry lot though, every one of them has glasses and braces and is uncoordinated as hell. They all trip about like newborn calves. Too bad she married that Merle Strickland, such a muench he is!"

Mindy shook her head in disbelief. Glued to her head, her black teased mane was immovable. Chattering nonstop like a magpie, she gabbed on and on.

"And I know you heard about Libby Furleigh! Right after she won prom queen, she and David Pearson were arrested for-"

"Well Mindy," I quickly broke in as she took a breath. I knew there were years of gossip Mindy had to catch up on, and knowing she would yak on never-ending, I nudged Julia with my elbow and pointed to the dance floor.

"Look Honey, there's Mike and Sandy, we must trot on over and make our salutations." I smiled at Mindy and Morey.

"Hey, it's great seeing you folks again and nice to hear you're doing so well, but there's so many people I'd like to see. Maybe we'll sit together at dinner!" Secretly I was praying our reserved seating was miles from theirs.

I steered Julia towards Mike and Sandy Casey. As we moved away, I turned to wave goodbye to the Goldfabs, but Mindy was already hailing our college newspaper editor, Violet Wyatt.

"Hey dude!" Mike bellowed, pumping my arm. I leaned in and kissed Sandy. Mike and Julia greeted each other.

"How's it going?" I asked Mike.

"Eh, it's okay." Mike shrugged. "I ain't gotten a drink yet, and I can truly live without squeezing into a monkey suit and making small talk to a bunch of losers I don't even know."

Sandy glared at him.

"But, uh," he quickly said. "I heard the chow is supposed to be primo, and Sandy's dying to two-step on that dance floor that goes out over the ocean. She's been talking about this night continuously since we got the invite in the mail."

He put a fleshy finger in his collar, yanking it looser. He'd already unbuttoned the top button and his mottled tie was askew.

"C'mon girl," Mike grasped Sandy's hand and pulled her with him as he moved away from us. "Let's show off these spiffy duds we're wearing. I'll prove to you I can still whirl you around the floor like I used ta!"

They disappeared through the crowd making their way to where other brave souls were stomping and hopping old, out of fashion dance steps to even older once popular music. I decided not to reveal to Julia how ineptly my two left legs non-rhythmically moved.

"Would you like a drink, sweetie?" I asked my wife. When she nodded affirmatively, I took her elbow and guided her towards a bar. I wanted to revel in the jealousy and envy I'd see on the old gang's faces when I presented the knockout wife I managed to land.

Julia and I drank Screwdrivers and mingled for thirty minutes or so when the maître d' announced dinner would be served shortly and guests should begin seating themselves. I fished the invitations out of my pocket and looked for our table reservation number. We had table 25.

Holding Julia's hand, we slowly made our way through the pool of intermingling, nervously jabbering people.

Smiling and nodding to past acquaintances, we finally found our table. I pulled out a chair for Julia and she sank gracefully onto it. Pushing her chair in, I sat down on my own, setting my drink on the lace tablecloth.

"Isn't everything so beautiful?" Julia said breathlessly in my ear.

I grinned at her. "You certainly are!" I saluted her with my drink.

Julia giggled. "You're so silly, Rusty. Cut it out now, you know how embarrassed I get! I expect you to behave yourself tonight Mister!"

She playfully waggled her finger at me.

The seats all around us began filling up as guests found their places. It was becoming louder by the minute. Some people were already on their way to getting smashed. I wondered how many would still be standing and coherent by the end of the evening.

I didn't recognize anyone at our table, so I introduced Julia and myself to our companions. There were two empty seats still. I looked up as I heard a familiar voice.

"Rusty broster, and Julia as well, long time no see!"

Chapter Sixteen

"Hey Steve, it's great you could make it!" I stood up and gave Steve a 'manly' hug, barely touching but showing our affection for each other.

I gave Heather an imperceptible bow, she and Julia mumbled unenthusiastic hellos.

Steve looked pretty dapper in his obviously new blue suit. The gold buttons on the sleeves of the jacket were engraved with his initials.

Heather was poured into a skin-tight, sheer black dress. The front was so low cut, if she moved in the slightest you could see clear down to her navel. The dress could be considered sexy if she had anything to fill it out, as it was, I couldn't see how the darn thing was even being held up!

One could see right through the dress, it was so transparent, if one desired to, which I sure didn't! Black certainly suited the witch, I thought meanly.

I was hoping Heather and Sandy wouldn't run into each other. I didn't want to see Sandy get all hurt and upset again. She had looked so happy earlier while hanging onto Mike's arm.

The couple had been gazing at each other like the young lovers they once were. I'd hate to see Heather destroy the delicate threads that were holding the Caseys' marriage together.

We chatted with the Hazelhursts and occasionally with the other couples at the table. The conversations around the room continued to rise in volume. I heard 'oos' and 'ahs' as the waiters brought out the first course.

I looked down, my mouth watered as a plate of honey-glazed pears was placed in front of me. Rudely, I didn't wait until everyone was served, I delved right in. Yum yum the pears were stupendous!

When I had eaten the last of the fruit, using my spoon, I scraped up every ounce of juice and drizzled honey that was left swimming in the china.

Next, the servers brought brimming plates of steamed lobster, and juicy, char broiled filet mignons. A silver boat of melted butter was set next to my right hand.

Arranged on the plate like a ribbon-tied bouquet of flowers, were crisp sweet asparagus. The greens were lightly blanketed with a peppery cheese sauce. Nestled next to the steak, scrumptious apricot colored new potatoes were just waiting to be eaten!

Tucking my napkin into my belt, I reached for a garlic-drenched dinner roll, shoving it whole into my mouth, ahhh, crusty and flaky on the outside, soft and hot on the inside. I thought I'd died and gone to heaven!

Now it was pretty quiet in the room. Mostly all I heard outside of my own chewing and swallowing were silverware clanking on plates, and other orgasmic sounds of people savoring the delightful meal.

Waiters invisibly filled the crystal wine glasses with a robust Pinot Grigio that held up nicely to the steaks. The goblets were never allowed to be empty. I took some huge gulps to see if I could beat the waiters to the bottom, but alas, they were just too darn efficient!

I was feeling warm and slightly tipsy from the pleasant wine and marvelous food.

I glanced over at Julia. She was demurely cutting her food into bite-sized morsels before placing them with care into her invitingly open mouth. I looked around at the other women seated at our table.

Some were gluttonously gorging themselves, zestfully relishing the sumptuous feast like cows led out onto a lush pasture.

There was one woman though, just skin and bones that only pushed her food around on the plate while sipping soda water. Poor thing. I continued to plow through my food with gusto!

"Ladies and gentlemen, may I have your attention?" A microphoned voice burst into the room, halting the eating activity.

Our prior dean, August Treymane, was standing on a small stage vying for our attention.

Mr. Treymane used to instill swift and intense fear in me the second I laid eyes on him in my college days. But as I took in the few strands of dyed black hair he combed over his widening forehead, and the rotund figure sweating like a stuck pig, the only thing instilled in me now was the concern as to what was for dessert and where was it!

Treymane cleared his throat then began, "My dear Florida Suncrest College alumnae, I want to welcome you here tonight to celebrate your tenth year reunion! While we're waiting for the servers to clear the dinner plates away and prepare dessert and coffee, we would like to begin the awards part of the evening's program.

"First, I'd like to bring out the class president of your senior year, Colleen Stewart. Colleen will take over from here. I'm sure you'll have an exciting and memorable evening! So nice to see you all, -Colleen?"

Mr. Treymane made a hasty exit as he waved Colleen Stewart on, passed her the microphone then slipped off stage right. There, he was met by Celia Bridgend; the school's female of the worst reputation.

Apparently things never change, because Celia, barely wearing the shortest dress and highest heels I'd ever seen, was gushing all over Mr. Treymane while rubbing her extremely exposed, exceptionally enormous breasts all over his arm.

Treymane was buying it all. Staring like a teen-aged schoolboy down her endless cleavage, he put his arm around her waist and ushered her out the side door. Hmm, I thought, I sure can guess where they're going. I wonder where Mrs. Treymane is tonight?

Colleen, looking like the cheerleader she always was, took the microphone and started reading what she thought were cute anecdotes of our college days.

She'd say something she thought was terrifically funny about an incident, such as the time Alan Matthews tripped going to his seat in the lunchroom one day and falling face first into a Boston Crème Pie that was on the table he was planning to sit at.

When Alan stood up, his face oozed white cream. He tried to act nonchalant by licking the pie off his mouth and declaring it delicious, but he sure looked the fool.

So Colleen called Alan up to the podium and presented him with the Clown of the Class award. Red-faced, Alan, who used to be the skinniest guy on the campus, was now quite the opposite.

He accepted the award good naturedly, made a comment about hoping we're not having pie for dessert and went back to his seat.

The rest of the awards followed in like suit. Bored, I tapped my fingers on the table and looked around, still wondering where my dessert was. I turned towards Steve.

"Things look pretty good tonight, Steve."

Steve smiled, nodding in Heather's direction. "You are so right, Rusty, things are going really well!" He leaned over to whisper in my ear, "I think tonight's the night I might get to move back home!" Winking, he grinned like the Cheshire Cat.

"Hey buddy, that's great, my prayers are with you," I said to Steve. Heck, if that's what he wants, I'm happy for him.

Oh goody, the waiters were back, and one set a huge slab of key lime pie in front of me. I could hear snickering as people turned and looked at Alan Matthews.

Alan shrugged, just his luck there was pie for dessert. I grabbed my fork and dug right into the whipped topping and toasted almonds. I ate my piece then finished off Julia's for her.

We sipped coffees laced with Bailey's Irish Cream liquor, laughing infrequently as other classmates were made fools of by accepting goofy awards from our ex-class president. Having just enough to drink to forget I can't dance, I jumped up and tapped Julia's arm.

"Come on baby, let's boogie!"

My gorgeous wife acquiesced and followed me as I skipped to the dance floor to join the other dreamers thinking they were still hip as they twisted and leaped crazily all over the highly polished floor.

Julia and I lurched and turned, sometimes even in unison, secure in the knowledge that we were the absolutely coolest couple on the floor.

My eyes wandered around the floor as I judged my fellow mates. Sad, so sad, I thought. Most had gone to paunch and wrinkles already. A few of the guys still had hair. Geez, they look this bad now I hate to see what they'll look like when they hit 40!

Actually, the women had held up the best. I could tell some of them were hitting the gym pretty regularly, their firm and probably cosmetically altered bodies didn't show how many kids they've had. None of course could compare to the raving beauty in my arms!

The music switched abruptly from rock to a romantic slow dance. I reached for Julia's slim hand and drew her into my embrace.

Julia rested her head on my chest, her hand tenderly cupping my neck as we drifted slowly around the room, in a loving world of our own. I felt a tap on my shoulder. Breaking apart from my wife, I looked up.

Mike was standing there, one hand in his pocket, legs apart. "I'd like to dance with Julia," he said.

'Oh!" I stepped back, surprised. I looked at Julia.

She shrugged her shoulders indifferently and said it was okay with her. I handed Julia over to Mike and went in search of Sandy.

Glancing back, I couldn't even see my petite wife. She was completely hidden by Mike's thick girth.

I found Sandy sitting alone at their table. Most of the other guests were dancing or outside enjoying the view of the water. Sandy was absently stirring a spoon in her coffee; her eyes followed the progress of the two dancers I had just left.

"Hey girlie," I said to her cheerfully as I sat in the empty chair next to hers. Mike must have vacated it some time ago since it wasn't warm.

Surrounding an empty coffee cup, were at least a half dozen beer bottles. Mike must have been pretty bored because most of the labels on the bottles had been peeled off and were crumpled and littered all around the table.

Sandy greeted me gratefully, she probably felt like a sore thumb sitting there all by herself while her husband danced with another woman. Albeit the other woman was a good friend of hers... hmmm... that sounded familiar...

I chatted comfortably with Sandy, but I seldom took my eyes off the pair on the dimly lit dance floor.

Sandy and I conversed amiably for a few minutes when I noticed that it appeared Mike and Julia were arguing. They were still holding each other, but they were stretched an arm's length apart.

Julia's face looked thunderous, while Mike looked smug. Sometimes Mike had a snide way of peering down at you, like he thought you were a worm he could crush beneath his boot.

Suddenly, the couple broke apart. Julia had her hands on her hips and was shaking her head negatively at Mike.

His arms were crossed in front of his brawny chest, he was nodding and smirking.

Julia shook her finger at Mike and started to turn away, but he reached out and grabbed her wrist, holding her taught, he ground out a few more words. Julia tried to yank her arm free from Mike's grasp, but he held her tightly.

Alarmed, I stood up, ready to go to my darling's rescue! Mike is a strong man, but I was fueled with indignant anger.

Sandy's head shot up as she took in the scene up front. As I took a step from the table, Mike released Julia's wrist with parting words, his head nodded up and down on his thick neck, apparently pressing home his point.

Julia jerked away and stormed from the dance floor. As she neared the dining area, Julia realized I was watching her. She slowed her pace, the vexed expression cleared from her face. Her gentle, timid smile returned as she rejoined me.

"What the hell was that all about?!" I exploded. Mike must have ducked out a side door as I didn't see him anywhere in the room.

"Rusty, please lower your voice, people are staring." Julia hushed me as she reached up to smooth her mussed hair.

Slightly quieter, I said, "I'll be damned if I'll lower my voice! That son-of-a-bitch just manhandled my wife and I want to know what the hell is going on!"

I was so mad I was cursing. I can swear like a sailor if I want to, but I respect my wife and seldom do I curse in front of her. Except for now. If Mike were standing here I'd punch him in the nose!

"Oh... it wasn't that big a deal." Julia moved to our table and gathered up her purse and silk stole. She was acting as if nothing had happened. I grabbed her shoulders, halting her in front of me.

"Honey, tell me what happened between you and Mike." I squeezed her arms in anxious urgency.

"Now Rusty," my wife smiled up at me, "really, it was nothing. Mike is just an uncouth savage with an atrociously vile sense of humor. He told me a stupid tasteless joke, and I told him I didn't appreciate dirty stories.

"He's just a barbaric Neanderthal who needs to return to the jungle with the other animals, where polite society doesn't have to tolerate him. I feel sorry for Sandy. C'mon let's go, have you had enough reunion for this decade?"

She stood back, her head tipped to the side, waiting for me to come with her. I looked back for Sandy but she had disappeared.

"Okay sugar pie, let's blow this popsicle stick!" I wrapped my arm around Julia's shoulders and led her out of the ballroom.

When we stepped outside the entrance to the hotel, we stood momentarily on the marble landing as I helped Julia with her wrap.

Breathing deeply, we inhaled a hint of brisk freshness in the autumn air. The sun had long set, and a cool ocean breeze tickled our faces, still warm from the stuffy ballroom.

"Hey Baby," I suggested, "let's nip down to the ocean, we're hardly ever here in the evening."

We held hands as we slipped down the steps of the Golden Gill then followed the pebbled path that led around to the back of the hotel.

The path disappeared into the sand. Giggling, we held onto each other as we clumsily took off our shoes. Holding hands again, we gleefully pranced like schoolchildren, kicking up the cool sand as we dashed down to the water's edge.

We stopped, letting the surf roll up to us, lick our toes gently, then suck back in a roaring rush to its vast eminence.

There was a sprinkling of lights near the hotel. We could see people up on the terrace, the orange tips of their cigarettes moving and glowing in the dark.

Out on the beach near the water, it was black as pitch, and just a tad chilly. We snuggled, wrapping our arms around each other. Julia shivered. I rubbed her arms, loosening her light stole. Dipping my head, I captured her silken lips, plundering them with mine, kissing her fervently, rapturously, endlessly, until she broke off the kiss, shakily pulling back.

My young wife's eyes were cloudy with lust, her lips swollen with passion. I was drunk with erotic furor; my brain was a frenzy of sensuous carnal pleasure. Oblivious to our surroundings, I pulled my wife closer to me.

Julia put her hands up, fending me off. I pulled her more urgently, more ardently. Julia firmly pushed away from me. I blinked, trying to clear my muddled mind. It was hard to push down the emotion that filled me and focus on Julia's voice.

"Rusty, Rusty, calm down, we're not alone here." Julia's voice was softly pleading. She had taken a few steps away from me. I shook my head, wiping my brow with the back of my hand. Looking around us, I noticed other folks meandering along the water's edge. I smiled at my wife.

"I'm sorry baby," I apologized, closing the gap between us. "You just get under my skin so badly sometimes, it's hard to control myself. I'm okay now, I promise I'll behave like a gentleman."

I reached for her hand. She had her shoes and purse in one hand, and was trying to keep her wrap from completely falling off onto the sand with the other. I took her silver slippers and purse and tucked them against my chest along with my shoes.

Holding hands, we stood side-by-side, our intense emotions quieted now. We gazed briefly, lovingly at each other before turning to drink in the vast magnificence of the phenomenal ocean.

The frothy surf rippled and winked, surging, thrusting in then dragging back out. The water sparkled so much from the moonlight that my eyes imagined a burst of a thousand fireflies, euphorically scampering along the frosty tips of the amethyst water.

The ocean, a liquid forest, preened undulant with glorious patterns and mixtures of colors. A melding of topaz and garnet, the dark night brought out the deepest kaleidoscope of shifting hues.

Hauntingly beautiful, the magical waters merged with the blackness of the sky. The line dividing the Atlantic and the horizon became invisible, mysteriously melting together. Phew, talk about feeling insignificant!

"I'm exhausted sweetie, are you ready to go home?" I handed Julia her shoes and purse. We made our way slowly back to the pebbled walk that led to the hotel. Sitting down heavily on the steps, we put our shoes back on.

Looking down the length of the beach, it was difficult now to see the ocean. Our topaz tryst was over.

Driving home I could barely keep my eyes open. I glanced over at Julia. She looked happily sleepy, her head resting against the window bumped gently.

I was thinking about how comfy our bed is...I shook my head as I pictured hitting my fluffy pillow.

Chapter Seventeen

An incredibly short weekend was followed by a laboriously long week. I had to work late every night.

Sighing, I set my miniature pliers down and reached for the phone. I tried calling Julia to tell her it was going to be another late night. She probably had already figured that out since it was after 8:00 p.m.

The phone rang five times before the answering machine clicked on. Julia must be out walking the pups or taking a bath. I left a message telling her I'd be home around eleven. Oh well, we hadn't seen much of each other this past week. I was sure looking forward to this weekend.

At least it was Thursday, only one more day to go. Maybe we could take in a movie on Saturday. I needed to check and see which teams were playing football on Sunday. Yeah, a beer, pizza and football weekend, my favorite! I rubbed my eyes behind my glasses and got back to work.

Finally Saturday arrived and I was ready! I rolled over stretching, and then quickly covered my head with my pillow before any daybreak light could sneak in and fully wake me up.

Sniff... sniff... What's that?

Sniff... smells like bacon. I pulled the pillow down more tightly. Didn't work. Bacon, toast and coffee were sifting in and slinking up my nose. Groan.

I tossed the pillow aside and looked over at the clock. It read 9:00 a.m. It was later than I thought, seemed like I'd only been asleep for a few minutes.

"Rusty?" Julia called from the bottom of the stairs. "Wake up Rusty, there's a lot to do today and the morning is half over. Come on honey, get up!"

I waited until I heard her move back into the kitchen then I padded into the bathroom in my bare feet and splashed cold water on my face. Peering at myself in the mirror, I decided I was really quite a fine looking guy.

My hair was thinning a bit, but then it always was baby fine. I gazed into my bleary eyes. They were a little bloodshot with the late nights, but still a nice bluish-green color. My teeth were still pearly white and I only had tiny laugh lines around my eyes and mouth.

My eyes traveled further down, towards my chest. I really need to get started on a weight lifting program, tomorrow perhaps.

I caught a glimpse of my belly- time to go. I hate to keep Julia waiting when she's cooked my breakfast and all. Dashing into the bedroom, I yanked on a shirt and shorts then zipped down the stairs to my awaiting breakfast, uh and Julia too.

After pigging out on a farmer's style breakfast, I wandered into the den to read the newspaper before perusing the list of chores Julia had written down for me to do today. I could hear the water running in the kitchen; Julia must be washing the dishes.

Harrumph. I plopped noisily onto the couch that was soft and squishy from age and use. I brought the furniture that's in the den with me from my dorm in college. Julia wouldn't allow it in the living room.

I remember reaching for the paper when I must have dozed off. The ringing telephone jerked me into full awakeness.

"I'll get it!" I hollered to Julia.

Snatching the phone off its cradle I put it to my ear. "Hello?" I said, not too friendly, after all, I had been in a deep snooze when the rude-

"Rusty?" A vaguely familiar voice, rusty with age and sobbing, croaked unintelligibly into my ear.

"Hello?" I repeated. "Who is this? You have to slow down, I can't understand what you're saying."

"Rusty, this is... this is... sob... Amy... Amy Richards... sob... Sandy Casey's grandmother... sob" The voice kept breaking up into heart wrenching sobs.

"Grandma Amy? What's the matter? Where's Sandy?" She was scaring me with all the horrendous crying.

"Grandma Amy?" I said again. All I could hear was crying. The crying finally quieted somewhat... I could hear her gulping and breathing deeply.

"Grandma Amy, are you all right? Where are you? Are you home? I'll come right over-"

"Rusty, sob, it's Mike... Mike is dead!" she cried out then she broke down into torrents of sobbing.

"What?!" I ejaculated, "What's going on? What are you talking about Amy? Where is Sandy?" I blurted questions into the phone. I could only hear crying and hiccups of breath.

"What's wrong, Rusty?"

I could hear Julia's concerned voice behind me. She could tell I was upset by my screaming into the phone.

I turned to Julia and said, "I don't know what's going on. It's Grandma Amy. She's hysterical and practically incoherent. She claims that- that Mike is dead."

Julia's eyes widened, her mouth parted. "She must be mistaken." She shook her head in disbelief. "Maybe Mike has been in an accident and she's afraid he's badly hurt."

"I hope you're right." I turned back to the phone. "Now Amy, calm down and tell me exactly what is going on. Where is Sandy?"

I tried to speak calmly and soothingly, the elderly lady was beside herself. Now I was worried that she'd gotten herself so stirred up she might have a heart attack.

I could hear Amy breathing more slowly and deeply, trying to get a grip on her emotions.

"Sandy is at the hospital with the police." She sounded dreadfully haggard. She took some more deep breaths then sniffed. "I'm here watching the baby."

Her voice tightened again, shakily she said, "An hour or so ago, the police knocked at the door and asked for Sandy."

In stuttering, gulping breaths she continued, "They told Sandy that they had found Mike in his boat... and that.... he... he had been shot!" She burst into crying again.

"Oh my God!" I shouted.

"What? What?" Julia asked, tugging on my sleeve.

"Amy says Mike has been shot!" I ran my hand through my hair and thumped down on the couch, my legs suddenly became too wobbly to hold me up.

Julia stood anxiously, gaping at me. I waited a minute.

"Are you sure he's... uh, dead?" My voice squeaked. Maybe he was wounded cleaning his rifle or something. Mike liked to get drunk and sit around playing with weapons; he could be a big dope sometimes.

I put my hand to my brow. What a great guy I am, maligning my friend who might actually be dead - damn! I couldn't take it in, there has to be a mistake.

"Sandy went with the police to the hospital. She... she asked me to watch Bonnie and to call you. Rusty." Amy wailed, "I don't want to be alone and I don't know what's happening! Please, please come over here!"

"Okay now Amy, you calm down, Julia and I will be right there."

The tinny, weeping voice begged me to hurry. I repeated that we were on our way over then hung up the phone. I went in search of my shoes. I couldn't find them. Julia followed me around the house, wringing her hands.

"What happened Rusty?" she kept parroting as we went from room to room. My brain was totally dysfunctional. I couldn't think straight. I tried to sort out what Amy had said. How could Mike be dead? Who shot him? Was it an accident? What was he doing at his boat?

I thought he and Sandy had made up and he was back home. Questions, questions swirled around in my head. I could hear Julia repeating herself, but I couldn't find the words to answer her. Mechanically I found my shoes and put them on.

"Go get dressed," I said to Julia as I grabbed the truck keys off the counter. Julia ran off to the bedroom.

I was in my truck, starting the engine when Julia came out of the house. She flew down the steps and jumped in.

Still in shock, I drove blindly to the Caseys' house. Amy must have been watching for us through the closed curtains because the door opened as we pulled into the driveway.

I hurried to the front door, not waiting to help Julia out of the truck like I usually do. She slipped down off the high seat and ran to catch up with me.

Amy fell weeping into my arms as I entered the house. I put my arm around her and led her to the sofa then gently helped her to sit down. Julia quietly closed the door.

Clutching her purse, she stood awkwardly in the foyer.

I hugged Amy to my chest, patting her gently on her back. "Shhh, shhh," I tried to quiet her. I let her cry for a few minutes.

The weeping finally subsided, she sighed deeply several times. Sitting back on the couch, she removed her glasses and wiped her eyes with a tissue. She looked so distraught; I could feel my concern in my throat, choking me.

"Can I get you something, Amy? A glass of water, or some tea perhaps?" I patted her knee. She smiled crookedly and sniffed.

"Actually, a good two fingers of scotch would probably do the trick!" She almost chuckled.

Quickly obliging, I got up and went over to the Caseys' liquor cabinet. Setting a glass on the counter, I poured in about two shots of Dewars and carried the drink into the kitchen. Adding a good ounce of water, I plunked in a couple of ice cubes.

Returning to the living room, I noticed Julia still standing in the foyer. She was at a loss as to what to do.

Fumbling with her purse, her gaze traveled around the room then she looked at Amy. She didn't know Grandma Amy as well as I. Usually she's a great comforter, I couldn't understand why she just stood there now, blankly staring at Amy.

"Honey, why don't you sit down?" I motioned to an easy chair beside the front window.

Julia moved silently to the chair. She sat down, staring out the window. It was almost as if she wasn't even there.

Some people are good in a crisis. I'm normally pretty useless, but, looking at poor distressed Amy, well my heart just ached watching the old lady cry. I handed her the scotch.

"Thanks, Rusty, I'm so glad you're here." She accepted the drink from me and took a few quick sips. "Ahhh, I feel better now." She sighed and propped the glass on her lap.

"Can you tell me now what has happened, Amy?" I gently prodded her. She sighed again, deeply.

"Well, I'll tell you the little I know." She took a sip, let it roll down her throat and warm her frail body, then she took a bigger sip. Her blue eyes, large and watery behind her thick glasses turned up at me.

"Mike and Sandy were getting along pretty well lately, since their separation, you know." She looked at me and I nodded.

"Mike had been staying here again at night for the past few weeks, but his things were still on his boat at the marina. Well," she shuddered, taking a big swallow of her scotch, she pushed a lock of white hair behind one ear.

"After the party you all went to the other week, the fighting started again. You know how Mike can be, hard-headed and belligerent."

I gave a lop-sided grin in agreement.

She went on. "Sunday night they were yelling and screaming at each other. I took Bonnie into my room and turned the TV on so we couldn't hear the hollering. Poor Bonnie, it's so traumatizing to a baby to see her parents fighting like that."

I nodded, grimly bemused.

"Anyway," sighing, she continued, "Mike was furious and he grabbed his keys and jacket and slammed out the door. Sandy ran off into their bedroom, I could hear her crying though the walls.

So could Bonnie. I guess Mike went to stay on his boat because he never came back the rest of the week, and the lout never called either. Sandy was fraught with nerves.

"She kept having crying jags that would sometimes turn to anger, then she would curse the man." Amy smiled, her thoughts going back in time.

"I remember when they were teenagers and dating. My son and daughter-in-law tried desperately to keep those kids apart. Rob never thought Mike was good enough for his baby girl, and Sarah had high hopes of a good career for her daughter. But alas," she took another sip.

"You can't keep two hot-blooded kids apart. If they want each other badly enough, they'll find a way to be together!" The old lady shook her head, dispelling her recollections.

"After they were married and little Bonnie came along, Rob and Sarah finally accepted Mike and tried to be more friendly and welcoming. But he knew, mind you, he knew how they felt about him. That had to be hard for the boy, knowing your in-laws think so poorly of you.

"I'll grant you though, that young man worked hard and supported his family. I think it was the ill feelings and lack of respect that contributed to Mike's low self-esteem. He used alcohol and other women to boost his ego.

"Unfortunately, we all know how that really undermines and eats away at a person. Mike may be big and gruff, but inside he was so fragile..." Amy stared down at the glass in her hand.

"The only thing I know is," she looked from me to Julia.

Julia was gazing out the window, not acknowledging us at all. She must be trying to keep her feelings in, I thought.

Amy looked down at her drink again. "We hadn't heard a word from Mike all week until the knock at the door this morning." She gulped loudly, tears filled her eyes again.

"The police asked for Sandy, and I went and got her. Sandy started trembling the second she saw the police in the doorway. They suggested she sit down, but she was frozen with fear. She stood with her hands clenched in front of her mouth, expecting the worst." She sucked in a trembling breath.

"The police confirmed it. They told her Mike was dead."

Julia and I gasped.

I tore my eyes from the old lady and looked at Julia. Her face was white and her eyes wide. I know I mirrored her. Amy brought the tissue to her eyes. She coughed a bit.

"They said a buddy of Mike's had come over to the boat at dawn this morning. Apparently they had plans to go fishing down in the Keys for the weekend. When Mike didn't respond to the man's hellos, he climbed into the boat, calling Mike's name.

"The boat was strangely silent. The man figured Mike was still sleeping so he went to knock on the cabin door. Expecting the door to be closed and locked, he was surprised to find it wide open.

"He said he stuck his head inside the cabin and called for Mike again. When he heard no sounds of greeting or movement, the man stepped inside the doorway. It was still semi-dark in the cabin as the sun hadn't quite risen yet.

"But with the door open there was just enough light to see inside the cabin. The man wished there hadn't been any light. He could see Mike sprawled on the floor, his shirt a mass of dark goo. The man said he took an involuntary step back. His shoe stuck slightly to the floor. He looked down. He was standing in a congealed pool of Mike's blood.

"Terrified, the man ran screaming from the room. He told the police he hurt himself trying to climb out of the boat on that rickety ladder. He kept slipping, getting splinters in his hands, and cuts and bruises all over his legs from scrambling in terror and his urgency to get off the boat and away from the nightmare he had witnessed." Amy sighed heavily, taking a big gulp of scotch.

Removing my glasses, I lowered my head to my chest and put my hands to my eyes. *Oh my God*, I cried. It was true; Mike was really dead. The truth hit me like a ton of bricks. I wept.

Suddenly Julia was beside me. She pulled my head to her bosom.

Stroking my hair, Julia uttered comforting words, although I couldn't understand them. Grief overwhelmed me. All the anger I had felt towards Mike was seeping away in each tear that poured down my face.

The front door opened.

A weary, shell-shocked Sandy dragged slowly into the room.

I struggled to my feet and went to her. Putting my arms around her plump shoulders, we sobbed together.

I leaned back, still holding her. "Amy told us what happened. Oh my gosh Sandy..." We sat down on the couch.

Julia left to make some tea. Amy held her drink in one hand and Sandy's hand in the other.

Sandy sat slumped. "The police said they really don't know anything yet. They're investigating. I didn't see the guy who found him, H- Herb Myers. They were done questioning him by time I got there and he had gone home."

She looked at the tissue she was crushing in her hand. "I wish I'd gotten to talk to him, Rusty. I wanted to know more. Mike was alone... if only we hadn't fought! It's all my fault!" she cried.

"Now, now," I lightly chastised her. "It certainly is not your fault! We all know how difficult Mike can be. Do the police know how it happened? Was it an accident? We figure he was probably cleaning a gun or something while drunk, and the damn thing went off."

Sandy turned anguished eyes to me.

Shaking her head she said, "The police said Mike was murdered."

Chapter Eighteen

Standing at the back of the church with Julia by my side, we waited in silence for people to come in and sit down.

Sandy's brother and parents had arrived for the funeral. Surrounded by family, Sandy was led in a dark cloud of mourning to a pew up front.

I couldn't see her face, a dense black veil covered it. She sat arrow straight, unflinchingly facing the coffin that crowded the small space in the front of the room.

"Let's sit down," I whispered to Julia. She nodded. I guided her to a seat close to the front.

Once ensconced in the pew we sat motionless. We were still numb with shock. Mike was dead. Mike had been murdered. My brain still couldn't fathom it. He was such a large, lively man, I couldn't believe he was gone.

Noticing movement next to me, I turned and saw Steve and Heather sitting close by.

Steve and I nodded, silently sharing our grief. I know how Steve probably felt. He had been livid with Mike over the affair. He forgave Heather, but he said if he ever saw Mike again he'd kill him. I'll bet he regrets those words now!

He probably feels guilty over wishing the death of his close friend, and then suddenly there he is, stiff as a board. I was teed off at Mike for his behavior at the reunion. He had been somehow inappropriate with Julia, she wouldn't tell me specifics, but I sure didn't wish him any harm, and I had still considered the big lug to be my friend.

Heather leaned past Steve and waved gaily to me. She was actually smiling! What kind of an ignorant, cold-hearted gnome is that woman? She never ceases to amaze me.

Here we are at the funeral of a dear friend, one with whom she had an adulterous affair, breaking the heart of her husband and her best friend, and the hussy sits there, grinning from ear to ear and dressed like a floozy!

Does she have zero class? Shaking my head in disbelief, I looked her up and down. What does Steve see in that girl? It just bewilders me.

At least she was wearing black, what little there was of it. Short, tight and low-cut as always with slits up the sides. She had pinned a small black mantilla to the side of her head like she was at a freakin' London horse race or somethin. I guess she was going for the rakish, funeral look. She looked like a tramp. I turned away in disgust.

Sandy had asked me to say a few words about Mike during the service. Nervously going over what I had prepared in my mind, I pulled out a slip of paper upon which I had written some things about Mike. Crib notes.

It was going to be hard enough to stand up there in front of all these people, in my desperate sorrow, and try to speak eloquently about the dearly departed.

Knowing me, I'll stand there babbling like an idiot until the priest takes pity on me and hauls me off the podium. *Sigh*, oh well, I'll do my best.

After the service, we gathered by the burial plot. Sandy was holding Bonnie's tiny hand and softly crying. My poor bereaved friend tossed a red rose onto the coffin as they lowered it into the earth. She then encouraged Bonnie to throw her rose as well.

Bonnie was way too young to comprehend what was going on. Which on one hand was a good thing. She wouldn't experience the grief and pain of losing her papa. She was old enough to wonder for a while where he was, but soon she'd forget all about him. That was the sad part.

Baby Bonnie would never get to know her daddy, and what a great guy he was... hic... and Mike would never see what a darling his daughter would grow up to be... sniff... he'd never walk her down the isle- oh God... I wiped my eyes with my sleeve.

Julia pulled my handkerchief out of my breast pocket and handed it to me. She has been a tower of strength, my little one. I gratefully took the hanky and blew my nose.

Julia stood stoically. She glanced around at the people, but then she never took her eyes off the coffin as it was lowered, finally disappearing into the black hole.

The priest read a few scriptural passages, then closing his Bible, he turned to Sandy. Touching her arm, he murmured a few consoling words before he left, walking up the small grassy hill to his car.

Grandma Amy, looking like she'd aged ten years, took Bonnie's hand and brought her over to an elderly man that was leaning on a cane near a shady tree. The old man held out his hands and drew Amy and Bonnie into his arms.

Julia and I made our way over to Sandy. Her family had dispersed to get their cars. Just as we approached Sandy, a white car pulled up at the top of the hill.

The cemetery was in a tiny valley, set at the foot of an underground coral reef ridge. I recognized the cheap suit as a man exited the car. Detective Patterson.

There was another plain clothed officer with him. The two men just stood, hands clasped in front of them, silently observing the scene below them. Patterson stared at me.

I glared back at him for a moment then ignoring him, I turned to speak with Sandy. She hugged me.

"Thanks so much for speaking at the eulogy, Rusty. You said so many lovely things about Mike."

"You know I loved the big guy, Sandy." My eyes welled up again. I tried to distract myself from the pain. "Did you notice the cops on the hill watching us?"

She nodded. "They were at the house last night asking a million questions. 'When's the last time you saw your husband? Does he have any enemies? Does he gamble? What did you two fight about? Was he fooling around? Do you know who might have done this?' For a few minutes I thought they actually suspected me!"

She sounded amused, but irritated as well. "For Pete's sake, the wife is always the first one they grill! I think Grandma Amy was getting ready to pack hers and Bonnie's bags, it looked for a while like I was on my way to the Big House!" She snorted.

"I've been furious with Mike many times in my life, but certainly never angry enough to do away with him!"

Her eyes drifted back up to the police. "Actually, they seemed to be leading in another direction. They said there was something unusual about the bullets... uh... that they took out of, uh... at the uh... autopsy... some at the boat..." Sandy fumbled in her purse for a Kleenex.

"That's okay Sandy, let's not talk about it." I handed her my slightly damp handkerchief.

At that moment, overlarge dark Chanel sunglasses covering her face and her bony butt sashaying, Heather came strutting over to us. She pushed the glasses on top of her head, unaware that she had shoved the mantilla back with the glasses and now it was dangling sideways off the back of her head. I swallowed back a snicker.

"Darling Sandy, I am sooo sorry about your loss." Even to my unjaded ears she sounded insincere. She set one hand on her hip and swung her tiny beaded purse back and forth with the other.

Her tone flat, Sandy thanked her for her condolences. She didn't smile in return to Heather's saucy smirk.

"Oh well," Heather said. Uncommonly at a loss for words, she shifted her feet and pursed her skinny lips painted a brash red. "Now at least you can find yourself a real man!"

I gasped! My eyes flew to Sandy.

A deep, dark red crept up her neck, it quickly covered her face. Her lips pressed tightly together, her eyes narrowed.

"I think you need to go now, Heather," Sandy hissed through clenched teeth.

"Well! You needn't be so snippy!" Affronted, Heather sniffed, both hands on her hips her purse dangled from one wrist.

"Come on Sandy, you know what a big, smelly dope Mike was. I should have told you before, but I didn't want you to be hurt, but..."

Heather held her hand up, studying her nails she said, "Mike was going to leave you. He asked me to divorce Steven and marry him."

I heard Sandy's quick intake of breath.

"Why you wicked witch!" Sandy hauled off and slapped Heather so hard across the face Heather's head snapped back and the lace mantilla jerked hard but it still managed to cling inelegantly to a few spiky hairs.

"Get out of here! Get out of here now before I kill you too!" Sandy screamed at Heather. "You lying bitch! Mike told me when he tried to dump you, you threatened to tell me about the affair. When that didn't work, you swore you'd commit suicide."

Everyone present sucked in an aghast gasp. Sandy wasn't done.

"You spiteful slut, Mike never would have left me and Bonnie, and you knew that, didn't you? Mike said you were so infuriated that you just screamed and shrieked, cursing like a fishwife and throwing things at him until he left. Did you ever tell Steven about that?" She jabbed a finger at Heather's bony breast. "Huh?" Jab, jab, "Well, huh?"

Rubbing the slapped side of her face, Heather stepped out of Sandy's reach. There was a nasty purplish imprint of a hand streaking across her cheek.

With a guilty expression, she quickly looked around to see where Steve was. She sighed in relief when she spotted him standing half way up the hill talking with Julia.

They were too far away to hear, but they hadn't missed the scene. Neither did the police. They were making their way down the hill towards us.

I could hardly contain my glee. It was about time someone smacked that skinny little shrew. You go girl! I silently applauded Sandy. Patterson walked up to our group, the other detective tagged along.

"What's going on here?" Patterson questioned. His eyes flitted from one of us to the next. His voice was gruff, legs rigidly akimbo, his hands were laced together and held stiffly behind his back.

"Look Detective," I said, "this is private business. People are upset, this is a funeral after all and emotions are high. Why don't you run along now and give us a little time and space to deal with our grief?" Last thing needed was for Sandy to get arrested for battery.

"You listen here, Dixon," Patterson was in my face. "We're in the middle of a murder investigation and I'm looking at a yardfull of suspects. Now I want answers and I want them now. Anybody who doesn't want to cooperate can drag themselves down to the station and be treated more formally. Bring a lunch though, it always takes hours longer there!"

Patterson took out a small notebook and pen. His expression impassive, he looked around to each of us. "Now, what was that fight about?"

We reluctantly answered his questions. The other cop just watched us. He never said a word nor jotted down any notes.

At this point, Steve and Julia joined the group. As stories were told, Steve started to fume. When Heather grabbed his arm, trying to explain that everyone but her was lying, Steve jerked his arm away and stalked off up the hill.

Julia stood next to me, her cold hand clasping mine.

Finally, the coops finished their questions and the grieving group broke up and everyone went on their way.

Sandy's parents propelled her into their car where Grandma Amy and Bonnie were already waiting.

Julia and I hopped into the truck. Heather stood alone, unsure of herself for a change, apparently her ride had left without her.

Oh well. Turning on some music we headed for a restaurant, boy was I famished!

Chapter Nineteen

We had spaghetti and a tossed salad at Zititella's then went home.

I felt drained, empty. The murder, the funeral, the slap climaxed the week. I hadn't gone to work since that Saturday we first heard about Mike.

Fortunately, Artie understood. After resting tomorrow, I'll go back to the shop on Monday. I know the work has been piling up for the past week and I need to think about something other than the murder.

Random thoughts constantly spun around in my head. It was like having a merry-go-round in my brain, swirling and bobbing, never ceasing. Who killed Mike? Why?

The police told Sandy the door to his boat's cabin was wide open. He was killed on Thursday night. It gets dark around 6:00 p.m. now, why was his door open? They must have made a mistake, it must have been closed.

It's not very safe where he docks his boat. He can't afford much, so the marina he uses isn't in the best area of town. The place is not too clean, and there's mostly only old or small fishing boats there. They have a night watchman, but he's known to drink heavily and sleeps most of the time.

In south Florida, if you leave your lights on and doors open, you're welcoming every bug and crook in town to visit you. No, Mike would have had the door closed.

So... why did he open it? Late on a Thursday night he probably wasn't expecting anyone. He gets up pretty early for work, and now earlier still, for him to get to work on time he'd have to leave earlier because the marina is further outside of town than his house is.

I doubt he would have even answered the door if a stranger had knocked, it was just too dangerous out there. Mike was wild and uncouth but he was street smart.

Unless he was expecting someone. A woman? Was there another woman in his life? Mike was turning out to be quite the Romeo!

Yes, it had to be a female. Mike wouldn't have lost sleep over a male friend visiting him. So who was it? I wondered if I knew her. And the big question, how and why did she kill him? A lover's quarrel perhaps?

Ah ha! I've got it! I snapped my fingers. It has to be Heather! She must have come around, begging to be taken back and Mike spurned her again. A woman scorned and all that! Of course it was Heather.

I need to call the police and inform them. Patterson calls himself the detective, ha! I've certainly bested him, the condescending egomaniac. We'll see who looks down whose long nose now!

I jolted when the doorbell rang. Geez, all this thought about murder is making me jumpy! I peered through the peephole first. Strange how unexpected death makes one more cautious.

What a coincidence. Detective Patterson and his sidekick, Officer Penny what's-her-name, were poised on my doorstep. Patterson was reaching up to impatiently ring the doorbell again when I yanked the door open.

"Oh do come in, Officers." I swept my arm, magnanimously inviting them in. Closing the door, I ushered them into the living room. At least this time I was looking forward to the interrogation!

Officer Penny said stiffly through her meager lips, "Good evening, Mr. Dixon." I looked at her nameplate. Officer Newman.

Patterson nodded his greeting.

"Hi, c'mon in and sit down." I motioned to the sofa. "Can I get y'all something? Coffee? A cold soda? Beer? Wine for the lady?" I smiled winningly at Officer Newman. At least I was pretty sure she was a lady.

Trim, but with those muscles, and in certain lighting I could swear she has a mustache- and it didn't look like she was too endowed in the breast department-

"Uh, no thank you, on duty and all," Newman said, shaking her head. Patterson only grunted. It sounded like a decline to me.

I shrugged, we all sat down. I plopped onto a chair kitty-corner to the sofa.

"Harrumph," Patterson cleared his throat. "We have a few brief questions to ask you, Mr. Dixon." He pulled a pen and a small notebook out of his suitcoat's inside breast pocket.

"Actually," I eagerly cut in. "I've solved the mystery! I know who killed Mike Casey!" I smirked smugly at the pair.

"What?" they blurted in synchrony.

"Yup. Got it all figured out. Used the little grey cells, as Poirot used to say." I pointed to my head.

Patterson leaned in. "Do tell all," he said, slightly sarcastic.

"Well," I leaned forward also, my elbows on my knees. I told them how I deduced that it was Heather who had killed Mike.

"Motive, opportunity, and, I'm sure she could easily have obtained the means. Every K-Mart and flea market in town readily sells guns to whoever is tall enough to see over the counter! Heather is such a ditz, she would kill someone in a fit of rage or jealousy and be dumb enough to leave a trail a mile long."

The pair of cops stared blankly at me.

"Yeah, Heather has fluff for brains. The only thing going on up there," I tapped my skull again, "is hair, clothes and money! Plus, I've seen her mad. Boy, we were at the Hazelhursts' one time," I rattled on excited with my detective work.

"She and Steve had this horrific fight! She practically clawed his eyes out, screeching obscenities as she threw dishes at his head. We ducked and ran for home! Oh yeah, our little Heather has quite the temper!"

I sat back, a self-satisfied sneer on my face.

The officers were quiet for a moment. Patterson pulled reading glasses from his inside pocket. Putting them on, he flipped through his notebook. He stopped and read through one of the pages.

He grunted. "Hmmm."

I sat up. "What?"

Patterson removed his glasses, tapping them on the open notebook. "It says here that Mrs. Hazelhurst spent most of the evening on the day of the murder going over architectural plans with some foreign guy named Dimitrius."

He put the glasses back on and referred to the page.

"Something about a shop or store or something they plan on building. He was also helping her review some inventory of clothing she had already purchased for the place. Apparently, they were together late into the night."

"But-"

"This Dimitrius can vouch that Mrs. Hazelhurst was never out of his sight. He said they shared business and um, pleasure, for most of the night. We checked with the restaurant they claimed to have had dinner at and it was confirmed by two waitresses that they were there for hours. It seems she has an alibi."

Patterson flopped the book closed and looked at Newman.

I sat back feeling foolish. Heather the whore scores again. I was so sure... who then?

My voice came out strident, "Ah, well then," I coughed and lowered my tone to a more acceptable macho level. "Do you have any suspects?" I tried to act cool, like I wasn't a total bonehead who had just accused an old friend of murdering her past paramour.

Patterson slid his glasses back on, opened the book back up, looked down at it, then squinted up at me.

"Usually our first suspect is always the spouse, wait-" He held up a hand as I moved to object.

"But in this case, there's something unusual. Do you remember a while back in the news there was a story about a double murder in Sherwood City? It may have stuck in your mind because of what was done to one of the bodies." He took a breath as I stared quizzically at him.

"Two petty criminals were murdered, a male and a female. They were both shot while in bed, but the female had been dragged onto the floor. After she was already dead, someone had bashed her face in, totally beyond recognition with a glass snow globe."

He took his glasses off again and patiently watched me.

"A snow globe?" I echoed stupidly, not sure what the significance was.

Penelope Newman sitting with her back rigid and a totally void of any kind of expression on her face or in her voice, cleared her throat then spoke slowly and stiltingly like a teacher explaining to a student. "Yes. Snow globes are round glass objects with various scenes in them that you tip upside down then upright, then the snow inside the globe falls on the scene."

"I know what the damn globes are," I snapped at her. "What was the point to obliterating a person's face with one?"

Patterson said, "That's a good question that we don't know the answer to. That's not the odd part."

My brows furrowed. Smashing someone's face in with a snow globe isn't odd?

"What we're looking into is, that the bullets that killed these people were painstakingly hollowed out by hand. That is extremely uncommon. So uncommon, that when a person does that, they leave their own sort of 'signature'. No two people hollow out a bullet by hand quite the same way. In fact, the murderer has a habit of gouging out the bullets in circles going clockwise, indicative of a left-handed person."

"Wow." I never heard of such a thing! "Why would someone go to all that trouble when you can buy premade bullets off the shelf?"

Patterson crossed his legs. "Normally it's done to make sure the bullet will splinter or explode when it enters the body, thereby insuring maximum damage resulting in certain death. People are usually taught how to do it from someone else."

"Oh." My voice was barely discernible, I could feel my face drain of color. They looked at me. I looked at them.

"Listen Patterson," I said, "that sounds like a professional hit man to me. I sure don't know anybody like that!" Thank goodness! I shivered. The thought alone gives me the willies. Goose bumps popped up on my arms. Oh my gosh, Mike!

"The bullets are the reason you're including those dead thugs with Mike's murder?" I was astounded.

"What do they and all this hollow-point business have to do with Mike? I mean," I swallowed hard, "Mike doesn't hang with violent thugs." I could feel my eyes twitching.

There were only the side table lamps on as the sun was still on its way going down. I got up and nervously went around switching on every light in the room and in the hall.

The officers sat silently waiting for me to return and sit back down. I nervously crossed then uncrossed my legs. If I'd had a pen I would have been clicking it obsessively to distract myself.

Occasionally Patterson and Newman would look at each other and then at me.

"Your friend was killed by the same type of bullets." As he spoke, Patterson looked away, his voice low.

"I... I... he... what?" Stunned, I dropped my arms on the arms of the chair, my mouth fell open. Shaking my head I brought my hands to my eyes and covered them. I was afraid I was going to embarrass myself and cry.

Patterson and Newman sat quietly, politely waiting for me to get a grip on my emotions.

I smoothed my hair that Julia said looked like wheat shining in the morning sun, back behind my ears with both hands. I breathed deeply a couple of times to calm myself.

I leaned forward with my fingers laced and my forearms on my knees. First I stared at the floor then I looked up at Patterson.

"I don't understand. Mike was a good guy. He had a wife and baby girl. He didn't violate the law. He worked with his dad for Pete's sake! You guys must have it wrong. You need to trot back to your lab and do your tests over again. Y- you've made a mistake!" I know I sounded like a whiny kid, but gee, I couldn't imagine, poor Mike. I felt so confused. I plopped back against the sofa cushions.

"I know you're upset, Mr. Dixon. This has to be very difficult for you, losing a close friend and all. But," Patterson smiled sadly, "it's true. Michael Joseph Casey was killed by the same kind of bullets as those lowlifes in the city I was telling you about, and almost certainly with the same gun."

My head swung up, my startled eyes met his. "How do you know that?" I was thinking that someone had found the weird bullets or bought them from a crook or something.

"Really, Mr. Dixon. You watch television. Everyone knows about ballistic tests these days." One side of his mouth pulled back in a half smile. He looked at me like I thought the moon was made of cheese, same old patronizing Patterson.

"Yeah, I know about that ballistics stuff. What kind of gun was it?" I asked, although knowing what kind of gun it was would mean absolutely nothing to me. I don't own a gun, they scare the heck out of me!

Putting his glasses back on, the detective lowered his eyes to the notebook. He licked a finger and pushed a few pages until he found the description the lab had faxed to him.

"It's a Fabrique Nationale. The Fabrique is a small handgun made in Belgium, it has only a two-inch barrel. The guns were manufactured between 1931 and 1983. This one will be tough to trace. It may have even been used in World War ll. That means it could have passed through a lot of hands and never been registered. And," he searched the notebook for more information.

"We believe this particular Fabrique is called a '*Baby*'. It's small, light and square with no safety or slide lock and can be easily hidden in a purse or a pocket. The gun is a semiautomatic and obviously quite deadly."

Patterson took his glasses off again, his brown eyes seemed to bore a hole right through my head. I liked it better when a thin pane of glass was between us. The glasses awarded me a feeling of protection even if they weren't much of a shield.

Newman sat on the couch. She didn't contribute to the conversation, but she nodded her head vigorously at every word Patterson uttered.

"So, Mr. Dixon, do you or anyone you might know own a gun such as the one I just described?" The detective crossed his arms and tapped his glasses against his side while waiting for my response.

Laughably, Newman unknowingly mimicked him. She crossed her legs when he crossed his; she even leaned forward when he did. I would have chuckled if the subject matter wasn't so serious and painful.

"How can you possibly know what typed of gun was used? The bullets couldn't tell you that?"

"Ah," Patterson's brow wrinkled. "We pulled tons of surveillance tapes all over the area of the death of the couple. The person stays well out of range of cameras, but there was a fleeting shot of the pistol that was caught by a camera outside of the motel room."

My eyebrows rose. "Really? But no pic of the perp?"

He shook his head. "The person was drawing the gun just as the door to the motel room was opening. The camera was angled wrong, it caught the gun, but missed the body and the hand that held the gun. Didn't get a good shot of the clothes either. We're lucky it at least captured the weapon."

No, lucky would have been a good clear photo of the killer. Then they would have been arrested and possibly Mike would still be alive.

Somewhat annoyed, I said, "No Detective, I do not own, nor do I know anyone that owns a gun like the one you've described. What kind of people do you think I hang around with for heaven's sake?" I was a little peeved that he even asked me that.

"Gee Mr. Dixon, it wasn't my friend who has just been shot to death." Patterson sneered sarcastically.

I jumped up. Choking on my words I spat out, "I've had enough of you talking down to me like I'm a moron. I don't need this. Don't you have any compassion? I've just lost a best friend! You can leave now if you're done with your cruel inquisition!"

Angrily, I gestured towards the door. Boy, what a creep this guy is, and his sidekick Pocahontas the mimic or whatever! They didn't budge.

"Sit down, Mr. Dixon. I'm sorry if I've hurt your feelings. It's been a long day, and we're only doing our jobs. We are trying to solve these murders you know." His attempt at placating me was admirable.

"I have just a few more questions to ask you." He clicked his pen.

Very slowly I sank back down onto my chair.

"Where is your wife, Mr. Dixon?" Patterson queried.

"She's gone to the grocery store. What do you want with her, anyway? She hasn't known Mike very long," I said defensively. Crossing my arms in front of my chest, I glared at him.

Patterson said, "We need to question everyone who has ever been involved with the Caseys or the deceased couple in Sherwood City. After all," he smiled, "someone was peeping at your wife, remember? We don't know if any of these incidences are related."

"Right," I said sneering, "you guys never did find the peeper, or the guy who broke into my house. Maybe if you were doing your job, Mike might still be alive! Think about that." I nodded my head triumphantly at the two of them.

Patterson rubbed behind his ear with his pen. He asked, "Are you familiar with any of Mike Casey's gambling habits?"

Chapter Twenty

$\mathcal{I}$ shook my head. "No. Other than local football pools at the Turquoise Bar and Grill, and the Florida Lottery, we all buy tickets for that."

"Uh huh." Patterson examined his notes, jotting down what I said.

I relaxed a hair; the glasses were back on.

"We believe the two people that were killed in the city were heavy into gambling. We found quite a few bookie numbers, and horse race bulletins scattered around the man's apartment. The bookies we questioned didn't know much.

"But they did recognize the male victim, although they didn't know much about him, just his first name, Tom, or Tommy. He called in most of his bets, probably from the bar at the corner of the street he was living on.

"There was a phone in the hotel room he was staying in but it was out of order and we didn't find any cells on him or the lady. The suspect likely took them with them."

I stared blankly at the detective, I don't know why he was telling me this.

"Let's see the bar next to the hotel is the," he flipped a few pages back in the notebook. "The Posh Pub it's called." He smirked. "Hardly posh, the place is a dive."

Beside him, Newman snickered, then straightened her face when Patterson frowned at her. Apparently he was the only one allowed to be amused at the information.

Anyway," he read on, "we sent a couple of flatfoots over to Gulf Stream Park, Hialeah and Calder Race Tracks. Apparently, Tom Allen was a regular at Gulf Stream, and a couple of people recognized his picture at Calder."

He glanced again at his notes. "When they found his body, the remains of a buxom blond female," he referred to his notes, "we identified through her prints as Annabelle Grace Cranston, was located on the floor next to the bed." He closed the notebook and removed his glasses.

"Now," Patterson said looking up at me. "When we flashed around a picture of the deceased female at the track, no one recognized her. But, witnesses did say Allen was occasionally seen with a woman. Unfortunately, not one person could describe her very well.

"They said she never came up to the counter with Allen, and she wore big hats and sunglasses. All the men agreed she was a looker, but they couldn't specifically say why." Patterson reached into an inside pocket of his suitcoat. He pulled out a dog-eared photograph and held it out to me.

Uneasily I took it, barely holding it between my thumb and forefinger as if it could bite me. I didn't want to touch it, feeling as if the bad karma could reach out and get me. Timorously, I looked down at the picture.

Phew. I had been afraid it was a photo of the woman after she was found dead. Of course that would be silly because the paper had reported that her face was bashed in, that they had needed fingerprints to identify her.

I studied the picture. It was a grainy mug shot. But I knew I had never seen her before in my life. She was one of those lowborn, big blowsy kind of girls. Fried and dyed, with unhealthy looking bottle-blonde hair, gobs of make-up, fake eyelashes, the whole nine yards.

She was wearing a prison uniform in the picture, but you could tell she was extremely voluptuous, just on the verge of fat, and her face was hard. The old saying came to mind; she looked rode hard and put away wet. She gave me the creeps.

I thrust the picture back to Patterson and shuddered. "I don't know her, never seen her before."

Patterson took the photo and stuffed it back into his pocket. He handed me another picture.

Reluctantly, I took the picture from him. Hmmm. The man was average looking. Dark hair and eyes, beady eyes, at least they looked beady to me, he looked pretty muscular.

"Hey…" Curious. "How big is this guy?" I asked.

Patterson took the picture from me and looked at the markings on the back.

"He WAS," he emphasized the was, "around 6'4 and 220 lbs. The picture is deceiving. He looks like a little weasel in the photo, but he must have been quite a large man. The people at the pony races all said they remembered him because he appeared menacing to them just because of his size. They described him as imposing and threatening."

"You know," I said thoughtfully, "actually he seems familiar to me. I think he could have been the guy that broke into my house." Holy cow.

This is really freaky. Looking at a picture of a dead guy that might have actually been in my home! Oh my God! Julia and I could have been murdered!

"Patterson," my voice shook, I was truly afraid, "what's going on? I'm suddenly totally scared!"

I stood up and looked at the clock over the television. Where in the heck was Julia? I raked my hands worriedly through my hair and started pacing. Running to the window, I pulled back the curtains and peered out into the black night, panicking.

"Calm down Dixon." Patterson stood up, Officer Newman leapt up with a snap next to him.

"We have an officer sitting out in front of your house. He'll stay for a few days until we get a handle on what's going on."

161

He looked at his watch. "Well, I had hoped to speak with your wife." He folded his glasses and closed the notebook, tucking them and the pen inside the breast pocket of his suitcoat. He patted both trouser pockets then reached into one and pulled out a card.

He handed the card to me. "Please have her give me a call tomorrow. I have just a few questions to ask her, standard stuff."

The pair turned towards the door. But now I didn't want them to leave! I stepped between them and the door.

"Don't you have some more questions of me? More pictures to view? Perhaps I didn't look closely enough at the Cranston woman, maybe I have seen her before!" I anxiously reached out for the picture.

Ignoring me, Patterson opened up the other side of his suitcoat and slipped the photographs inside.

"Mr. Dixon, you'll be okay. Officer Henry Roberts is parked right out front. Just holler if you need him. It's late; we've got to go. Come on Penny." He motioned for Officer Newman to follow him.

He opened the door and the two stepped out into the darkness.

"Remember, please have Mrs. Dixon buzz me in the morning. You have a good night now." He moved down the steps, Newman followed, practically glued to his back.

"Yeah, bye, thanks a lot," I called bitterly after them. "Yeah, see ya, don't worry about us, we'll be fine, really." Harrumph. I watched until they drove off.

A patrol car was parked on our swale. A uniformed man waved a brief greeting at me. I hailed him back.

Feeling somewhat safer, I closed the front door, leaving the porch light on.

Backing inside so no one could sneak up on me, I realized the house was lit up like a museum. I had every light in the place burning. Prowling about like a caged hamster, I opened every door, looked in every room, every closet. I even looked under the bed.

Dashing around the house, I checked every lock and all of the windows to make sure everything was securely closed and locked.

After thoroughly re-checking everything twice, I returned to the brightly lit living room, and sat huddled in a terrified lump on the couch, waiting petrified with fear for my wife to return.

Fifteen minutes later, she came in the front door carrying two empty leashes in one hand, and a bag of groceries in her arms.

Closing the door, she said, "Hey Rusty, there's a police car parked out front. The cop waved at me when I got out of the car. What's going on?"

"Where are the dogs?" I asked nervously, but didn't move off the couch. She set the bag on the coffee table, laying the leashes next to it.

"I let them out to the backyard, I think they ran straight to their doghouse. Why?" She sat down next to me on the sofa.

I told her about Patterson's visit, describing the photographs, and told her he wanted her to call him in the morning.

She frowned. "Why does he want to talk to me? I've only known your friends less than a year." She sounded apprehensive.

"It's okay honey." I patted her knee. "He said he has to question everybody that has known Mike in the past few years, and you are of course part of our tight knit group. He can't have too much to ask you."

"Well, I hope I don't have to look at any awful pictures, that would be so gross, you know, looking at dead people. Ick." She shivered. She twisted a lock of hair, a habit I've noticed she does when she's worried or nervous or has something on her mind.

"What did the people look like?" she asked. She was staring at the top button of my shirt. Her face was tense.

"Don't freak out, baby. It wasn't that morbid. The photos are of the people when they were alive. Now I don't want you worrying your pretty little head about all this. I'll take care of us, everything will be fine, you'll see."

I smiled brightly at her, hugging her to my chest. "It'll all be okay." She snuggled against me.

We sat for a long time, staring wide-eyed at the front door.

Chapter Twenty-One

Boom!

A huge crash coupled with a terrifyingly brilliant bolt of lightning blinded me. I jolted straight up in bed. Wow! That was a close one!

I padded to the window and pushed the curtains aside.

Crooked fingers of crackling lightning zigzagged and streaked across the sky followed by deafening crashes of thunder.

I could see the police car still in front of the house. The car and officer shone clear as a bell every time the lightning flashed around them in the sky.

Normally the lightning wouldn't unnerve me, but I was feeling a bit skittish these days. I looked over at Julia. She was sleeping like a baby.

I could hear soft, gentle snores from under the tumble of hair and pillows. Lucky her. The drunks and innocents never have a problem sleeping.

Yawning, I glanced at the clock. The display read 5:00 a.m. Still drowsy but too edgy to sleep, I wandered downstairs. Already the storm was moving off. The time lapse between the thunder and flashes of lightning grew greater and greater.

I went into the kitchen and puttered around making coffee. By the time the coffee was ready, the rain had let up and the thunder was only a vague rumbling in the distance- just like a typical Florida storm. Hitting hard and nasty, then gone in less than thirty minutes.

I'd rather have it like that, crash, boom and over. Not like it is up north where it piddles and drizzles for dreary weeks on end, staying cold and damp for so long the chill creeps right into your bones. That is so depressing.

There's something excitingly violent and cleansing about our storms here in the south, although I can live without the darn hurricanes.

I slurped a little coffee then decided I would use up some of my nervous energy and take the pups for a walk. I decided that murders don't happen in good neighborhoods with cops watching out front, and the sun beginning to rise. I cringed when I remembered Mike was found at dawn with a security guard nearby.

Oh well, I'm sure I'll be safe with our two lively dogs. Retrieving the leashes from where Julia left them on the table last night, I opened up the back door.

"Here puppies, come!" I shouted. Within seconds the pair came bounding out of their doghouse, ears flapping, tongues flopping, tails wagging. They bounced and jumped around me as I tried to put their leashes on.

"Behave now Boris, get over here Muffy!" I commanded the pups. The dogs finally tethered and leashes clasped tightly in hand, I took off out of the yard and down the street.

The dogs strained at their ropes, sniffing every scent in town. I waved a jaunty hello to the cop in the car. I felt a little silly now, acting like a frightened fawn last night.

It's a lot easier to be brave in the daylight, walking down your own street with two dogs by your side than it is in the dark alone at night.

We scooted along the river, so serene and lovely. It was hard to imagine such horror and brutality had occurred so close to home. I tried to shove the thoughts of Mike and the murdered hoodlums out of my mind.

It was too nice a day to have gory thoughts of killings encompassing me like an ugly aura. Determined to enjoy the day, I surged on following the walk that wound along the river. I admired the water flowing smoothly, the emerging sunlight twinkling in paths dimpling and curling across the river.

With one hand in my pocket and the other firmly clutching the leashes, I let the dogs lead the way. Soon they were yapping as another early riser advanced towards us. A boisterous Terrier struggled to get closer and check out my babies.

"Hi Joan, how's things?" I greeted a neighbor. She attends the same church as Julia and I. Hopefully she's a more regular attendee than we are. After the baby is old enough, I'm sure we'll be more regular then.

We chatted for a few minutes, allowing the three dogs to sniff each other. When Boris started becoming more amorous with the Terrier, I decided it was time to move on. I just don't know where Boris gets it from, he's been fixed. Like stepfather like son I guess.

We walked down to where the mouth of the river mingled with the intracoastal as the current moved towards the ocean. There were already quite a few boats barely bobbing lightheartedly on the almost smooth as glass water.

Pelicans and gulls circled and sometimes bombed the water around the boats searching for escaped bait. Since there were still empty lots at the dead end of the street, I let the pups off their leashes. They played happily in the tall grass, chasing each other and butterflies.

I could feel the weight of the tragic past few weeks shed like a snakeskin. I drew in deep, cool breaths of clean air, in with the good, out with the bad.

I decided that Mike's death must have been an accident. It was more comforting to think that a deliberate killer wasn't that close to home. Maybe Mike had been innocently involved with the wrong people, gamblers and the like.

We hadn't really seen a lot of him since that last Saturday night before all hell had broken loose. That night was certainly a harbinger of things to come!

I thought about Sandy, wondering how she was getting on. Mike had been such a huge part of her life for so long, I'm sure she's having a hard time functioning without him around. Poor girl. She has Grandma Amy; that should help.

Amy is good support and Sandy won't have to worry about Bonnie. That reminded me about Amy's nocturnal sojourns. I wondered what's up with that? Could her secretive jaunts have anything to do with Mike?

What on earth would an old lady be doing out for hours late at night? As much as I liked and respected Amy, I think I'll mention her suspicious outings to the police.

I shook my head. "Don't be ridiculous," I scolded myself. Picturing an elderly Amy, knee-highs showing under her long flowered dress, brandishing a huge firearm in her withered, age-spotted hand and saying something like, "Your money or your life!"

What a sight! I broke into peals of laughter. I'm such a fool and so easily amused. I looked around quickly, hoping no one had seen me standing alone in the middle of the road, laughing like an idiot to myself. If Julia were here she'd tell me what a big goof I am!

"Boris! Muffy! Come on pups!" I called the dogs. If I were lucky, breakfast would be sitting on the table waiting for me to devour! I ran all the way, well at least a couple of yards, up the road and over the ridge.

When we finally reached home, I bent down and scooped up the paper that was lying in a muddy puddle. Things are back to normal, I can breathe easily again!

I took the dogs around back. Unleashing Muffy's collar, she immediately ran free. Then, as I was unhooking Boris' leash, I managed to drop the paper and the dog snapped it up. He ran towards the back of the yard.

"Boris!" I yelled, "bring that paper back to me!" I was exhausted and in no mood for games!

The dog ran up to me, and just as I reached out for the paper, he hopped back and then took off again. I was sure he was laughing at me. Muffy sauntered over to the doghouse and went inside. Time for her mid-morning nap, and mine too!

"Okay Boris, now I'm serious, get over here with that paper!"

He must have noted the threatening tone in my voice because he zipped right over with the paper and stopped in front of me.

"Good puppy," I praised him. While scratching his head with one hand, I pointed to the ground with the other. "Drop the paper, Boris. That's a good boy!"

He was just about to open his mouth and drop the paper, when he turned and took off hell for leather to the doghouse.

"Damn!" I swore under my breath, so much for my being the master. I trod heavily over to the small white house with **The Pups** painted in black across the front.

Kneeling down on the wet grass, I poked my head through the small arch that was their doorway. I could see the two dogs sitting against the back wall, drooling, watching me make a fool out of myself. Geez, sometimes life is sooo hard!

I put a hand on the ground inside the house to steady myself. The paper was lying just inside the door. Quickly, I snagged the paper before either doggy could make off with it again.

Yeah, I needed to let go of the newspaper and stick with the net. Some day. It's just, I liked the feel of the inked paper in my hand, I can fold it and flip it, and go back and forth through articles. I get more of a tangible feel of the words I'm reading when I can tough them.

Crouching, I bent backwards out of the house. I felt something on my hand. I looked at my palm. Something was stuck to it. A stamp. I peeled it off and looked at it.

Expecting to see the run of the mill postage stamp, I was taken aback when an unusual looking stamp lay cradled in my palm. I picked it up carefully by a corner.

Pushing my glasses up to peer through the bifocals, I studied the tiny square. I had never seen a stamp like that before.

A winter scene was depicted on the face. A man and woman in colorfully warm attire were pictured sitting in a sleigh that was being pulled through the snow by two horses. Up in the corner was printed: 10 Cents, U.S.

Wow, I thought, I wonder if this is worth any bucks. Hey, I could be a millionaire! I carefully placed the stamp in my shirt pocket. Dragging the paper through the slushy grass, I tried not to groan as I stood up, my knees creaked like an old geezer's.

Julia was in the kitchen whisking eggs and milk together in a bowl.

"Hey! Look what I found!" I grabbed her around the waist, kissed her hard on the lips then presented the stamp.

Julia glanced at the stamp as she set the bowl and whisk down. She pulled open a drawer, took out a gingham yellow apron and tied it around her waist.

"Hmmm," she mumbled as she poured the yellow foam into a pan gurgling with hot butter on the burner, "that's nice." She smiled absently as she sprinkled salt and pepper over the already bubbling omelet.

Striding over to the counter, she picked up a bag of bread, removed two slices and quickly buttered them.

When she popped open the toaster oven, I slipped out of the room. Julia was obviously not as interested in my find as I was! First thing tomorrow, well right after work anyway, I'm going to check out some stamp collecting stores in town. I need to know how many thousands, maybe millions I'm gonna be worth!

I put the stamp in my wallet where I knew it was safe. Then I booked up the stairs to change my clothes before breakfast was ready.

Chapter Twenty-Two

$\mathcal{I}$ could hardly wait for the last computer on today's work order to download.

I spent the past few hours painstakingly trying to retrieve lost material. You always know that it's in there somewhere, but where?

Finally, I found the customer's missing document in a different file than he thought he'd saved it in. I locked up my equipment, wrote some paperwork detailing what I'd done and then practically ran down to Art's office.

"Hey Jill!" I grinned ecstatically at the secretary. "Here's my entire completed work-order for today! Finished! Finito!" I tossed the paperwork onto her desk.

Jill removed the earpiece that connected her to the phone and swiveled her chair to face me.

"You know Rusty, when you speak that Spanish so eloquently- like a swashbuckler- it really turns me on!" Laughing at her silliness, she reached for the papers.

"I can't believe you're done already! I've never seen you work so fast. What, do you have a hot date or something?" She leaned forward and winked lasciviously.

I laughed. "No, that's not until much later tonight. Right now I need to see a man about a stamp!" I pulled out my keys from my pants pocket.

Jill frowned. "A stamp? You have a date with a stamp? Last time I looked, their figures were pretty square!" She outlined a square with her fingers in the air.

I shook my head. "No, silly woman. A stamp, a collector's stamp I think. I found this stamp in the dogs' house at home. It must have gotten stuck on one of the pups' paws. The ground has been wet from all that rain. When they got inside the doghouse and dried, the stamp probably loosened and dropped off. I found it this morning."

Taking the stamp out of my wallet, I turned it around in my fingers examining it. "It looks brand new, not at all damaged. I'm hoping it's worth a fortune and I can retire and live on the French Riviera!" I held the stamp out so Jill could look at it.

"Wow!" She said, "I know absolutely zilch about stamps. It is pretty though. I hope it keeps you out of the doghouse and brings you into a Big one, Rusty!"

"Jill," I said seriously. "I already have the 'Big One.' I'm hoping for some money!" I laughed uproarishly at myself.

Jill threw her head back in mock disbelief, rolling her eyes she laughed at my foolishness as well.

"Okay, I'm outta here. Say goodnight to the boss for me!" I tucked the stamp back into my wallet and high-tailed it.

I sailed out the front door and back around to the parking lot to my truck. I found the Bronco where I always park it, under the biggest Black Olive tree in the lot!

The tree drips sticky sap all over my paint job, but it's worth it when the car is ten degrees cooler than if it had been baking in the hot sun all day.

As soon as I got in the truck, I pulled out a list of stamp collecting stores I had written down. During my lunch hour I scoured the yellow pages for some shops. I figured I'd hit the small local places first.

The stamp might belong to someone in the area and I sure didn't want to be accused of stealing! I probably should put an ad in the paper as well. The first store on the list was called Stamps for the Memories. It was the closest store to me right now, right over Cactus Creek Road, off I-95.

The **Stamp Pad** was next nearest. I could hop right on the main boulevard to Federal Highway. Punching the truck in gear, I roared off. Traffic was outrageously heavy. The snowbirds were flocking down in droves and it's not even really that cold up north yet.

Seeing my exit notice, I turned off the expressway.

Traveling slowly down the boulevard, I read the address on my list -1212 NE 5th-hmmm, the 12th block crossing 5th...There's a string of strip malls. I saw the sign for Honeyhill Plaza. The shop I'm looking for should be in there.

Pulling in, I scanned the names of the stores while avoiding plowing over pedestrians. I spotted it. Such a teeny shop, I'd almost missed it. Parking the truck in front of the store, I got out and went up the walk to read the sign.

It said, **Stamps for the Memories and other Memorabilia. We buy and sell stamps, coins and baseball cards.** A smaller sign below it said Closed.

I went up to the door anyway and tried to turn the knob. It was locked. The lights were off inside. Darn.

Cupping my hands around my eyes, I pressed against the glass and peered in. The shop was hardly bigger than a closet. There were two glass counters displaying mostly stamp books, but I could see coin books as well.

There was also a lot of miscellaneous junk piled around. Comic books and baseball cards were showcased in the window, so was a lot of dust. I looked at the sign on the door.

Open Mon-Sat, 9:00 a.m. to 7:00 p.m. I glanced at my watch, 6:30. Hmmm, they must not be too busy. Oh well. I climbed back into the Bronco and looked to see where The **Stamp Pad** was located. I had also written down another store.

Let's see. I unfolded the paper I'd brought. **Stuck on You, Stamps and More.** That was further out west. It would take me

40 minutes to get there from here. I'll just check out **The Stamp Pad**.

Back on the expressway, I could see cars coming towards me with their lights on. It was black behind them in the distance- right where I was heading. Within minutes the rain struck.

Even with the wipers on high, visibility was poor. Cars were pulling over to the side of the road to sit out the worst of it. Persevering, I forged on. It looked clear beyond the dark storm clouds that had gusted in so quickly.

Struggling to see through the foggy, streaming windshield, I rubbed my sleeve across my forehead, wiping away the perspiration.

The clouds soared overhead, whipping across the sky. They moved so fast it looked like someone was blowing them along. I had slowed the truck down during the worst of the deluge, but as it lessened, I accelerated rapidly, dashing past the scaredy-cats that were plodding along in the far right slow lane.

Now I was moving so fast I almost missed my exit. Veering east, I raced down the ramp to the main road that runs north and south. Slowing down, I looked for Turtle Trail Drive. It was supposed to bisect the main road.

Oops, there it was. Passed it. I moved into the left lane to make a U-turn. Turtle Trail Drive was a busy little street lined with souvenir and antique shops.

The area was quaint in a funny way. Many of the buildings were designed in a western motif. A burger joint actually had a hitching post out front for horses. Hay and chickens were sold along the road. It was like I was driving through a whole different state!

The Stamp Pad was pocketed right between a country diner advertising the best apple pie in town and a convenience store that was dolled up with butter churns and milk cans.

Parking the truck, I hustled up to the 'Pad', hoping it wasn't closed too. Upon opening the glass door, I heard a bell tinkle overhead, announcing my presence.

Hesitating in the doorway, I looked around. This store was also small, about the size of a postage stamp. Ha ha. Amused at my own joke, I took in the metal displays of comic books and baseball memorabilia. The shop was a twin of the other one. Except this one had customers in it.

I stepped up to the counter. Behind the glass table, a white-haired, rotund fellow was gabbing with a customer. It appeared that they knew each other well, because they both were leaning on the glass fairly close to one another, and were obviously just shooting the breeze.

The bell at the door chimed again as a customer left. The store clerk never looked up nor made a break in his conversation. Fishing seemed to be the important topic.

Wandering around, I checked out the merchandise. Stopping in front of the baseball card display, I could have kicked myself. All those Mickey Mantles and Henry Aarons I used to trade with the other kids. Now they're gold mines, if I'd only kept them.

Thinking of big bucks, I moved along, skipping the coins. Tucking my hands into my jean's pockets, I made my way back to the stamp counter. It was the biggest display.

There were books and books and more books! Personally, I thought, as I gazed at the stamps, they're pretty boring. I mean, a stamp is just a stamp after all. There's got to be a gazillion of them on the earth.

"Can ah hep yew?" a voice drawled.

I was so intent on the stamps I didn't notice the two men had stopped talking and were looking at me. They hadn't budged an inch. They were still leaning on the counter, but now they were watching me with a distinct lack of interest.

"Oh, uh, yeah, uh..." Feeling my shirt pocket, I fumbled for the stamp. There was only a comb there. I patted the front and then the back pockets of my jeans, spare change in the front. Oh yeah! Now I remember, I put it in my wallet.

Pulling out my wallet, I opened it and rummaged through an accumulation of bits and pieces of pretty much useless papers. I thumbed through old receipts, phone numbers, lottery tickets, oh, there it was. I pinched the stamp and held it out to the clerk.

"I found this stamp. I was wondering if it's valuable."

The clerk moved away from the guy he had been talking with. The buttons on his shirt were straining over his huge belly, ready to pop off any second. Ten to one the guy plays Santa at Christmas. He moved closer to me and held out his hand.

I placed the stamp carefully into the old man's pudgy palm. He pushed his glasses to the top of his head and reached for a magnifying glass. Holding the glass over the stamp, he brought it closer to his red-veined face.

Muttering, "Hmmm," he moved the glass back and forth. The customer he'd been yakking with yawned loud and long.

Scratching his thinning pate, the clerk left the counter and disappeared through a door that was behind him.

Looking around nonchalantly, I whistled tunelessly. The customer next to me had pulled a catalogue in front of him and was indifferently leafing through it. We were the only people in the shop now. I smiled at the man.

"How ya doin'?" I asked politely.

Never looking up from his catalogue, he snorted, "Middlin'."

I strummed my fingers on the glass counter, humming. "Dum de dum de-"

The man turned and looked at me, his face expressionless. I cleared my throat. Where'd that clerk go for Pete's sake?

Finally, the fat man eased back through the doorway. He had a thick book opened and held in his hand. The stamp was resting on a page. Moving ponderously slowly, he reached the counter.

Setting the book on the counter, he picked up the stamp and shuffled through the pages. Hesitating at a page, he ran a sausage-plump finger down the pictures.

He stopped suddenly and leaned in, scrutinizing the book. Holding the stamp between his thumb and forefinger he examined it again under the magnifying glass.

"Well?" I was getting impatient. It was irritating being ignored while I watched this portly gentleman at an agonizingly snail's pace, search up and down, page after page.

The man peered at me through his eyeglasses. He shoved his thumbs through each suspender. The customer looked over with interest.

"Sonny," the old clerk drawled, "what's your name, boy?"

I gulped. "Rusty Dixon."

He thrust his hand out. "Hi," (Although it sounded more like 'hah'). "Ah'm Graham Archibald Cahtah the Third." We pumped arms. His fleshy hand almost completely enveloped mine.

"Please to me you Mr. Carter," I said.

"Mistah Cahtah was mah daddy. Call me Gray or Gravy. All mah friends call me Gravy. Righty Andrew?" He winked at the customer who had turned back to the catalogue he was reading.

"Harrumph," was Andrew's response as he hunched his shoulders.

"Well boy," Gravy Carter started to say.

I interrupted him. "That's uh, Rusty, sir."

"Uh huh. Now, this'n stamp here, boy, well, it wuz printed in 1974 by Krause. It's paht of three stamps that were ah special Christmahs issuew. The title of the issue was called 'The Road-Winter' or sum such, done bah Currier and Ives. It wuz worth ten cents in '74 and about 25 cents now."

"Oh." I was disappointed, big deal, 25 cents. Bummer.

"But," Gravy Carter continued. "If'n ya'll had the full panel of 'The Road', or sheets of all three stamps of the issuew, well," he put his thumb and finger to his bottom lip, tugging on it in thought.

"Well?" I encouraged him to go on.

"Hmmm." He beamed at me. "Could be worth a couple a hunnert dollahs!"

Not exactly the gold mine I was expecting.

He closed the book with a thud.

"Oh, Mr. Carter," I asked. "Do collectors keep records of what and to whom they buy and sell?"

"Sure Sonny. We hafta keep track of sales for the IRS, and fer shows, ya know, exhibitions and the like. Lotta customers ask us fer somethin' special and we may know who has that particular stamp and we give 'em a call."

"Could you tell me the previous owner of this stamp? I mean of course if it was purchased here." He handed the stamp back to me.

"Sure Sonny. In fact, ah know ah've seen that'n before. But it'll take sum searchin'. Ah have a huge inventory and mah record keepin' ain't the best! Need a secatary I do!" He laughed.

"But raht now ah'm about to close up and get me a cold 'un next door and jaw sum more with Andrew there. Raht Andrew?" He looked at the man standing with apparent boredom beside me.

"Yup." The man of many words never looked up from his magazine. I quickly jotted down my name, and both home and work numbers.

"Thanks Mr., uh, Gravy. I appreciate your time. Please let me know if you find anything." I handed him the slip of paper.

Nodding to Andrew who was now watching me through half-closed lids, I turned to leave as he was putting a cigarette to his lips. It's closing time *fer sher*. Leaving the dark shop, I felt as if I was emerging from a dank cave.

I strolled to the truck enjoying the still bright sunshine. I-95 had lightened up since it was well past the rush hour. Disappointed that I wasn't on the verge of becoming a millionaire, I scurried home.

Chapter Twenty-Three

$\mathcal{I}$ had pretty much forgotten about the stamp by the end of the week. Alone it wasn't worth anything. Even if I had the whole series, it was only valued at a few hundred dollars.

Not that I'm knocking a couple of hundred bucks! But it makes no difference anyway because I don't have the other stamps.

Julia and I were arguing about going to Sunday dinner at my folks' house when the phone rang. About the only subject Julia and I ever disagree about are my parents. Dad thinks Julia is cute and all, but he says she's standoffish.

I've told him she's extremely shy, but he still says she acts snooty. My mom says she has no 'people'. What are 'people'? I always ask. What was she, hatched? It's not like we're not all human for Pete's sake!

When I was in college, my grandparents used to get me invitations to debutante parties all the time. I hated to go! I had to dress up to the nines and make small talk with superficial dolls that had no direction in life except to get married to money.

It was like being in a room filled with Heathers with no escape! Talk about claustrophobia! I reached for the phone.

"Hello?" I know sounded a bit exasperated because I was dreading the tug-of-war it was going to be to get Julia to my folks'.

"That you, Sonny?"

I recognized the drawl. "Hey Mr. Cart- er, uh, Gravy! How are you?" The guy sure was a character!

"Hello, Boy. Well," he spoke achingly slowly, dragging out every word with long pauses between sentences. "Ah found that information ya'll wanted son. Are ya'll still innersted?"

I wasn't really, but I appreciated the trouble he'd gone through.

"Sure Mr. Carter, sure I'm interested."

"Okey doke," he replied. I could hear paper rustling as he read slowly into the phone.

"Uhhh...here it is...okay...the previous owner of that'n stamp ya'll found was bought from me back almost Christmahs tahm last year. Regulah customer he is too."

"Uh huh..." I waited. These southern folk. It takes them forever to spit out a few short sentences. You're never sure if they're done talking or not. I'm always afraid I'll say something and then realize they were still in the middle of a sentence. Patience Rusty, patience.

"Yep. Sure did belong to a bloke name of Mike Casey. Mike's a good ol' boy. Pops in every three or four months or so...whenever he gets the itchin' to add to his collection. Apparently, his daddy got him started when he was just knee-high to a bumblebee and the boy still loves the stamps today!

"He don't buy expensive stuff, jes picks a few up when he has the extra cash. Now I 'member him sayin' he liked the stamp you found because it had a winter scene and since he lived most of his life in Florida he dreamed of the coolness and pristine snow of the North. Nice feller he is..."

Carter rambled on but I didn't hear a word he was saying. Mike? Mike? I put my hands to my head and squeezed my temples. Mike? I don't get it, how could it be? I couldn't think with the old codger babbling.

"Wait Mr. Carter, wait. Are you sure it was Mike, uh...Mike Casey you sold the stamp to?" It had to be a mistake. I found the stamp weeks after Mike was killed.

Closing my eyes, I thought back. I hadn't cleaned out the doghouse since...let's see...since, oh my gosh, I remember cleaning the house the weekend before Mike was shot. I remember because Julia was on me that the pups had fleas and she thought scrubbing the doghouse would help.

I cleaned it thoroughly and then gave both the dogs a good wash and flea dip as well. The flea problem disappeared...

The fat man continued jabbering, "Yep, I sure know ol' Mike. Big guy, black wavy hair, real loud. Will prob'ly be in soon. Seems he's been comin' up with a lot of extra money lately. Told me bizness wuz a'pickin' up and he had more bread ta throw aroun'."

Carter lapsed into silence, but I could still hear the labored breathing of an extremely overweight man.

"Mr. Carter, when was the last time you saw Mike?" I questioned.

"Hmmm, now let me ponder on that...ah think it wuz aroun' three or four weeks ago, son."

I realized the guy didn't know Mike was dead and I didn't have the heart to tell him. "Did he have the rest of the 'Road' series?" I asked.

"Um, he had sum a' them if I recollect rightly, not all, but maybe sum." I could almost hear him nodding and scratching his head.

"Well Mr. uh, Gravy, I want to thank you for all the trouble you've gone to for me, looking up your records and calling me and all. If I ever know of anyone who's collecting stamps, cards or coins I'll be sure and give them your name."

I thanked the old guy and hung up. I was sitting staring blankly at the phone when Julia came into the room.

"What's wrong, Rusty?" Mild concern laced her voice.

Sitting on the rocker, I struggled to smooth my furrowed brow. Briefly, I explained about finding the stamp and Mr. Carter and then about Mike. It totally blew my mind that I found Mike's stamp in my backyard. Somehow it had gotten there shortly before he died. How?

"That's pretty weird," Julia said. She sat next to me on the couch and opened up her sewing box. She adeptly threaded a needle.

Smokey Robinson was singing in the background. Holding the needle with two fingers, she picked up a button with her other hand and said, "One of the dogs must have gotten it stuck to their paw the last time we were at the Casey's and brought it home."

She turned her attention to the blouse and started to sew the button on it.

"Makes sense," I agreed, but I knew that wasn't true. We hadn't been over to the Caseys' with the dogs since way before summer. But then again, Carter did say Mike had bought the stamp around Christmas. So then where has it been hiding all this time?

And how did it suddenly show up in the doghouse in the past few weeks? I don't see how the stamp could have traveled home on a dog's paw, fell somewhere unseen for over nine months, get miraculously stuck on the paw again and then fall off in the doghouse.

The stamp was in way too good of condition for all that activity on a dog's paw. But I didn't want Julia worrying about it.

"Let's have lunch now, honey," I said. "I've got some work at Carpathian I need to check on." I hated to lie to my trusting wife, but I wanted to go to Mike's boat and look for the other stamps and I didn't want her to worry.

Maybe there's a clue there that the cops missed and I can find. After consuming a bowl of tomato soup and a toasted cheese sandwich, I telephoned Sandy.

"Hey girl," I greeted her when she answered the phone, "how are you doing?"

She sounded weary but not as distraught as she has been. "We're hanging in, Rusty," she said. "My family is leaving us alone a little more since you called last week. I was about to put Bonnie in a daycare to get her more used to other kids, but since, uh, you know, Mike and all," she took a deep breath.

"I think it's best right now to keep her close to home for a while. We still don't know exactly what happened. We could be in danger as well. The police still have someone watching the house. I'm glad for that, you know, but it is unnerving and it keeps the horror alive." She sighed.

"That's what I wanted to talk to about, Sandy. Do you know anything about Mike's stamp collection?"

Julia had finished her sewing and went outside to pull weeds, so I felt free to question Sandy.

Julia would just think I'd lost my mind anyway and tell me to leave the investigating to the police. She still chastises me for following our housebreaker that time. But really, how dangerous can it be to just look for a couple of stamps?

"Well, you know he's had those stamps since he was very young." Sandy sighed sadly. "They were about the only thing his father ever showed any interest in. I really don't know anything about them myself.

"I tried to buy him one a long time ago for a birthday present, and he admonished me, said I paid way too much for it. I didn't really know what he liked or what particular collection he was working on. I guess it's a personal thing like taste in art or music."

"Do you know if he took the stamps with him to the boat?" I tried to keep the query nonchalant.

"Let me think, Rusty. Hmmmm." She was quiet for a moment.

"I remember the first time he left, he took his Jim Beam of course, and beer, just a few clothes, and... oh yes! After he left the second time, you know, after the fight about the reunion... did you know he left me there and I drove home alone? He didn't show up for hours later that night. I was frantic something had happened. I guess I was right to worry!" she said wryly.

"Anyway, when he took off the second time and didn't call or come home, after a week I went and searched his closet and drawers to see how much stuff he'd taken to gauge how long he planned on being gone.

"Actually, all he took with him that time was a jacket. I'm pretty sure he took the stamps the first time. He hadn't brought anything back to the house after he'd taken them to the Bonnie

Lass. I guess he was checking the waters first to see if I had truly forgiven him." Her voice cracked a little. "What's this all about, Rusty?"

"I don't mean to upset you Sandy, you've been through enough. I just would like to look into something, nothing critical. If it means anything then I'll let you know. Have the police finished with the boat yet?" I tried to sound blasé, matter of fact.

"I think they have. I haven't really asked them. I guess I need to start looking into selling the heap." She sighed deeply again.

Still trying to sound casual, I asked, "Is the key to the cabin still there in the horn?"

"Sure, I think so. What's going on Rusty?" She was becoming curious.

"Nothing, really, Sandy, just a little something bugging me, no big deal. I'd feel foolish even telling you. Do you mind if I go to the boat and look around?" I didn't need to have her worrying about probably nothing.

Quickly losing interest and sounding tired, she said, "Go ahead, Rusty. Do whatever you want. I really don't care. I've got to get Bonnie's lunch now."

I could hear tot talk in the background. "Grandma Amy went to the store earlier. So I'll talk to you later. Say hi to Julia for me and let me know if you find whatever it is you're looking for. Bye Rusty." She hung up.

I left Julia a note telling her I'd gone to the shop. It was Saturday and I never go to the shop on Saturday. But I didn't want her worrying about nothing, so I didn't feel too guilty about my little white lie.

I put the peppershaker on the note as a paperweight, grabbed my keys and took off for the boat.

I'd been to Mike's boat numerous times over the years. Parking the Bronco, I walked along the deck that was badly in need of repair until I got to Mike's slip.

The Bonnie Lass was bobbing gently in the water. The marina was pretty secluded and well off the beaten waterway track. The guy who owned the boat in the slip next to Mike's was usually there. Ed must have seen me pull up because he came out of his cabin, hopped off his boat, and strolled towards me.

"Hey Rusty, how're ya'll doin'?" He shook my hand cheerfully. Then he looked sad. "You here to check on the boat? I'm so sorry to hear about Mike. He was a really great guy. I'm the one who called the police, you know."

"You called the police?" I was surprised. "They told us the guy who found Mike called them."

"Hell no, man. I heard the man pull up in the lot. He had a loud muffler, hard to miss. The place is so deserted most of the time that a car engine attracts my attention."

Ed and I were standing on the deck in front of Mike's slip.

"The night Mike was, um, killed, I was out at a bar, unfortunately, or fortunately for that matter. Same person coulda killed me too, or, I coulda saved Mike's life, we'll never know."

We nodded sadly together. I felt Mike's loss strongly. It must give Ed Thomas the creeps living next door to a ghastly murder scene.

"So why'd you call the police, Ed?" I asked him.

Ed stood with his hands in his pockets, staring at his boots. His face paled, his eyes darted around the marina until they lighted on Mike's boat. He hastily looked away, then back up at me.

"Hell, I heard this hideous bloodcurdling scream. It was spine chilling, man. I can still hear it at night sometimes, in my dreams." He shivered even though we were standing in the warm sun.

"I have 911 on my speedial since the marina is so remote. Kids come around in gangs, drinking and drawing graffiti all over the buildings and do drugs and have sex in the unoccupied boats. Down yonder, through those bushes near the end of the dock is a frequent make-out haven." He pointed to a thick patch of green scrub.

"The kids trash the place." He gestured to a mess of beer bottles and garbage scattered all over the area. "But, when I heard that frightful screech man, I punched that speedial without a second thought. Cops musta been in the area already, 'cause by time I was out on my bow looking over, they were pulling up, and some strange guy was running like a bat out of hell, straight to them.

"To be honest, it looked to me like the man was running for his life and the cops just happened to be in front of him by accident." He shrugged his shoulders.

"Did you tell the cops what you saw?" I asked.

Ed shifted his baseball hat on his head and tucked his loosened shirt into well-worn jeans, then shoved his hands back into his pockets. He swayed from one foot to the other.

"Naw, I didn't think nothin' of it so I didn't say nothin' to the cops. I went back inside before they saw me and watched out the window. The guy was sure shook up, though. He was shaking like an antenna on an old '47 Ford! Face as white as rice! Kinda funny now," he chuckled, "but then I had no desire to see what had spooked him!"

"What happened then?" Mirroring Ed, my shoulders hunched as I shoved my hands deeply in my pockets.

"Well, the cops, a couple of them, poked their heads in the door of the cabin. They quickly pulled right out though!" He laughed as he described some rookie cops jumping off the boat with their hands clamped over their mouths as they ran off the deck and out into the tall weeds where no one could see them.

"Could sure hear 'em, though." Snickering some more, he pulled his hands out of his pockets and crossed his arms in front of his chest.

Looking over his shoulder, I could see the Marina's sign. **Koko Kove Marina** could still be read, although the paint was badly peeling. Any windows it used to have, had all been knocked out by teens and rocks.

Graffiti in varying colors and styles was plastered all over the building as high as the kids could reach. Weeds and grass had grown up all around the building and the docks. I had had to shuffle through knee-deep grass to get to the pier. It smelled swampy.

Ed Thomas continued, "Three or four cops immediately closed off the entrance to the cabin with yellow police tape. Soon after, a van showed up, and a bunch of people in white coats hopped out while putting gloves on. The cops even had those plastic baggie booties on their feet. They looked hilarious, like big bunnies!"

Thomas sniggered, picturing the scene. Immediately he sobered. The smile left his face, his eyes shifted to the floor. "Ahem." He was ashamed of his mirth when he remembered Mike.

"Anyway, I came out and ambled on over and moseyed up to one of the rookies and asked him what was up. After I told him who I was and that I lived next door; he explained to me what was...uh...what they had found inside.

"I'm sorry buddy." He reached out and patted my shoulder awkwardly.

The anguish I kept tightly suppressed, tried to bubble up and choke me. I swallowed, breathing shaky deep breaths to get a grip on my sorrow.

"It's okay, Ed. Life goes on, you know?" I looked away quickly so he couldn't see me blinking back tears. I didn't want the guy to think I was a sissy.

"Yeah. So, uh, what brings you here, man?" He looked away too. He was probably embarrassed at my boo-hooing. Although he didn't look too great shakes himself. His eyes looked watery and a corner of his mouth quivered.

"Uh, nothing really. I just want to have a look around. Mike's wife asked me to see if there was anything of value on the boat that she might want. Otherwise she'll hire someone to clean it out and put up a for sale sign."

I shuffled my feet back and forth. I'm not used to being so untruthful to people. I'm usually so tactless I tend to blurt out the truth even if it's inappropriate. At least that's what people tell me.

Ed adjusted his hat again and fiddled with a button on his fishing shirt. It was obvious he was uncomfortable. He coughed.

"How's his wife and little girl doing?" he asked.

I shrugged my shoulders. "They're doing as well as can be expected you know, under these morbid circumstances. It's such a horrid experience for them to have to go through. Their daughter is really too young to comprehend what's happened. Sandy says the baby cries at night and first thing in the morning for her papa."

Again I had to bite my lip and sniff back tears.

Thomas looked even more uncomfortable. "Yeah, well... um, well go on about your business. If you need anything, give a holler, I'll be right inside."

"Hey, sure, thanks Ed." We shook hands and Ed Thomas wandered back into his in the slip beside Mike's. I walked the few steps to the boat and hesitated.

It looked harmless enough, calmly rocking on the sky-blue water. There was little current, barely even a ripple on the river. I was stalling. I feared what sort of macabre scene would meet me inside the sinister looking cabin.

I had never thought of it that way before. It was always just Mike's get-a-way. We went fishing on it, and took the girls snorkeling. It was fetching and fun then. Now it looked gloomy and haunted.

Pushing aside my grim thoughts, I pressed my tongue tightly between my lips and stepped over onto the boat. It rocked slightly, tilting in as I climbed on the deck.

Standing on the stern, I looked around.

Tossed carelessly in a corner ages ago, a lifejacket laid fading in the sun. There were worn ropes and a couple of well-used wooden paddles stuck in the side wells.

The brown vinyl seats were also faded from age and sun. They had rips and tears in them. Beer bottles were stuffed in a trashcan next to the captain's seat.

It was so terribly quiet. Dragonflies buzzed around, the sun poured down, the boat listed and bumped as an occasional minuscule wave pushed it against the pier.

The only sound was the squawk of a seagull soaring past the shore. The absolute stillness on what would normally be a lovely southern winter day, now felt somehow evil.

Noting nothing unusual on the deck, I turned towards the cabin. The police had closed and probably locked the door.

Next to the steering wheel on the dashboard was the horn. Moving towards it, I reached in the large grubby horn and felt around. My hand touched a key. Mike kept the key there for years. I don't think he even remembered it was there or ever used it.

I pulled it out. It was quite rusty and dirty. I blew the dust off it and walked back to the cabin.

I brushed my hand over my forehead, took a deep breath to calm my nerves then stuck the key in the old lock and turned. It unlatched. Holding my breath, I apprehensively turned the knob. The door creaked ominously as I slowly opened it.

Pushing it open further, fearfully I stuck my head in. Surprisingly, it was light in the cabin. Duh. I thought to myself, you idiot. It was broad daylight and there were only worn skimpy curtains covering the small windows.

Somehow I had expected it to be dark and scary. My skin was crawling, I rubbed the goosebumps that erupted on my arms.

I looked down before I stepped inside, remembering the description of a shoe stuck in blood to the floor. Someone had tried to wash the blood away. The dark stain was still there though, but it looked black, not red. Gag.

I almost tossed my cookies right then and there. Gulping air to quell my queasy stomach, I tried to count to ten to distract myself.

Getting a grip on my fear, I glanced around the small cabin. It hardly looked any different than the last time I was there. Some of the cupboards were open, and clothes spilled out of drawers. The police had obviously searched the place.

Stepping quickly around the dark shadow on the floor, I moved over to Mike's desk. There was a glass on the desk with a small bit of amber liquid in it. I would have thought it all would have evaporated by this time. The liquid looked like scotch or bourbon.

There were books, papers and a can of peanuts cluttering the desk as well.

Uh huh... I could see some unusual stamps peppered across the tabletop, and... well looky here.

I knelt down, knees cracking. A stamp book was face down on the floor next to the desk. The chair in front of the desk had been knocked over and lay on its side, and what looked like stamp collecting implements, a pair of tweezers, glue, and more stamps were scattered all over the floor.

After he was shot, Mike must have fallen on the desk, dragging the contents there with him to the floor. I pressed clenched knuckles to my eyes.

Oh Mike. I wondered if he was scared. Did he even see the murderer? Did he know he was going to die? He had to have seen and known the murderer, I remembered I had deduced that believing Heather had committed the crime.

I figured the door had to be closed and locked, Mike wouldn't have let just anyone in. Not at night, and not here. Plus, he must have felt comfortable with the person that was there, because apparently he had been sitting calmly at is his desk working with his stamps.

Tears started streaming down my face. I swiped at them with the back of my hand as I picked up the stamp book. Standing up, I took the book and went over to the miniature table in the galley.

I pulled a white plastic chair close to the table, sat down and studied the book. Flipping through page by page, I realized I had no idea what I was looking for. I knew zero about stamps.

Searching through the book, I figured I should look for stamps like the one I'd found. After examining the entire book I found zilch. Nada. He probably had receipts or records somewhere. I'd have to look for those too.

Maybe Mike got a hold of some big wig's stamp and he wanted it back so he killed him for it. That sounded pretty unlikely. His records were probably still at Sandy's house.

I was so engrossed in the book, that I didn't feel the boat rock, or hear the footsteps behind me.

I did hear the low, gruff voice suddenly growl, "Who the hell are you?"

My head jerked up. Standing just inside the doorway of the cramped cabin, was a scruffy looking man and he was holding a gun. I stared in instantaneous terror at the barrel.

Even in my fright I realized that he was probably not holding the murder weapon.

The police said that the gun was very small and square. This gun looked HUGE, and the barrel was at least six inches long and aimed right at me! It looked very powerful. My eyes bulged, I couldn't take them off it!

"I... I... I'm, uh... uh.. R-R-Rusty D-D-Dixon" I spat my name out, stuttering in total alarm. My body was quaking with fear! His arm rigid, the man held the gun straight at me.

"What the hell are you doing here?" Where's the money?" he snarled.

I sat immobilized in abject terror, I couldn't squeak out another word. My throat was paralyzed. Frozen in fear I gawked at the gun. My knuckles gripping the chair seat were bone white; my mouth hung wide open. At least my mouth was too dry to drool.

He must have been able to hear my heart pounding, it was beating so hard and fast I thought it was going to burst right out of my chest! He waved the pistol at me; his voice grew louder and he sounded even angrier.

"Where the hell is the money?!" he repeated, his nasty bark was probably as bad as his bite.

His taught face saw its last shave days ago, his lips were pulled back in tight fury and dark eyebrows were drawn down so hard his eyes almost disappeared, which was a good thing- I'm sure I would have fainted if I saw the evil inside him shining in his eyes. He was so mean looking he'd give Frankenstein nightmares!

My mouth opened and closed spastically, without forming any real words. "Wha...wha...wha..."

The man stepped closer. "I know there's money here. Mike was waving it all over the bar that night. I was sure he had more, that's why I tried to surprise him early Saturday morning. But I was the one surprised, wasn't I? Eh?" His laughter contained no humor.

He raised the gun and pointed it directly at my head, aiming it between my terrified baby blues. "Tell me where the money is right now or I'll plug ya and look for it myself!"

"I- I- I don't know... I.." stammering, pretty sure I was about to wet my pants, I held my shaking palms up in front of him, trying to ward off the bullets I knew were about to slam into my head, exploding my brains and splattering my blood all over the dingy walls.

Visions of Julia, pregnant with my child tossing a red rose on my coffin flashed before my eyes as I squeezed them tightly closed. I pictured my shattered body crashing to the floor, twitching violently, then lifeless eyes staring up, my blood mingling with Mike's... I tried to think of prayers, but my mind was too busy screaming.

The screams were out loud now- "Aaaaaaaaaa-"

Chapter Twenty-four

"Drop the weapon!" An authoritative voice suddenly boomed from behind the vicious thug.

I opened one eye slightly and warily peeked out.

Police had burst through the narrow doorway and were now standing akimbo with guns drawn and aimed steadily at the man in front of me.

The thug whipped his head around to look at them, but he never moved the gun from pointing at my head. I expected to hear an explosion any second blowing my brain matter all over the wall behind me.

Slamming my eyes closed again, I tried to compress myself into the chair I was on, making myself as compact a ball as I could. I figured the smaller a target I made, the less damage there'd be.

"Drop the gun now or we'll shoot!" the voice bellowed, the command ricocheted loudly off the walls.

I heard a whoosh, then an expulsion of breath. There was a whimper, but I realized that was me. When I didn't hear the deafening thunder of shooting and felt no bullets piercing my body, I cautiously opened my eyes.

There were no less than four cops in the tiny cabin, their weapons aimed directly at the thug.

Realizing he wasn't going to win the standoff, the criminal lowered his weapon to his side with a shrug.

I slumped back in the chair; relief seeped through me, relaxing my stiff body. Dropping my head back, I stared up at the stained ceiling and mumbled a prayer, thanking the Big Guy for saving my life.

"Well now, look who we have here." A familiar voice jolted my head up. Oh no, Detective Mark Patterson. I don't believe it, I groaned.

"You have some explaining to do, Mr. Dixon. Get him out of here." He motioned to the uniformed policemen to remove the hood they were handcuffing.

I dropped my head into my hands, propped my elbows on my knees and moaned.

Patterson dragged a chair over and sat down, straddling it. He rested his arms on the back of the chair. "Exactly what do you think you are doing here, Dixon?" His eyebrows rose in question.

"Uhhhh..." I sat back. "Nice to see you, Patterson. Pretty good timing, although the rookies beat you here. I owe them my life, I think." I smiled weakly at him, becoming more relaxed as I realized my demise was not imminent.

"The 'rookies' as you call them, responded to a 911 call. When I heard on the radio the location was this particular marina, I decided to see what was up. Again," he repeated, "what are you doing here?"

"Always the inquisitor, Detective," I said derisively, my arms crossed in front of my chest. "It's really no big deal." Blandly, I explained to him about the stamp and what brought me to Mike's boat. "I do have the widow's permission," I advised as I ended my story.

"You haven't explained the situation we walked in on. Remember, man with gun pointed at your melon head?" So sarcastic this detective, I wonder if he speaks to the missus in that tone.

"I don't know who the guy is. I was in here, minding my own business, with permission," I reminded him, "and suddenly, this ruffian was standing there waving a pistol at me and asking me something about money." I clasped my hands, putting them under my chin to prop up my head. I was exhausted. What an ordeal I had just been through!

"What money?" Patterson asked.

Shaking my head I replied, "I have no idea. He told me he'd seen Mike drunk as a skunk, waving a wad of money around at some bar one night, and he figured there'd be more. At least that's why he said he was here this morning.

"He said he hadn't come before because of the cops. He figured now they had cleared off the premises, it was safe to come and search. You see, *he's* the murderer. Mike wasn't killed the Thursday night like you guys said, he was killed early Saturday morning." I leaned forward, smug in my clever deciphering.

"And another thing, the guy who lives next door, Ed Thomas, well he said it was he who called the police that morning, not the hood you just arrested. Your guys have it all wrong. Ed said he saw the man arrive.

"Then minutes later he heard a horrible scream, which must have been... um... Mike... just before he was shot to death. Mike must have let him in because he knew the man from frequenting the same bar. Ed called the police the second he heard the scream.

"They got here so fast, that by time the man could scramble out of the boat, the cop cars were right there. The killer inadvertently ran straight into their arms!"

Patterson sat silently, patiently letting me explain my theory.

"Your officers had the murderer right in their hands and they let him go!" I slapped my hand into my fist in disbelief. I was astounded at their stupidity, and it showed in my voice.

"For some reason, they believed him when he said he had only discovered the body when he came to pick up Mike to go fishing. They believed his ridiculously innocuous story!"

"Did you notice the gun the suspect had, Dixon?" Patterson asked calmly.

I hesitated before saying, "Yeah, well sure, it was aimed right between my eyes for heaven's sake! The thing was the size of a canon, it darn near blocked the whole room!"

"Mr. Dixon, it's not the murder weapon, it's a totally different gun." He spoke slowly, enunciating each word carefully like he thinks there's a dunce cap stapled to my head.

"I know. So what? So the guy has more than one gun. He's a criminal, maybe he likes a variety depending on what type of job he's pulling that day." I rolled my eyes. Boy, Patterson sure could be obtuse for a detective!

Patterson patted his breast pocket but didn't take out anything.

A few officers remained. They seemed unsure of what to do next. Apparently they were waiting for orders from Patterson. And, as usual, he was grilling me, the innocent bystander!

A corner of his lip tugged in, Patterson advised me with the usual sarcastic tone, "The coroner said Casey died Thursday night, sometime between the hours of 7:00 p.m. after he was last seen buying beer at the Easy Liquor Store on the corner of Cork and Flamingo Road, and about 2:00 a.m., according to the autopsy.

"They can't pinpoint the exact time, only approximate. But he was definitely killed the night before. The coroner used medical science to arrive at his conclusions, not amateur reasoning." He watched me for my reaction.

I thought for a minute.

"Listen Detective, that guy could have shot Mike, maybe he didn't mean to. Maybe he didn't think Mike would be there for some reason, and Mike surprised him as the guy was ransacking his boat. Maybe they struggled and the gun accidentally went off.

"Then, worried that someone might have heard the shot, he got scared and ran off. Returning a day or so later, he carefully noses around, checking things out. It was quiet and deserted. No one around, especially no police.

"Satisfied that the place is vacant and no one has discovered Mike yet, he gets brave and ducks inside to continue looking for the money. Then, he must have heard the police cars coming down the road, so he panics. He has to get out of there or he'd be caught.

"Frantically, he tries to get away quickly from his crime. He's obviously petrified, frightened to death. He's scared all right, scared of the electric chair! He's a criminal, I'm sure he's a great actor! He fell right into your officers' welcoming, gullible arms.

"They kissed his boo-boos and sent a daring, ruthless, dangerous killer back out into the world. Pitiful, Patterson, just pitiful." I shook my head at their naiveté. They're trained cops for Pete's sake! Weren't they thinking?

His eyes narrowing in annoyance at me, Patterson replied, "We know who the suspect is, his name is Jack Ramsey. He's a small time hood that drinks too much to do any big jobs. We didn't find any connections between Casey and the two murdered lowlifes found in Sherwood City.

"Besides, Ramsey had an alibi for the night of the murder. He claimed he was shacked up with his ex-wife, Lola something or other. We've taken him in for more questioning, and-" He held up a hand as I opened my mouth.

"We will also charge him for numerous offenses such as attempted murder, firearm in the possession of a convicted felon, trespassing, and I'm sure we can come up with a plethora of other misdeeds he committed today." He was humoring me.

I was getting cramps in my limbs. I stood up and stretched, shaking the pins and needles out of my arms and legs.

"By the way," Patterson held out a hand, palm up, "can I see your driver's license?"

"What?" Confused, I took out my wallet, pulled out my license and handed it to him.

He didn't even look at it before he handed it back to me. "I see you're left-handed." He nodded. "You're free to go, try to stay out of trouble."

Dismissing me like he always does, like yesterday's news, he turned and stalked out the door, calling out to his people to follow him.

What in the heck was that all about? I wondered. It was time to leave this morbid place. I climbed out of the cabin and pulled the door to the cabin closed behind me, making sure it was locked.

I had no desire to ever see the depressing boat again. "Goodbye my friend," I murmured solemnly to myself, "rest in peace." Shading my eyes from the sinking sun, I made my way across the wooden deck and climbed gratefully back onto the dock.

Ed Thomas was talking to the police. I walked up to where they were standing and joined them.

"Rusty man, I'm glad you're all right! The second I saw that ugly looking creature slinking suspiciously towards the boat, I called the cops! I knew he was up to no good!" Ed vigorously shook my hand, slapping me hard on the back.

I was so grateful, I hugged him. The cops scattered to their respective cars.

"You saved my life, Ed! Thank you from the bottom of my still blood-red heart!"

"Anytime buddy!" He grinned, wiping his perspiring forehead in relief.

We chatted about the event for a while, watching the police drive away. I thanked Ed again profusely, then said goodbye, figuring I would never see him again.

Wanting nothing more than to be safe in my own home, hugging my beautiful wife as tightly as I could, I steered the Bronco recklessly, splashing through puddles and bouncing over rocks, I raced home.

Chapter Twenty-Five

$\mathcal{J}$ulia was beside herself with fear and concern when I told her what happened at the boat. Her hand pressed against her heart as her knees buckled. I caught her as she crumpled to the floor.

"I'm okay honey, really, everything is okay!" I squawked. I carried my wife to the sofa and gently set her down.

Sitting next to her, I put my arm around her and hugged her tightly to convince her I was fine.

"Oh Rusty, I can't believe the danger you keep putting yourself in! I don't understand what possesses you to get involved with gangsters and murderers and...and-" she burst into tears. Pushing me away when I tried to comfort her, she jumped up and ran into the bathroom and slammed the door.

I could hear her crying behind the door.

"Julia! C'mon honey, I'm okay. Come on out of there, sweetie." I tapped on the door.

"Listen," I said to the closed door, "I didn't go anywhere looking for trouble. I just wanted to check something out at the boat. I didn't know some hoodlum was going to show up there and try to blow my brains ou-..uh...anyway, everything turned out just right!

"It's all over baby, they have the killer behind bars. We're safe and sound and can get on with our lives. So please baby, come out of there!" I cajoled and whined while continuing to knock lightly on the door.

Hearing water running, I waited a minute. The faucet squeaked as it was turned off. I could hear Julia shuffling around inside.

"Baby?" I whispered, "are you coming out?"

"I'll come out Rusty," she said through the closed door, "if you promise me this is it with the detective work. No more investigating or 'just checking something out' stuff. If you act like James Bond one more time, I'll... I'll... well I don't know what I'll do but you will regret it! Do I make myself clear?" She threatened, sounding quite angry. I could imagine her pointing her finger at me behind the closed door.

"Yes dear, I promise, no more 007, I'm sorry." Feeling pretty sheepish, I acquiesced. I was hardly giving in reluctantly; the ordeal on the boat frightened me to death!

I'm sure when I look in the mirror, there'll be ten new grey hairs! Probably a few white ones as well, I was totally petrified when that mobster aimed that gigantic gun at me. I've had more than enough police work. From now on, I'll leave all the detecting to that jerk Patterson. The guy probably has nerves of steel, ice water in his veins, all that kind of stuff.

The lock clicked and the door swung open. Julia swept out of the bathroom with her cute nose in the air and stalked off down the hall.

"I'm going into the kitchen, we can talk later, after you take out the garbage and mow the lawn," she instructed.

I wasn't about to argue. I hate it when my precious darling gives me the cold shoulder. That usually results in a cold bed as well!

I followed swaying red hair that just brushed the tops of her shoulders, and that sassy butt swinging side-to-side in skin-tight denim shorts into the kitchen. She ignored me and went to the refrigerator, I headed for the trashcan.

The brisk air hit me when I got outside toting the garbage. What a beautiful day it turned out to be. After all that ugliness at the boat, I was grateful just to be alive!

Whistling, I dumped the garbage into the trash bin and went to get the lawn mower out of the garage. The cool air smelled wonderful, a welcome relief after the long hot summer. Even the fall had been still sweltering during the days.

Opening the garage door, I had to push a bunch of junk out of the way to get to the lawn mower. Humming, I dragged the mower out and turned it on.

By time I was done trimming the entire yard, I was a sweaty mess, and very hungry. It'd been over an hour since I left the house, so I figured Julia was over her snit by now and it was safe to go back inside.

I put the mower back, kicking the junk back in front of it and went in through the kitchen door, making a beeline for the refrigerator. I reached in for an ice-cold beer.

Greedily flipping one open, I chugged half the bottle before taking a breath. Wiping my sweaty forehead with a towel, I trotted off to the living room in search of my bride.

Julia was sitting on the couch. There were colorful papers spread out all over the coffee table. She was studying them in earnest. I flopped down next to her. She bounced slightly when my weight hit the cushions.

"What'cha doin'?" I asked.

She turned to me and thrust a handful of the pamphlets into my hands.

"What are these?" Looking down at the papers in my hands I saw they were brochures for vacations and cruises. Looked like someone was planning a trip.

"We need some time away, Rusty, a breather, change of scenery. It's been way too morbid and scary around here lately. I want to relax and feel safe and have some fun. What do you think of Tahiti?"

She opened up a pamphlet that had clear blue water and palm trees on the front, and held it under my nose.

Actually, I could use a little escapism myself. But I wasn't too sure about Tahiti or Bora Bora, we're on a budget!

"That's a good idea, sweetie, I'd like some R&R myself. But I think we need to choose something a little closer to home. How about Key West or Disneyworld, or maybe St. Augustine or someplace like that?" I gathered up a bunch of pamphlets and started leafing through them.

"Rusty, I want to go somewhere tropical where there's sun and they bring you drinks with little umbrellas in them!" Julia sat back, pouting.

"Gee honey, hello, we already live there! How much more tropical can you get than Florida?" Smiling at her I handed her a brochure on Sanibel Island.

"This isn't too far away, but it's a little more exotic than Ft. Lauderdale. Or here, Captiva Island, doesn't that sound mysterious and romantic? What do you think?"

She frowned, pushing the brochure away. "I want to get out of Florida, Rusty. I'm feeling claustrophobic and I think we've had quite enough of 'mysterious', don't you think?"

I ignored the slight sarcasm in her voice.

She continued, "I want to go someplace totally different than here, foreign but still tropical, intriguing yet relaxing. How about Bermuda?" She asked hopefully. I scanned the ads until one caught my eye.

"Here, this is perfect! Exotic, tropical, foreign, out of Florida, everything you want and it's affordable!" I handed her a brochure that had an orange parrot on the cover. She unfolded it and read it silently.

"The Bahamas... hey, Rusty, this would be great! We can sun on the beach, go snorkeling, sailing, I want to go here!" Excitedly, she shoved the pamphlet back under my nose.

"Look Rusty, look at the picture of the pastel colored hotel, it's huge and right on the sand! And look at the marlin leaping out of the water! We can go deep sea fishing too! When can we go? How soon? I've got to go get a new bikini!"

Julia jumped up and down, clapping her hands in glee, just like a little kid about to get an ice cream cone. Her cheeks were all aglow with pink and her eyes shined such a pretty green, damn but her excitement was contagious!

I was already picturing myself lounging on a beach chair, basking in the sun and drinking a frozen strawberry daiquiri. I need to get a broad straw hat and new sunglasses.

"Hey, let's call a travel agent honey and see how quickly we can get a reservation!" I quickly suggested, jumping to my feet. We could only stay for a few days because of work and money, but it'd be a great, inexpensive get-away! I was pumped to go!

"C'mon honey, let's go shopping!" I grabbed her hand and we danced happily around the living room.

Hours later, we returned laden with our purchases still buoyant with eager anticipation of our trip. The travel agent booked us for Saturday morning- we had to get packed! We would only be staying three days.

I called Mrs. Anderson next door. She said she'd feed the pups and keep an eye on the house for us. She's really a jewel when she's not harping on Julia's occasional nudity.

"Hey! Wait for me!" I exclaimed when I saw Julia dashing up the stairs to try on her new outfits. Taking the stairs two at a time, I quickly caught up with her.

She tossed her packages on the bed and was pulling things out haphazardly, trying to decide what to try on first. There were shopping bags, clothes, boxes and tissue paper strewn all over the bed. I ran into the room, grabbed my tiny wife around the waist, and threw her onto the bed.

Lying on her back amidst the jumble of items she giggled and held up a gauzy negligee for my perusal. Teasing, she said, "Can you wait until you see me in this, Rusty?"

"Listen honey, if you wear that wisp of nothing I'll be able to see ALL of you!" I jumped on the bed and straddled her hips. I tickled my honey until she begged me in between squeals of laughter to stop.

Breathless from the horseplay, I rolled off Julia and plopped down next to her. Her giggling subsided, she sighed happily. I turned towards her.

What a beautiful sexy sprite she is. Julia's head rolled on her pillow as she faced me. Turning on my side, I leaned in and kissed her. Her full lips parted as mine pressed ardently against them.

I swept our new clothes off the bed and pulled Julia closer...

Chapter Twenty-Six

My flip flops slapped down the steps and out to the driveway. My straw hat falling over my eyes and my arms full, I had to blindly judge my way to the Bronco.

I found it easily after banging my knee into the front bumper. Feeling my way around the side with an elbow, I finally found the door. Using my only free finger, I managed to open the door.

Geez. Only a three-day trip and we had three suitcases, hats, suntan lotion, even extra sunglasses. Now I know where they got all that stuff on Gilligan's Island!

By the time I finished tossing the suitcases into the truck, Julia came skipping down the steps. She was wearing a new sundress, big straw hat with a wide brim, and enormous sunglasses that covered half her face. Her arms were full of stuff as well.

"Julia! Be careful!" I yelled to her. How could she see where she was going with all that paraphernalia she was wearing, and carrying! "Wait for me, I'll help you!"

I rushed over to her to take some of the things she was holding. "Gee, Julia, what on earth do you have here?" The bags weighed a ton. She pushed her hat back, and huffing and puffing followed me to the truck.

"Just stuff, Rusty, you know, we need some sodas for the ride over, and some sandwiches. I got some magazines and books to read. The boat trip over is like four hours long Rusty. We need to have things to do during the trip."

I put the bags into the truck and opened the passenger door for her. She got in, smoothing her ruffled skirt as she sat. Realizing the hat she was wearing was pretty big, she pulled it off and set it on her lap. She clutched the hat it tightly, twisting it in her hands.

I climbed in and stuck the key in the ignition. Then I caught a glimpse of myself in the rear view mirror. I looked kind of goofy in my straw hat. Deciding it would be pretty difficult to drive with it on, I removed it and tossed it behind me into the back seat.

We pulled out of the driveway, taking off for the port to catch our ship. Patting Julia's knee, I realized she was nervous, not elated. "Honey, you've never been on a ship before, have you?" I asked glancing over at her.

She shook her head. Biting her lip, she looked out her side window.

"No, this is the first time. I'm little scared Rusty. I don't have a passport or anything. Aren't we leaving the country sort of? What if they turn us away at the port because we have no passports?" Her chattering showed how anxious she was.

Laughing, I reassured her. "They let you use your license or even voter's registration card, honey." We got to A1A quickly. It was easy to find the port. There were signs all along the winding road.

We passed a million advertisements for rental cars and cruises. The airport was opposite the port on the other side of Federal Highway.

"By the way, you didn't need to pack anything to eat or drink, they stuff you the whole trip. You're constantly chowing. I swear, every hour they're announcing over the loudspeaker to come and eat some more! We will probably have each gained ten pounds by time we come home!"

My mouth started watering. I was already thinking about all that glorious food they're going to force on us! Just the thought caused my foot to press harder on the gas pedal, urging the truck to go faster!

"I see." Julia said, relaxing some. "That's why you wanted to skip breakfast. Now I understand, it's so unlike you to miss a meal!"

"You betcha!" Turning at the next street, we could now see some ships.

Julia's eyes widened. "Oh my gosh, Rusty! I've never been this close to a big ship before, they're huge!" Being with my wife was like being with a child. Everything was always new and thrilling for her. It was a great aphrodisiac!

"Look at that one!" I pointed to an exceptionally large cruise ship docked nearby. People were hanging off the ship, cheering and yelling to friends on land.

"And, sweetie," I said, "you don't need to worry about being bored on the way over and needing something to read. They have constant entertainment! There's games and shows, movies and swimming, skeet shooting, believe me, there's a lot to do!" I drove around the port for a few minutes.

Finding a place to park, we hopped out and started removing our suitcases.

"Listen, honey," I said, "we can only carry so much. We don't need the food or books so let's leave them here in the car, okay?"

Julia stood there, pushing back her large hat with one hand and trying to hold a suitcase and paper bag with the other. "Okay, here, put this back in." She handed me the paper bag. Locking the truck, we dragged our suitcases over to the elevators.

There was a group of people there waiting for the elevator. They were all brightly dressed and chatting excitedly. One stout man was wearing red shorts, a non-matching, flamboyantly flowered shirt and a safari hat. He had an unlit, fat cigar stuffed in his fleshy face.

Chomping on the cigar, he jabbered loudly into a cell phone while his wife kept pushing things into his hands as she emptied out her purse. Evidently someone couldn't find their tickets.

"Baby," I bent and whispered into Julia's ear, "if I EVER leave the house looking like that, PLEASE shoot me!" Julia laughed.

"Don't worry Rusty, that's a promise!" Giggling we joined the noisy group. The elevator door opened just as we arrived. Everyone boisterously crammed in.

The fat man bounced off me then smushed Julia against the wall. "Sorry girlie," he said, spitting around the gnawed, gushy cigar. He stomped on my foot as he finally settled on one spot. We were so packed in, I couldn't move.

A plastic flower on a hat was stuck up my nose. I couldn't move my head to look for Julia, so I glanced around moving only my eyes but I couldn't even see her!

Finally the door opened and we all rushed off the elevator. We pressed on in a mass group, more people joining us as we traveled closer to the big glass doors that looked like our destination.

The group pushed through the doors and people ran up to booths. We stood in line until it was our turn to go up to a booth.

"Hello, how are you folks today!" A man cheerfully greeted us we approached the booth. He wore a sailor type uniform, very clean cut and spiffy looking. His voice had a singsong rhythm to it.

He held out his hand, smiling at us. "I need to see some type of identification please." Setting down the suitcases, I pulled my wallet out and handed the man my driver's license and my voter's registration card.

"Oh my God, Rusty!" Julia cried, as she fumbled frantically through her purse. "I... I think I left my wallet home! What are we going to do?" Her face crumpled, she looked like she was about to cry. Her bottom lip trembled slightly, she looked up at the man in the booth.

"Sir, do we have to go all the way home and get my license? We might miss the boat and we've looked so forward to this much needed trip. Is there anything we can do?" she pleaded, gazing up at the man with her big green eyes, so sad and so pretty. One tear slid out of her eye and slipped slowly down her rosy cheek.

The poor guy doesn't have a chance, that's what I was thinking!

He looked a little uncomfortable. He tore his dark Island eyes from Julia's pleading ones. "Can you vouch for her, sir?" He looked at me hopefully.

"Hmmm, let me think about it..." I said.

"Rusty! Cut that out!" Julia hit my arm.

Laughing, I said, "Yes, sir, I can vouch for my wife. We're married and she is carrying my son."

Julia must have been really scared because usually when I say son, she jumps in with 'daughter'! She never said a word; her eyes remained unwavering, glued to the man's face. He looked back and forth from me to Julia.

"Okay," he sighed. "You know I'm not supposed to do this, PLEASE don't tell anyone, I would lose my job! Go ahead." Smiled broadly, he waved us through.

We were so grateful, we thanked him profusely and zipped through fast before he could change his mind.

"I'm so sorry, Rusty. I thought I had everything. I changed purses and I always forget something when I do that!" Julia said as we looked for the signs for where our ship loaded its passengers.

"It's okay honey, we're on! That's the important thing! C'mon, let's find our ship!"

Julia pulled the tickets from her purse and looked at them like she hadn't memorized them already! "We're on the 'Sundew Jubilee', Rusty. Look!" She pointed excitedly, "There it is over there!"

She waved the tickets at the sign that directed us to our ship. We got in line at the gate outside of the plank that crossed to the ship. Cool, I thought, we get to 'walk the plank' but without anything horrific happening!

I always wanted to be a pirate. They got to live exciting lives! Sailing and killing and pillaging, cool!"

Friendly, polite people dressed in sailor suits herded us along the plank and to the stairs leading to the boat. I had butterflies in my stomach! I love sailing! They ushered us onboard, telling us to feel free to wander throughout the ship. We could go anywhere except where there are signs posted advising us of no entrance.

We followed groups of people up the stairs, where we eventually spilled out onto the outside deck. There was a beautiful, sparkling pool in the center of the deck. A lot of people were already in bathing suits, some were splashing in the inviting turquoise water with dozens sitting around the Olympic sized pool.

Numerous bars were near the entrances and exits, and lounge chairs were spread out all around the entire deck.

"C'mon, Julia, let's grab some chairs before they're all taken!"

We had checked our luggage at the gate, so we were unencumbered. I dashed in and out of lounging, yakking people and got us two chairs near the railing.

Plopping down on a chaise I spread my arms and legs out. "Man!" I sighed, "This is the life!" Although it was winter, with the sun beating down on the wooden deck, and the railings blocking the wind, it was comfortably warm.

Settling herself ladylike and carefully onto her chaise, Julia pulled her chair back to a sitting position. She sat back relaxing, stretching out her legs. We sat quietly for a few minutes, drinking in the sights.

I looked over to the huge pool.

Some model types of girls were perched provocatively on the glistening green and blue tile that encircled the pool. Wow! All of them were gorgeous, and wearing Band-Aids for bathing suits.

With practiced nonchalance, they studied their nails and primped their hair, pretending they were oblivious to the throng of men gathered around them that were vying for the babes' attention.

My eyes wandered around the crowded deck. Everywhere there were happy, laughing people, drinking, lounging, chatting, standing, it was really great to be here! I turned to Julia. She was looking all around with wide-eyed interest as well.

"Honey, you want something to drink?" I asked her.

Her grin was ear-to-ear. "Sure, I want one of those drinks with the little umbrellas in them!" She pulled off her straw hat and let her vivid red hair swing free.

Yes, I thought, I could have guessed, that's all she talked about all week! I hailed a waiter. He hurried over.

"Hello young man," I greeted him. I was trying to sound like a seasoned, man about the world traveler. "We would like two of those pink drinks you're giving everyone, but we want little umbrellas in ours."

The waiter sniffed. "Sir, we don't have 'little umbrellas'." His nose tipped up in the air.

'*Well*', I thought, '*excuuuuse me*'!

Julia wailed, "I want a little umbrella in my drink! You have pictures of drinks with the umbrellas in your brochures!" She pushed her sunglasses up on top of her head and glared at the server.

"Okay, okay, miss, I'll see what I can do!" Shaking his head and mumbling to himself, the waiter moved away.

"Well!" Julia harrumphed. "They shouldn't advertise them if they don't have them!"

A voice came over the loudspeaker, "Hello everyone!" It called, "Is everyone happy?!"

People on the deck cheered loudly. The voice continued, "As soon as we're underway, we're going to start some games. Prizes can be won during these games, and everyone is welcome to play!"

More cheering.

"At 8:00 a.m., we will start the announcement for first seating at breakfast. So get ready for food and fun!" Joyful shouts of hooray covered the rest of the announcer's words.

"Are you hungry, honey?" I asked Julia.

She smiled indulgently at me. "I'm not hungry yet, Rusty, but I know you are. I'll come with you when you go though. I can have some coffee." Julia knows I'm always ready to chow!

"Sir, miss," a haughty voice interrupted us. It was the waiter. He handed a pink foamy drink to Julia and one to me. Mine had alcohol mixed in, but Julia's didn't.

Neither drink had an umbrella in it, but they both did have sticks poking out with things crowning the ends. "This is the best I can do." The waiter sniffed.

"They look cute, what are they?" Julia asked.

I touched mine. Oh! "They're fruit honey! Look, they're little folded up paper fruit. Here, give me yours, I'll show you."

She handed me her drink, curiosity drawing her brows together. The waiter shook his head and left. I unfolded the colorful paper, wrapping it backwards, using the tiny clips to hold them open.

They were various types of paper fruit. Mine were a pineapple, orange and lemon and Julia's were cherries, an apple and peaches.

"Ooo!" Julia clapped her hands merrily. "These are perfect!" Satisfied, she bent her head and sucked noisily on her straw. "Yummy!" She declared. I tasted mine. She was right! The drinks were delicious!

I noticed though, people around us were watching us. As the waiter passed them, they grabbed his arm, and pointing at our drinks, they all demanded to have the same paper fruit decorations in their drinks! The waiter turned and glared at us each time a different patron pointed at us.

"Uh oh, I guess we started something!" Julia laughed. "I don't care," she said, "they should give us what they advertise! I'm happy with my fruit!"

About the time we finished our drinks, the ship started underway. Most of the lounge chairs were taken. Big blobby people were sunning themselves all around us.

I watched as Julia sensuously spread sun tan lotion on her arms and legs. She turned her back to me and handed me the bottle of lotion, I eagerly obliged. The lotion was cool and creamy in my hand, I touched her back, it was warm.

When I put the lotion on, she shivered slightly. I smoothed the lotion in circles until it disappeared into her skin. With such fair skin and prone to freckles, Julia needed to be careful and screen her delicate body.

Replacing the lid on the bottle, I handed it back to Julia. She leaned over and tossed it into her beach bag then shoved the bag under her chair.

She put her straw hat and large sunglasses back on and sat back with a happy sigh to soak in the rays. The second she settled, closing her eyes and stretching out, the intercom announced the first seating at breakfast.

I looked over hopefully at Julia. She never moved her head, but smiled and said, "Go on Rusty, I really don't want anything. I'll wait here, you go pig out."

"Thanks baby!" I jumped up and gave her a kiss on the tip of her elfin nose. "Want me to bring you back anything sweetie pie?" I asked, feeling a smidge guilty for leaving her alone.

Without moving a muscle she said, "No thanks, I'm fine, have fun."

"Okey dokey. I'll be right back!" I skipped, well not really, but it felt like I was skipping, down to the dining room.

Wow! What a smorgasbord! Every breakfast food in the world and then some was there. What a dream come true, food laid out a mile long in front of me, just sitting there, waiting to be chosen! I grabbed a hot plate and got started.

When my plate was piled as high as I could get it without stuff falling off, I looked around for a seat at a table.

A waiter appeared at my elbow. "Coffee, sir? Juice? Water?"

I already had a huge forkful of food in my mouth, so I just mumbled, "Yeah, everything," and motioned to my coffee cup and empty water and juice glasses.

The waiter asked, "Orange, tomato or grapefruit, sir?"

"Okay." I grunted. Pretending not to notice when the waiter rolled his eyes, I kept forking the food in as he poured orange juice, water and coffee, and then went on to the next scavenger. I gobbled up tons of scrambled eggs, grits, ham, bacon, sausage, toast dripping with butter and grape jelly and on and on.

"Oh my gosh, Rusty!" A surprised and familiar voice came from behind my right shoulder. Halting the fork with hash browns clinging to it, I turned my head. It couldn't be!

Steven and Heather Hazelhurst stood there, grinning at me like a couple of buffoons. Well Steve was grinning, Heather appeared bored, half a smile and one raised eyebrow was her greeting to me.

"What in the heck are you guys doing here?" I blurted as I jumped up to pump Steve's hand. I nodded to Heather, trying to keep a straight face. Every time I remember that slap at the funeral I get quite a chuckle.

They both had plates piled with food that they set on the table.

"Hey, join me!" I said, pointing to two empty chairs as I plunked back down on my seat.

Steve sat next to me and Heather sat on the other side of Steve, as far away from me as possible, good move I thought!

"What are you doing here, Rusty? Where's Julia?" Steve questioned as he nibbled on a chunk of cantaloupe.

Heather pierced a strawberry then she languidly pulled it off the fork with her fingers and put it to her lips. Sucking on the end of the ripe strawberry, her eyes roamed around the room.

Visions of the story Steve had told me about the night in the hot tub with Mike and Sandy came to me. Heather had been feeding green olives to Mike just before the wife-swapping debacle. Conniving seductress, that's what the skinny little snit is! Poor Sandy, she-

"Hello-Rusty-earth to Rusty, come in." Steve was yammering in my ear.

"Oh! Sorry Steve. It's just so hard to tear myself away from this dynamite buffet!" I politely set my fork down and drank some juice.

213

"Julia is basking on the deck. She's not an early morning eater. She has to have pots of coffee before her stomach can stand the sight of food. Have you guys been on deck? What are you doing here, anyway?" I demanded to know!

Somewhat sheepishly, Steve looked down at the table then back to me, "We, uh... well, we're trying to give it another shot, kind of like a second honeymoon. I mean, we've invested a few years in this relationship you know, we hate to waste them, throw everything away. And..." he hesitated.

"We're thinking about starting a family!" His face lit up with joy. He put his arm around Heather and squeezed her to him.

"Oh cut it out Steve, you're hurting me," Heather snapped irritably. She sipped some coffee. "Can you smoke in here, or do we have to go out on that windy deck like dogs sent to the porch?"

Waspish as always, our darling Heather certainly hasn't changed!

Steve snatched his arm off her shoulder as if it was on fire. "I'm sorry, sweetheart. I forget how sensitive you are in the morning. I guess you have to go outside to smoke, I don't see any ashtrays, and no one is smoking in here. I'm sorry, honey," He apologized again.

'*Oh Steve, what a doormat you are*'! I thought. I just can't believe the way that guttersnipe treats him, and he keeps coming back for more! But, not my business. Eating is my business, and I'm damn good at it! I attacked my remaining food with gusto!

"We haven't been out on the deck, yet. We've been visiting the boutiques they have on board," Steve told me. He was wearing an obviously brand spankin' new garishly flowered shirt and khaki pants.

Heather had been shopping as well. She was squeezed into a white, one-piece halter thing that tied around her neck. The shorts to the outfit were so tight they went right up the crack of her butt!

No kidding. Heather, shopping, the story of her life and Steve's wallet! "Well!" I exclaimed, unabashed. "It's terrific on the deck! You can't feel the wind, just a slight sea breeze, and it's sunny and there's a fantastic pool! As soon as I digest this breakfast and take a nap, I'm hopping right in! You guys have to come and see it!"

Draining my juice glass and water, I started on my coffee. "Where are you staying in the Bahamas?" I asked Steve.

Steve turned to Heather. "Where is it we're staying, sweetheart?"

"Uhg," Heather groaned impatiently. "How many times do I have to tell you, for Pete's sake? We're staying at the Blue Brythonia Inn by the Sea. Can you remember that or do I need to write it down for you?" Heather spoke down to Steve like a peevish schoolmarm to a short-panted middle schooler.

Embarrassed, Steve said, "Uh, no honey. I think I can remember the Bruthonna Blue Inn…"

Heather rolled her eyes heavenward and grunted again. "I'm going to go have a cigarette. I'll see you later." She grabbed up her purse and swept away from the table.

Steve followed her thin figure with his eyes as she made her way, undulating around tables, and out through the front entrance. He stared wistfully at the door even though he could no longer see her.

Trying to cheer him up, I said gaily, "C'mon Steve, come and say hi to Julia! We'll buy you this fabulous pink drink. They put little paper fruit in them, and a lot of rum, you'll love 'em!"

I nudged his arm as I stood up, my chair scraped loudly on the linoleum.

His head hanging down like a beaten dog, Steve stood up and slowly followed me from the room.

Chapter Twenty-Seven

Steve and I strolled silently along the hallways.

We passed dance rooms and a gym. We stopped and peeked inside the gym. There were lockers, towels, and a bunch of men in all stages of dress. Sure, I want to go on a vacation and exercise!

Flocks of merrymakers shoved past us as we continued making our way up to the deck. Stopping in front of the 'Coral Cornucopia Room', we watched a guy blowing up balloons and musicians setting up equipment.

"Looks like quite a show they're planning on," I said to Steve. He shrugged noncommittally, his hands shoved deeply in his pockets.

"I guess..." he sighed. He absently watched the man blowing up the balloons, his eyes and mouth drooped sadly, his shoulders slumped and his head still hung down. I couldn't keep quiet any longer.

"Gee man, why do you let her do that to you? I don't get it." I leaned against the doorway of the locker room, turning towards him.

Steve stared down at his feet. Then he looked up at me, his eyes narrowed. A little angrily, he said, "You know Rusty, I have tried and tried and tried. I give her anything she wants and she repays me by cheating on me. I really thought this could be a second, no a third, maybe even a fourth chance, like a second honeymoon... you know, get close again..."

He ran a hand through the side of his blonde hair. It was growing a little long in the back, it looked good. I bet it's a passive rebellish act to Heather.

She always made him keep his hair cut short and spiky to match hers. She told us she thought it was cute that they looked more like brother and sister than husband and wife. But now his slightly longer hair gave him a more rakish look.

He trailed off... the steam was running out of him. "Well," his voice suddenly strengthened. He said, "I have really had it this time. Her whining, and pouting, and her petulant attitude about everything I do or say, she's the most querulous, ungrateful woman I have ever known!" He threw his hands up in the air in frustration.

"I don't know how you take it, Steve." My face displayed my sympathy for the position he's in. We both watched as a group of teenybopper girls giggled their way past us.

Steve smiled wryly, practically oogling the young females. "Yeah buddy, this is it. I am done with her for good! The word divorce has always scared the hell out of me, but heck, I'm young, not too bad looking... I think... I think I can do better!"

He stood away from the wall, spread his legs apart and slammed his hands on his hips. He looked ready for battle! "And if I get lonely, I'll get a dog or a cat or a bird or something, anything that doesn't grouse at me twenty four-seven, and that will greet me at the door when I come home with a happily wagging tail!"

"You know what Steve, I think you're finally ready to move on, and Julia and I will be more than happy to help you begin your new life!" I slapped him on the back.

"What hotel are you guys staying in?" Steve asked me.

Our hotel was right on the water according to the brochures. "We have a lovely cabin overlooking the aquamarine waters of the spectacular Atlantic-"

"Yeah, yeah, cut out the advertising crap, Rusty, you never were a good salesman! Just tell me the name of your hotel. Is it the same as the one we have reservations at? The Blue... uh...

Blue... Blytherma... whatever, it's a stupid name anyway for a hotel! I should have told her so too!" Enigmatically nodding his head, Steve crossed his arms in front of his chest.

Hoping he sticks to his guns, I said, "Our hotel is the Island Vistique. We're supposed to have a room right on the ocean side. What are you planning to do now?"

Steve looked a little mischievous. A smug smile crossed his face. "Our hotel room is already paid for. I think I'll let Heather go ahead and stay there, and I'll see if I can book me a room at your hotel. What do you think about that?"

"You go Steve!" I cheered. We high-fived, then quickly backed away from each other. There were flocks of partymakers coming down the hall. We didn't want to look too geeky!

"C'mon, let's find Julia!" Motioning to go with my head, I led the way.

Just as we reached the top of the stairs, we could hear music blaring and mixed conversations. Easily blending into the loud group that was obviously already enjoying the alcoholic rum drinks served on the Lido deck, we made our way through the multitude of half-dressed people swarming the deck.

I pushed a path to where I'd left Julia. When we were a few yards away from her, I could tell someone was sitting on MY lounge chair, chatting with MY wife!

I started to steam, gee, you can't leave a beautiful woman like Julia alone for long, some drooling sap will always quickly move in. I need to put up a No Trespassing sign!

As we got closer, I realized there was something vaguely familiar about the man talking to Julia. Oh no, no, it can't be... it just can't be! Am I to be plagued forever by that man!

I recognized the flopping chestnut hair and muscular body of Detective Patterson! Un-freakin'-believable!

Steve pointed to him. "Hey, isn't that-"

I cut Steve off. "Yeah, that's that crummy supercilious son-of-a-" My teeth were gritting by time we reached the pair.

"Honey!" Julia waved at me brightly. "Look who's on the boat too!"

218

"Yeah, I see." Neither my voice nor my face was welcoming. I stared coldly at the detective. I figured I didn't have to be polite to this guy. We were on a luxury liner on the way to the Bahamas. I'm sure he had no jurisdiction out of the states.

Besides, as far as I was concerned, they caught the hoodlum that was peeping at my wife and killing everyone. They hadn't charged him or tried him yet, but as far as I was concerned, the police had the guilty party, no thanks to Patterson!

Over my shoulder I heard, "Ahem..." I'd forgotten Steve. "Hey honey, look who else is here!"

Steve stepped from behind me and leaned down to kiss Julia on the cheek.

I heard a snicker. "Well, Hazelhurst as well... it is a small world after all, isn't it?" Sarcastic as always, but he did stand up at my arrival, vacating MY chair.

"I know why we're all here, Patterson, but what brings a big, fancy, Florida detective on a cruise? Some big international smuggling ring you're investigating?" I can be sarcastic too!

Julia pulled her sunglasses down and glared at me over the tops. I was being silently chastised to be polite.

A little ashamed at my bad manners, I shut my mouth and smiled politely at the officer. "I-"

"Daddy!"

As Patterson opened his mouth to respond, a small whirlwind of noise and dirt hurled itself at the detective, squirming and clutching at his neatly pressed T-shirt. The creature jumped up and down, shrieking at the top of its lungs.

Steve and I stood back, trying to decipher what sort of beast was attacking, and to get out of its way.

"Okay Frankie, settle down, calm down boy, Frankie settle down..." Patterson tried to hold down the rambunctious object that appeared to be a small boy. At least I thought that's what it was.

It had a very grimy face and some red and orange gunk all over its clothes and hands.

Tightly gripping the small, active boy, Patterson introduced us. "This is my son, Frances Douglas Patterson, he's five. Frankie,

Say hello son, to the nice people. That's Mr. Dixon and Mrs.-"
Patterson was pointing to each of us as he announced our names,
but the creature was tugging at him and leaping up and down on
the detective's Nikes.

"Daddy!" it shrieked. "I wanna play videos! I wanna hot dog!
I wanna soda pop!" The child had quite the piercing voice, went
right through one's ears.

"Why are you here anyway, Frankie, where's your sister?
She's supposed to be watching you." Patterson questioned the boy
as he continued to squirm and struggle out of Patterson's grip.

I don't think the detective could have let go if he wanted to.
The child seemed to be dripping in stickiness and goo. I think they
were pretty much stuck together at this point.

Whatever red and orange slop that was on the boy, was now
clinging to Patterson's once crisply clean shirt. The boy pointed a
grungy finger towards the pool.

"She over der, Daddy, she tol' me to go play 'cause she
wanna talk wid da sail guy."

Patterson followed the boy's finger. "Damn! Can't let her out
of my sight for an instant! Here, watch him!" The detective thrust
the boy at me.

"Ick-" I cringed and tried to back away from the dirt devil,
but Patterson threw him at me and stalked off towards the pool.

The boy immediately tried to run after his father.

Reluctantly, I reached out a hand and snagged a tiny, sticky
arm. The kid screamed and struggled pretty good for a minute or
so, until Julia pulled out a grape lollipop from her purse and
handed it to him.

Julia said, "There's another one in here for you if you behave
and stand still until your Daddy returns."

The boy grabbed the sucker, ripped off the wrapper tossing it
aside and stuffed the candy into his mouth. His already plump
cheek burst out even more with the candy in it.

Julia settled back again in her chaise. She pulled her knees up
and set a paperback against her thighs.

"Do you think it's okay to give the youngster candy without his parent's permission?" Steve queried. Concern mapped on his thin face.

"Do you want to hold him, Steven?" Julia smiled at Steve, her brows arched.

Steve had pulled up a chair, which he placed next to mine, with Julia's chaise between him and the child. Eyeing the little grease monkey warily, "Uh, I guess he'll be okay," he muttered, sitting down.

"What are you doing here?" Julia asked Steve. She was still sipping her pink drink.

Steve explained to Julia why he was there and about Heather and their problems.

"Poor baby," Julia commiserated with him. "You stick with us, we'll take good care of you! You don't need that... woman." Julia patted Steve's hand. She was too much of a lady to verbalize what she thought of Heather.

We observed Patterson's progress across the deck.

He had reached the pool, and was in obviously angry conversation with a teenaged girl and it looked like a crewmate.

The boy dressed in sailor togs looked pretty sheepish as Patterson appeared to be giving him a tongue-lashing. The boy quickly disappeared out the door.

Patterson then grabbed the young girl and dragged her unceremoniously across the deck and back to us. I was scared for a minute he might forget about the mini monster, and I had no desire to get stuck baby-sitting the terrible tyke!

As he approached us with the girl in tow, the boy, Frankie started getting excited and agitated again.

He chomped on his sucker while screaming, "Daddy! Daddy!" at the top of his lungs. People were looking aghast at us, like we were torturing the child.

Others were frowning, giving us the eye. Apparently they thought the little hellion was ours and we were not doing a very good job of controlling him.

Patterson stopped so abruptly in front of us that the girl he was gripping almost tripped and fell into him.

"This is my daughter, Trixie," he introduced her, but before he could say our names, the boy kept screaming and jumping, and now the girl was screeching as well, shaking her long blonde hair, both hands balled into fists were planted on her hips.

Patterson was trying to hold onto his son, argue with the girl and explain to us why they were there.

I almost, but not quite, felt sorry for the guy. If anyone deserved a squalling boy and nubile teenaged girl, well, it couldn't have happened to a better guy! Better him than me! I relinquished all control of the kid.

Thankfully, Patterson moved away with the two screaming children. Eventually they also disappeared off the deck and out the door. Probably going to throw the kid in the bath, beat the girl, and slug down some full shots of scotch!

As far as I could make out, with all of that screaming and yelling going on, Patterson and his wife are divorced and it's his turn to have the kids, so he decided this trip would be a good distraction. Again, better him than me!

Steve was smirking, and even Julia had a slight grin.

I couldn't help it, I laughed out loud! "Poor slob!" I choked.

Julia and Steve burst out laughing. We shared our amusement at Patterson's sorry life for a while.

We could see some crew people setting things out up front. A pretty Asian girl had a microphone and was asking for our attention.

"Hi everyone! Welcome! My name is Thi Ling and I will be your cruise director for the brief time you're on the ship. We are going to start the games now, and for people not interested in sun or games, we have plenty of activities elsewhere!

There are duty free shops all over the ship, gambling can begin as soon as we are three miles out, and our first 'way, way off-Broadway' show will begin at 10:00. We are happy to present the 'Glitz Girls' dancers in the Athena Room, and in the Coral

Cornucopia Room on deck two, 'Tilly's Troupe' will start at 10:20.

"Both exercise rooms are open, on the second and fourth decks. And for you sports enthusiasts, we have skeet shooting set up off the aft deck." She drew a deep breath and grinned widely at the crowd.

"I'm here to answer any questions you may have, and our crew is at your disposal to help you have a happy and safe time! I'm going to turn you over now to Suzy Santia who will lead you in the games!"

The cruise director handed the microphone to a bouncy blonde girl. Pony-tailed and perky, Suzy, dressed in a tiny pleated skirt and sparkling white sneakers, excitedly explained the game that was about to begin.

Apparently, the idea of the game was something about who could eat the most crackers while trying to blow up a balloon. Peculiar. Well, I'm up for it!

Julia and Steve were chatting, at least Steve was talking, she appeared to be sleeping.

"Hey," I said to Steve, "I'm gonna go play the game. You coming?"

Steve looked to the front of the deck where mostly men were gathering. He shook his head. "Naw, I think I'll check out the action around the ship."

Heather hadn't shown up yet. I noticed Steve looking around anxiously, expectantly, but as time went on, he seemed angrier and angrier. Apparently Heather had already made new friends on the ship. And, undoubtedly they were all of the XY persuasion.

"Okay, I'll see you in a while, I need to work off my breakfast so I have room for lunch!" Grinning at Steve, I pecked Julia on the cheek.

She was breathing very lightly, sound asleep. I headed for the gang of guys up front; I could see a blonde ponytail bouncing up and down in the middle of the group.

Chapter Twenty-Eight

We played games for at least two hours.

Finally, exhausted, hot and sweaty, I'd had enough. We had started with about 30 people and now there were only around 10 of us left.

Suzy's hair was losing its pertness, her little face was flushed, and her cute voice was starting to get an edge to it.

I headed back to where I'd left Julia. There were plenty of people splashing in the pool, but it looked like a lot of folks were snoozing. Good idea, I thought.

Julia was reading a book when I flopped down on the chaise next to hers. "Hi baby, miss me?"

She murmured, "Mmmm..."

Groaning, "Ahhh," laying my sleepy head back, my eyes closed automatically. "Where's Steve?" I asked.

"Mmmm... um, he was kind of mad that Heather never came around, so he said he was going to go look for her. Says he has something to discuss with her. He said he'd try to catch us at lunch," Julia advised never taking her eyes from the book in her lap.

"Oh..." I was already drifting off, huge tables piled high with bounteous food swam in my head...

"Rusty, wake up Rusty..." Somebody was pushing my shoulder.

"Wha...?" Rubbing the sleep from my eyes, I sat up. My gorgeous wife was sitting next to me.

"Come on Rusty, they're calling for seating at lunch. I'm absolutely famished, let's go!" She was gathering her purse and slipping into her sandals.

No one ever needed to tell me twice to go eat. Shoving into my flip-flops we took off for the dining area.

Just as we stepped inside the door of the buffet room, we caught a glimpse of the Patterson trio. Fortunately, they were clear across the crowded room. Julia grabbed a table close to the front entrance and I went to fill up our plates.

Joining Julia shortly after loading our plates to the max with a bevy of food, I could just start to hear little Frankie Patterson's infrequent shrieks.

I pushed Julia's piled high plate in front of her. She would never be able to eat it all, but then I used her plate as a reservoir for mine! A little extra lasagna, a few rolls, some cold cuts, minor things that I had no room for on my plate.

"Wow Rusty, everything looks incredible! We'll never be able to eat it all!" Julia exclaimed. She watched me for a second, I was already shoveling my food in. Laughing, she picked up her fork and worked at making a dent in her load of lunchables.

We could hear a commotion from the back of the room. I didn't look up, but when I saw Julia's head turn, I asked her what was going on.

She chuckled. "That poor detective. He's got a hold of the boy's wrist, the kid is screaming and struggling to get away. He already looks like he was doused in a pile of ketchup and mustard. The mustard is smeared all over his face, and ketchup is practically dripping from his hair!" Julia put her hand to her mouth so no one could see her laughing.

"The girl, Dixie, Pixie, whatever her name is" Julia giggled, "well, she's wearing like a tube top, and skin tight Capri pants! Whew! I'd hate to be that girl's parents, she's trouble brewing! Anyway, the girl took the opportunity of her dad's distraction with the kid, and she's bolted for the door. The detective is trying to go after her, but he's trapped with the boy! Ha ha ha..." Julia laughed.

Peering over her juice glass, she said, "He's trying to clean the kid up. They're all dressed in different clothes than earlier, they must have gotten a cabin for the ride over. He's hollering at the girl as she's running out the door.

"I think I see that young sailor fellow she was so cozy with this morning at the pool, just outside the door. Patterson's going to flip his lid when he catches up with them! Uh oh-" Julia quickly turned her head. "Don't look, here he comes!" Julia dropped her eyes to her plate. I kept eating.

We could hear the noise and practically feel the noisy activity as the father and five year old passed by us. We kept our heads down in case the detective saw us. Once they were safely out the door, Julia peeked through her lashes, "They're gone, we're safe!" We laughed and continued our lunch in peace.

After stuffing ourselves to our heart's content, we discussed what to do next over coffee. "I'd like to see some of the ship, Rusty, and a show!" Julia said excitedly, "And I want to check out some of those duty-free shops."

"Don't you want to gamble, sweetie?" I asked her. I'm pretty sure I'd be really good at Blackjack!

She frowned at me. "I don't think so Rusty, we've had too many 'gambles' lately for my peace of mind!"

I had the grace to look sheepish. Life had been pretty daring recently. And it's not like we have a lot of money to throw around either. Oh well. "Okay, let's go, where to first?" I stood up and pulled Julia's chair out for her.

"Shops!" she said gleefully and led the way out.

We didn't buy anything, everything was very expensive. Wandering in and out of shops, we eventually came to the Athena Room. Peeking inside, we could see it was dark, and loud with music.

"Let's go in, Rusty," Julia whispered, tugging on my sleeve. Cautiously we entered the dark room, slowly allowing our eyes to become adjusted to the lack of light. We could make out tiny tables with candles slightly lighting them, scattered throughout the room. I could barely see the people at the tables with drinks in front of them.

But, the stage was sure lit up! Dancing girls were prancing across, their flashy costumes glittered as they wiggled and kicked to the music, loud, raucous music. We found an empty table. As soon as we sat, a waitress was there.

"What's your specialty?" I asked her.

Cupping her ear and leaned down close to me, "What?" she said. I repeated my question.

"Hailstorm Hurricanes!" she yelled at me.

"Okay," I shouted back as I took out my wallet. "We'll have one regular, and one virgin!" She nodded and left the table. We enjoyed the show and our drinks for a while.

We watched the show for about half an hour or so, and then decided we'd had enough. Leaving the dark, noisy room, we emerged into a quiet, bright hall.

Following the hall to the stairs, we decided to go up as high as we could. We popped out onto the outside of the fifth deck, the strong sea wind hit us in the face, whipping our hair and stinging our skin.

"Eek!" Julia shrieked as she grabbed for her hat. She almost lost it in the wind. We made our way, struggling against the wind, around the side where we were a little more blocked from the elements.

"Whew! Man, that was rough!" I exclaimed as we leaned against the railing. We looked out over the vast ocean, no land in sight. All blue as far as the eye could see. Enormous waves crashed all around the roiling sea. Ooh, my tummy got a little queasy when I realized we were out in the middle of nowhere.

"Isn't this marvelous, Rusty?!" Julia raved.

Gulp, "Uh yeah, sure, awesome..." My fingers gripped the railing. I could feel the boat swaying. Uh oh, I'm not usually susceptible to seasickness... always a first time for everything.

"Wow Rusty! Look down! It's so cool!" Julia proclaimed exuberantly. She snatched her hat off her head and let the breeze ruffle wildly through her hair. The sun sparkled over the water, it was a brisk, clear day.

Looking down over the railing as instructed, I almost fainted. We were way high up... the dark ocean was far below us... The water rushed up and splashed mightily against the ship. The sea hit the hull and the walls so hard, we could feel the salty spray hit our faces.

"Oh yeah, how, uh, nice..." I muttered. "Uh, didn't you really want to buy that cute little purse in that last shop we were in honey?" I asked hopefully.

I was more than willing to run up the charge card more if it got me away from this perilous edge and roaring ocean. Out of sight, out of mind, I thought. Figuring if we were inside, away from the view, my fear of the churning deep would go away. "Let's go," I urged Julia.

Reluctantly, Julia pushed away from the railing and took my hand. Trying to walk as nonchalantly as possible, I didn't want my wife too know what a scaredy-cat I was, I led her back to the stairs, to the safe, secure, inside.

Strolling along the maze of hallways and decks, we rounded a corner, and stopped dead when we saw Steve nestled in a love seat by a window, with none other than our cruise director, Miss Ling!

"Shhhh" I held one finger to my lips to quiet Julia as she was about to say something.

I didn't want Steve to see us and break his rhythm. He seemed to be doing quite well with the black-haired beauty. They were leaning in very close together, their lips were almost touching. Miss Ling giggled at something Steve said, throwing her long mane back, she had a pretty laugh, tinkled as they say.

At that point, Steve put his arm around the girl's shoulder and stroked her cheek. Why the little Romeo, I thought, he doesn't even have his glasses on! I hope he kisses her in the right spot! It sure looked like they were about to kiss.

"C'mon honey, let's go, if he spots us the mood will be spoiled!" Very quietly we slipped past the duo on the divan and hurried down the hall. As soon as we were out of sight, we stopped, leaned against a wall and burst out laughing.

"Wow!" Julia declared, "I didn't know he had it in him! I'm so happy for him!"

I agreed. We stood for a minute, giggling and catching our breaths. Uh oh...here comes trouble, I thought as I looked down the hall. Heather was coming right towards us! She was wrapped around some strange guy herself!

Heather and her 'fella' didn't notice us until they practically ran into us.

"Oh!" she gasped, startled, and looking a little like the kid with her hand in the cookie jar. "Rusty, Julia! Um...." Her eyes shifted about guiltily.

"I've been playing, uh, roulette in the... uh.... gambling room... this is um, this is Kenny... uh... honey what's your name?" She glanced up at the tall guy she had been clinging to moments ago. The man sighed, bored.

"Hello, Kenneth Klibano... hmmm... pleased to meet you," he held out a limp hand, shook ours and then turned away indifferently. He had some sort of a foreign accent, greasy, slicked back, black hair with a mustache to match. Yuk.

The guy gave me the creeps. I bet he was hanging around with Heather because he either thought she had money and he was a gigolo type, or he figured she was just easy.

Heather had on a ton of makeup, although a lot of it was smeared at this point, especially her hot pink lipstick. She'd changed her clothes. Her shorts were still just as short as they could be, and she'd tied her white blouse tightly beneath her breasts, exposing her skinny midriff. She reeked of perfume.

This girl has no morals at all! Talk about an alley cat. I could only hope that Steve dumps her fast and hard!

"Have you, uh, seen Steven? I've been just looking everywhere for him!" Heather asked, though obviously actually finding for Steven was the last thing on her mind!

"Uh, yeah," I answered, pointing down one of the various halls I knew Steve wasn't in. "We just saw him in the forward lounge, that way."

"Oh good... I must speak with him, I'm practically out of money and he has the charge cards. Well, uh... we'll... uh... I mean I'll see you guys later, okay? Have fun now, toodles!"

Heather pushed her hand through the gigolo's arm and guided him down the opposite hall to where I had said I'd seen Steve.

Taking Julia's hand, I led her away from both the Hazelhursts. "Man, that woman makes me feel dirty. I feel like I need a bath when I'm near her."

Nodding silently next to me, Julia clung to my hand.

"Hey Rusty, look at this! This is so neat!" Julia proclaimed. She stopped at a door with a tiny window in it. Opening the door, she stepped inside.

"C'mon," she urged me to follow her. I obliged and walked into the tiny room behind her.

"I've never seen anything like this before, Rusty, this is way cool!" Julia danced around the minuscule room. It was a telephone booth, but an old fashioned kind. It was about eight feet long and four or so feet wide, and there was a small table and chair under the phone. On the table was a pad and pencil for the occupant's use.

"This is great, unique," I agreed. "I feel like I'm in a foreign spy movie!" Julia giggled and pressed into my arms.

"It's kinda romantic, Rusty. There's only a teeny window, and-" I hushed her with my lips. We started making out, hot and heavy. As I pulled apart the top button of Julia's blouse, never taking my lips off hers, I caught some movement behind her head.

"Damn!" There were sailor people watching us through the window. I pushed Julia behind me so they couldn't see her lipstick smeared, flushed face and opened blouse!

"We're not alone, honey, we have an audience," I warned her quickly passing her my handkerchief. Wiping her mouth, Julia peered over my shoulder, "Oh!" She ducked behind me again.

"Oh Rusty, I'm so embarrassed, we gave them quite a show!" She tried to smooth her mussed hair with her fingers.

"That's okay, it could have been worse, it could be five minutes from now!"

When Julia realized what I meant, her mouth opened, horrified at the picture we would have presented. Then we started giggling. After all, we are married, and it's not like we showed any skin or anything!

Straightening our rumpled clothing, we casually opened the door, and calmly and collectedly, we strode past the gawkers gathered outside the booth.

Safely around the corner, we collapsed into gales of suppressed laughter. Our hands were pressed tightly against our mouths, we didn't want those people to think we were affected by them seeing us fooling around in the phone booth!

Languidly making our way back to the top deck where we left our jackets and magazines, we realized we were getting tired. Four hours is a long time, I needed another nap!

As soon as we reached the chairs we had staked out earlier, an announcement came over the loud speaker. By the entrance of the deck was a calypso band that had played nonstop since our arrival. They were packing up their equipment.

The person on the speaker, sounded like Miss Ling, announced we would be docking soon, and we should be preparing to leave the ship. She said she hoped we'd all had a fun time and that perhaps she would see us again soon!

Chapter Twenty-Nine

$\mathcal{I}$ looked over the railing. "Hey Julia, look! Land!" I waved excitedly.

Humoring me, Julia smiled, nodding. "Yes Rusty, the Bahamas, we're finally here!" She stood next to me holding our windbreakers and hats. Our excitement increased again, now that we knew we were getting off the ship and onto our destination.

I couldn't wait to get to our hotel! "Let's go see if we can get to the exit level honey." I ushered Julia towards the hordes of people already gathering at the exit of the deck.

Hurry up and wait. We stood, crammed in a wall-to-wall mass of people. We were lined up on the stairs, but we had two decks to go down.

Uhh, I groaned, this is going to take forever. We would have been better off sitting at the bar upstairs waiting for the crush of guests to leave. Now we're stuck, standing, pressed against smelly strangers. I had my arm around Julia, I was scared I'd lose her in the crowd.

She wriggled slightly against my side. I quelled the erotic feeling that welled up in me at her body pressing against mine- not the time to get romantic!

Finally, the crowd moved, slowly. It took us forty-five minutes to get off the ship.

Emerging into the bright tropical sunshine, we followed the scores of visitors into the building on the dock. Our tickets were checked again, and everyone's suitcases were scattered all around the cavernous room. It didn't take too long to find our cases, I'd tied yellow ribbons on them back at the house. We went back outside to wait our turn for a taxi.

Wearily sitting down on our cases, we waited another thirty minutes for a cab. Six other people crammed in with us, how delightful. I told the driver the name of our hotel. "Don't they have shuttle buses here?" I asked.

'Ya mon," the driver cheerfully replied, "At de 'otel." He had the same sing song voice as the crewman at the port.

Julia had her face pressed against the window as we drove from the port and through a tiny village. I've been here before, but this was all new for my wife.

Julia turned to me, but kept her eyes out the window, "It's different, but kind of the same as Florida, Rusty. Look at the little children in their uniforms!" She pointed as we passed a school.

Children were running and playing in the schoolyard. They all looked alike, dressed in blue skirts or shorts and white blouses. Swiftly we drove through a rural, heavily wooded and floral section before we entered a small city.

We passed fruit stands, and other places where the natives were selling homemade baskets and trinkets along the street.

We continued just a few more minutes or so, when I saw the sign advertising our hotel. "We're here!" I exclaimed excitedly. We turned into the driveway.

The driveway curved up a grassy hill. The hotel was pastel yellow with white trim. Luxurious flowers decorated the front. I could see the beautiful aquamarine color of the ocean calmly pulsating behind the hotel

The cab driver stopped under the sign that announced The Island-Vistique. The entire front of the hotel was enclosed in glass.

As soon as the cab stopped, Julia and I hopped out. Well, I climbed out slowly, my muscles had cramped after being squished in the car. I paid the driver and we retrieved our luggage he had removed from the trunk.

The glass doors to the hotel automatically slid open at our approach. When we stepped inside the lovely air-conditioned lobby, a woman dressed in a uniform came forward and greeted us. She pointed to the front desk.

In a pretty, lilting voice, the woman said, "Please check in at the desk. As soon as you've seen your room, please join us outside by the pool. There are free refreshments and our recreation director will be happy to explain everything that we have here that is available to you." She smiled warmly as she gestured towards the pool outside the back of the lobby.

Continuing, she said, "The recreation director will explain breakfast and transportation to the towns and activities surrounding the area. Please have a pleasant stay here with us at the Island-Vistique Hotel!" she ended as she motioned us to the front desk.

Then she turned swiftly to greet the guests that had entered behind us.

We signed in at the desk, received our keys and instructions to locate our room. We were around back to the right. We had bungalow three. Following the signs and directions, we made our way to our room.

"Here it is!" I announced as I saw the number 3 on the door. Sticking the key in and opening the door, we tiredly entered the room.

"Ooh…" Julia moaned as she set her suitcase on the bed.

The room was tropically pretty with soft pink walls, a small round table with two chairs was placed in front of the window next to the entrance and a king-sized bed.

The curtains matched the bedspread, tiny pink and yellow flowers were printed on them. There were two paintings of beach scenes, one hung over the bed and one decorated the wall over the desk and dresser.

The hotel room was like most others, it had a TV, miniature bathroom and separate dressing area. It was a good-sized room and very bright. I could see bird-of-paradise flowers peeking in the back window.

"Ahhh," I exhaled happily as I flopped on the bed. "We're finally here!"

"Oh no you don't Rusty! You just had a nap on the ship. We're only here for three days, let's go out and see the place! They have free refreshments - remember!" Julia tugged at my hand, trying to drag me off the bed.

Reluctantly I sat up. Well, refreshments always get my attention, "Okay, let's go." I pocketed the room key as we left the suite.

Following the walk that led around the back of the hotel, we curved around the beach. The sun blazed on the sand and water. The reflection was so brilliant we put our sunglasses on so we wouldn't be blinded.

Spotting the pool, we strolled towards it. The pool glowed sea green, rippling from the children that were playing in it. We headed to the table with the food. There were chairs set up in front of the table, and lounge chairs were strewn around the pool. Most were already taken.

As we approached the table, a beautiful young lady greeted us. "Hi, my name is Trish Van Dolan." She shook our hands. "If you'll take a seat, we will have a brief documentation of the island, how to get around and what to see. Then you're free to indulge in the refreshments."

She gestured towards the table with the food on it. "Please have a seat in the viewing area." We followed her motion, and sat down on the chairs that were set up in front of the table.

"Oh good," I murmured. "We're being held prisoner and have to earn our food."

Julia admonished me in a whisper, "Shh, they're just going to tell us what there is to see and do, be patient!" She settled back.

Grimacing, I crossed my arms and legs and sat back. I hate when they hold you hostage and make you wait to eat.

The presentation wasn't very long, about five minutes. It told us how to get to the cities and shopping areas. They described the best beach places, where to rent sailboats, snorkeling equipment and ski-doos. We could obtain a list of restaurants and maps at the front desk.

They advised how to use the transportation. I remembered most people rode those little scooters or moped things. They were easy to maneuver. The bad part was the Bahamians drive on the wrong side of the road! The British influence I guess. Takes a while to get used to.

The film and speech ended with instructions on our breakfast. At the crack of dawn, they will deliver little baskets with muffins, eclairs and fresh fruit.

The waiters deposit the baskets on the porch outside the room door. That way the guests can eat at their leisure, without dressing or having to get to a dining room by a specific time. What a great idea! Coffee and tea services were already in the hotel rooms. They would be replenished daily.

As soon as the presentation was over, Julia and I leaped up and went to the table. Bananas, apples, kiwi, all types of fruit were pleasingly displayed. Salsa and chips, pastries and party sandwiches were arrayed across the dazzling white tablecloth.

After getting our food, we made our way to some chairs under an umbrella by the pool. Just as we sat, Steve wandered up and joined us.

"Hey guy, what's happening? You sure look rested and cheerful," I said to him as he sat down. He was drinking a soda, chock filled with ice.

Steve smiled widely at Julia and me. His grin was so huge, his teeth gleamed in the sunlight. "I am doing great!" he responded happily.

I winked at him. "Yeah, we know man. We saw you on the ship with the cruise director. Way to go!" We high-fived.

"You looked pretty involved, Steven," Julia smiled shyly at him, "we didn't want to disturb you so we slipped past."

"So what's up with that?" I leered, questioning Steve about the girl.

Steve looked bashfully at his soda. But he couldn't contain his smile. "That was Thi Ling, she's really nice." He looked slightly embarrassed.

"We know who she is man, what's up with her? You guys looked like you were about to get hot and heavy when we saw you. That was hours ago, man. C'mon," I urged him, "tell us all the wicked deets!"

Steve's grin practically took up his entire face! He ducked his head, embarrassed, his cheeks turned pink. "Geez Rusty, she's just a nice girl. We hit it off, you know... uh..." he broke off, not looking us in the eye. Steve's not used to being a Don Juan.

"C'mon Steve, inquiring minds want to know!" I laughed, begging him to spill his guts to us. Julia sat quietly, smiling and sipping her drink.

"Oh, we just made out a little, she has a cabin on the ship. It's not going anywhere guys." He looked at me, then Julia. We were at rapt attention, this behavior is so unlike our Steve.

"After all, I am married, and she lives on the ship. We're uh, just good friends. It was a brief encounter, we could only see each other every few months or so if we dated...." he trailed off wistfully.

"So, what's wrong with that?" I asked.

"Rusty!" Julia scolded me.

"Well, I see nothing wrong with Steve here sowing some wild oats. A girl in every port as it where!" I said. Julia hit me in the arm. She turned to Steve.

"What happened with Heather? Did you guys ever hook up?" She asked.

Steve looked sad. "Yeah," he said, "that's kind of what precipitated my rendezvous with Thi." He looked around before continuing. People were swarming all over the pool area and beach.

We could see boats out on the water, para-sailors, and there was this yellow thing people were sitting on. It looked like a huge banana. Six or eight people were riding astride it, they bounced wildly up and down as a boat dragged the banana through the waves. Even thought they were pretty far out, we could hear their screams and laughter wafting ashore.

"Yeah," Steve repeated, squinting up at the sun. "I came across Heather and some swarthy foreign guy making out on one of the decks. They were outside, and because it was so windy, they didn't hear me when I opened the door on them. They were pretty well occupied, too much to notice me or much of anything else!" he said wryly.

"I was so furious, I was afraid I might hurt someone, so I left without saying anything. She didn't even know I saw her. A while later, I ran into her outside of a gambling room. She apparently had just come out of the ladies room. I let her have it. I told her off so bad..."

He hesitated, closing his eyes. "I think she was going to cry, but with Heather, well, it's usually crocodile tears. I'd had enough. I told her we were through for good. I called her a slut and threw the hotel reservations at her. Told her she was on her own from now on."

Sighing heavily, Steve continued, "She wasn't fooling me, I could see that dark bastard inside the gambling room waiting for her. I recognized her red jacket on the seat next to his. I told her she could stay at the hotel, that I was going elsewhere, and as soon as we got home, I was getting a divorce. She," he chuckled weakly.

"She stood there, mouth unattractively agape, eyes wide in disbelief. I left her there like that. I don't care anymore... that's it, finito. She's lucky I didn't smack her silly lying face!" Shaking his head sadly, he sipped his cola.

"I'm sorry Steve buddy. I really am. You know how I feel about Heather, but I just want you to be happy." I patted Steve on the shoulder, Julia was stroking his arm, trying to comfort him.

"So, anyway... just after I left her, I ran into Thi again. We started chatting and she said she was off for a few hours. We walked and talked for a while, I told her what happened. I think she felt sorry for me... I mean she's so pretty and all, and look at me, you think she'd be interested in a geek like me?" He laughed derisively.

"C'mon Steve," I said.

"You stop that right now Steven Hazelhurst!" Julia interjected angrily. "You are a very handsome guy! A girl would be lucky to be with a man like you," she scolded, shaking her finger at him.

"Well, to be honest," Steve hung his head sheepishly. "I kind of have a date for dinner tonight."

"What? Who?" We stuttered together, surprised.

At that precise moment, Trish Van Dolan, the recreation director of the hotel stopped at our table. She smiled at Steve.

"Hi, Stevie, I'm ready whenever you are!" She tapped his shoulder lightly. She had changed from her uniform into a little black dress. Her blonde hair was done in a twist up the back of her head. Stevie?

His face turning red, Steve pushed his chair back and got up. "Uh, yeah." He introduced us, then turned to the girl.

"Okay Trish, I'm ready. Uh," he said awkwardly, "uh, I guess I'll see you guys later, okay?" He took Miss Van Dolan's arm and guided her from the table.

Julia and I just sat and stared after him. "He seems to have a predilection for leader-type women. I'm surprised the hotel lets their employees date the guests. Can you believe that guy?" I asked Julia.

She simply shrugged. "It looks like our little Steven is growing up!" Julia quipped.

"Yeah," I laughed. "Growing up from Steven to Stevie." We giggled together. More power to him. I can't wait to see Miss Heather and her expression when she gets a load of her Steven and the sexy bit of fluff he just strolled off with.

We turned to each other. "Well?" I asked, "What shall we do first?" Julia pondered for a moment.

"C'mon, I want to check out the markets." She grabbed my hands and jerked me up off my seat. We went back inside the hotel to inquire about the transportation.

A hotel staff member suggested we take the small tour bus that stops at the common touristy places. We got tickets and went out front to wait for the bus. It showed up in less than ten minutes.

As we were boarding, Julia said, "Do you have the camera, Rusty?" She knows I always forget things like tickets, keys, important things. But, she is never going to live down the fact that she forgot her ID and the whole trip was almost canceled!

I patted the pocket of the jacket I was carrying. "Right here sweetie, we're all set, I'm right on the ball!" Julia hopped on first and found us a seat together.

We stayed on the bus for an hour, just touring around and seeing the sights. People got on and off the bus at various stops around the city, visiting shops, museums, beaches. We finally got off at a market when our tummies advised us it was time to eat.

Quickly gobbling down some jerk chicken sandwiches, we decided to wander around the outdoor market. The Bahamians had outlandishly colorful paintings everywhere for sale. Straw hats and baskets and fresh fruit were in abundance.

Native women kept coming up to Julia and asking to do her hair. They wanted to put teeny braids all over her head.

"Go on honey, I think it'd be kind of cool," I urged Julia. I like the look, little braids with tiny colorful beads throughout her auburn hair would be neat.

Julia waved off one of the women as she approached her with her singsong voice.

"Do your hair lady?" the woman asked with a wide grin.

Julia said, "I'll think about it, maybe later. I'm not sure if I'll get a headache from the tight braids."

We strolled along the market, so many things to look at! I bought Julia a beaded bracelet and anklet to match. We got back on the bus and took a ride over to an advertised park.

Leaving the bus and entering the park, Julia hurried to a dirt path that led into the woods.

"This is so beautiful!" Julia exclaimed as I hurried to catch up with her.

"Look it! What is that?" Julia squealed, jumping back as she pointed to the ground.

What looked like a giant lizard, its huge tail curled completely over its back, scurried over the path and into the grass.

"Wow, that could have been a dragon!" Julia said, carefully sidling past where the animal had disappeared in the lawn.

Laughing, I said, "It's just a different type of lizard than we're used to at home, honey. It's hardly a dragon." I ducked as she swung her purse at me.

"Quit teasing me, Rusty, if it was any bigger we could have been its lunch." She giggled and ran off down the path as I chased her growling and snarling, pretending I was a monster.

We almost ran smack into a party coming around a turn. They had to have heard Julia's screams and my growling. They looked at us funny as we passed by.

"You must behave yourself, Rusty. Now act mature or they're sure to throw us out of the park." Julia pretended to reproach me.

Patting her on the butt, I grabbed her hand. Strolling along, we held hands as we appreciated the lovely nature surrounding us. Crossing over a tiny wooden bridge, we entered into a lush, wooded area. A small waterfall splashed down over rocks and through some dense trees.

"Take my picture Rusty." Julia said as she ran and stood in front of the cascading water. The splashing was louder as we got closer to it.

The sound of the water drowned out all the other sounds in the park. It felt like we were completely alone, on our own private island. I took Julia's picture, then pulling her into my arms, I kissed her.

She responded by melting against me, turning her head slightly as her lips parted softly. Hearing voices up the path announcing we were no longer alone, we reluctantly separated.

Enjoying the exotic flowers, we wandered slowly, admiring wild anthuriums and the striking orange birds-of-paradise.

Snapping pictures of birds and exotic plant life, we soon crossed back over the bridge. Stopping on the top, we looked down.

"Ooh, Rusty, look at those pretty water lilies." My wife gestured to the floating green pads, looking so soft, like they were made of felt.

White and pink flowers bedecked the center of the pads. The sun streamed dappled through the trees, lighting on every other flower, brightening them. The small brook barely moved, except when a frog swam underneath only lightly disturbing the green, swampy water.

"I think we should gather up a bunch of them, Julia," I advised her, "and we can make them into hair ornaments for you to wear."

"You're so silly, Rust." She laughed, kissing me as we stood on the bridge.

Suddenly, we heard a man's yelling and a young boy's loud, piercing voice.

"Uh oh, time to go," I said, recognizing the father and son's caterwauling without having to see them. Julia nodded. Wincing in agreement, she quickly covered her ears.

Not even waiting for me, she bolted down the bridge, running along the path, opposite to where we could hear the ever-increasing shrieks. I hurtled after her.

Soon, we left the cool shadowed woods and re-entered the bright sunlight. Without hesitating, we hurried to the bus stop area. Climbing on the bus, weary now, we plopped down heavily onto the leather seats.

Julia rested her head, her red hair softly curling from the humidity on my shoulder, and somehow, tuning out the gabbing going on around us, the jouncing bus lolled us into a light sleep.

When the bus stopped, I said to Julia, "Let's go have a drink on the beach, enjoy the ocean for a while before dinner." She caught up my hand as we made our way to our hotel room to change.

Even though it was winter, it was warm on the beach. We snatched up two lawn chairs, pulling them side-by-side. Julia spread her hotel towel on her chair, then sitting on the edge she took out her suntan lotion.

Sprawled out on my chaise, watching her slather her milky white skin with cream, I said, "Honey, don't you want a little tan?"

Smiling slightly, she shrugged. "The sun causes wrinkles, Rusty. You don't want me to look old and haggardly do you?" Settling back, she put on her straw hat and over- large sunglasses.

Sitting back and closing my eyes as well, I said, "You hardly need to worry about that for a long time, baby. You're young and beautiful! Look, you're pregnant and in such good shape, you're not even really showing yet!" I heard her snort.

"We all grow old Rusty, and, since I'm still early in my pregnancy and I work out, I won't begin showing for probably another month. But when I do start to age, I plan on doing it gracefully! Face lifts, hair dye, massages, I have no problem with any of it!"

At that moment, a native woman approached Julia and asked her if she wanted her hair braided.

"Oh, go for it honey, I think it'll be cute!" I encouraged her.

She gave in. I paid the woman and Julia sat up so she could work on her hair.

Knowing it would take a while for the braids to get done, I took off to get us some drinks. Kicking through the hot sand, I made my way to the tiki bar. People were sitting around the bar, drinking and socializing. A calypso band played by the pool area. Kids were splashing and laughing in the pool.

I bought two piña coladas, one virgin, but both had umbrellas in them, and made my way slowly back to Julia.

I laughed out loud when I saw Julia! She scowled at me. The native woman was just about done with her hair.

Nodding to me as she picked up her basket of bands and beads, the lady sauntered away, down the beach she stopped at every lounger, trying to sell her wares.

"You better not laugh at me, Rusty Dixon! I did this for you!" Scowling, Julia shook her head and picked up a magazine, pretending to ignore me. A million tiny braids, all with beads interspersed in them, swung around her head, rattling as they bounced and banged into each other.

"No, really sweetie, you look, uh... different!" I started laughing again, teasing her. Julia held her magazine up in front of her face so I couldn't see her.

Leaving my chair, I moved over and sat next to her on her chaise. Pushing the magazine down, I chuckled as she tried to move away from me.

"Cut it out, Rusty!" she whined.

Holding her shoulders so she couldn't move, I said, "Baby, I think they're really sexy, I honestly do!" I gazed into her eyes as sincerely as I could. I really did think they were sexy!

The beaded braids swinging around her head, made her look like that girl in that movie '10'. I couldn't wait to get her alone in the hotel room! "You look like a very young Bo Derek, honey, you know she was a babe!"

Julia turned her head away from me, crossing her arms. "I want to look like me, not some movie star from the forties!" She turned her nose up in the air.

"It wasn't that long ago Julia, and the woman still looks fine today. Anyway," I said, as that wasn't making her any happier. "I was just kidding you, I really really like the braids! Let's go back to our room and I'll show you how much!"

Grabbing her chin, I turned her head to face me, kissing her gently on the lips. "C'mon," I cajoled. "Let's see how those braids look lying against a pillow."

Julia laughed. "Okay, in a few minutes. I want to enjoy the beach for a while, and we haven't even drank our drinks yet!" She pushed me away and sat back in her lounge chair.

Getting the hint, I moved back to my chair and picked up my drink. Slurping the coconut-flavored beverage, I asked my wife if she wanted to go swimming in the ocean.

"I don't think so, Rusty. I think I'll just sit here and listen to the music and relax." She sighed blissfully.

"Okay." Sitting for a minute, I watched the other people frolicking in the salty water. "I think I'll go in," I announced.

Kissing Julia on her forehead, I jumped up and ran like a kid down the beach. Splashing noisily, I moved clumsily through the small waves that were crashing on the shore.

"Ahhh…" I moaned, floating on my back, this is the life! The water was surprisingly warm for the winter. Ducking my head, I dove under the water, swimming below the surface, I moved along until I couldn't hold my breath anymore.

Popping up through the surf like a rocket, I bobbed, treading water for a few minutes.

I wished Julia had joined me. I pictured her in her tiny bikini, the emerald green color of it matching her eyes, her legs would be wrapped around my waist. Light as a feather, buoyant from the water, I could move around holding her easily as I plastered her face with kisses, her water soaked half naked body pressed against mine… no one could see us from the shore, we could actually-

Whew! Enough of that thinking, now I have to wait a few minutes now before I can leave the water!

I could hear the shrieks and screams from the people that were riding the yellow banana. They were laughing as the banana bounced roughly through the water. It looked like fun. Maybe we could try it later.

"Ooo!" What was that? Something brushed my leg. Glancing down, I peered through the crystal clear, sea green water. There! I saw an angelfish swimming away from me. How pretty!

Its iridescent body shimmered as it slid silently through the sun-streaked water. I wish I had a snorkel and mask. Oh well. Making my way slowly through the flowing water, I emerged and trudged up the beach to Julia.

A man was standing next to her chair, talking to her. She didn't look too pleased.

He looked up as I approached, then moved away before I reached them.

"What's going on?" I asked Julia as I sat down, dripping water all around me. Reaching for my towel, I dried my arms and legs and ruffled it through my hair.

"Oh," Julia sounded peeved. "They don't leave you alone here, Rusty, everyone is constantly trying to sell you something!" She closed her magazine, shoving it into the straw purse she had purchased at one of the markets.

"Yeah, I know. Walking back up the beach, three people stopped me to ask if I wanted to buy jewelry, a soda, snacks, whatever... I guess they make their livings on the tourists," I said.

"Well, it's annoying, I-" she cut off as a man stopped next to her and asked her if she wanted to look at his bracelets for sale.

"No!" she shouted at him. "Go away!" The man didn't even look affronted at her rudeness, he just moved away, on to the next person.

"Come on, let's go shower and take a nap before dinner," I said, wrapping the towel around my neck and standing up.

Julia stood up as well, and we went back to our air-conditioned room. The drapes were closed, it was dark and cool inside.

We took a shower together, made slow, romantic love on the king-sized bed, then fell asleep still entwined in each other's arms.

Chapter Thirty

The taxi dropped us at the entrance to the Coconut Cabaret where we had dinner reservations.

Steve's friend, Trish, had told us that the Cabaret was one of the best restaurants on the island. Fresh fish was their specialty, and supposedly, one could order any type of seafood one could think of, and have it cooked anyway you desired.

Trish said they put on a spectacular show as well. Belly dancing and flamethrowers were the best around, all glitter and flash. Trish suggested we get reservations.

I hoped it wasn't too commercial, I was looking forward to a little mystery and suspense. We came to the Bahamas for a bit of a different experience than the sameness of the white monotony of Florida.

After paying the taxi driver, I helped Julia out of the car. Boy, green never used to be a favorite color of mine, but that sure is changing fast! My beautiful wife was wearing a silky dress that clung to her in all the right places.

I don't know what shade of green it was called. When I was sixteen, I went on a trip to Hawaii with my folks. The mountains there were subtly majestic, the peaks softened by mists and grass.

The color towards the top, was at first dark forest green. Then, as your eyes moved up further, the sun lightened the grass, filtering it through clouds to a mellow emerald with whispers of saffron peering out.

That pretty much described the color of the dress Julia was wearing. Her eyes danced with the identical shade, the orbs picked up the nuances of the shimmering outfit. Julia clung to my arm as I ushered her inside.

Wow! The place was stupendous! The restaurant staff was all dressed in island clothing. Gaudy flowery shirts on the men, and the waitresses were wearing flowery bikini tops with tiny flowered skirts. All the girls had flowers in their hair.

Torches lit the main dining room as we entered. The tables were glass and rattan, lush plants covered walls and floors. It looked like we were square in the middle of a tropical jungle!

In the back behind the restaurant, I could see and hear a waterfall. It looked like it flowed into a fountain. I bet they even had goldfish in the water. We have to check that out before we leave, I decided.

Apparently, we were sitting family style. There weren't many separate tables. All the seating was together in long lines.

We were seated quickly, and promptly ordered some tropical drinks. The drinks arrived quickly, they were neon yellow, with giant red hibiscus popping out of them.

I had to remove my flower and straw so I could get a good swallow. Besides, watching the other men around me, it looked kind of sissy to be drinking a cocktail with a flower in it. It was bad enough it was yellow for Pete's sake!

I looked at Julia. She was glowing. This was a perfect setting for her, pretty and flowery. I took my hibiscus, dried it in a linen napkin and then tucked it in her hair, pushing it behind her ear.

"Except for the sienna brilliance of your hair, baby, you fit right into this magical place!"

She rewarded me with a dreamy smile. Then her eyes opened wide.

"Oh dear," I heard her say, "we're in for it now, look who's sitting at our table." She nodded to the right.

I looked over, damn, Patterson was sitting a few chairs down. I didn't see the boy, but his daughter, Mixie or Trixie, whatever it was, was next to him. She was scowling, and from where I was sitting, she wasn't wearing much either.

Patterson was yakking in her ear, but he saw me look over. Picking up his glass, he saluted a hello to me.

I nodded and turned back to Julia. Last thing I wanted was to get into a conversation with him!

"Uh oh, Rusty, here comes real trouble!" Julia exclaimed in my ear. She nudged my arm with her elbow, nodding towards the door.

Heather was sweeping through the entrance, latched onto the arm of that smarmy gigolo she was smooching with on the ship. Heather saw us and pointed in our direction to the hostess.

Oh great. The hostess brought them to our table, and there was nowhere to run. What a way to ruin our evening, Heather the Hussy and Pablo the Gigolo all night, oh no...

Heather slinked over and sat right in front of us. She had a tight hold of the virtually transparent, white gown she was wearing. You could see right through the material, made me think of the sheer curtains you put on your windows behind the drapes.

The dress had slits up the sides that went clear to her navel, I think. That's why she was holding onto the dress so tightly. The material was so revealing, it was obvious she wasn't wearing any underclothes, and as she sat, the slits opened and her entire lower half was exposed!

Her date was wearing a tux. The shocking whiteness of his shirt accentuated the darkness of his skin, the black of his eyes gleamed as he perused the area. Reminded me of a ferret.

The second the gigolo sat next to Heather, his right hand disappeared under the table. Immediately, Heather turned and giggled at him, brushing his chin with her short spiky hair.

Blech, made me ill to watch them, it was all I could do not to look at her nipples almost fully visible in the slight material. Heather turned her attention to us.

"Rusty, Julia, you remember my friend here, Kenny Klibano," She stroked his arm as she introduced us.

He nodded a greeting, then stared back at Heather. He grasped her chin with his left hand, pulling her face close to his, kissing her outrageously, like they were the only two people in the joint!

His right hand stayed under the table. Heather moaned, squirming in her chair, she wiggled closer to him, rubbing her chest against his jacketed arm. Revolted, I turned away.

Julia had a smirk on her face. She was staring at the front entrance. I followed her gaze. Uh oh, now there really was going to be trouble!

Steve was standing at the bar. He wasn't alone. Perched on the stool next to him, was a brunette. The female wasn't Trish, the recreation director from the hotel, Trish was blonde. But they were definitely together, the girl was smiling sweetly at Steve, and he had his arm draped around the back of her chair.

I looked at Julia. Now she was watching Heather.

They were still making out, exposed tongues slobbered all over each other's mouths, ugh.

They stopped briefly, Heather turned half closed, lust filled eyes to us. "Oh" She giggled. "We're embarrassing them Kenny!"

Kenny, his tongue in her ear, mumbled something.

Heather pushed Mr. Mustache away as she reached for her drink. She sucked her martini, ogling the olives marinating at the bottom of the triangular glass. Her lipstick was smeared already.

Unfocused eyes reflected that the martini she was imbibing wasn't her first of the evening. Pablo the Gigolo, kept trying to force his tongue in her ear.

Heather pushed him away more forcibly, evidently she was becoming annoyed at the wetness slopping into her ear. "Quit it," she ordered, her words slurred slightly.

Out of the corner of my eye, I could see Patterson watching her with interest. He looked from her to me. I wondered what was going on in that brown haired cop brain.

Returning my gaze to Steve, I noticed the hostess approaching him. She tapped him on the shoulder. He reluctantly tore his attention from the girl he was chatting with.

"Have you seen Steven since you've been on the island?" Heather whined, breaking the silence at our table. "He's not staying at our hotel, and I haven't heard a word from him."

After being pushed away twice, her slimy partner had turned his attention to the rest of the room. His black beady eyes traveled around the room. He looked like a wolf searching for a stranded lamb.

His feral gaze seemed to settle most often on the older women sitting with only other women. They appeared to be single, and most were dripping in jewels. His game was pretty obvious to everyone but dull witted Heather.

"Well, Heather," I said. "We've only seen Steve once or twice since the ship, but I think that's about to change." I couldn't keep the snideness out of my voice.

"Huh?" Heather muttered obtusely. The alcohol was making her response seem in slow motion. Her mouth was drooping open, her eyes looked vague and confused.

I couldn't believe that we were all going to be sitting at the same table. Providence perhaps?

It was really weird, I was thinking as the hostess was bringing Steve and his date directly to our table. This ought to make things interesting!

Julia turned to me, her mouth was open as well, she had been watching Steve and now realized where they were heading. She turned to me, her eyes wide in question.

I shrugged. What could we do, but sit back and enjoy the show! Although now it looked like there's going to be two shows, one on stage and one at our table!

"Hey Rusty, Julia! What a surprise running into you guys here! Cool hair, Julia!" Standing behind Heather, Steve greeted us enthusiastically.

Recognizing his voice, Heather's head whipped around. Her mouth opened, smiling, she was about to say something to Steve. Abruptly her lips snapped shut as Steve introduced the girl at his side to Julia and me.

"This is Diana. Diana, these are my friends Rusty and Julia."
He ignored Heather completely. Diana smiled shyly.

Diana was very pretty, in a sweet, simple way, and she had
to be at least five years younger than the rest of us. Her shiny
brown hair hung poker straight past her shoulders. Black lashes
fringed big, dark blue eyes.

Her eyes were her best feature, the blue was the color of the
deepest part of the ocean. She had a friendly smile, shy but
welcoming, revealing perfect white teeth.

Almost as tall as Steve, she was wearing a midnight blue
dress, demure but sexy in a subtle way. Steve had his arm around
her, he pulled out a chair for the girl.

They managed to sit two seats away from Julia and I, kitty
corner from Heather and her date.

When Heather had heard Steve's voice, she had moved her
body away from the gigolo's. As soon as she realized he wasn't
alone, she pressed back against the macho hunk as tightly as she
could.

Unfortunately, Pablo, Kenny, whatever the creep's name
was, had lost interest in Heather and was busy scoping out new
territory. His beady glare was aimed a few feet away.

Sitting at a private table, a matronly woman, encrusted in
gems was conversing with two younger, equally bejeweled
females.

The younger women, slightly more attractive than the older
lady, were both sporting huge diamonds on their wedding fingers.
That must be why the gigolo was staring intently at the obviously
wealthy older woman, whose ring finger was bare.

Every other pudgy digit was covered in expensive stones,
except the one. That one finger was like a beacon of light, along
with the ostentatious jewelry of course!

Steve was in deep conversation with his date, Diana...I'd
already forgotten her last name. They were flirting lightly with
each other. The way they were giggling, I could tell they didn't
even notice anyone else was in the room. Ahh, I thought, young
love!

Julia was snuggled against me, sipping on her virgin Yellow Zinger. As soon as we all finished ordering our dinners, the room darkened, the show was beginning.

Immediately the stage glowed with burning torches, and girls wearing hula skirts bounded out onto the stage, dancing rhythmically to the beat of drums. It was like being in Hawaii!

The show was great, a lot of frenetic dancing and music. It was hard to watch the performance and eat at the same time.

Thankfully, our food arrived just before the intermission. Alaskan king crab legs, piled at least a foot high, sat in front of me, steam pouring off them.

Shoving the lemon off the end of my cocktail fork, I grabbed the nutcrackers and dug in. Clanging cutlery around the room let me know I wasn't chowing alone.

As soon as the lights came on, conversations began. It got loud around the immense hall. It was sort of awkward at our table. Heather and Steve were trying to ignore each other.

At first, Heather had tried to show how little she cared that Steve had a date by throwing herself all over the gigolo. But, Pablo already had other plans. When the lights came on, he removed Heather's manicured fingers from his sleeve.

With barely a, "See you later, it's been fun," he slithered from our table and made his way to the rich patroness a few feet away.

Diana stood up, clutching her matching blue purse, and excused herself. Steve watched her walk all the way to the entrance where she disappeared, assumedly on her way to the little girl's room.

The girl had a curvaceous body and quite the provocative little walk. Steve was certainly doing okay lately, he was sure coming up with some babes! Each one was better than the last! That is so unlike him, he's not exactly Brad Pitt or anything, how was he getting all these bodacious women I wondered. Maybe he won a lot at the gambling tables or something and didn't tell us.

When Steve's attention returned to our table, Heather used the opportunity to strike up a conversation with him.

LOUISE FURLEY

I tried to pretend I wasn't listening while loudly cracking the shells of my crabs. By the way she was idly poking at her stuffed shrimp, I could tell Julia was listening too.

Heather leaned in, trying to reveal more of her already exposed tiny bosom. Diana made Heather look like a ten-year-old girl in the figure department.

Heather took a healthy gulp of her martini and licked her thin lips. It might have helped if she had repaired the damage that the gigolo had done to her lipstick. Glaring red was smeared around her mouth. Someone give the girl a mirror, I thought to myself.

"Uh, so Steven... what are you... uh... how's... um... where are you staying?" she stuttered, unsure of herself for the first time in her life. It didn't do her ego much good seeing Steve with a pretty young girl all goo-goo eyed at him.

Steve turned indifferently to Heather. His eyes took in her slutty outfit, raking up and down her practically naked body. He barely concealed a yawn as he dismissed her, looking away in disgust, like she was a bug.

"I'm staying at Rusty and Julia's hotel, the Island-Vistique..." Steve hesitated, then wickedly sneered, "on the water!" he said as he picked up his fork and speared a broiled scallop.

Steve told us that the hotel he had booked first was more in the city, about five miles from the ocean. Heather had complained at the time of the reservation, but Steve was watching pennies then. I wonder what caused the change.

Affronted, Heather sat back. Then she tried again, "So who's the little girl you're with? A friend of yours daughter? Are you baby-sitting tonight?" Jealousy curdled Heather's words.

Steve's bored look in Heather's direction was like a slap in the face. "No darling," he said, sarcasm dripping from his very being, "she's my date. We plan on continuing our relationship when we return to Florida."

He had turned away from her, missing Heather's curled lip.

But his gaze returned as he said nonchalantly, "Oh, dear, by the way, since our house is only rented," Julia and I looked at each other, surprised. I didn't know they didn't own the house. No wonder he paid so much out each month!

He continued, "I called the owner from the hotel. I've canceled the lease. We have thirty days to vacate. Is that enough time for you to remove your belongings, honey? And don't forget, dearest, the furniture is rented too, so make sure none of it follows you out the door."

At Heather's sharp intake of breath, Julia and I set our forks down, it was too hard to pretend not to be listening.

There was a commotion down the table from us as well. Patterson was arguing with his teenaged terror. He was trying to hold her wrist and she was writhing and yanking her hand, trying to get away. We could hear his deep voice instructing her to sit down.

"You are going to stay here Trixie. Now, sit down and act like a lady, at least as much as you can in that minuscule dress you're wearing! You look like a harlot with all that paint plastered on your face. I'm sure your mother doesn't allow that!" Patterson gave her arm a vicious yank as he tried to pull her down onto her chair.

The girl refused to budge. She continued struggling, trying to pry the officer's grip from her hand. "Daddy," she pleaded, "let me go! I promised Clark I would meet him at the Carousel Club at nine! Come on," she kept jerking her arm.

"I'm not a little girl for heaven's sake, I'm sixteen, almost seventeen! I'm old enough to go out on a date, Mom would let me go!"

"I refuse to let you out in the night in a strange place with some punk named Clark," Patterson growled. "What kind of a silly name is Clark anyway? Now sit down and finish your dinner before the show starts. You've hardly touched your pasta and calamari."

Patterson gave her wrist a final jerk, slamming her onto her chair. Her face thunderous, she crossed her arms and glared at her plate.

The detective returned his previously tossed napkin to his lap and picked up his fork. Just as he took a bite of steak, his truant temptress leaped up and ran from the table, making her escape from the room before Patterson could blink.

Quickly, I averted my eyes to my plate. It was too late, Patterson had observed me watching his fight with his daughter.

He shrugged. Picking up his drink, the detective left his seat and moved over to us, sitting down in the empty chair next to me. Oh great.

"Mind if I join you Dixon?" He asked, not waiting for my reply. "I hate to eat alone, the boy's with a baby-sitter." He gulped his cocktail. It looked like he planned on drinking the rest of his dinner.

The way things have been going lately, I could picture lonely Patterson and the equally abandoned and intoxicated Heather hooking up. I shivered, ick, what a thought.

I shoved the ugly picture I had envisioned of a skinny, nude Heather, and hairy, muscled Patterson about to fall into bed together-ugh- I turned quickly to Steve.

Heather had given up on him, she was smoking a cigarette, staring at the vacant stage. I was pretty sure there was no smoking in our area, but I don't think Heather cared. Wary of the dark glower on her pinched puss, I wasn't going to be the one to break the news to her.

Quickly, before his current date returned from the ladies room, I asked, "So Stevie, what happened to Trish, the girl from the hotel?" That got Heather's attention.

She hadn't known about Diana's more recent predecessor. Heather's bleached blonde head swiveled around, her eyes narrowed as she studied him. I bet she was thinking, what is it all these girls see in him that she didn't see?

Now that she realized other women were interested in her man, she was looking twice at him with renewed interest.

Steve had told us when we saw him at the hotel that he had been sitting at the bar with the cruise director on the ship, in a lip-lock, when Heather had passed by with her gigolo.

She had pointed her nose in the air, pretending she hadn't seen him, but there was no way she could have missed them, he and the girl were the only ones at the bar.

Steve grinned at me. He was still timid, but confidence was beginning to invade and push out his base shyness. "Trish and I only had dinner together. She's nice, but wasn't really my type. She's into going to live wrestling matches and mud fights, stuff like that. Actually, she kind of introduced me to Diana."

Totally ignoring the smirk on Heather's pointy face, he continued, "Diana is a guest at the hotel-"

Heather interrupted with a snide comment, "What, she can't get a guy so she vacations with a bunch of girlfriends?" She sucked on her cigarette. Blowing out smoke she snorted, "What a chick, sounds special." Reaching for her drink, she flicked her ashes on the floor.

Ignoring the biting bitch's sarcasm, Steve confided to Julia and me, "Diana is here with her sister Kathryn. Kathy just broke up with her husband and needed some consoling and change of scenery. Diana thought taking her on this trip would help smooth things over, let her sister relax and get her emotions back in check. She's a terrific girl, kind, compassio-"

Heather's ugly snort interrupted Steve's dialogue again. "So big deal, Steven, you have a brief fling with a little girl that's going to have to end as soon as you leave the Bahamas. Really, where's she live, Montana or something?"

She blew smoke at the side of Steve's head, since he refused to acknowledge her existence. I could hear a chuckle coming from Patterson, but when I glanced at him, he was staring at his empty glass.

Waitresses in their gay outfits, swooped in and started clearing our tables, asking who wanted coffee and dessert. I remembered seeing hot blueberry cobbler topped with cold vanilla ice cream, I ordered that with coffee.

Steve said eagerly, "You won't believe this, Rusty, but Diana owns a small boutique." With difficulty he didn't look in Heather's direction, he knew she was listening.

"It's right on Seagrape Drive, a block from the ocean, practically in the heart of Ft. Lauderdale. She couldn't be any closer!" He beamed, proud of his new girlfriend.

"I'm a lucky guy!" Steve crowed setting down his fork. The server removed his plate.

"In fact," he almost whispered, "since I pulled out of bankrolling another store, not mentioning any names," he ignored Heather's hiss of denial, "I was thinking of maybe investing in another one! I seem to suddenly have an excess of money now that I don't have exorbitant rent, clothes, hair salon, manicures, pedicures, building a new shop, gourmet food bills etc. etc. etc..." he trailed off just as Diana returned to her seat.

Steve jumped up and pulled out her chair for her. Heather looked away quickly, disdain pushed her sharp nose further in the air.

As Diana re-joined the table, the waitress returned, but not with my coffee and dessert. She had an ice bucket, bottle of wine and seven wine glasses. She set a glass in front of Patterson, Julia and me, Steve and Diane and Heather.

The place where the gigolo had been sitting was empty. The waitress kept the seventh glass on the tray.

We all looked questioningly at each other. I told the server, "We didn't order any wine." Confused, we continued watching her as she proceeded to pull the cork out of the bottle and pour the wine into each of our glasses.

She nodded towards the direction of the front of the room. "The wine was sent from the gentleman at the bar." After filling our glasses, the bottle was almost empty, she placed it in the ice bucket and wrapped a towel around it.

Relaying the message, the waitress continued, "He said, 'give my compliments to the table, tell them I said hi', or something to that effect." She left the table right as she completed delivering the message. She disappeared before we could ask her any more questions.

I looked at the bar. I didn't recognize anyone at the bar and none of the people sitting there appeared to be even looking in our direction, must less interested in anyone at our table. Maybe the waitress had made a mistake. Oh well, I thought, as I reached for my wine glass, someone's loss is our gain!

The room darkened again as the second half of the show started. My dessert and coffee showed up. Contentedly, I spooned ice cream into my mouth, my arm around my wife's shoulder. Her head rested on my arm.

The show went on for another hour. One by one, everyone at our table left to go to the restroom. Some returned, some didn't. By the time the performance was over and the lights came on, only Julia, Patterson, and I remained.

Steve and Diana had left shortly after the show had started again. When Heather realized Steve wasn't coming back, she packed up her cigarettes, and taking her fourth martini with her, she left without saying goodbye. Good riddance, I thought!

Suddenly, the peaceful quiet was shattered by bloodcurdling screams that reverberated through the room as the front door was opened.

We all sat straight up, sobered by the screeching.

Patterson jumped up from years of training, and dodging tables and chairs scattered around the room, ran out the front door.

I took Julia's hand, we might as well check it out too. The few people remaining in the restaurant were pouring out the door, eager to see what had caused the hideous screaming.

Spilling out the door with the rest of the patrons, we saw a tiny crowd of gawkers gathered by the outside pond. We moved towards the pond with the other rubberneckers.

More screams were heard as people viewed the sight that awaited us. We pushed people aside and peered through the crowd. Those closest to the fountain gagged then turned away covering their mouths and eyes. It looked like a lady or two was going to faint.

It was dark outside, around one in the morning. The moon was out, full, and a few outside lamps cast an eerie glow. Shadows moved as people flowed to the pond and then quickly away. We moved through the crowd and looked down.

A man lying on his stomach was sprawled across the rim of the fountain. His body was on the outside of the pond, but his face was under water. Blood circled his head, and the coy were nibbling at his flesh. My stomach turned, but I couldn't pull my mesmerized eyes away.

"Rusty! Rusty!" Julia was violently tugging at my sleeve. "I want to go! Let's go Rusty!" she wailed at me.

Patterson was kneeling by the pond, he was looking at the body but not touching it. Without turning, he hollered out to anyone listening,

"Someone call the police!" No one moved. "Now!" he yelled.

A couple of waiters jumped at his command, startled, they ran off towards the hotel's entrance. Julia moved to the back of the crowd.

I took a couple of steps closer to the pond, coming to stand next to Patterson. I tried to peer into the inky water.

Without disturbing the body, the detective was attempting to push the fish away from the apparently dead man's head. "Stay back!" he barked at patrons that were pressing in to see.

Leaning in closer, I could see the man's head and shoulders were submerged, and something was sticking out of the guy's neck. Wow, gross. "What happened Patterson?" I asked.

"Stay back, Dixon," he ordered. "Where the hell are the police? Did any of you knuckleheads call the police?" he shouted over his shoulder, still kneeling and shooing away the fish.

I told him a couple of waiters had called the cops. The crowd was getting bigger, fluctuating from people joining the group, then dropping back groaning in horror when they realized what gruesome scene they were viewing.

Some diehard onlookers, like myself, stayed close, trying to see the dead guy in the black, bloody water.

With sirens blaring, the police arrived within ten minutes. I looked around for Julia. Not spotting her, I figured she went back inside the restaurant. Standing next to Patterson, I listened as he described to the cop in charge what he knew, which was very little.

The police were wandering through the thinning crowd, asking if anyone had seen anything. I could see people shaking their heads in the negative. It seemed like a long time before they finally pulled the body out of the water.

He didn't look too pretty, the fish had done a job on his face. I sure didn't recognize him. It's not too likely I'd know some dead guy in the Bahamas anyway.

I heard a shriek, "I recognize him!"

I turned as a waitress was pointing in my direction and screaming, "He knows him! He knows him!" I looked over my shoulder, no one was behind me. The crowd paused, all eyes were on me.

"He was sitting at the bar and he bought that guy a bottle of wine!" the waitress screamed, still pointing an accusing finger at me.

What?

My mouth dropped open. "Me? I didn't know the guy! I've never seen him before in my life!"

Patterson stepped away from me, his hand went inside his coat pocket. Oh my gosh, was he reaching for a gun?!

"I didn't know the guy Patterson, cut it out!" I yelled in terror, scared to death the nut was going to kill me!

"Him too!" the waitress screamed. "He was sitting next to the killer, he knew him too!" She was pointing at Patterson.

Patterson's head jerked up in shock. He squawked, "What?"

Several police officers ran over, aiming guns at both of us, they ordered us not to move. Not a problem, I thought. My shaking hands shot in the air.

Patterson moved more slowly. "I'm a police officer in the states- I-"

"In the air!" the cops commanded him.

Reluctantly he raised his hands. "I have a badge and ID in my right breast pocket," he informed the officers. One came over and carefully reached in Patterson's jacket. He pulled out his ID. Reading it, he lowered his weapon.

"It's okay," the policeman told the other men. "He's Detective Mark Patterson, Indigo Isles Police Department." Handing back his ID to Patterson, he told the detective he could lower his arms.

"Hey!" I yelped. "What about me?"

Patterson frowned at me. "I know this man," he said, "take him in for questioning."

"What? Hey! Patterson! Hey!" I cried as I was roughly handcuffed and then quickly shoved into a police car.

"My wife, Patterson, tell Julia!" I yelled out the open window as the police car drove off.

Chapter Thirty-One

The Bahamian police interrogated me for three hours.

After removing the handcuffs they said I wasn't under arrest, I was just brought there for questioning. They refused my request for a lawyer, claiming that since I was only being questioned, not arrested, I didn't need an attorney.

They had fingerprinted me as soon as we had arrived at the police station even though they continued to state that I was not under arrest. Then I was thrown into a tiny cement room that contained only a table and two chairs.

I was pushed down onto one of two chairs. They were pretty rough to someone not under arrest, I'd sure hate be arrested!

A fat guy with a bald head, and a thinner, short guy with a beard entered the room.

The fat guy had a file folder in his hand. He set the folder on the table and sat down on the only other chair in the room.

The thin guy leaned against the door, his ankles and arms were crossed. I guess he was the guard dog. Waiting for the 'bad cop-good cop' routine, I nervously braced myself for a verbal beating.

The fat guy opened the file and leafed through the three or four pieces of paper that were in it. He looked at me, then down at the file, then back at me.

No one made a sound for about five minutes. I guess they were trying to make me sweat, hoping I'd spill my guts from the tension.

"Mr... uh..." the fat man looked down at the file, then up at me, "Dixon," he said. "How did you know the deceased, uh,.." back to the file, "Gil Cooper?"

Anxiously, I squirmed in my chair. These foreign police scared the hell out of me. I'd always heard about people getting arrested on bogus charges in other countries, they get locked up, never to be heard from again.

I was sweating like a pig the day before a big barbecue. Trying to control the quaking in my voice, I said, "I do not know the dead guy." I looked earnestly over at the fat guy, then to the other guy, then I turned my eyes down, staring at the file. There were photographs in the file.

"Hmmm..." the fat guy flipped through the file. He sat back and silently stared at me for a few minutes. "Mr. Dixon, we've been talking with the officer that was with you at the restaurant, uh... Detective Patterson."

I nodded, hoping Patterson wasn't hanging me out to dry.

"Mr. Patterson has informed us that you could be a possible suspect in some unsolved murders in Florida." The officer squinted at me, apparently trying to affect a 'piercing glare'.

Taking a deep breath to calm myself, I clenched my shaking hands together. "Sir, one of the people that was murdered was a best friend of mine that I'd known for years. I'm even a godfather to his daughter. And the other people that were killed were some thugs from the city that I never heard of." I pleaded with my eyes for the fat guy to believe me.

He looked me straight in the eye, "Mr. Dixon, people quite often murder people they know."

The guy by the door shuffled a bit, leaning his other shoulder against the doorframe. He rubbed his beard with his free shoulder. He didn't utter a word.

"I did not murder my friend," my voice squeaked like a baby's. "I did not murder those criminals in the city, and I certainly did not kill some stranger here in the Bahamas!" I tried to sound serious and convincing. But I know my voice shook and I sounded whiny and probably guilty.

The fat man pulled a sheet of paper from the file. "It says here that the deceased man bought you a bottle of wine. Why would he do that if he didn't know you?" he questioned me with one eye squinting.

"He didn't buy ME the bottle of wine, he sent it over for the entire table. The waitress brought six, no, seven glasses, and said it was compliments to 'them'." I explained.

"If you're suspicious of anybody, you should investigate Heather Hazelhurst's date, some playboy named... uh.." I couldn't think of the gigolo's name. "Uh... Kenny I think she said. That guy has to be crooked, take one look at him, he's shady as heck!" Feeling more confident, I sat back, crossing my arms in front of my chest.

"Besides," I added, "he left our table early in the evening, he could have easily killed the guy. As dark as he was, no one could have seen him in the night, he-" I stopped in mid word when I realized both officers were staring at me.

Forgetting they were Black, I had blundered on about the dark, smarmy foreign guy, what a dope I am! Jeepers, I thought, just bring me a blindfold and a cigarette, let's get this over with.

The cops did not respond to my faux pas. "What did you have for dinner, Mr. Dixon?" the fat guy inquired.

"Huh?" What did that have to do with the murder? "Um... I had the, uh, king crab legs. But I don't see-"

The fat guy cut me off, "Cooper was killed with a skewer," he said.

"What? A what?" I asked, leaning forward, my elbows clunked on the table.

The fat man reviewed his paperwork. Looking back at me he repeated, "A skewer. A thin metal rod with a point on one end. Commonly used for shish kabob. It was stuck into his neck," he explained. "Did they give you a skewer with your crab legs?"

"No, you don't get a skewer with crab legs, you get a tiny cocktail fork and some nutcrackers," I replied, shivering when I remembered the medal rod sticking out of the side of the guy's neck and the coy chewing on his flesh- gross.

"Did anyone at your table get a skewer with their dinner?" the cop asked.

I tried to remember what everyone had. Julia ordered stuffed shrimp... Heather had the salmon... Steve and Diana shared a mixed seafood fajita platter... the gigolo had left before dinner was served...

"Hey!" I announced. "Detective Patterson was eating a steak! He wasn't sitting with us when he was eating, but he could have kept the knife and hidden it in his suit coat!"

That was interesting, I thought. Patterson could be a suspect in the murders too, he was around during all the killings just as much as I was.

The fat cop looked at me like I was dense. "I said the murder weapon was a metal shish-kabob skewer, not a knife. It had been wiped clean, there were no fingerprints on it."

"Oh." Feeling stupid, I stared at my hands. I looked around the room thinking hard.

I looked up at the fat man. "You know, those people that were killed in Sherwood City were into gambling and stuff. The newspaper said they thought the murders may have been mob related." I tried to sound intelligent, informative.

"Uh huh..." the fat guy mumbled. "What about your friend then, why was he killed? Did he owe someone money?"

I felt the grief hit me anew. Mike. I tried not to think about him these days. Sometimes I missed him so much, especially during football season. We used to go to the Dolphin games together a lot. I blinked rapidly, staring at the ceiling. I didn't want to cry like a sissy in front of these burly cops.

"I honestly don't know what was going on with Mike," I answered. "We've all thought and thought about it, what he could have been into, but we just don't know. Mike was a loud, sometimes obnoxious, but super friendly guy. He liked to play hard.

"He and his wife had been having problems, they were separated for a while before his murder. We don't know what kind of people he was hanging out with. And...ah," feeling guilty I said, "I was a little.. uh... ticked off with him and hadn't been really speaking to him for some time before he was killed."

"Ticked off?" The cop raised one eyebrow in question.

"Um... uh... I was a little mad at him," I explained. "He had acted crudely towards my wife at a social function our circle had attended. And he had been treating his wife pretty shabbily lately. Sandy, Mike's wife and I have been close friends since practically birth... and-" I broke off, why was I telling these guys so much personal information?

It was none of their business, and I was probably hanging myself further. Clamping my big mouth shut, I sat back in my chair.

"Go on," the fat guy said, "how well were you and this... this Sandy woman getting along?"

"Sandy and I, like I said, we're good friends. I'm the first person she called when she was told about Mike's death."

The cop by the door acted totally disinterested in our conversation. I looked at the man in front of me, with what I hoped was an innocent expression.

"Were you and Sandy having an affair?" the fat man asked.

"What?! How dare you!" I sat bolt upright, furious. "Sandy and I are friends, I would never do something like that! I am happily married to a beautiful woman!"

"Wouldn't be the first time a 'happily married guy' got it on with his friend's wife!" the cop said with a cutting glance to his friend by the door.

"Well! Not me! I couldn't... wouldn't... not in a million... I just would not!" I declared, highly offended at the suggestion of any kind of impropriety between Sandy and me, the nerve! Crossing my arms again, I slumped back in my chair.

"People have killed for less than sex, Mr. Dixon. You could have wanted this woman for yourself and murdered her husband to get her," the cop suggested.

"Well, I did not. I am insulted that you are even saying such a thing." Leaning forward again, I shook my finger at the fat man.

"Sandy and Mike Casey were good friends of mine that I'd known for years. I never had any *designs* on Sandy, ever, and as I said, I am actually a newlywed, married to a wonderful, gorgeous woman that I am madly in love with!" I trumpeted- so there, I thought.

"And anyway, I repeat, I did not even know those hoods that were killed in the city. The Florida police don't know what the connection between Mike and them was."

Muttering noncommittedly, "Uh huh," The guy shuffled the papers in the file.

"And…" I said, "if you want to know about affairs, my friend Mike was having one with Heather Hazelhurst. Furthermore," I tattled, "Heather was really mad at Mike for breaking it off, and she also was sitting at our table when the stranger sent over the bottle of wine."

I sniffed, put out that anyone would accuse me of cheating! I kept my arms tightly crossed in front of my chest and crossed my legs as well, putting myself in the most protected position I could get in.

The fat cop looked over at the thin one. They shared a silent agreement. The fat man wrote something in the file.

I craned my neck slightly and strained my eyes trying to peek at his notes. Heather's name was there, but he quickly covered the rest with his arm when he saw me looking.

The thin man pushed his hands into his pockets but didn't move from the doorway. "You know Richard," he said casually to the fat man, "last time I had crab legs, I was given a long, thin metal rod-like utensil that was used to help push out some of the meat that clung to the inside of the shell."

Oh my gosh, I thought, stiffening in sudden fear. I remember now, they did give me one of those. I never used it so I didn't think about it. Oh no! Both cops were watching me.

They had to have observed my instant panic. Hiding my feelings was not something I was ever good at. I still blush at off-color jokes, especially if a woman tells them.

"Listen Officers," I pleaded holding my palms up. "I... I was given one of those skewer things, I remember now it was on the plate with the legs. But... but I didn't even touch it. I set it to the side, I think, and never thought about it again! I swear!"

Anxiously I looked from one cop to the other. "Besides, isn't that metal rod smaller than a shish-kabob thing?"

Richard reviewed the file. He picked up a paper and read it. "Hmmm... oh, here it is... yes... metal skewer - eight inches in length."

"See!" I yelped excitedly. "I think the one on my plate was a lot shorter than that, maybe like six inches or less." Boy that was close, I thought with a sigh of relief. They were probably all ready to lock me up and throw away the key.

The thin guy with the beard said, "I don't know, that's pretty close in length. Who's to know that on that night the cook ran out of small skewers and used a long one on your plate?"

Richard, the fat cop, stared at me for minute, silent. Then he wrote something in the notes.

Scared again, I said, "Even if that were true, and I'm sure it isn't, anybody really could have taken that skewer from me without me noticing. The room was very dark, and people were constantly getting up and down from our table, going to the restroom or taking pictures. Also," I scrunched my eyes closed trying to picture the restaurant.

"There was a stand with a bus pan on it right at the end of our table. Anyone could have surreptitiously picked one out of the pan and hidden it inside a long pocket or a purse."

Richard made some more notes. He looked at me. "Did you notice anyone from your party approach anyone at the bar?"

Shaking my head, I said, "First, it was not MY party, people I know just happened to be sitting at the same table that I was. And no, I never saw any of the people I knew go to the bar..." I hesitated, my eyes dropped quickly to the wooden table I was leaning on.

The fat man's brows arched in question. "Yes?" he asked.

I looked away, I know I looked guilty. "Um, uh... nothing... you know... uh nothing," I stammered.

"Mr. Dixon," the fat guy glared at me, his voice stern, "you are in absolutely no position to keep anything from us. You are a hair's breadth from being arrested for at least one murder. We have opportunity, and possibly the weapon - that we believe came directly from YOUR plate. We can easily come up with a motive, like for instance... the guy looked funny at your wife, or offered her an indecent proposal."

He laid his pen down, and clasped his pudgy hands in front of him on the table. "You already got pretty hot about how beautiful your wife is, and how madly in love with her you are. You said you were estranged from your friend because he'd been inappropriate with your wife.

"That makes us suspicious as to how far you'd go to keep other men away from her. How scared are you of losing her? Scared enough to commit murder?" His eyebrows rose higher in accusation.

"Yes," the thin guy moved to the table, and stood in front of me. He smacked his fist on the table for emphasis- I jumped at the sudden sound- "Was your wife attracted to this guy? Did he put the moves on her?"

The fat cop leaned closer to me, glaring at me. "Have you been having problems? Has she 'wandered' before? It's okay, you can tell us. We're men, we understand how angry a fellow can get seeing another man hitting on our woman."

"No! No! No!" I yelled. "You have it all wrong! Julia loves me! She would never cheat on me, she would never leave me. I wasn't worried... I... I... it was Steve at the bar!" I blurted- oh my gosh, I can't believe I was giving up my best friend!

"But- but Steve would never in a million years do anything against the law." Lowering my head to the table, I ran my hands over the back of my hair. What the heck was going on here? How did this horrible thing happen to three happy-go-lucky couples?

The fat man sat back and crossed his thick arms over his bulky chest. "Steve? Steve who?" he inquired. The thin man still leaned over me, one hand was flat on the table, the other on the back of my chair.

"Ohhh..." I moaned. Sitting back, I closed my eyes. "Steven Hazelhurst is my best friend. He wouldn't, couldn't, hurt a fly. The only time I saw him at the bar, he was making goo-goo eyes at his date. I didn't see him talking to anyone else. He doesn't know anyone else here... uh, except his wife."

"His wife?" Both cops asked in unison.

Richard the fat cop said, "This Steven was on a trip to the Bahamas with his wife, but he had a date at the bar?"

Oh dear, with friends like me, who needs enemies? What have I done? I tried to explain, "Steve is a good guy, really, it's his wife that's the problem."

The thin guy sat on the edge of the table.

Richard leaned back, his hands were now folded in front of him like a schoolboy, ready to listen. "Why don't you start at the beginning," he suggested.

"Uhhh..." Rubbing my eyes, I sat back and told them all about the wife swapping, then the affair, Mike's death. I told them what a little tramp Heather was, I even told them about the stamp and the crook on Mike's boat that was going to shoot me.

They listened intently, asking a question here and there. The thin guy's name was Donald. Actually, they seemed to be pretty nice guys for police officers. It took me a while to tell the entire story, and explain what coincidences brought all of us here to the Island.

By the time I was done talking, we were all stretching and yawning. Richard and Donald wrote notes sometimes, occasionally referring to something in the file.

They showed me a picture of the dead guy. It was totally gross. His eyes were closed, thank goodness, but his face was bloodless and bloated, and there were cuts and tears all over his skin. Damage done by the coy I figured. They couldn't show me a DMV photo?

I tried to be cool while perusing it, but I could feel my stomach protesting. Looking away quickly, I said I'd never seen him before in my life.

The police said he was an American. His name was Gil Cooper and his ID said his address was in Titusville, Florida. They didn't know what he was doing in the Bahamas.

Apparently he had a record for minor crimes. His specialty was scams, so the cops figured he was hanging around the restaurant looking for an easy score. Richard said with all those old, rich widowed women the pickings were easy.

Finally, Richard closed the file and tucked the pen into his pocket. "Well Mr. Dixon," he said to me, his voice kind. "I'm pretty satisfied that you had nothing to do with the murder of this American. Although it's quite a coincidence that you are involved in some unsolved murders back in the States," he held up a hand as I started to object.

"Mr. Cooper was probably here up to no good and someone found out and killed him for whatever criminal activity he was involved in. I don't see any tie between you and him. We're going to let you go, we have your address, and we assume you would return and cooperate if we have further inquiries." He raised an eyebrow in question.

They were letting me go! "Yes! Oh yes!" I exclaimed, "Anything you want, I'm at your disposal!" I grinned while nodding vigorously.

Richard stood up, Donald was already at the door. I shoved my chair back, eager to get the heck out of that cramped dank room.

The officers shook my hand at the door. Richard pointed down a hall.

"You can exit that way, I think your wife is at admitting waiting for you. You are free to leave, but we are going to want to talk with your friends, the Hasselhoffs."

"Steven and Heather Hazelhurst," I corrected him. I had already provided their hotel names to Richard. I reminded the officer about the gigolo Heather was hanging around with, and Detective Patterson.

Patterson was starting to look suspicious to me at this point. Maybe he killed someone and was trying to frame me! I could make a pretty good patsy. Between my gullibility and my big mouth... sometimes. I need to learn to be more careful.

I thanked the officers for being so easy on me and hurried down the hall, I wanted to leave this place quickly behind me. The two officers were shaking their heads and grinning at my fright and eagerness to leave. I must have looked pretty greenly unworldly to them.

As soon as I rounded the corner, a beautiful little bundle of red hair and softness detached itself from a chair and hurled its warm body at me.

"Oh Rusty, I've been so worried!" Julia cried, hugging and kissing me. "I didn't know if I should get a lawyer, they wouldn't tell me what was going on, only that you had been brought in for questioning. I tried to reach Steven but he's not at his hotel. I didn't know what to do!"

"I know baby, it's okay now, I'm all right. Let's get the hell out of here! I want to go home, and I mean America, not the hotel." I grabbed her arm and we ran for the exit.

Chapter Thirty-Two

The ship ride home didn't seem as long as it did on the way over. We sat in our lounge chairs and barely moved from them the whole return trip.

Fortunately, we did not run into anyone else, no Steve, no Heather and no Patterson with his sticky son and truant teenager.

An hour before the ship was due to dock, we made our way to the exit, insuring we'd be among the first to get off.

Thoroughly exhausted, we exited the ship and never looking back, we walked through the glass enclosed greeting area and made our way to the luggage area. I glanced over to see if the guy that had let us on without Julia's ID was working.

Yeah, there he was, I could see his gleaming smile 100 feet away. Sure, I thought, thanks for nothing. If he'd been doing his job, he wouldn't have let us on the boat and we wouldn't have had to go through that horrible traumatic experience!

I had half a mind to go over and punch him right in the nose! But, the vision of the jail I narrowly escaped, loomed in front of my eyes and I thought better of it. Impatiently, I led Julia quickly out of the departure room and hurried us to the parking garage.

It took us 20 minutes to find the Bronco. Unlocking the doors, I threw the baggage in as Julia jumped into the front seat. Joining her, I stuck the key in the ignition and turned the engine on.

I reclined my head back and briefly closed my eyes. Sighing in relief, I realized I wouldn't feel totally safe until we got home. Shoving the gear hard in drive, we zoomed out of the garage and roared out of there, eager to head for the sanctity of home.

We didn't even unpack the suitcases, we just tossed them in a corner and stumbled into the den, where we plopped down happily on the soft leather couch. Sighing heavily, we turned to each other. Julia gazed at me through half closed lids.

"There's no place like home," she sighed contentedly. Closing her eyes, she let her head roll back on the sofa cushion.

We didn't move for hours. Sometime, around eight o'clock, Julia sat up, groaned softly and said, "I guess we should have some dinner. I'll go check and see if we left anything in the refrigerator."

I called out to her, "Anything would be fine with me!"

"No kidding!" I heard her mumble.

I'm easy to cook for, I'll eat whatever is put in front of me, especially if someone else has prepared it! A blinking red light caught my attention from the corner of my eye. The answering machine, we had a message.

Stretching and shaking my head to clear my mind, I moved to the easy chair that was next to the phone. Three messages awaited us, the machine said. Pushing the play button, I sat back and listened.

The first message was on Saturday, it was from Sandy. She sounded a little lonely. "Hi guys, I just wanted to see how you're doing... um... Grandma Amy took Bonnie to Walmart, so I have some time to myself... uh... maybe you two can come over tomorrow night for Sunday dinner. I was thinking I could make a roast with stuffing and sweet potatoes, maybe some greens.

"I know Rusty, you love apple pie... I guess..." she hesitated, sighing deeply. "I guess around these holidays I'm really missing Mike. Well, give me a call and let me know... um, okay... um... bye now."

The phone beeped and said "Second message, Sunday night, 10:00 p.m." It was my mother.

"Hi Honey, it's Mom. Are you there? Pick up... are you there? Oh... okay... we're just calling to see how you are. Daddy twisted his ankle the other day, he's okay, hobbles a little but the doctor said don't worry, a day or two and he'll be right back to normal." A second or two of silence then she continued.

"So, do you think you and Julia will be able to visit for a day or so around the holidays? Let me know okay, so I can make some plans. I'd like to have Dave and Sherry stop by as well, and maybe Aunt Harriet and Aunt Dorothy, we haven't seen them in quite a while you know. Well, um... I guess I'll talk to you later dear, give me a call, all right? Take care, love you baby, oh, and say hello to Julia for me, by now."

I made a mental note to call my mom. I hope Julia doesn't have a problem with going there for the holidays. Maybe she wants to visit her parents, it's been quite some time since she's seen or talked with them. I'll ask her later. Beeping, the machine went on to the third message.

The message stated the call was from Wednesday, apparently the night before we left for the Bahamas. We'd been so excited about our trip we must not have checked the machine before we left.

The message was from Detective Patterson. Geez, that guy is going to haunt my darn dreams!

His gruff, low voice came into the den. "Dixon? You there? Detective Mark Patterson here. We've come up with something. I need to ask you and - stop it Frankie, Daddy's on the phone, be a good boy and go play in your room. Come on Frankie, cut it out, Daddy doesn't want a Twinkie on his leg, Frankie-"

I could hear the minor menace shrieking in the background. Patterson must have put his hand over the phone because the sound was suddenly muffled, but it didn't totally block out the piercing screams and whining of his heir.

He spoke again into the phone, yelling over the screams of the boy, "I gotta go Dixon, I'll give you a call on Tuesday, I'll be gone on a trip over the weekend and - Frankie! Daddy said don't feed Twinkies to the dog! Stop pulling King's ears you're hurting him! Frankie stop-" A sudden click ended the message.

Boy, no one deserved a horrible offspring more than that guy. There is justice in this life after all.

"Honey! Dinner's ready!" Julia called from the kitchen.

Wow! That was fast! I hurried into the kitchen.

"Is this okay?" My radiant redhead asked me. She set a frozen pizza on the placemat in front of me.

"Uh huh, mmmm good," I murmured. I could eat pizza three times a day. Plucking a black olive off the pie, I popped it into my mouth and relayed our messages to Julia.

She didn't say anything while I yakked away. Quietly, she cut off pieces of pizza with a knife and fork. That is something I never could understand. Your whole life you're looking for food you can eat with your hands, and pizza comes along, perfectly fitting the bill.

And then what happens, people eat it with utensils, I don't get it. Grabbing the hot pie with two hands, I shoved it into my mouth, biting off as big a piece as I could uncomfortably fit, my cheeks bulged to accommodate the food.

Continuing to chat with my mouth stuffed full, I asked Julia what she thought about spending a couple of days during the holidays with my folks.

Pushing pieces of pizza around on her plate, she drank some cherry soda before she answered me. "Rusty, I understand you want to spend the holidays with your family. But I had kind of hoped we could celebrate our first Christmas together here in our own home, just the two of us.

"You know, decorating the tree, then later sipping hot chocolate, we could sit cozy together and watch one of those old fuzzy Christmas movies, you know like with Fred MacMurray or something..." her voice trailed off wistfully.

When she looks at me like that, all doe-eyed and sultry, but with little girl charm mixed in too, well, I just melt. I felt like the oozing cheese on the pizza, my insides got all warm and mushy.

Picturing us trimming the tree, getting a little tipsy on some eggnog, making love right on the floor amidst gaily wrapped presents and decorations strewn all around I- my dream bubble was immediately popped as two furry bodies hurled themselves against the door.

Apparently Muffy and Boris could hear us inside and wanted in. The mood broken, I was brought back to our conversation.

"Julia," I whined, "you know I haven't seen my folks in months, and it is the holidays. We can spend time together here, and then visit with them for just a day or so. It's not like they live that far away. They're only a few hours north you know. Unless, of course, you may want to see your folks. You haven't seen them since we met." Watching her expression, I forced more pizza into my still full mouth.

Expelling a deep breath, she said, "I would love to see my parents, it has been a long time. But, that would entail plane tickets and more time off from work for you. I don't think that's feasible." She looked up at me. "And I don't want to go anywhere without you honey."

I smiled warmly at her. "Does, uh, does that mean it's okay that we go to my folks', baby?" I pleaded.

"Oh Rusty," she sighed, giving in. "Fine. If that's what you really what, fine."

Quickly changing the subject from visiting my family, nibbling on a bite of eggplant, she asked, "What were the other messages?"

"Oh, that son of bitch Patterson called. Can you believe it? That guy won't leave us alone," I complained.

"Rusty!" Julia frowned. "Your language! I am not a construction worker you know."

I hung my head in shame and apologized. "He just really gets on my nerves, baby. They have the guy who killed Mike, I don't see why he keeps coming after me," I said mournfully.

"He's just doing his job Rusty. What did he want anyway? Hey," she said, "how did he get home before us? You drove like a bat out of hell, with those kids there's no way he could have beat us home."

Sure, I thought, I can't swear but she can say hell. Swallowing a huge gulp of cola, I said, "No, the call was made on Wednesday night, before we left. I don't know why he called, he didn't get to say. Little 'Dennis the Menace' was sticking Twinkies in the dog's ear or something and he had to go. He said the police had discovered something suspicious or something, I don't know. Said he wanted to grill me some more. Did you ever go see him at the station?"

"No, I never seemed to find the time. I'll be honest, Rusty, the whole thing just scares me to death. I wish they would just arrest that man and get it over with!" She shivered.

After consuming four pieces, I decided I'd had enough pizza and pushed my plate away. Sitting contentedly back in my chair, I drained my soda.

"Oh, I almost forgot, Sandy called too. I think she's feeling lonely. It's the holidays and Mike is not there, she sounded pretty sad. I feel so bad for her, I wish there was something we could do."

Julia stood up and closed the cover on the pizza box. She picked it up and put it in the refrigerator. Coming back to the table, she stood and finished her soda.

While picking up our empty plates and glasses, she hesitated then said, "I know Rusty, I feel badly for her too. You know it's going to take a long time for her to get past this. At least she has Bonnie and Grandma Amy, she's not entirely alone." She carried the dishes to the sink.

"Actually, I think that makes it worse," I said. "She has to celebrate Christmas with the baby. The whole time, she's going to be looking at that little girl and thinking how horrible it is that her papa isn't there to be with her." Mike was one of those fathers that would stay up all night Christmas Eve, putting together a doll house or... my eyes filled with tears.

Damn the guy, dying and leaving us all here to miss him. I looked away, clearing my throat. "Um, anyway, Sandy invited us to dinner today but it was too late to call her by time I heard the message. I'll give her a ring tomorrow."

Julia had left the dishes in the sink and came to my side when she heard the sorrow in my voice. She put her arm around my shoulder and laid her head on my head.

Hugging my neck, she said softly, "I know you miss the big lug, baby. I'm so sorry for you guys. Why don't you give Sandy a call back now, and make some plans for this weekend with her, you'll both feel better."

She stood back with her hands on her hips. "You know, we could try to fix her up. Nothing gets a girl over a guy faster than another guy! Don't you know any single men at the shop?" She asked leaning over and putting her face directly in front of mine.

Her lips curled up slightly, her head tilted to the right. Her hair fell, covering half her face.

Picturing Sandy with another man made my stomach twist up. "No, I don't know any single men except Ted, and he's not ready to settle down yet. He just wants to sleep with women, not marry them!" I snorted.

Julia moved back to the sink. "Listen," she said as she turned on the water. "I'm not saying Sandy needs to get married, heaven forbid! On the contrary, that girl needs to sow some oats and live a little! She got married so young to that jerk-" She bit her tongue.

"Uh, I'm sorry honey, I mean, well, Mike wasn't all that great to her. I'm sorry to say it, but you of all people know that's true." She turned back to the sink and poured in soap then turned the water on full blast, bubbles filled the sink.

Shoving back my chair I stood up. "There's no way baby, that I'm going to match-make anyone. Until I got you, I dated the worst women," I admitted.

"Oh yeah?" Julia swung her head around, laughing at me. "Tell me about them!"

She turned the water off and danced over and slipped into my arms. She wrapped her arms around my waist and looked up at me. "Come on baby, tell me all about your prior conquests!"

I shook my head and leaned over to kiss her on the tip of her nose. "I don't think so. I went out with some real dogs, Mike used to make fun of me. He'd say, 'Rusty, you need to get yourself a broad with big ti-'" I clamped my big mouth shut and set my pretty wife aside then pushed in my chair.

"Uh, never mind. Anyway, I am no way a good judge of people, and I'm certainly not going to start learning with Sandy. She can find her own guy when she's ready. That is none of my business, nor," I said swiftly as her head turned quickly towards me, "is it any of your business either. Let her find her way, in her time, we're staying out of it, you understand Miss 'Dolly'?"

Julia returned to her suds. "Oh sure, Rusty, I understand, uh huh." She started humming.

I left the room. Women! I knew she would totally ignore my instructions and do whatever she darn well pleased. I figure in about two weeks we'll be having a dinner party. Sandy of course will be there, and I'm sure we'll have a surprise guest, a single guy around Sandy's age will be sitting right next to her at the dinner table.

Since there was not a damn thing I could do about it, I wandered back into the den to watch TV.

Chapter Thirty-Three

$\mathcal{I}$t was almost a pleasure to be back at work Tuesday morning.

After the bedlam in the Bahamas, I was more than happy to be safe and sound, sitting on my stool in the workshop, busily working, repairing a computer.

Ray Ducey, a co-worker, was chatting away at me, inanely describing the movie he had seen Sunday night. Listening with more than my usual patience, content at my workstation, I was so thrilled that I was not sitting behind bars in a foreign country, nothing was going to bother me for a long time to come!

Ray was putting away some tools, and signing off the computer he had finished downloading. Glancing at the clock, I realized the morning had flown by and it was already well past time for lunch.

"Hey Ray," I said, "what do you think about getting a couple of beers and hamburgers over at Flanagan's?" The small restaurant was close by and their burgers were the juiciest.

Covering the computer with plastic, Ray turned off the light over his station and grabbed his keys off the countertop. "Some other time, Rusty." He said smiling. "I gotta meet Paula at 'Diamond Lil's'. We need to get her engagement ring adjusted. I hope by adjusted, Paula means enlarging the band, not the stone!"

We laughed at his quip.

"You'd better bring your checkbook anyway, Boy-o, you know how these ladies are once they think they've nabbed you!"

Laughing again, Ray agreed as he left the repair shop. Alone, I finished what I was working on. The Burger Binge will suit me just as well as Flanagans I decided.

The phone rang just as I was about to hit the lights and close the door. I was going to ignore it, but then I thought it might be Julia. Unlocking the door, and turning the lights back on, I reached for the phone.

"Hello, Rusty speaking," I said, answering the phone.

"Dixon. Detective Patterson here." The gravelly voice scraped along my spine like nails on a blackboard.

Oh no, what now? Groaning, I held the phone away from my ear, but I could still hear his low voice, barking out of the receiver.

"What? What'd you say Patterson, I didn't hear you." With a moaning sigh, I sat back down on the stool to listen to whatever imagined travesty I had committed now.

"Listen Dixon," Patterson ordered. He sounded anxious, unsettled, very unlike the calm, condescending man I normally knew. "Something's happened."

Sounding more urgent, he said, "There were shots fired at me today, I'm pretty sure they were at me, but I wasn't hit."

What? Wow. "I'm sorry to hear that Patterson, uh, I mean that the shots were fired, not that they missed." I was quick to correct myself.

The detective grunted. "They missed me Dixon, but my partner was hit."

"What? Oh my God, Patterson! Officer Penny uh," I could never remember her last name. "Is she okay?" The pair was annoying, but I sure didn't wish them any harm.

"It wasn't Officer Newman who was shot, it was my partner, Rodney Miller. We were getting into the car at the station when I dropped my keys. Just as I bent to retrieve them, a shot rang out. I heard Rodney behind me cry out. He'd been shot in the shoulder and fell to the ground. They think he'll be all right. I need to talk to you." His voice had lost some of its tenseness. He sounded authoritative again.

"What does this have to do with me, Patterson? I have been here at work all day, I have tons of witnesses if you need them." Aggravated, I started thinking about a bullet to his head....

"There's something we discovered, I have to speak with you. I'm at the hospital now. You need to meet me at the station. Do you have a car? I can send over a unit to get you if you don't."

I hate being ordered about, how dare he! That was his way though, even with his partner lying wounded in the hospital, he was still in charge, directing everyone. Well, no one was pushing me around!

"I haven't eaten lunch yet Patterson, and it's way after 3:00," I heard the whine in my voice and didn't care.

"Listen Dixon, this is important, I'm telling you. I expect to see you at the station in one hour. Do not go home, do not go to a restaurant, do not pass go, go straight to the station. You got that?" he thundered so loudly into the phone. I had to hold the receiver away from my ear.

Well! Very bossy today. "Fine," I grit out. "I'll be there, don't get your panties in a twist," I said sarcastically.

I was figuring the station was only a couple of miles away. There's plenty of time for me to grab a sandwich or sub somewhere, and still get there before he does. The hospital was way out west, I was much closer to the police station.

"Just make sure you do as I say Dixon. Straight there, got it?" he said gruffly, rudely slamming the phone down in my ear.

"Jerk!" I yelled into the dead phone. That's telling him, I thought. He can't order me around and tell me what to do. Besides, what could be so gosh darn important anyway, that he couldn't tell me over the phone, or even wait a few hours or days to discuss?

He probably just wanted to tell me to my face that I was right, that they realized that thug at Mike's boat was the real perp and they were going to prosecute him. Well. Patterson can wait to eat crow. Speaking of eating, I was starving.

I turned off the lights and locked the door. I took a minute to stop and visit with Lisa before I made my way out of the shop and to the Bronco.

I decided to go to Fleur Bistro and have a crepe Angelique. It was light yet filling. Consuming the crepe as slowly as possible, I helped it on its way with a dry, light Chardonnay. Boy, can these French cook, I was thinking as I ordered dessert. Inelegantly, I hid a burp behind my hand as the waitress wrote down my request.

Glancing at my watch, I realized I had already killed the hour Patterson had given me to get to the station. Against my will, my stomach involuntarily fluttered in nervousness.

It was not like me to deliberately go against what people ask of me or instruct me, as Patterson had. I was feeling guilty. Better gobble that dessert up fast, and get going, I was thinking.

That thought zipped right out of my head, as the waitress set the gooey, caramel and chocolate brownie, smothered in ice cream in front of me. Wow! Snatching up my spoon I dug in. Orgasmic! Delicious! I was in heaven.

"Oww!" I cried as ecstasy turned to agony! I had bitten down hard on a nut, and then the caramel stuck to my tooth - what the heck? I held my hand to my mouth in pain.

Gingerly I felt around the inside of my mouth with my tongue. Uh oh. I opened my mouth and pulled out a filling. Great. Just what I needed.

Instantly, thoughts of meeting Patterson flew out of my memory. I had to get to a dentist pronto! Paying my bill hurriedly, I ran out the door to my truck.

Running red lights, I tore down Long Pond Road to my dentist. I had to go out west, that's where she had her office. I hoped she would take me right in, I was in agony!

Holding my jaw with my left hand, I maneuvered around traffic, as the Bronco rapidly ate up the road to Dr. DeBellita. Dr. DeBellita has been my dentist for years. She's a wonderful woman, compassionate, kind. She's never hurt me in all this time.

Even when she fills a cavity, no one has gentler hands than her. And, she has the tiniest hands I've ever seen on an adult, just perfect for a dentist. I hastily parked the truck in the lot and ran into the office.

The receptionist, Patricia, greeted me. "Rusty! What are you doing here?" she asked, puzzled at my rushed entrance. "You don't have an appointment today."

"I know Patricia," I mumbled painfully through my aching jaw. Pointing at my mouth, I said, "I lost a filling. I might have even broken a tooth, it hurts so bad!" I wailed.

Embarrassed at my sniveling, I forged ahead. "I hope," I begged, "I hope Dr. DeBellita can see me right away."

Patricia shook her blonde head. "I'm sorry Rusty, the doctor is on vacation."

"Oh no!" I cried. "What am I going to do?"

"We're only open today because Lucinda is doing cleanings. You're going to have to go to Dr. DeBellita's partner, Dr. Larette. Here," she said, pulling out a pad and pencil. "I'll give you directions. But let me call them first, and make sure the doctor is in." She reached for the phone.

I stood there holding my jaw, praying they would answer the phone.

Patricia was talking into the phone. "Yes," she said, nodding at me, "this is Dr. DeBellita's office calling. I have one of our regular patients here who believes he lost a filling and might have broken a tooth..." she listened for a minute.

"No... no," she said, looking at me, "no, I don't think he can wait until tomorrow. He seems to be in quite a lot of pain. Do you thin k you can squeeze him in?"

I must have looked like a big baby standing there, holding my jaw and pleading for the doctor to say he'll see me. But I didn't care, I was in too much pain!

"Okay, I'll send him right over... okay, sure... uh huh... thank you so much Justine, I'll give him some," Patricia said into the phone.

"Yipee! Ow!" I yelped gratefully.

"All right Rusty, let me write down these directions." She scribbled down some lines and words, and handed the paper to me.

"Wait Rusty, Justine said the nurse said to give you some aspirins, they'll help relieve the pain. Hold on a second and I'll get you some." Patricia moved from behind the front desk and disappeared down the hallway.

Impatiently I shuffled my feet back and forth, I wanted to go!

"Here you are Rusty, take these, they'll help you feel better." Patricia quickly returned with two white tablets and a cup of water.

Tossing the pills into my mouth, I washed them down with the cold water. Profusely thanking Patricia for her help, I fled to the Bronco, and was soon speeding down the highway to Dr. Larette.

Chapter Thirty-four

Doctors' offices seem so hushed and slow moving to me I always feel like I should whisper, and sit patiently and quietly, waiting for the god of medicine to deign to see me.

I ran to the front door of the office, but as I entered, I crept casually into the waiting room, acting like I was not screaming inside with pain.

Actually, now that the aspirin had time to work, I really wasn't feeling half bad. The pills had definitely dulled the pain, lightening to just a small throbbing in my jaw.

Patients in the waiting room looked up at my entrance. They watched me move to the window to sign in then turned back to their magazines and conversations.

Moving up to the closed window, I wrote my name on the waiting list and rang the bell. This office was cold. Dr. DeBellita's office was warm and welcoming. Pastel colors and earth tones radiated warmth in her waiting room. Pretty paintings hung on her walls, and silk flowers festooned the tables.

This office was painted brown and olive green. Yuk. Posters decrying tooth disease blasted from the sides of the receptionist window, and there were no pictures to look at, just old torn magazines. The place gave me a chill. I had to wait several minutes before the window finally slid open.

A young woman with a tart, unwelcoming smile, snatched up the board with my name on it. She read the list and tossed the board back into the window and reached for a file.

"The doctor will be with you as soon as he can. There are people here ahead of you that have appointments." She emphasized the word *appointments*. "Have a seat," she snapped as she slammed closed the window.

Sure, I thought, who's going to argue with that! At least the pain was a lot lessened by now, the agony reduced to a mild twinging.

Making my way to an empty chair, I picked up a magazine from the side table. Settling into a seat, I discreetly looked around at my fellow partners in pain. Only three other people shared the room with me.

An elderly couple sat together. The old lady talked extremely loudly to the old man, who never said anything, just nodded his head.

Huddled in a corner with a magazine clutched in her hands, was a middle-aged woman. Periodically she would glance at her watch, huff in annoyance and return to reading her magazine.

It was twenty minutes before the nurse opened up the door and called out a name. "Manny Feinstein," she said, holding the door open. Her foot tapped on the floor as she impatiently waited for the elderly man to detach himself from the chair.

Sighing, I looked at my watch. Geez, I'm going to be here for hours, I can't believe this. I should have called Julia. She'll probably think I'm working late anyway. I'd hate for her to worry. Then I realized I'd left my cell at work.

I got up and went to the receptionist window. I tapped lightly on the window. No response. I could hear the nurses talking on the other side of the window.

Why did I feel like I was being treated like a child or a criminal for Pete's sake?! I tapped more boldly. The talking continued but the window was shoved open.

The same young lady peered out at me like I was a rodent. "Yes?" she asked impertinently.

"Uh... I was uh wondering if you knew how long I have to wait... uh… I mean... I just want to call my uh-" I stuttered. These people in doctor offices really made me nervous. I was always scared if they got mad they could kick me out without seeing me.

"I really don't know Mister," the little snot said to me in a bored voice. "No one knows how long a patient will take. I told Miss Cannon when she called that you would have to wait. You don't have an appointment you know!" The window slammed closed in my face.

I reached up to touch my nose to make sure it was still there, then I crept self-consciously back to my seat. Nothing to do but wait.

Thumbing through a National Geographic, I hesitated at pictures of Bermuda. They resembled the Bahamas way too much. Quickly I turned the page. Whatever happened to those shots of naked women I enjoyed during my youth?

The next page was an article on an antelope-like animal, the dik. Hmmm, cute little critters, look something like a tiny deer with big brown eyes. I read a few sentences. How interesting... apparently the male dik covers the females' poop with his, so other predators can't tell there's females there, and won't try to move in and take over.

The animal is so tiny and fragile, it tries to have as few territory fights as it can. Huh. There's always some dude out there somewhere trying to take over your home. Boy, even the animals of the forest have to worry, not just us humans.

Nothing else in the magazine interested me, so I tossed it aside and picked up a People. Shuffling through pages and pages of fifth marriages, and movie stars running for political office, I glanced at the clock. Another thirty minutes had passed by, and they had called no one else into the other room, and no one came out.

After reading a long article on some guy in Washington that had 23 monkeys as pets, I started thumbing through the magazine again.

Oh, I stopped. Those are pretty... an advertisement for snow globes caught my eye. Hmm, Ivan Hammondstone's Special Series Six.

There were pictures of reproductions for sale. Beautiful female figurines, all dressed in a colorful theme. My eyes zeroed in on one of them, the title was **The Belles of the Ball**. Hey, it sounded familiar... but I couldn't recall why.

The article describes the globe: '**The Beauteous Jade**, she is made of extraordinary fine, imported bisque porcelain, attired in green velvet, she holds an emerald fan to cover her demure expression.

Second in the series is **Crimson Rose**. Lovely Scarlet, the glazed finish heightens the gleaming colors of her passionate red gown, she carries a ruby parasol.

Third, **Sparkling Sun**, Dahlia, a diamond tiara adorns her crowning glory of blonde hair.'

The dolls were spectacular! I stared at the rest of the ones there, trying to remember why they seemed so familiar...

'The fourth globe, **Golden Girl** contains Shannon, dressed in transparent gossamer, her lovely face with its gently blushed cheeks and hand painted, wide blue eyes, is mistily hidden by a gold veil.

Fashioned with incredible skill, the fifth lady to be revealed was Tania, titled, **Twilight**. The voluptuous contours of her face, and her richly bold, ebony skin, brilliantly displays the sheen of her silvery gown. A black pearl necklace, dreamy in reflected colors, drapes her tender neck.'

The pictures of the snow globes were fabulous. Boy, if I wasn't a guy I'd be tempted to purchase one. Hmm... perhaps Julia would like one for her birthday. I read on.

'Treasure always these china figurines, their expressive features, the folds in their clothes, down to each tiny button on the sleeves, all artistically crafted with separate loving care.

The sixth in the series, the last one to be created and the end of the collection, is **The Sapphire Bell**. With jet-black hair, she is cloaked in a sumptuous sapphire gown, a white petticoat peeks out coyly at the bottom. Stunning Selena has matching sapphire slippers and gloves. A satin ribbon, capturing a miniature sapphire bell, hangs seductively above her exquisitely sculpted bosom.

Each figurine is showcased in a dust-free, crystal clear dome. With one tip of the hand, the entire scene is flowered in a soft dusting of snow.

The globes are hand-numbered in 24 karat gold. Issued in this limited edition until the end of this year, custom designed, the dolls are priced at $165.00 each, local sales tax excluded.

Order yours now, make 4 easy installments... start your own, or someone you love's collection... imported from Austria, you can't get this collection in stores...'

Whew, the babes were sensational! Still... what is it? Something was niggling at the back of my mind. A half-listened to conversation about a newspaper article slipped into my mind.

"Oh my God!" Until I heard the gasp from the lady in the corner, I hadn't realized I'd said that out loud. I had to get home!

Hurling the magazine onto the side table, I jumped up and ran out the door. There is no way... what was going on?

Incomplete thoughts chased around in my head. An inkling of suspicion crawled in, but it couldn't be... pushing out the thought, I grabbed it again and forced it back into my brain.

Driving recklessly and totally erratically, I couldn't concentrate on the road. Thankfully the other cars managed to stay out of my way!

My mind jumped about like it had been electrocuted. I had almost an idea of what Patterson wanted. He probably was warning me of danger- ideas were forming, scary, petrifyingly frightening thoughts pressed my foot hard against the accelerator.

My knuckles were white, clutching the steering wheel, my throat constricted in fear. Home... I had to get home...

Chapter Thirty-Five

Turning onto my street, I was practically frozen in thought. My limbs felt paralyzed in foreboding. The closer I got to my house, the harder my heart pounded.

Slamming the Bronco in park, I sat for a minute in the driveway. I was scared to death to go into the house. Julia's car wasn't there. She must be shopping.

My legs felt like they weighed ten tons as I laboriously got out of the truck. Treading heavily, I moved slowly up the steps to the front door. My hand shook as I stuck the key in the lock.

Entering the semi-dark house, though strangely still, it screamed out in malevolent silence. The dogs were probably sleeping out in the back yard. Great watch dogs, not a peep at my entrance.

My body trembled in dread as I left the living room, and made my way down the hall. Thinking about turning on a light, but never making the effort, I warily opened the door to the nursery.

Breathing deeply, I tried to calm my nerves. My heart still pounded, straining with every wrenching beat, it thumped so hard against my chest, I thought it was going to leap right out of my throat.

Of course that couldn't happen because my throat was clenched so tightly in fear, I could hardly swallow.

The nursery had no windows so it was very dark inside. I could barely make out the outline of the Pooh pictures on the wall and the small dresser near the closet. There was no crib, no stroller... where were all the baby things my wife has been purchasing?

Stepping inside the room, my hand brushed the light switch. I flicked it on. A single light instantly came on, but it only dimly brightened the small room. I looked around, trying to make out objects in the slight light.

The Piglet lamps and Pooh pictures I once thought so cute and charming, now loomed spookily, watching me. Shaking my head to clear the feelings of permeating evil, I moved with trepidation to the dresser.

My hands tremulously pulled open the top drawer. Some baby clothes were folded neatly, stacked in short piles. I shoved the clothes around, looking for something... yet I had no idea what I expected to find. There was nothing but clothes in the drawer.

I closed it quietly and opened the second drawer. More clothes, although less than what were in the top one. I picked up a couple of infant undershirts, tossing them around the drawer, it was soon apparent there was nothing out of the ordinary in that drawer.

The bottom two drawers revealed nothing as well, just more newborn clothing. Still not knowing what I was searching for, I moved to the closet.

The door opened easily. I thought it might be locked, but there was no need to rummage for a key. There was no light in the closet. I peered into the dimness, trying to make out objects. I could really see nothing in the shadowy darkness of the interior.

Reaching into whatever precarious peril awaited me, I grabbed some items and pulled them out to examine them in the light. Opening a shoebox, I nervously looked in. Shoes.

Setting aside that box, I reached into the closet again. Some sweaters fell off a shelf onto the floor.

I felt some more boxes. Cradling several boxes in my arm, I moved to the center of the room and placed them on the floor. I sat down next to them on the hard tile floor, apprehensive of what they might contain.

Removing a lid and viewing the inside of the box, my eyes opened wide in confusion. There were old, rusty dog leashes inside. What the heck?

I picked them up and tried to read the grungy labels. 'Muffy' was engraved on one, and 'Boris' on the other. I don't understand. Scratching my head, I tried to read the minuscule writing on the tags.

The only words I could make out were 'Tho- and Alle-' the address and rest of the words were worn too smooth to decipher. The tags were obviously for our pups, but we've only had the dogs for less than a year. What on earth were these tags for?

Perplexed, I returned the tags to the box, and replaced the lid. Setting that box aside, I reached for another.

Inside the third box I had found what I feared would be there.

Reaching in, I grasped a black case and pulled it out. Opening it carefully, I studied the object. It was a gun case. Empty.

The nightmare increased as I read the inside cover. The letters stamped on the soft fabric were worn as well, but readable. My heart squeezed in pain as I read:

'Fabrique Nationale d'Armo de Guerre.' The second line said, 'Societe Anonyme, Herstal-Liege (Belgique).'

A wrenching moan from deep inside me escaped as I stared at the words.

Remembering Patterson sitting on my couch describing to me the gun used in the killings, I recognized my worst fear, this is the case of that gun.

Oh my God. My head drooped down. Wiping the confusion from my eyes, puzzle pieces started to hook together. A picture was forming.

Reluctantly I looked up, I could see in the low light, a collection of glass globes were lined along a shelf nailed to the wall. I set the case on the floor and wearily stood up. Painfully, I walked over to the shelf.

I had seen the globes the few times I'd been in the nursery, but they hadn't clicked in my brain until now. The Series Six Collection. Minus the last one, 'The Sapphire Bell.'

Again, the half-heard conversation blasted into my head, crushing my spirit and breaking my heart. I strained to recall the article in the newspaper Aaron had been reading months back.

Something about a grisly double homicide, the female's face had been bashed in by a glass snow globe.

We had tried shushing him... but his words came back now, they'll haunt me forever...

"The snow globe used in the brutal disfiguring was from Ivan Hammondstone's Special Collection... it was called 'The Sapphire Bell.'"

Patterson had said that those vile murders had been connected to Mike's.

Tears welled up in my eyes, it was too unbelievable, how could-

Chapter Thirty-Six

"You finally caught on, you moronic idiot."

My head swung sharply towards the sarcastic voice at the door. The voice was familiar, yet not. It almost sounded like my loving wife's melodious voice, but it was pervaded with snarling viciousness.

The sound chilled me to the bones.

I turned my back to the figurines and faced the door.

Julia was standing there.

My eyes dropped to the small, square gun she held in her hand. It was aimed at me. Her once pretty features were drawn down in a repellent grimace. Her smile, so lacking in warmth, was repugnant in its attempt at mirth.

My fear escalated.

"Julia, I don't understand. What is going on?" I begged her to tell me this was all such a huge mistake, that I would suddenly awaken from this ghoulish nightmare!

"You fool Rusty, you wouldn't recognize the devil if she was sleeping right next to you." Julia moved slowly into the room, never moving the gun from its beeline to my head.

"Do you think that I married you because I thought you were Mr. Right? Mr. Perfect? Ha!" She spat on the floor.

"Love? Is that why I married your sorry ass? You are the poorest excuse for a man that I ever met!" She laughed humorlessly.

Cringing backwards at her nasty onslaught of words, I bumped into the shelf of dolls. The shelf shook slightly, the globes jostled, clanging into each other.

I put my hands behind me, bracing them on the wooden shelf. "But baby," I started to say.

"I am not yours, nor anyone else's 'baby' Rusty, except to this gun maybe." She turned the gun sideways and moved her palm off it slightly. The word 'Baby' was revealed, carved along the side of the handle of the gun.

Covering the handle again with her hand, she stepped closer to me. Her eyes glowed with feral intensity. Her lips were pulled back so tightly her teeth were exposed. She resembled a snarling jackal, about ready to rip my throat out.

I clenched the shelf behind me so hard in fright, some of the globes rolled off. I could hear breaking glass shattering below me. I didn't dare look down.

Petrified to take my eyes off Julia, I was afraid she'd shoot me or attack me. I just stared at her, totally scared out of my wits.

"What do you want with me, hon- uh... Julia?" I stammered, quaking against the shelf.

"So gullible, Rusty, so easy." Julia laughed meanly again, stepping even closer to me. "My name, you jerk, isn't even really Julia Maria Da Nisi as I told you when we met."

She snorted foully, words ground out from between her teeth. "At birth, my useless mother named me Julie Susan Bloggs. Lovely, huh? How would you like to live with that handle?" She waved the gun at me.

"I don't understand Jul- Julie... uh... what does this have to do with me?" I knew I was petulant but I couldn't help it! Nothing was making any sense. Who was this snarling stranger?

I stepped back and bumped the shelf again, I heard more crashing of glass behind me. Glass crunched beneath my feet as I awkwardly moved away from the gun aimed at my head.

"Okay stupid, I'll tell you my story." Vulgar words and twisted features marred her very being. Where was the beautiful, happy girl I'd married?

Standing in front of me was only an ugly, shell of the woman I'd known. Barely suppressed fury laced her words, as she began with her past. It seemed like she wanted me to know what she was really about.

"I was born in Titusville, actually several years earlier than I told you. I'm really older than you Rusty. Remember how desperately I tried to stay out of the sun all the time? Wrinkles tell you know."

I had never noticed the fine lines around her eyes and mouth before, but now that they were turned down so hard in contempt, it was easy to see she was a lot older than she had said.

I guess I was so astonished at my good fortune of finding such a beautiful girl interested in me, I pushed aside anything that hadn't fit the pretty picture. I had wanted so badly to love her, and have her love me, I never noticed the incongruities.

She continued with her story, moving around the room, but staying an arms-length from me. No worry there, I was too scared to raise a finger!

"Anyway, I had been living for the past ten years with my boyfriend, Tommy Allen." She looked intensely at me to see if I recognized the name. It was familiar, but I couldn't remember why.

"Tommy and I did some jobs together," she said, she said with lowered brows.

"Jobs?" I nervously croaked out.

"Oh yeah, I forget how green and sheltered you are," she mocked me.

I winced at the truth. My sheltered childhood kept me shielded from…whatever this was.

"Yeah, you sad sack, jobs like shoplifting and scams were our specialty. You know, conning old people out of their savings, the stupid old codgers!" She shook her head with a sneering wink.

"Sometimes we had to lie low from working the scams because the police would get close. Then I would make ends meet with dancing... stripping actually. How do you like that dopey? Your loving, adoring wife is really a nickel and dime hustler that takes off her clothes in dingy bars for sick perverts." One hand was on her hip, the other clutching the gun never moved.

My queasy stomach was doing summersaults. I could feel bile rising in my throat. What kind of a monster had I married? My parents were going to kill me, that was of course if Julia, or Julie, whatever her name was, didn't shoot me first!

"So one day, Tommy and I were reading the Society Page in the newspaper, just for kicks, and we saw this article written about your grandparents. That's when the idea came to us.

"Your grandparents are quite wealthy, and old. We figured out this scheme, and you are such a sucker, you fell hook, line and sinker!" She shook her head back and forth, her contempt for me shone so wickedly nasty from her sneering eyes.

Her hair, I had thought so thick and fiery, hung scraggly over her shoulders, the red had dimmed to a dull wine color. I had always thought the color was natural, but like the other information I was learning, apparently that was also a lie. I was a sucker and a fool!

She described how she'd plan to meet me, by accident of course. She and her boyfriend followed me, learned my habits and schedule. Most Friday nights I hung with my friends at the local pub.

On that fateful night at the Turquoise Bar, I fell completely enamored with her. She had captivated and conquered me so quickly, I hadn't known what hit me.

"Anyway," she continued, "we planned to trick you into marrying me. I couldn't stand to be with your skinny oafish self for long, so I pretended to be pregnant to move things along. Surprise, you jerk!

"Do you think I would get caught dead carrying your sniveling little heir? I don't think so!" She shrieked in witchlike laughter.

Looking at me with cruel indignation, she wandered around the room, occasionally waving the gun at me. I shrank back against the wall from the harrowing sight.

"The scheme was to marry you then kill your grandparents. That would be easy, they're old, ancient, anything could happen. The house could catch on fire, a car accident, Tommy was great at carrying out a good plan!" She sounded proud of the criminal scoundrel.

"So, after they were dead and you inherited, I'd wait awhile, then you would suffer some sort of tragic accident, and I would get all your money, including that hefty insurance policy I talked you into getting.

"I don't think the police would get the connection between your deaths, after all, your grandparents are old and you'd probably have your accident while vacationing in another country or something.

"We hadn't worked out all the details, an accidental drowning perhaps, or a fall off a cliff while sightseeing. We were just going one step at a time." She was quite confident of herself and her paramour.

I interjected timidly, "What about my parents? They would have inherited before me, five accidents in the same family would seem a bit suspicious, I would think."

She stopped dead. Her eyes narrowed as she thought. "Damn! How could we have forgotten them?" Shrugging her shoulders, she continued circling the room. "We'd a' thought of something." Her cultured, lilting voice had disappeared into a guttural, slanging arrogant mutter.

"What happened?" I asked. "We're all still alive. I would have discovered soon that you weren't pregnant. Were you planning a miscarriage or something?" I was curious.

Julia scowled. "Things didn't go quite according to plan, stuff happened. I used to use the dogs as an excuse to go see Tommy in the city. You're such an idiot, you believed I'd brought them home as strays.

"Tommy and me had them dogs for years, but when he moved to a hotel room in the city to be closer to me, they didn't allow pets. We had to figure out a way to get them here, without arousing your suspicion. Not like we EVER had to worry about that. You are thick as a brick, you know that Rusty?" she jeered.

I nodded in total agreement. Sucker was branded across my forehead.

"Well, one night, I remember the awful, rain, I decided on the spur of the moment to go see Tommy. He didn't know I was coming. I wanted to surprise him, so I crept up the stairs, and quietly unlocked the door with the spare key he'd given me. I was the one surprised though, that's for sure!" She wiped at an eye.

"There he was, naked as a jaybird, in bed with some blonde bimbo. They were sound asleep. Both were snoring loud enough to wake the dead. I was furious! The bastard! Here I was, breaking my neck to be nice to you, I had to have sex all the time with you and pretend to like it, well! I just exploded!"

Angrily, Julia strode about the room, waving the gun, wrath poured from her mouth, her eyes looked deranged. I shriveled further against the shelf, my feet crunched on broken glass.

Julia aimed the gun at the Piglet lamp, and squinted through the scope. I was steadying myself, preparing for a gun blast. She swung the gun back at my head, I ducked.

She yelled, "I plugged them both! The son of a bitch!" She dropped the gun to her side, suddenly deflated.

"I couldn't bear for Tommy to be next to any other broad, even in death. So I dragged the big blonde off the bed onto the floor. She weighed a ton. I had to pull the sheet, dragging her body with it to move her." She shrugged dismissively with an irritated sniff.

"When she landed on the floor, I stared down at her to see what Tommy saw in her. She wasn't nothin' special. I thought she was fat and she had big ol' craters in her face from acne."

Julia started pacing again. "But she still pissed me off being with my man. I didn't want no one to see her with him, so I... I looked around for something to wipe away her face. If she had no face, she couldn't have existed, you know?" She sounded insane, shrugging glibly again.

"I wandered around the room, looking for a weapon, like a hammer or somethin'. Then I found the box, he'd had it hidden in a drawer. The big dope had bought me the last snow globe in the collection for my birthday." She blinked, her eyes rounded with regret.

Sniffing back tears, she said, "I took it out and admired it. He'd bought me all the other ones. One a year for the past five years. I know he really loved me. Why he had to be with that slut-

"I grabbed the globe and went over to the dead bitch and knelt next to her. I raised the globe up high, and I slammed it into her stinking face. I smashed it and smashed it in a mindless fury, until it broke.

"I don't know how the glass didn't cut me, because it shattered all over, pieces of it stuck in her face. But, she was unrecognizable, the bitch. She'll never steal another girl's man!" Julia swiped at her tearing eyes with her sleeve, gun still in hand. Her shoulders slumped.

I tried to edge away from the shelf, imperceptibly moving towards the door.

But, she swung around and faced me again. Her eyes shone with madness. All traces of my darling wife were gone.

Chapter Thirty-Seven

"You never realized, Rusty, that the night you followed that guy from the house into that alley, that was Tommy. You had been working late for a while, so he took a chance and came to our house to see me. We made love in our bed, Rusty." She grinned meanly at me.

"The same bed you and me had sex in. I never even changed the sheets after so I could smell him and think of him…" She looked away, her eyes dreamy.

"We had fallen asleep that night. When you pulled in the driveway, your truck lights woke us, but it was too late for Tommy to get out. So we waited, giggling and smooching, with you unknowing downstairs, until we thought you were asleep.

"It never took you long. Thank goodness you decided to sleep in the den that night!" Her once tinkling laughter sounded so coarse, ugly.

"You mean you knew the stranger that was lurking in our house?" I asked her incredulously, although nothing would surprise me at this point. If you asked me what my name was right now, I would not be able to tell you.

Laughing loudly, Julia said, "Yeah, you are so stupid! Somehow you woke up before Tommy could get out the door. You must have heard the stair squeak or something. Anyway, when you followed him out the door and down the street, I was right behind you. You're so easy Rusty, I'm surprised some other scam artist has never got you before."

"I agree. I'm a big gullible dope." I nodded. Since she was glaring at me, I stopped moving towards the door.

"Yeah, that was me that clobbered you over your thick head and left you in the alley, and you never knew." Hysterical laughter cackled from her throat, she threw her head back and shook it over my idiocy.

I stared at her, stunned that this tiny terror I had married was really Satan incarnate!

I had to know, "What was the tie in with Mike? Were you involved in that as well?"

She walked around silently for a minute. Stopping inches from me, she said smugly, "Mike was the peeper, you know."

"What?" Another surprise! I guess I never really knew Mike as well as I thought either. Am I still on the planet Earth? Did I get off somewhere and not realize it?

"Heather wasn't the only one he was hitting on. Every damned time we were alone together, he'd be all over me like white on rice, the pig!" She spat again.

"I could not stand that vulgar yahoo you all loved and adored. He had grimy fingernails, and love handles you could haul a boat with," she stuck her tongue out in a grimace and rolled her eyes.

"I never told you, you're such a coward. I just kneed him one day and that did it. He left me alone." She leaned her back against the wall, one knee bent, her foot propped against the wall. The gun was still aimed in my direction.

"The candy wrapper should have clued us in," she said matter-of-factly

My eyes widened in puzzlement.

Giving me a 'you are so stupid' look, she said, "Remember Mike had quit smoking and was chewing gum, and sucking on candy all the time? When we called the police about the peeper, I didn't know then it was Mike.

"After he learned the cops were nosing around, he started hanging out in Sherwood City. He happened to be peeking in the

exact hotel Tommy was staying in. He saw me come out the night
I... the night I killed Tommy..." Julia's voice cracked, she wiped
at her eyes with the sleeve of her blouse.

"He put two and two together when he heard about the
murders on the news. He was much quicker, and way more clever
than you, Rusty."

Nodding in agreement, I was beginning to think I was the
dumbest person on the earth. Everyone was smarter than me. And,
apparently I was the only one that wasn't two-sided either.

"The son of a bitch started black mailing me. He was
bleeding me dry! In the beginning, I had been taking most of the
money you thought I was spending on baby stuff, and giving it to
Tommy to pay his bills. Evidently, I was paying for his gambling
and prostitutes as well!" she said wryly.

"Then Mike started sucking money out of me. The night of
your college reunion, Mike was upping the price. That's the
argument you witnessed. The pig. More, more, I knew he'd
always ask for more, he'd never quit. Normally, I'd have had
Tommy take care of him, but..."

She looked forlornly at the gun in her hand. "I had to do it on
my own. Mike told me to bring over the money on that Thursday
night. He was expecting me, so the door was unlocked. He never
heard me come in.

"I think he was drunk, and working on those stupid stamps
of his. I crept up behind him. A boat must have gone past, because
suddenly the floor moved and I was thrown off balance." She
paced a few steps in either direction but didn't take her eyes off
me.

She glanced at her feet then back at me. "I fell into a cabinet.
The noise alerted him, but he was dull with booze, his reflexes
were slow. He started to get up, to come at me. I regained my
balance, I still had the gun in my hand. Thank goodness I hadn't
dropped it when the wave jostled the boat."

Her hands on her hips, Julia was swaying back and forth as
she so casually described killing my friend.

Anger and grief welled up in me, but I was helpless to do anything except glare at her in hate.

"I jerked the gun up fast and pulled off a couple of rounds. I think I fired like four times, but I guess I only hit him like twice." She shrugged uncaringly, like his death meant nothing to her.

"The stupid cops, they think that jackass that came on Mike's boat Saturday did it. He only saw Mike waving MY money around in a bar and figured there was more hidden somewhere, big jerk. There was no more, Mike always spent the money just as soon as I gave it to him. Anyway, that took care of that big slob." She shrugged again, like flicking a bug off her arm.

"You know Rusty, when you came home that day, whining about that guy that almost killed you on Mike's boat? I had to leave the room, not because I was crying so hard over fear for you, I was laughing so hard I thought I'd lose it!" She broke into gales of laughter, shrieking in mirth at the remembrance.

"When we were on the deck of that ship going to the Bahamas, I was just about to try to push you overboard! But you turned too quickly, you seasick sap. Your weak stomach saved your life. But actually, your grandfolks still had to go first, but I was so tempted..."

Greatly amused at her attempt on my life, she covered her face with her hand, trying to control her laughter.

"What about the stamp, Julia, how did Mike's stamp get in our doghouse?" I asked. I wanted all the pieces of the puzzle before I left this world. It was obvious I was not to leave this room alive.

"Geez, Rusty, how do I know? Figure it out for yourself!" She snapped, impatient at my thick-headedness.

"It was raining the night I killed Mike. I had brought the dogs so you wouldn't be suspicious. I thought I'd tied them up securely on the deck, but when the gun went off, they got so startled they broke loose and burst inside the cabin.

"They were stomping all over, they were terribly agitated. The stamp probably got stuck to one of the dogs' paws by either the water, or maybe Mike's blood. I had to freakin' crawl around on my hands and knees wiping with a rag to make sure there were no paw prints in the blood on the floor that could lead back to me."

I cringed at the picture of her cleaning Mike's blood off the dogs' paws and the floor with Mike dying beside her.

She smirked at me. "But those stupid cops would probably have pinned the murder on you anyway, they were already suspicious of you. Anyway, the stamp must have stuck on the dog's paw all the way home until it dried out, and fell off in the doghouse." She was uninterested in the stamp. She found everything she did fascinating though.

"You know," she said bragging, "I never had any ID in the name I told you. I couldn't tell you my real name, so I never had a driver's license or anything. I figured I could sweet-talk anyone like I did that guy on the ship.

"It worked with him, it would have worked if a cop had ever stopped me for speeding or something. Men are idiots, they believe anything if you appeal to their pride- or any lower area of their anatomy."

She laughed derisively, shaking her head. "Remember that jerk on the beach in the Bahamas that you thought was hitting on me? You should have recognized him Rusty. He was the dead guy at the restaurant. You saw him talking to me on the beach when you were swimming. He took off as soon as he saw you coming!" She frowned.

I looked at her confused, trying to remember what the guy had looked like, he ran off before I got to them. And there hadn't been much left of the dead guy's face in the pond because of the coy-

"Unfortunately," Julia said, "he recognized me from when I was a stripper in Titusville. It's a small world like they say. It was only a matter of time before someone blew my identity. But it was too soon. I had to kill him.

"When he stumbled upon me, I tried to pretend I wasn't who he claimed I was. He quickly figured out I was trying to disguise myself, and soon he would have figured out my scam. Then I'd have another blackmailer.

"His sending over that bottle of wine was his way of telling me he knew what I was up to. He had to go, and fast! I didn't want you accused of the murder, though. Locked up for a murder rap wouldn't get me any inheritance!"

Pacing the small room again, she never took her eyes off me.

Chapter Thirty-Eight

Julia held the gun loosely in her left hand. Turning it over and over, she admired the blue shine. Tiny as it was, the gun fit neatly into her small hand.

Now I thought about the times we talked about how much harder it is to be left handed. We thought it was funny then, us having that in common.

Again, now I remembered a talk I'd had with Patterson. He had said the killer was left-handed, even tricked me to see what I was. Vaguely, I recalled he said something about the bullets.

"The bullets," I said, "what's up with the bullets? Patterson told me there was something weird about them."

Julia ducked her head down, but I could see she had a sweet, child-like smile on her face. Some of the wicked ugliness dissipated, smoothing her face back into the pretty innocent I thought I'd married.

"Uhhh..." she murmured, her voice sounded a long way away.

"My granddaddy was in World War Two. He was mean as they come. A bullet had crippled his one arm. He drank to ease the pain and the horrible memories. According to my dad, once or twice a week, the old guy would get blasted and something would set him off.

"He'd grab a two-by-four and go after everyone in the house. My daddy was the youngest, therefore the easiest to catch. Going by the way he acted sometimes, Daddy had probably gotten brain damage from being bashed in the head so many times. Every bone in his body was broken at some time or another.

"But in those days, folks minded their own business. The neighbors never reported the screams they heard to the cops, and the doctors pretended they believed the stories about him falling down the stairs accidentally. Hah." She snorted.

"People never notice when you're in pain. They only stick their noses in when you don't want them to." She sounded tremendously sad and burdened.

I had to catch myself from feeling sorry for her. She was a cold-blooded killer that had premeditatedly planned to marry, and then kill me and my family! My heart hardened again as I listened to her disturbing tale.

She wasn't looking at me. Her eyes were in the past. "Daddy learned good, all right. He learned how to beat us kids black and blue, but where it didn't show. He made sure a suspicious teacher would never get a glimpse of our home life!" Her smile was coarse, hard. She grimaced as if in pain as she recalled her childhood.

"But, I didn't have to endure it long, Daddy left us when I was eight. I guess he got tired of molesting me and my sisters and moved on to younger territory." She huffed a maltreated sneer.

I gasped. I never suspected her abused childhood. Yet now, I recalled a couple of conversations when she'd get suddenly sad or angry when we discussed parents and their children. The poor kid, she never had a chance at a normal life.

Her smile turned suddenly tender. "There was one thing Daddy and me shared though, other than when he touched me... Granddaddy brought back a gun with him from the war. This one." She held it out for me to see.

I leaned over to catch a better glimpse of it, but she quickly pulled her arm back.

She petted the gun lovingly. "Daddy got ahold of it one night when the old bastard was beating his mother with the board, and...

he told me he fired straight into his father's skull. Emptied the gun into his head, he said.

"He wanted to make sure the old bastard couldn't get up and come after him. They cleaned up the house and buried the body deep in the woods. Never was found. No one went looking for him.

"The local police knew him as one of the town drunks. The authorities figured he just hopped on a train one day, and moved on down the road, far away from his familial responsibilities- and sick abuse. That's what the cops told my ma when she made a missing person's report." She shrugged, cradling the gun in her arm, she stroked it as if it was a beloved pet.

"Anyway, when Daddy would take the gun out every so often, I'd watch him clean it. He took great care with the gun. He caressed it, explaining to me how to take care of a weapon." She was caressing the gun herself, gently rubbing it against her cheek, as she told me about the only happy times she'd shared with her father.

"What about the bullets?" I asked, breaking into her reminiscing.

Foggily, she looked up at me. Blinking back from the memories, she told me, "My daddy's daddy had taught him to hollow out his bullets with a knife. He said it made him feel as if he was part of the bullet- that when it would strike someone and slice through their body it was almost as if Granddaddy was the bullet and he got to personally kill the person! Sick, huh?" She grinned crookedly.

"Anyway," she shrugged. "I watched Daddy do it so many times, I could have done it in the dark. When Daddy left us, he left behind his gun. I don't know if he had to go in a hurry, or just didn't care. I didn't find it for years after he left though, but I had always hoped he'd left it for me. A present. Something to remember him by. Something to say I was special, loved, important." Her eyes filled with tears, her voice melancholy.

"But Julia, you were always chatting happily away with your mother when she called. We were supposed to go to Boise for

Christmas, but your dad got sick. Was that your step-father?" I didn't understand, did she have two families? A pleasant one and a horrific one?

She regarded me in amazement. "Rusty Dixon, I cannot believe how stupid you are! My old lady lives up in Titusville with like her fifth husband. Husband two and three also got turns at me. If I'd found the gun by then I would have long been locked up I'm sure.

"By husband three, my sisters had left home and I got to enjoy my 'special' times alone with my stepfathers. I still don't speak to those coward-bitches, they ran out and left me there with no one to talk to, no one to share the pain..."

She turned her head, I think she didn't want me to see her tears. But I could still hear the anguish catch in her voice.

I took a step towards her. I don't know what I was thinking, perhaps to comfort her. Immediately she swung the gun up and aimed between my eyes.

"Don't move loser! It's not at all hard to kill, especially after you get the first one under your belt." She laughed moronically.

"I can't believe I was ever worried about you catching on to my game, what a joke! It wasn't my mother or brother that called those few times you answered the phone, that was Tommy, my boyfriend. He pretended to be my brother Cliff.

"I don't have any brothers you dope, just wussy sisters. I can't believe you never figured any of this out, you were never once suspicious." Shaking her head at my lack of guile, she stepped back from me.

"Julia," I begged, "you can't hope to get away with killing me. Don't you have any feelings at all for me? After all, we've been together for almost a year..." My hands were clenched. I held them out and opened my palms up, holding them out in pleading.

"Ha!" She said, "Feelings for a wimp like you? You've got to be kidding. My Tommy would put you to utter shame!

"He's bigger, stronger, braver and ten times more handsome than your freckled-faced, pot-bellied hairless butt. And my name is Julie, not that prissy 'Julia'! That was for your benefit. I needed you to think I was from a fancy ho-de-do family so you'd more easily believe my lies!" She doubled over again as peals of mean laughter filled the room.

I was not as amused. "How can you kill a human being so easily, Julia-Julie?" I asked.

Snorting, she answered, "I don't really remember killing Tommy so much. I was in a terrible blind rage. When I saw him in bed with that tramp, I just saw red. I wanted to obliterate them from the earth. If they were gone, they could take my pain and betrayal with them. It was over so fast, they were dead before I knew it. I regret killing my Tommy now, I... I miss him all the time..."

She sniffed, then her face grew hard again. "Once I had killed them I figured, what's the difference in one murder or twenty? It's the electric chair either way. I thought about it, I can act real good, and I'm easy on the eyes, you were always saying that yourself. Always saying how pretty I am."

I nodded. It was true, I used to think she was the loveliest thing on this earth. Now, she had turned into a demon, and it has actually altered her features, or I was truly seeing her for the first time without love clouding my vision.

Her nose looked sharp, her hair dull, and the once puffy lips were dry and cracked. Her eyes were totally flat, devoid of any goodness or shine. I used to think they were the most expressive eyes, beautiful shining emeralds... now, they no longer reflected the light. It was as if she was dead inside, and you could see it in her vacant eyes.

"I won't have any problem killing you Rusty," she bragged, waggling the gun in my face. "I have waited for this day since the moment we met, and I knew I was going to have to touch you, and let you touch me. You used to make my skin crawl, you little weasel."

Hey now, she was becoming quite insulting. I didn't think I deserved this, but I wasn't going to engage her in an argument. Last thing I wanted was to make her mad and shoot me quickly in anger. I needed to stall for time, to figure a way out of this!

Thinking humor might disarm her, chuckling weakly, I said, "You know, at one point I thought even Grandma Amy was somehow involved in the murders! Isn't that ludicrous?"

Julia rolled her eyes to the ceiling. "How can you be that stupid and unimaginative? Sandy told me months ago what was going on. She had called to talk to you, but you weren't home from work yet. Granny it seems, was getting 'a little action' of her own." She giggled like it was a dirty little secret.

"She met some sugar grandpappy at Bingo, and they were going hot and heavy! They didn't want anyone telling them they were too old for 'shenanigans' is the way she put it to Sandy.

"Amy was sneaking out late at night because she didn't want anyone busy-bodying into her business and telling her what to do." She shifted her weight from one foot to the other and crossed her arms, but still kept the gun aimed straight at me.

"I deliberately didn't tell you because I figured the more suspicious you were of other people, the less you'd be looking in my direction. Obviously, that was no problem, you couldn't see the glasses on your own face." She said derisively.

Waving the gun at me again, the harridan ordered, "Move away from the wall, it's too dark in the corner. I don't want to miss you, or give you the opportunity to try to escape. Like you would even try, you big scaredy-cat." It sounded like she was trying to goad me into attempting to run so she could shoot me and get it over with.

I tried to think of ways to stall for more time, maybe the cops would show up, when Patterson realized I hadn't come in- maybe he'd come looking for me.

"Uh, wait a minute Julia-Julie, uh, tell me about your mom. Did she know about your abuse?" I was throwing out words, anything to stall her.

She raised the gun again, her arm rigid. "My ma was a drunken two-bit whore. She would have sold me herself if she coulda stayed sober long enough to make a deal! She did not care what happened to me, I was just a mouth to feed, and she barely managed to do that."

Oh crap, I could see her finger tightening on the trigger!

"Okay, I've had enough of this," she said. "I'd like to torture you some more because you're such a sissy, but I gotta go, I got things to do. It's been 'real' knowin' ya Rusty, goodb-"

"Wait!" I held my hands up in front of my chest. "Wait!"

Her finger eased off the trigger, but she didn't lower it.

"I think Detective Patterson is on to you! He called me earlier today, and told me he needed to speak with me about something urgent!" Boy, now I sure wish I'd heeded his warning and not gone home.

I'll never eat anything with caramel and nuts in it again! That's if I live of course, and my chances of that seemed slimmer by the second.

Sneering at me, she said, "See how slow you are Rusty? When you told me about that phone message the other day, something about Patterson wanting to see you and - but he hadn't finished. There would be only one reason he would want to see us, and I assumed he meant us.

"He was finally suspicious about me. I could tell the last time he saw us in the Bahamas. He kept looking at me, his eyes narrowed like he was thinking of something or- maybe he got my prints and ran them or something, I don't know.

"So I hid by the station earlier this morning, and I waited for him to come out, totally unsuspecting that I lay in wait." She sounded so proud of herself. Her eyes took on an insane look again as she described her stalking of the detective.

"I had my baby here with me." She patted the gun with a small smile. "I missed it in the Bahamas. I didn't dare take it with me. But I was pretty clever to improvise with that skewer, huh?"

She was quite pleased with the way she'd stuck the skewer in the guy's neck.

"When we were at that show in the Bahamas, I pretended to go to the bathroom. On the way, I snatched the skewer out of a bus pan and slipped it under my wrap then I stopped briefly next to the creep at the bar.

"I told him to meet me outside by the fountain and we'd talk about money. Such a sap. Men never think a woman can be dangerous. What a fool. I told him I was wearing a real diamond necklace, and that I would give it to him to shut him up temporarily, but he needed to help me get it off. As soon as he lowered his greasy head near mine, bam! I stuck him in the neck!" She clapped her hands in glee.

"It was easy to push him towards the pool before he fell. I made it back inside the restaurant and to our table with no one seeing me.

"The detective was a piece of cake compared to that guy. I just hung by the station since 6:00 a.m. You thought I was walking the dogs, what a moron you are Rusty. One shot- blam- the slob dropped like a rock.

"Before anyone could see where I was hiding, I took off and merged with the traffic on the street. Who would suspect a petite lady strolling along the avenue, window-shopping?" Her eyes were gleaming with glee now, as she recalled how she escaped capture.

"Listen Ju- uh, you didn't hit Patterson, you hit another deputy standing next to him. Patterson dropped his keys or something, and when he bent to get them you hit the other guy."

Her head swung sharply towards me, she frowned, then scowled. "What? Are you telling me the truth, cause if you're not- I'll-" she waved the gun threatening me.

I cringed and involuntarily held an arm over the side of my head as I ducked from the waving gun.

"Geez Julia, I wouldn't lie, but, I don't know what Patterson's suspicions are right now. B- but if you kill me he'll know for sure it was you," I advised her, my voice quivering with dire fright.

Still holding the gun in one hand raised at me, she crossed the other hand under her arm. At least she was listening to what I was saying.

Shaking her head, she said, "I can't believe I missed the bastard. But," she shrugged, "it doesn't matter, he has no evidence on me. There's nothing. I've been extremely careful, there's no way he could know who I am. I didn't leave any trace of myself anywhere.

"I hadn't planned on killing you yet 'cause of your grandfolks, so I figured the next best thing was to get rid of him and stall for time until I could make your grandparents' deaths look accidental. Then move on to you."

She wasn't even looking at me, it was as if I wasn't a real person that she had lived with and made love to this past year. I winced at her murderous words and impassionate manner towards me.

But," she sighed, "somehow something sank into your thick brain and you finally figured it out and I'm out of time. So, just give it up, Rusty. I'm going to shoot you. I think I can make it look like a suicide." She nodded sharply.

"Yeah, I'll type up a letter saying you're so distraught over your accidental killing of your friend Mike. That you didn't mean to do it... you had a fight over money, or me, or you found out he was the peeper and confronted him, whatever...

"That way I can still get your life insurance as your widow and I'll be off the list of suspects. I can forge your name to the letter, I certainly did that often enough to withdrawal cash from your savings account. Then I can take care of the rest of your family later-"

She held the gun with both hands to steady it and took a couple of steps back. "Okay Rusty baby, now's the time, say a prayer and close your eyes-" She squinted at me from behind the tiny barrel.

Squeezing the trigger, she waved a 'bye –bye' at me with her other hand, laughing. "So long loser-"

"Oh God! Julia- no- please-" I cried, holding my hands over my head.

She took another step backwards- suddenly she tripped backwards over one of the shoeboxes I'd left on the floor!

She tried to keep from falling- trying to gain her balance and not drop the gun. Her arms flailing, she stumbled all over the floor and the shoeboxes-

I saw my chance! Reaching out to grab the hand that held the gun, I tried to snatch it as her arms flailed. When I jumped forward to take a hold of the gun, my foot got caught in another shoebox.

I tried to shake the damn box loose from my sneaker while reaching for the weapon.

Julia tried to turn away from me while still falling- Grasping a handful of her hair, I tried to hold her still while I reached out and clamped my hand on her wrist.

Screaming, "Iiieeee- let go of me you son of a-" Julia cursed, "I'm gonna kill you!" she screamed.

Twisting and writhing, trying to get away from me, she shot her knee up fast and hard between my legs- I jumped out of the way of her jabbing knee just in the nick of time, but I still held her wrist.

She tried to bite my hand, but I yanked her arm up holding tightly to the hand that had the gun with both of my hands now. I shook her arm up and down as hard as I could to get her to drop the gun-

Julia was screaming and cursing as we both struggled and fought for the gun. Twisting together, we whirled around the room in a macabre dance, trying to keep our balance, neither daring to let go of the gun!

The glass from the broken snow globes was scattered across the floor and smashing beneath our struggling feet.

Then- I don't know who pulled the trigger, but the pistol went off! The bullet missed us both and shot out the window. I could hear spewing broken glass tinkling as it hit the cement path outside.

At the sound of the window explosion, Julia turned her head, my elbow hit her in the face, knocking her backward.

We both still grappled for the gun - throwing my weight at her, I knocked her flying, but when she fell, she pulled me with her.

Landing hard on the floor, I heard her breath loudly expel as I fell crashing on top of her. I swiftly snatched the gun out of her hand when it crashed on the floor over her head.

"Now I have you!" I exclaimed in victory. "Don't you move, I have the power now!" I aimed the gun at her head.

Still on top of her, I pushed back on my heels until I had a knee on either side of her hips and straddled her. Surprised that she wasn't screaming and struggling, I held the gun to her face and warily peered at her.

She didn't move. Her mouth was open but no sound came out. Not a scream, not a beg, not a breath. Her eyes were wide open, staring. There was no light in them. Even the color seemed to be gone, they looked lifeless.

"Julia?" I leaned back carefully, still holding the gun at her.

Repeating louder, "Julia?" I pushed her head with the gun.

Her head wobbled to the side, drooping oddly.

"Oh no... oh my God no... it can't be... Baby?" I whispered.

She wasn't breathing.

I dipped my head to her chest to listen for a heartbeat. I prepared to protect myself- was she faking? Would she suddenly lunge for the gun and shoot me dead?

Still straddling her hips, I held one of her arms to the floor, keeping the gun out of reach as I leaned closer to her putting my ear to her chest.

"Ow!" Something sharp poked me in the head. What the heck...? I looked down.

Her chest was a mass of blood. The dark red liquid was spreading so fast, it poured down her sides, already pooling on the floor next to her.

"Yikes!" I jumped back.

Blood clung to me. Sticking and stretching in strings between us, it kept me somehow bound to her!

Barely sticking out of her chest, was a small, red, crystal-like pointed object. I carefully rolled her onto her side.

She had landed on the snow globes that I had knocked over earlier when I backed into the shelf they were on.

Under her body were shards of broken glass. It looked like it was the *Crimson Rose* snow globe that was directly under her. Holding her up on her side, I could see something bright red attached to her back.

"Ick!" I dropped her slight body, it thumped back on the floor. The figurine had pierced her heart. Scarlet's ruby parasol had stuck her in the back and was now just barely protruding out her chest.

I sat back on my heels, and stared at what had been my beautiful, adoring wife.

Her face had smoothed out in death, once again resembling the lovely woman I had married. The ugly lines of meanness and spiteful anger had slipped away.

Tears of pain and betrayal poured down my face as I remembered Julia, vivacious and carefree at our wedding- But none of it had been real. It was all fake, an act.

My head dropped to my chest as I cried for the loss of the future I thought I'd have. I let the tears flow, weeping loudly, my soul poured out with them.

I hardly heard the sirens coming down the street.

Chapter Thirty-Nine

Police were buzzing around the yard and house as I stood with Detective Patterson.

He was actually quite pleasant and sympathetic as an hour later, I explained what had happened.

I got a grip on my emotions, the tears were under control now. We stood talking under a full moon and bright stars. It will be a long time before the romance of nature affects me again.

Turning my back to the translucent silver orb, I told Patterson who my wife really was, and that she in fact, had been the killer in all of the murders.

His arms crossed, and nodding his head in affirmation, Patterson advised he knew all about Julie Susan Bloggs.

"After the homicide in the Bahamas, I realized it was too much of a coincidence that the killer couldn't be one of your group. No offense Dixon," he said not unkindly. "I was pretty sure it wasn't you. I didn't think you could keep up the bungling act that long..." He smiled at me.

I grinned sheepishly. I had to agree with him and Julia. I'm certainly not the sharpest pencil in the pack. That point was made crystal clear as Julia relayed to me how foolish and gullible I had been.

"And," Patterson continued, "Heather Hazelhurst had good tight alibis for most of the murders. Her husband, Steven Hazelhurst had the motive of jealousy and adultery, but he was equally guilty of cheating, and he too had a good alibi for at least one of the killings. Plus, it was apparent he has moved on. When we questioned him this week, that new girlfriend of his, uh," he thought for a minute.

"Diana Delyo, has already moved in with him. They have a townhouse over on Dovelake Drive, just outside of Indigo Isles." His hands in his pockets, he watched the activity of the police and CSIs.

Officers were running about, back and forth from vehicles and around the house. Already the yellow tape was up, securing the place. That damn tape seems to keep popping up a lot lately in my life. I'll be happy to never see that again, except on TV.

I asked Patterson, "How did you know for sure it was Julia?"

His head didn't move, but his eyes followed the rhythm of the people moving around him.

He shrugged. "Actually, she was the only one it could have been once I'd eliminated the rest of you. Sandy Casey wasn't in the Bahamas. And, like I said, a guy getting murdered while we were all there was just too much of a coincidence. Besides, he'd sent over that bottle of wine, he was trying to tell someone something. That other guy on the ship Mrs. Hazelhurst was with, what was his name?" he asked me.

"I don't know," I said, "Paco or Taco, maybe Kenny, I wasn't interested enough in Heather or her smarmy gigolo to remember his name." Heather still left a bad taste in my mouth just thinking about the crap she put Steve through. She was definitely off my guest list!

"Well, at first I thought he might be mob connected and sent in to threaten, or even take out one of you. I was still under the impression that Mike Casey could have owed gambling money, or maybe a loan shark.

"I was looking for a tie-in with that to you or the Hazelhursts. But, we investigated, uh, Kenneth Klibano his name is, was just as he appeared, a cheap, conning gigolo. I don't know what he was doing with your friend Heather." Shaking his head, his shoulders bumped in pondering.

"At first he might have thought she had money, or he was using her to scope out the rest of the old, rich ladies on the ship. Maybe he just wanted easy sex with a young woman before moving onto an old one.

"He ended up with Kimberly Ruttwell, an elderly, but extremely wealthy widow. She was quite vulnerable. Her husband had only died a year ago, and she never was an attractive woman even in her youth, according to her friends, just rich. We warned off the small time hood when we found out his criminal history. He has a minor rap sheet, but nothing violent, so I ruled him out as a suspect."

We moved together, slowly crossing over the lawn to get out of the way of the loud and active officers.

Patterson continued, "The only other people with you in the Bahamas were me, and Hazelhurst's new girlfriend, Delyo. It obviously wasn't me, so I checked her out as well. She's a native Bahamian. Her mother is white and from England, and her father is black.

"She has no record, just a really squeaky clean past. She'll make a good mate for your friend, Steve. A little boring, but very nice. You were too obvious of a suspect, showing up everywhere and butting in. So, as I said, after eliminating everyone else, that left Mrs. Dixon." He paused, looking around.

Apparently he didn't want to look at me. He was hitting sensitive ground now, he knew how I felt about my wife.

"I was already becoming suspicious of Mrs. Dixon. She had refused all my requests to come into the station and answer some questions. That's why I called you. I wanted to know how long and how well you knew her... and to warn you.

"I had checked you out as well of course. Your family has been here for generations and you lived your life in Indigo Isles without ever coming afoul of the law, not even a traffic ticket. I was pretty sure you weren't in cahoots with your wife."

We stopped walking. Patterson called out some instructions to one of the officers. We started walking again.

"As soon as I discovered the dead body in the Bahamas, I had ordered one of those busboys that was flitting about wringing his hands, to go secure the table area we had all been dining at.

"Later, when the police took you away, I suggested they keep and itemize whatever glasses, utensils or plates were still at each of your places. I knew by then you probably weren't the killer, but I needed to keep you and Julia there, and out of the way."

He chuckled a little. "You were kinda funny, Dixon, as they hauled you away. Your faced was pressed against the glass, pleading with me to help you and to take care of your wife! Ahem."

He sobered quickly when he saw the expression of outrage on my face.

"It wasn't very funny from my end, Patterson. I thought I was going to end up like Midnight Express or whatever that movie was, never to be heard from again." I sniffed and turned my head away.

He patted me on the shoulder. "I know Dixon, I'm sorry. I knew you weren't going to be held, I just needed to stall for some time. And I didn't want to spook your wife, and have her run off and disappear before we had the 'goods' on her."

He continued more serious, "So, I had all of your prints made, and guess what I came up with?"

I shrugged. "What?"

"Except for the gigolo, all of you but Julia were clean as babies."

What a surprise, I thought.

Patterson explained, "Julia's, or rather Julie Bloggs, came up all over the east coast. She had 'wants' for her from Jacksonville to Miami. Most of her activity was in Titusville where she's from.

"She seldom gets caught because of the aliases she uses and she mainly commits misdemeanors so she's let go without fingerprints or mugshots taken. Two years ago she was known as Eleanor Stanson. She's a pretty good little actress as you well know. And like regular guys, cops can be sweet-talked too by a pretty girl."

Don't I know it! I nodded as he talked. I remembered the dope at the booth we had to go through to get on the ship. He was a sucker too, taken in by her girlish smile and fluttering eyelashes.

"She had over ten active warrants for her arrest to date. She's been a busy girl. Don't feel too bad, Dixon, for being duped," he consoled me.

"She was a seasoned conwoman. Her and her boyfriend Tommy Allen, had been pulling scams for at least the past fifteen years. She probably honed her wiles on men by the stripping she did between jobs. It was only a matter of time before someone around here recognized her and exposed her game."

"I know, she told me." I said. My head hung dejectedly. After all, that was my lovely bride lying dead in there, the pain was still fresh.

"I think that's why she was moving her scheme along quickly, before someone would recognize her and she'd have to flee, thereby losing her shot at my inheritance. She said she had thought about pushing me over the railing of the boat, so she was escalating her plan. She must have been panicking because she hadn't yet disposed... uh... of my grandparents yet." I cringed thinking about plunging to my death in that shark-infested, deep dark sea.

"Anyway," Patterson said, "as soon as we knew she had a record, and no discernible alibis for any of the murders, I called you to warn you. But," he pointed a finger at me, "obstinate as always, you refused to obey me. You did exactly the last thing I wanted you to do, come here."

Nodding my head in agreement, I said, "I know, I know. I was an idiot. Believe me, I'll never disobey a police officer again, and that's a promise." I held my fingers up in Boy Scout honor.

Patterson started leading me slowly to the street, to an awaiting police car.

"It's over now, Dixon. I just need for you to come in and fill out some reports so I can close the case. Then, you can get past this tragic episode, and move on with your life." He ushered me into the car.

Closing the door, he took a step back.

I leaned through the open window. "Thanks for your help, Detective Patterson," I said smiling weakly. "You turned out to be not such a tough guy after all."

"Aw shucks." He grinned, staring down at his shuffling feet. "It's okay, Dixon, it's my job. You take care and I'll call you next week after the coroner gets through with the autopsy to let you know it's completely over."

He slapped the car a couple of times to let the driver know he could leave. I waved at Patterson.

Then, turning, I faced forward, moving onward to work through my loss and build a new life.

Epilogue

"Brrrrrring!

The phone in the kitchen rang as I passed by it.

I had never gone to the police station to make the final report. I just wanted to get away and out of town as fast as I could.

Not even returning to get my car, I hopped on a train and headed straight for my folks'. I was staying with my parents for the time being in Vero Beach.

My Aunt Edna was there as well, so I had plenty of mother hens to watch over me.

My house was still sealed off by the police, and I had decided to take a leave of absence from Carpathian. I needed some time away to gather my thoughts, and to grieve.

Steve, Sandy and the police had left numerous phone messages, but I hadn't returned them. I wanted to not think about the whole horrific nightmare for a while.

I just get up every day, read the morning paper while Mom fixes me hot oatmeal with cinnamon and cream. Then later, I go for a slow stroll through the park nearby. I let one of Tommy Allen's relatives take Muffy and Boris. I just can't bear to look at them, the betrayals, lies and memories they invoke are too painful.

After my walk I eat lunch, take a nap, nothing too strenuous or thought provoking.

Then I watch TV, eat dinner, and watch more TV until bedtime.

Sometimes, late at night, when the thoughts sneak in, memories of Julia when she was still my loving wife, I can't sleep.

I get up in the semi-darkness. Since that last night, I can't take the dark. I don't care what people think, the shadows petrify me now.

I wander out and sit on my folks' verandah, and swing gently in the porch rocker, and remember when we were happy together.

The phone continued to ring.

One day I answered it.

Once again, a familiar voice boomed from it. "Dixon?!" It was Patterson.

"Yeah," I grunted.

"Hey, Dixon," he said, somewhat hesitantly. "Hey, uh, we got the results from the autopsy. I wasn't sure whether to tell you this or not. Uh... well, Julia, Julie, she did die from that glass thing piercing her heart... but... well..." he paused.

"I'd better come right out and tell you. She really was pregnant! I guess she denied it to herself, but... uh... you there Dixon?"

"What?" I couldn't believe what he was saying.

Apparently she was going to die with my heir inside of her like she had said to the contrary when we were in the nursery!

"I don't believe it!" I squawked into the phone. What a ghastly tragic shock!

"Uh... there's more, Dixon. Your wife was almost five months along. We can do a DNA, but we're pretty sure it's yours. And...uh...while you and I were outside talking that night," he coughed and cleared his throat.

"Ah, apparently the paramedics realized she was pregnant and they made efforts to save the baby, even though the mother was dead. And... the baby is alive! It's been in the neonatal ICU in an incubator. You're a father, Dixon! Dixon? Are you there? Dixon?"

I dropped the phone.

I could still hear his gruff voice emanating from the swinging receiver, calling to me as I collapsed in astonishment to the floor.

LOUISE FURLEY

That's where my mom and Dad found me hours later when they arrived home.
They asked me what was wrong...
Boy did I have something to tell them!

The End

Dear Reader, thank you for choosing <u>The Sapphire Bell</u>!

I know you could have picked any number of books to read, but you chose this story and for that I am extremely grateful.

I hope you enjoyed this novel, and if you did, **please leave a review** **where you acquired it,** *and look for other exciting titles in my name!*

About the Author

Louise Furley loves writing romance with a huge helping of suspense. Sunny Florida is home where Louise is a graduate of St. Thomas University with a master's degree in Mental Health and lives with Bob, her own hero.

Louise is the author of numerous published novels. When not researching or writing, she is dreaming of unique plots and discovering fresh ventures she hasn't yet experienced in the world.

Ride along with her as she travels new and thrilling journeys!

LOUISE FURLEY